Andrew Comes Home

A Mississippi Tale of Love and Recovery

Multi-award winning Contemporary Fiction

- **Louisiana** 2008 First place RWA
- **New Orleans** 2010 First place and Grand Prize Dixie Kane Classic
- **Florida** 2012 Second place contemporary fiction,
The Royal Palm, Florida Writers Association
- **Alabama** 2015 First place, Alabama Writers Conclave
- **Texas** 2016 Finalist, East Texas Writers Guild Book Awards

For Joan—
a story of Mississippi love
plg Chen
4/6/19

Philip L. Levin, MD

Doctors Dreams Publishing
Biloxi, MS

Doctors Dreams Publishing
PO Box 4808
Biloxi, MS
39535

ISBN: 978-1-942181-10-1
Library of Congress Control Number: 2017917365

Andrew Comes Home

A Mississippi Tale of Love and Recovery

This book is dedicated to those unlucky souls who have lost a loved one to a tragedy. Sometimes a loss-bearer feels that his or her own life was also lost in that tragic event. Yet life goes on, and with love, recovery is possible. So mourn the past loved ones, and take the time to cherish even more those still with us.

Philip

Saturday, June 7th

I pulled Andrew out of the Chicago psychiatric unit at noon, returning with him to my Mississippi condo an hour before the opulent red sun could sizzle into the gulf waters. Holding open the condo door, I watched him trudge past, his tattered T-shirt bragging of past glory, a science fair from two years and a lifetime ago. Sullen, shallow eyes peeked out from below his dirty bangs.

He dropped his lumpy canvas bag on the terrazzo floor and I watched him walk through the living room and out onto the balcony. With the glass door wide open, the heat rolled in like an open oven. Coming up beside him, I observed him staring out at the beach ten stories below. Dark circles stair-stepped down cheekbones whose sun-deprived skin stretched tight.

I laid my arm on his shoulders in a fatherly gesture of love. "Welcome to your new home."

Andrew scanned the beach, its white sands sparkling in the setting sun. The sun worshippers having retired for the day, the occasional car on Beach Boulevard offered the only sign of human life. Beyond the beach, the gulf waters lay placid and dark. He leaned out over the rail, pursed his lips, and let loose a spit-bomb. We watched it plummet to the sands below.

"This freakin' wasteland ain't never gonna be my home."

I gripped the rail with my free hand, listening to the wind chimes sing of disharmony. "Give it a chance, Andy. Enjoy the peace ... the solitude. Why, I bet it'll only be a couple of days before you're running on the beach, basking in the sunshine."

Andrew stepped back from the rail, glaring at me from below inflamed lids. "Got it all planned out don't you, Dad? Jeez." For long minutes I watched him stare out to eternity until he turned away and trudged back inside. Dr. Hopkins had said he wasn't ready, yet in that cold Chicago hospital lobby it had all seemed so obvious. Get the boy out of there and everything would be fine. Now ... now I wasn't so sure.

younger Andrew, a smiling Andrew. I traced the photo's edge beneath the glass, folded to tuck away the part lost forever. Picking up this most precious of treasures, I hugged it tightly against my chest.

Monday, June 9th

The noon sun glared off my Camry's hood as I pulled into an empty spot in front of Gulfport High School. The car's hundred-thousand-mile air conditioner struggled against the heat. Before us, the 1950s style glass walls shimmered. Showing through those windows orange and blue banners promoted school spirit.

"Sure doesn't look like Riverside," Andrew said. The anger in his eyes from two days before had softened into sadness. I wondered what memories of his old school flitted through his brain. Dances? Science projects? Track meets?

"Give it a chance."

He looked down into his lap and sighed. I touched him lightly on his shoulder, and he shrugged me off.

"What'd you find out online?" I asked.

He looked up again, focusing on the school's front door. "Over a thousand kids. Jeez. I won't know a single friggin' one."

"Sounds like a great opportunity to make new friends."

Andrew turned to me, his eyebrows tented. "My friends are in Riverside."

I turned away to check my watch. "We're going to have to rush a little. I've only got an hour for lunch."

"In Chicago you didn't punch a clock."

I turned off the engine. "This isn't Chicago."

"Hey, I've got an idea." He placed his hand on my wrist. "I hate being here. Your job sucks. Let's go home."

I shook my head.

"Why the hell not?"

I could feel my pulse rising as quickly as the car's temperature. "I'm never going back to Chicago. I had to rescue you, but I pray that'll be the last time ever." I forced a smile. "C'mon. Let's go."

We got into the refrigerated blast where I studied a map on a bulletin board, figuring out the directions to the counselor's office.

"Look over here!" I turned to Andrew's voice and saw him standing with his nose pressed to the glass of a case. Ambling over, I could see the metal athletes holding torches, the track and field trophies.

"Cross country regional champions 2002, 2003, and 2004," he read from the plates. "Nothing for the last four years, though."

"C'mon, it's this way."

Just down the hallway we entered the office where a plump teenager with heavy make-up told us to sit and wait. She handed me some forms on a clipboard, and Andrew and I settled into the plastic chairs. I glanced over at him, slumped with earplugs bringing him music. His bangs glistened from his morning shower. I reached over, popping out one of his earplugs and he looked up at me. "What?"

"You want a haircut? When we're done here I can drop you off at the mall on my way back to work. It's only a mile walk home along the beach. Tell you what; I'll even spot you an extra twenty bucks for entertainment."

Andrew shrugged, stuffed the earplug back, and slumped further into his chair.

I looked up as a woman with short brown hair approached, hand outstretched. "Good morning. I'm Sylvia Perkins." Her light southern drawl stretched her words until they seemed to sing. High cheekbones framed her full red lips, petite shoulders accenting her peach-size breasts. I followed the plaid summer dress down to where her shins came out, muscular, balancing easily on three-inch heels.

I rose to my six-two height and she stopped abruptly, staring up at me with her piercing brown eyes. "Rick Lewis," I said. "And this is Andy."

Sylvia turned to him. "Nice to meet you, Andy. You're coming to join us this fall, I understand?"

Andrew looked up, tucking his feet out-of-the-way under his chair. "Yeah." His gaze returned to the floor. "That's what Dad tells me."

I watched her study Andrew. *No doubt she's seen thousands of students like him; kids whose life issues make school seem irrelevant.*

"Let's go into my office." Her attention landed on my face and I flashed a smile. She winked and I wondered if maybe she was lonely too. I chuckled at myself – how presumptuous to think she'd be interested in me. We followed her.

Her office, hardly larger than an oversize closet, was a forest of file cabinets, its fallen leaves stacks of brightly colored folders, magazines, and mishmash. Dozens of certificates in cheap frames covered one wall. Another wall, papered with cork, held an ocean of photos, the two-by-three and wallet sizes sold in school photo packages.

We settled into the three chairs and Sylvia opened the folder topmost on the stack. She scanned the papers a moment and looked up with a smile. "What brings a couple of Yankees down to the Deep South?"

"I relocated," I said. "Working at Cuevas' Chemicals in Biloxi."

Her gaze fixed on Andrew. "No doubt y'all find this much different than Chicago."

"For sure."

"Hush," I said. "You only got here Saturday." *Yet, there's already been a big improvement.* "Naturally Andy's had some qualms about the move."

I watched Sylvia's eyes skip over Andrew, taking in his body language, his grim face, and his I-don't-care clothing. As she examined my son, I studied her; her confident smile, her glowing face, and her trim body. Too cute!

Andrew sat with one leg stretched out and the other tucked under his chair leg. He had chosen an old pair of tennis shoes, white-socked toe poking out of a hole worn in the hood. He now stared at that toe.

"Andy?" she demanded.

"What?"

"Andy, look at me please." A determined smile created tiny dimples in her cheeks.

Andrew's face rose slowly until he met Sylvia's eyes. "Why are you looking at me like that?" he asked.

"Because I care about you."

He slouched further. "You don't know me from a friggin' Eskimo."

"Just because I don't know what you've been through, doesn't mean I can't care how you feel. I've seen lots of teenagers who've had some bad luck. I can tell you, Andy Lewis isn't the first fellow who's been pulled across the country. Those boys made new friends, and you can too. Of course, you have to try. Are you a trier, Andy?"

Andrew remained silent, staring at the ground.

"Andy," I said sharply. "Mrs. Perkins is talking to you."

She held up her palm. "This is Andy's time." She continued watching him, but he didn't look up. "Listen to me, Andy," she said. "You may not feel like talking now, but when you do, I promise I'll make time for you. It may not be that exact moment, but it will be as soon as I can. Okay?"

Silence lengthened until all hope for an answer died. Sylvia nodded gently, and turned back to Andrew's folder in front of her. As she flipped pages I studied her face, trying to guess her age. Usually I was pretty good at that game, but she was hard to judge, clear skin and all. Heck, I knew I looked a lot younger than my fifty. I noted she didn't wear a wedding ring.

Placing her index finger on one spot she turned to ask, "You didn't finish your junior year?"

Andrew didn't answer, so she turned to me. My head filled with memories. "Don't know really where to start," I admitted.

"Mr. Lewis ..."

"Rick."

"Well, Rick, I'll be Andy's counselor this year. I'm looking at a boy who was making straight 'A's thorough his freshman year and first half of the following. By the end of his sophomore year, he had 'C's and 'D's. Those fell to 'D's and 'F's last Christmas, and then, by the end of his junior year, he'd dropped out."

I almost told her. I wanted to open up, to find solace in her compassionate eyes. My pain must have shown, because she placed both of her hands on mine.

"Rick? Are you okay?"

"We're divorced. His mother and me." I couldn't talk about Jenny yet. Not yet.

"Oh." She held up her unadorned left hand. "It's not so bad once you get used to it. So the divorce has been hard on Andy, of course."

"Yeah. Well, Andy was ill and missed taking his finals."

She turned to him. "Andy."

He kept his focus on his shoe.

"Andrew Peter Lewis. When I call your name, I expect you to look at me."

His face rose slowly. "What?"

"Would you be willing to come to summer classes and take your junior year finals?"

"Attend summer school?" Andy reached down and began relacing his shoes. His words echoed sadly off the floor. "S'pose. Don't got nothin' else to do."

"You'll be the teacher?" I asked.

Sylvia nodded. "Yes. Besides being his counselor and summer school instructor, Andy'll be in my Mississippi History class during the regular year."

"You teach history? I love history."

"Really?"

"Definitely." Our eyes locked, just a moment – long enough for electricity to spark the gap. "Right now I'm reading John Adams biography; the '03 Diggins one. Have you read it?"

A flush came to her cheeks. "Diggins? Oh, yes. I loved it."

"Me too. Right now I'm into the 1804 election. Diggins gives an interesting perspective on the animosity between Jefferson and Adams, don't you think?"

She stared at me a moment, before murmuring softly, "I swear you're the first man I've found who enjoys history since I came back South." She returned her attention to the desktop and stared at the folder until I cleared my throat.

"What other courses will Andy have in the fall?"

Sylvia flipped a few pages. "Let's see. How about organic chemistry and, oh, looks like he's ready for calculus? With English and the history that still leaves one slot for an elective. What do y'all like?"

Andrew glanced up, providing his first show of interest. "How 'bout cross country?"

Sylvia cocked her head at this sign of hope. "I know all the boys on the team and I'm sure they'll love to have you. However, that's extracurricular."

I glanced at my watch. "Maybe we can decide on the elective later? I'm sort of short on time."

She stood and we followed. "See you July seventh, eight AM sharp. Got it?"

Andrew nodded.

I took her extended hand in both of mine. "Thank you very much Mrs. Perkins. May I call you Sylvia?"

She stared up at me, her hypnotizing smile dancing on her lips. "Yes, please. Call me. That."

We stood staring until Andrew spoke. "Do you know when the cross country team starts their workouts?"

Sylvia turned to check some papers on her bulletin board. "No, but remind me when you're back in July and I'll check on it."

As I turned to close the door behind us I glanced back to her. She had her gaze fixed on Andrew's folder as she absent-mindedly rubbed her empty ring finger.

Saturday, July 12th

Andrew and I stooped over a dead jellyfish, its glistening translucent remains iridescent in the morning sun. He poked it with a stick, flipped it over, and dragged its stingers through the sand. "What makes them sting?"

"Not really sure. Some kind of chemical reaction I guess; an acid burn, or maybe an enzyme that dissolves protein. We could Google it I suppose."

He poked the creature a few more times before standing and stretching. Six weeks of running had filled him out, and the Mississippi sun had changed his skin tone. He glowed with health – all but his eyes. They showed his loneliness.

"So how's summer school going?" I asked.

He scanned the horizon, its blue on blue line hypnotizing. "Okay I guess. Mrs. Perkins tells me what to study, then I take the test. We did social studies Friday. The electoral college system sure makes it complicated."

"And a bit unfair. Big states like Illinois get plenty of attention from the candidates, while states like Mississippi will hardly ever see one."

"Why would a candidate even bother? Nobody here gives a crap." He reached down and picked up a seashell, looked it over, and handed it to me. Its spiral curves diminished to nothingness, making me wonder how its creature could live in such a small space. I placed it back on the beach.

As I watched Andrew dig in the sand, I thought about how good Sylvia had been for him: stimulating his curiosity, reigniting his interest in school. Sylvia. I pictured her cute smile, and how she had gazed into my eyes at the end of the interview.

"So you like Mrs. Perkins?" I asked.

"Yeah, she's cool. Sometimes we just sit and talk. She can trace her family back to the Mayflower and Daughters of the Revolution and the Confederacy. No wonder she cares so much about history."

"She ever talk about her family. Children?"

"No kids. Lives in an old mansion with her aunt."

I remembered my life before children. Mallory and I had been madly in love. By the time Jenny was born, almost ten years into our marriage, the bloom was off the rose. Still, if it hadn't been for the tragedy we'd probably still be together.

Andrew drew some designs in the sand.

"She says I gotta pick an elective soon." He got up again and we strolled down the beach, the sand squishing warm between my toes.

"How about something to do with engineering? Drafting?"

He shook his head. "Nah. I'm thinking of something more to do with people; you know, how they interact. Sociology or something."

"Sounds more like psychology."

He nodded. "Yeah, that sounds right. Psychology. I sure would like to know how these Southerners think."

We walked on a bit, the sweat soaking my shirt. I thought about the people I worked with and their strange habits. "Just because someone's different doesn't mean they're crazy."

He snorted. "Should've told Mom that. Jeez. Locking me up in the loony bin."

"Your mother ... "

His voice flashed. "Yeah! You've told me it was my mother's idea! Well, friggin' get over that. You could have stopped her!"

I winced at his accusation. "She said you were hallucinating – paranoid delusions about white vans chasing you."

I watched his anger collapse into misery.

"Maybe." He kicked the beach, creating a sand spray that blew away in the breeze. A seagull landed close by to see if we might be giving handouts. "Still," he continued, "You could have rescued me sooner. Jeez, that place was awful!"

"I came as soon as I could. This job isn't like the one I had in Chicago. It's a family owned thing, really backwards. I'm trying to suggest some improvements, modernization. But the boss, Henry Cuevas, is a real ... well, not the type of guy who likes getting suggestions." I gave him a half smile. "Sorry, Kid. I came as soon as I could."

He kicked again. "Whatever." He looked behind us. "We've gone over a mile. You ready to turn back?"

When we reversed face, the sun shone directly into my eyes. "Yow. Do you run against this every morning?" I asked

He gave a half grin. "I told you to bring sunglasses."

"So how are your times?"

He ran a few steps in place. "Pretty good. Tryouts are next month; August twentieth."

We walked on in silence, passing a couple setting up an umbrella. They were quite young, maybe Andrew's age. "You know them?" I asked, pointing.

He shook his head. "How am I going to meet anybody?"

"You just have to be friendly. People might be friendly back."

He spit on the sand. "I have friends. They're just not here."

Sylvia: Saturday, August 23rd

Sylvia added a bowl of fruit to the tray, already laden with pitcher, glasses, and a cup of pistachios. Grabbing a rag, she polished a smudge from the sideboard's surface, pausing to run her fingers on the warm walnut. Glancing up, her gaze wandered to the portraits leading into and down the hallway. She walked over to the one of her father, his face flushed over the white linen suit. Placing her fingers on her lips, she delivered a kiss to its surface, a slight smile settling onto her face.

Returning to the bar, she picked up the tray and carried it out to the garden. She set it down on the metal table in front of Aunt Frances, and bent to give the elderly woman's cheek a kiss. Sylvia poured the tea before settling into the other chair.

"I was just admiring the Encore azaleas," Aunt Frances said. "I do miss that old magnolia, though. Do you think we should hire someone to dig up the stump and put in a new tree?"

Sylvia scanned the garden, admiring the scattered spots of color the roses, chrysanthemums, and germaniums added. A pair of massive oak trees shadowed a small fountain where a bright red cardinal relished his bath.

"I loved that old tree, too," Sylvia said. "I suppose we should go ahead and plant a new one so when I'm your age I can be sitting here, alone, enjoying its flowers."

Aunt Frances patted Sylvia's wrist. "Alone? You're still young, Darlin'. You'll find someone."

Sylvia shook her head. "I don't see how I'm ever going to meet anyone – not anyone who'd interest me, anyway. I'm certainly not getting any response from that Yankee."

Aunt Frances took a sip of her tea. "Yankee?"

"I have this student, Andy Lewis; troubled boy from a broken home. Chicago."

Aunt Frances brushed a few leaves off the glass topped patio table. "Is this your project for the year?"

Sylvia pursed her lips. "He's a good kid, very smart, but terribly lonely. Wanted to run on the track team, but something happened."

"So what's the connection with the Yankee?"

"His father." Sylvia fidgeted with the nuts, rolling them around her fingers like worry beads.

They paused to listen to a mockingbird sonata. Aunt Frances stabbed a cantaloupe ball with her miniature fork and brought it delicately to her mouth, dabbing her lips afterwards with her napkin. "What about his father?"

Sylvia pictured Rick's kind face, the softness of his hands, and the gentleness of his spirit. "He has these huge blue eyes." She scooped more nuts onto the table, pushing them around until they formed a heart.

"Didn't Gus have blue eyes?"

With a sweep of one hand, Sylvia sent the nuts bouncing across the brick tiles. "You are so right, Auntie. Rick is just another Gus – just one more blue-eyed Yankee, a man who couldn't possibly understand our culture. One would have thought I'd have learned my lesson."

She stared out at a pair of doves pecking at seeds fallen from the birdfeeder until she heard a stifled sob and glanced over at her aunt, who had her head turned away. Sylvia reached over and touched her aunt's cheek, holding her finger there until the glistening eyes turned her way.

"Do you think I would ever leave you again?" Sylvia asked. "And for another Yankee?"

Aunt Frances shook her head, a sad smile gracing her face. "I'm afraid you won't allow your heart to love again because you feel beholding to me."

Sylvia took hold of her aunt's hand, giving it a light squeeze. "You do need me, Auntie. Look what happened."

"It's just a broken hip. I'll be up and around in no time."

Sylvia settled back. "I know you will." She looked out into the garden, watching a squirrel scurry along the grass, pick up a nut, and carry it to the flowerbed to bury it. "First off, he's a parent. You know how I feel about dating a parent!"

"Yes, Darlin', but, even so. There seems to be something about this Rick you find appealing."

Sylvia clucked her tongue. "Oh no. I don't find him appealing at all. My mind is made up. If he calls I'm not going to talk to him."

"You gave him our phone number?"

Sylvia shrugged. "I gave it to his son. If Rick wanted it, he'd have it."

They sipped their tea to the tune of the birds singing in the morning air. Sylvia stared out across the garden, her thoughts drifting on the Saturday morning breezes. "He's tall and gentle and reads history books."

"And has blue eyes?"

Sylvia nodded. "Deep blue."

was hallucinating, acting crazy."

"He doesn't hate you," I insisted, trying to sound convincing.

She sighed. "Every time I call I leave a message, but he never calls back. He won't call me this time either, will he?"

"I don't know, Mallory. All I can do is give him the note. I'll wish him a happy birthday for you, too. Anything else?"

"Yes."

I could hear her sob, creating images of her face as I'd seen it so often last year, mascara tracks streaking down her cheeks. "What?" I asked.

"Tell him I love him." She clicked off abruptly.

I hung up and walked down to Andrew's room where I knocked.

"Go away," he called.

"Please come out."

"I'm not talking to her!"

"You won't have to," I replied. "She's already hung up. She called to wish you a happy birthday."

He opened the door and brushed past me, and I followed him into the kitchenette. We settled back into our chairs and I watched him pick at his remaining dessert.

"Happy birthday from the wicked witch of the north. What else?"

"She wants you to call her."

"Ain't happening. Anything else?"

"She said she loves you."

He threw his fork across the room where it clanged against the far wall. "She loves me? Ha! How dare she say that after locking me in the loony bin? How freakin' dare she?"

I went across the room and retrieved the fork, rubbing off the chocolate it had left on the wall. As I brought it back, I thought of how Mallory and I had handled our grief so differently, and how it had destroyed our marriage. I thought of how the loss of his older sister had affected Andrew; only a year apart they'd been as close as siblings can get.

I handed him his fork and sat down next to him. "Andy, I know you're angry at your mother. I can't swear she did the right thing by having you committed. But I do know that she must have thought it was the right thing."

He stabbed the air with his fork a few times, fighting imaginary demons. "You say that now, but you never thought she was doing the right thing when you guys lived together."

I glanced out at the Pollock print hanging over my easy chair. In the early days I had loved Mallory so much, reveling in our shared interests of abstract art, jazz, ... so many things. What had happened? Was I truly such a disappointment to her?

"Andy, it's true the love between a husband and wife can die." I paused until he looked up at me. "But never the love of a mother for her son."

He hung his head, poking holes in his cake with the fork. Finally he pushed it away and I took the plates into the kitchen, rinsing them and stacking them in the dishwasher. When I came back he was still sitting as he had been, his face staring at the empty table in front of him.

"When I was in fourth grade we had this Christmas Play in school," he said, looking up at me. "Do you remember that?"

I squinted, trying to recall. "Was that the one where you wore the turban?"

He nodded. "Yeah. Remember anything else about that night, would ya?"

"I remember I almost missed it. Something about my flight being delayed."

"Yep. You had to take a taxi all the way from Springfield, but by golly you weren't going to miss it."

I reached over and tussled his head, now with hair kept short and clean. "Not going to miss my big boy's star performance."

He luxuriated in the rubbing a while, twisting his head back and forth like a puppy. When I stopped, he turned to me. "Yep, you made it. But you know who didn't? Mom. She was too busy that evening. It was always like that."

He got up and walked out to the balcony. When I joined him, he was leaning out over the rail staring into the night sky. I studied his face, dimmed by the dark night. Pointing to the eastern sky, he said, "Look. Orion."

"Sure is. Hey, look at that red one off the horizon. I bet that's Mars." I picked up the binoculars from the table and gave it a study before handing them over. I relaxed to the night sounds as he spent several minutes surveying the skies.

"Dad?" Andrew asked, "How come we're in Mississippi?"

I tightened my grip on the handrail as I formed my answer. "After Jenny's death I had a hard time concentrating. I began making mistakes, sometimes ... sometimes blaming others."

I took a few deep breaths. *Andrew deserved the truth, and maybe I needed to put it in words for my own good.* "You know I'd been with that company twenty-two years, chief engineer, so they were trying to let things slide. Finally, though, I was called into a meeting with the big bosses."

Andrew pointed and I paused as we watched a meteor burn up in the atmosphere.

"So what happened at the meeting?" he asked.

"I said some things I shouldn't have said."

"Yeah? Like what?"

"I told the head of the Human Resources Department that since she didn't know a damn thing about engineering she should keep her ignorant trap shut. I, uh, may have also made a reference to her having a similarity to an overweight uncomely female dog."

Andrew snickered. "Ha! That must have brought the house down."

I harrumphed. "She deserved it. Anyway, they let me go."

"So why didn't you just find another job in Chicago? That sure would have made everything a lot easier."

I watched the stars, letting the question percolate in my brain. "Changing jobs wouldn't have changed me, Andy. I needed to get away. Everywhere I looked, everything I touched, reminded me of Jenny. I just had to get away from all the terror."

"So you ran away."

I shivered in the October cool. "I moved here to find a place of solace, a site to lick my wounds. And it's turned out for the best because you needed this place too. We have our home now, far away from the maddening crowd."

Andrew spit over the railing, and we watched the water bomb plummet out of sight. "So you're happy here?"

I stepped away, settling into the deck chair. Stretching out my legs I slumped back, closing my eyes and relaxing to the sounds of the night. I thought about how different my life was now.

"There's good and bad. It's certainly relaxing. On the beach road down there people drive slower than the speed limit just 'cause they're in no hurry to get anywhere."

Andrew snorted. "That's no compliment."

I laughed with him. "Anyway, I sure love this condo."

"Yeah, it's nice. But you can find a nice home anywhere. How 'bout your job?"

"It's a job. That's about the best I can say for it. My boss is a butthead. He's always riding me, and then takes credit for everything I do."

"That's the pits. I'm gonna get some more milk. Want something to drink?"

"I'm okay."

Andrew returned with the drink, finished half, and put the glass on the table. He sat down across from me and took out his cell phone. I watched him fool with the buttons a bit.

"Going to call someone?"

"Nah. Just checking to see if maybe Travis texted." He put it back in his pocket. "You know, what I miss most is the great times with my buddies."

"I imagine. So what's up with the gang?"

He turned away.

"What?"

Glancing back at me, he shrugged. "Calvin got kicked out of school."

"Oh?" I remembered Calvin's parents had been very active in Riverside politics, PTA and such. They were the kind of family the school treasured. "Do you know what happened?"

Andrew reached up to scratch the side of his neck. "Got caught with Jack Black in his locker."

Images of the boys growing up flashed in my mind: in the sandbox, riding bikes together, having their adolescent swim parties.

"So what's he doing now?"

Andrew rose and stepped to the rail, staring out over the water. This cooler night air was my first experience with anything but hot and muggy since my arrival in March. The saltwater smell seemed lighter tonight, the air cleaner.

I got up and joined him. "You don't have to tell me if you don't want."

He glanced at me, his brow heavy. "Probably shouldn't. Supposedly sacking at Whole Foods, but really, he's pushing dope."

I felt my heart thump. Calvin had always been the wildest of the set, but I never would have predicted this. I started to blame his parents, about how they should be disciplining him better, but the words turned to ashes in my mouth. What right did I have to criticize, after what I had let Andrew suffer?

"What about the other boys?" I asked.

"You know Little Billy'll do whatever the other guys are into. I'm surprised he didn't get kicked out too."

"And your cousin?"

I saw Andrew's face stiffen, though I was unsure if in anger or resentment.

"Travis isn't doing all that stuff, is he?"

Andrew's silence gave me the answer. I struggled against my urge to call Peter and Celine right away, warn them to check into it. I wondered if maybe they already knew. I hadn't talked to Mallory's sister and her husband since I had left. This fellow, who had been my best friend most of my life, just as his son had been Andrew's, now was a stranger to me. But in this case, it was my fault. I'd ordered him not to call, had shut him out of my life.

"I'm sorry your friends have gotten into so much trouble. This must be hard on you, worrying about them, I mean."

He raised one shoulder in a half shrug and turned away from me again. "Yeah. So it goes."

I watched him kick at the rail a few times, his new Brooks getting their first scuffmarks. "So maybe you could make some new friends?"

He turned around and leaned back against the rail. "Me? How about you? You ain't exactly hitting the bars every night, would ya?"

"It's not easy to meet people at my age."

"Humph." He looked at me, an eyebrow raised in skepticism.

I shrugged. "Maybe, like you, I'm just not trying."

"Everyone needs a friend."

I reached out my arm and draped it over my son's shoulder. "Then I'm in luck. I've got the best friend of my life standing right next to me."

Andrew leaned into me for the hug.

Monday, October 20th

After the assembly let out, with the subsequent directing of parents to the teacher classrooms, I made Mrs. Perkins' Mississippi History my first stop. Two couples had beaten me there. As I stood in the background waiting my turn, I studied Sylvia. A simple print dress came to knee length, her marvelous calves stretching as she pumped one high-heeled shoe. With the three-inches she was a good half-foot shorter than me. Even without them she'd be tall enough for my liking. After five minutes I had her alone.

"Good to see you again, Rick. Hold on a moment." She opened a desk drawer and brought out the Davis book.

"I read it yesterday. My great-grandfather served in the state senate with Davis."

"And my great-grandfather served with Lincoln in the Illinois house. Quite a coincidence!" She held up the book but I waved it away. "It's a gift, from one history lover to another."

She nodded her appreciation. "Andy did a tremendous job on the Gettysburg paper he turned in today. I haven't had the opportunity to study it completely, but he's certain to earn another A."

"Another A?"

"Does that surprise you?" She placed the book back in the drawer. "Surely he's shown you his grades?"

"No, he hasn't mentioned them."

"He held straight A's at the mid-terms."

I glowed in his glory. "I can tell how you're inspiring him. At night we talk about the history he's studying, and occasionally share a book." I leaned forward, placing my fingertips next to hers on the desk. She didn't move away. "Thank you for encouraging him."

She looked down at her hand and slowly up my arm until she was staring up into my eyes. "I've found the best way to get my students to achieve is to give them high goals."

I heard the crowds buzzing in the hallways, and knew we'd be interrupted any moment. "You've made a world of difference in Andy's self-confidence. I'd very much like to show my appreciation by taking you out for dinner."

I watched her face; the nervous tick of her smile, dissolving into that cute pout. Her eyes flared, her pupils doubling in width. When reason fights desire, reason may win a battle, but desire always wins the war.

Her hand came to rest on my arm. "What would the administration think if one of their teachers started seeing a student's father?"

I covered her hand with my own. "Is it against the rules?"

She shook her head. "No, not against the rules. But it isn't done." She gently withdrew. Her smile returned to her face, but this time the smile didn't include her eyes.

"Thank you for coming by, Rick. Please give Andy my regards."

I nodded and made way for a pushy mother who had some loud complaints about the way her son was being treated. I stepped back, impressed with the diplomacy Sylvia used to calm the lady. Before that woman left, more parents came in, and then others. When I caught her eye, I waved, and she winked me a good-bye.

All his teaches confirmed Andrew's remarkable scholastic performance, two of them commenting on how well read he seemed. The calculus teacher mentioned the class was about to start some harder material. I assured him I could help Andrew, and made my departure.

Last on my list was Coach Dalton, the cross country coach. As Andrew had said, Coach Dalton's skin had that deep Central African look. He was dressed in white sweats with a whistle around his neck, talking with a group of big African-American men.

I made my way into the crowd and introduced myself as Andrew Lewis' father. I'm always afraid these macho types are going to try and crush my hand, and this guy's handshake was true to form. The other parents drifted off, leaving me alone with the coach.

"Andrew Lewis? Don't recognize the name. What sport does he play?"

"Cross country."

"I'm a bit confused here, Mr. Lewis. I'm sure I don't have Andrew on my team."

I nodded grimly, shaking my hand surreptitiously to return its circulation. Ever since that day two months ago when Andrew told me he wouldn't be on the team, I had been thinking of what I'd say to this man. "I know that. You turned him away."

Coach Dalton seemed confused. "I've never turned anybody away, Mr. Lewis. If the student shows up at practice he gets to compete in the event. Did your son ever come to any practices?"

I stepped back, struggling to change my perspective. "You never turn anyone away? I understood you already have a full team."

He smiled wanly. "We've had an off few years. I thought we might have a chance this year, but I lost one boy out as transfer and another is having knee problems. If your son's a runner I'd sure love to see him at practice."

"What time?"

The coach rummaged through some papers on his desk and pulled out a schedule. "Here. This lists the times of all the sports for the month. See right here, under cross country?" He pointed to the line.

I nodded. "Yes, of course. Wednesdays after school."

"Yep, though I expect the boys to run on their own every day. We have a meet the weekend after next. You think your Andrew would be ready to compete by then?"

"I'll ask him."

"Good, good. Tell him if he gives me two good practices he can compete in the upcoming Pascagoula meet."

I folded the paper into sixths and placed it in my shirt pocket. The coach's good-bye grip made me wince again.

Tuesday, October 21st

The next evening, I served Andrew's favorite dinner, spaghetti, watching with pleasure as he gobbled it down.

"Sauce sure is good," he remarked, pausing to chug some milk.

"Secret recipe."

"Thought it came from a jar?"

"That's just the stock. You remember when your mom and I used to argue over whose turn it was to make the sauce?"

"Yep. Both are great." He went back to shoveling down the noodles.

"How was school today?" I asked.

He answered without looking up. "Same old."

"How about Mississippi History? I thought you weren't doing well in it."

He glanced up before returning his attention to the plate. Between mouthfuls, he mumbled out phrases I translated into, "What gave you that idea? 'Cause I complain about the reading?"

He washed his swallow down with milk. "When Mrs. Perkins handed back my Civil War test, she said she'd make a Southerner out of me yet. I think she actually meant it as a compliment."

I chuckled at his joke. "I suppose there are worse fates."

"Did you know that General Grant's victory at Vicksburg cut the confederacy in half? It made him famous enough for Lincoln to appoint him General in Chief."

I knew the campaign against Vicksburg well, having read about it a dozen times. "Yep. That victory gave the North such a relief from its recent setbacks that Lincoln felt he had enough popularity to publish his Emancipation Proclamation. It would be fair to say without Grant's victory we might still have slavery in the South."

Andrew snorted. "I doubt it. The end of slavery was inevitable."

"Really? Did Mrs. Perkins say that?"

He nodded.

"Hmm," I continued. "I would have thought she'd be teaching you the Southern viewpoint on slavery."

Andrew shrugged. "Mrs. Perkins does have a different way of looking at things. She's nice and she's fair. She mentioned seeing you at the meeting last night."

I tried to sound casual. "Oh? What did she say?"

Andrew grabbed the bowl of spaghetti and spooned another large helping onto his plate, adding another ear of corn. I sat back, having nearly finished off the small portion I'd taken. I watched with envy as Andrew shoveled in the pasta. It hadn't been too many years ago I had enjoyed eating like that. Once I turned forty I realized I'd better learn restraint. Dieting and forty-five minutes daily on the exercise bike kept my belly fairly trim. Still, I missed the joy of unlimited eating.

"Um. I don't remember exactly. Something about you being a Yankee. Said something else." He paused to take a bite. "This corn sure is good. Where'd you get it?"

"Winn Dixie. What else did she say?"

"Sort of funny. She wondered if you'd asked for her phone number. She's mentioned it a couple of times."

"Oh? You have her number?"

"Yeah. Gave it to me back in the summer. Said I should call her if ... you know, if I needed someone to talk to."

"Did you?"

"Nah." Andrew resumed his spaghetti consumption. "Good food, Dad."

"How about giving me her number? I might need to call her someday – about your schoolwork or something." I wondered if he'd suspect I had ulterior motives, but apparently this one slipped by his teenage innocence.

"I suppose. Who else did you see? Did you meet the calculus teacher?"

"Yes, I saw all your teachers. I talked with someone else, too – someone who isn't one of your teachers."

Andrew put down his fork and took the corncob in both hands. "Making friends, huh? Good for you."

"No, I looked up Coach Dalton. He said he doesn't remember you trying out for the cross country team."

Andrew closed his eyes and put the corn down onto his plate. I waited, allowing the silence to insist on a reply.

"Maybe I didn't actually try out."

"What did you actually do?"

Andrew slumped into his chair. "On the day of the tryouts I went by and sat and watched them for an hour."

"Did you talk to the coach? Did you show him you could run?"

Andrew sat up again, picked up his fork, and put it down again. He stood and turned, looking out to the living room. He sighed and sat back down again, staring at his plate. "They didn't need me. I could see that. No point in butting in."

I leaned back, arms folded across my chest. "Have you been following the team?"

"Yeah. They're like tenth in the region. If they don't start winning soon they won't even qualify to run in the regional meet. It's the first weekend in December. Not much time left."

I took half of the one meatball remaining on my plate and stuffed it in my mouth. Chewing it thoughtfully, I twirled a small piece of onion around on my tongue before swallowing. "So, maybe your first assessment was wrong. Sounds like the team does need you after all. How are your times?"

"I beat my goal by thirteen seconds on this morning's run."

I watched my son pick 'up the corn again, biting off a long straight line across one side. "Thirteen seconds, huh?" I observed. "Maybe you should go to practice after school tomorrow."

Andrew nodded slowly. "Yeah, maybe I should."

He finished eating and we both stood, carrying our plates to the sink. "Your turn to do dishes," I remarked. "How's your homework looking?'

Andrew reached behind him to scratch his neck. "S'al'right. I got a paper to write for English, and, of course, the fifty pages for Mrs. Perkins."

"Tell you what, I'll take your turn and you go ahead and get your homework started."

His eyebrows raised in surprise. "Hmm? I don't mind taking my turn."

"It's all right." I went to work on the dishes, and by the time I was done scrubbing the saucepan Andrew was engrossed in his work, his books spread out across the kitchen table. I walked over to stand above him until he looked up.

"What?"

"How's it going?"

"Fine. You want something?"

"Just wondering if you had Mrs. Perkin's phone number handy."

He shuffled through a notebook until he found it, copied it onto a scrap, and handed it over. "Here. You gonna call her?"

I nodded.

"Tell her that I'm gonna join the track team, and maybe she could cut down the reading, would ya?"

"How long does it take you?"

He picked up a paperback and showed it to me, <u>Reconstruction in the South</u>. "It's not that I can't read it, but, Jeez, some of this stuff is boring."

He went back to his work and I grabbed the cordless phone from the kitchen, taking it out on the balcony. A front was coming in, dark clouds obscured the stars, and a strong wind rattled the hanging plants, sending the wind chimes a' clamoring. I considered taking the phone to the quiet of my bedroom, but the breeze felt too good after being inside all day. I snuggled up against the patio doors, using the light from the living room to read the phone number.

It rang three, four, five times until the answering machine picked up. "You have reached the Hewes residence. Please leave a message."

I hadn't really thought about what I was going to say. "Uh. Hi Sylvia, this is Rick. Um. Andy said he … uh… said he's going to go out for the track. And … uh … he wanted to let you know that he might not have time. To do all that reading … um. I mean … ah heck."

I hung up, embarrassed that I'd made such a mess of the call. Holding the phone loosely by my side I stared out at the water. Usually calm, with only the rare whitecap, tonight the winds had roughened it up, so that even with the heavy cloud cover I could see lights from the condo tower sparkling in the turbulence. The phone rang and I jerked it to my ear. "Hello?"

Sylvia's laughter made me smile. "You are so funny, Rick."

I joined in her laughter. "Heh. Sorry. I guess … uh, I guess I wasn't sure of what I wanted to say."

"And is that what you wanted to say? Tell me that I'm working Andy too hard?"

I shook my head, though, of course, I knew she couldn't see it. "No, that wasn't it at all. Actually, I was calling to see if you had reconsidered my offer to go out on a date? I'd prefer to take you out for dinner, but we could start with coffee. We could talk about history, and, well, you know, about our lives."

I listened as the silence lengthened. I figured this was a good sign. At least she wasn't saying "No," and slamming down the phone. I looked in the living room, where Andrew had moved to the couch, his head on one armrest, his big tennis shoes hanging off the other. The *Reconstruction* book was in his hands, his ears filled with iPod buds.

"You remember what I said about dating parents, don't you Rick?"

"Of course I do. You said it wasn't against the rules."

I delighted at the melody of her laugh. "You certainly are bold, sure enough. Tell me about Andy and the track team."

"I talked with the track coach at the meeting last night," I told her. "He said he'd welcome Andy, so I've talked Andy into trying out. They practice on Wednesdays."

"I hope he makes it. In my experience, teammates often become good friends."

I hadn't thought about that. "I certainly hope so." The conversation seemed to have reached a lull, so I dragged for a new topic. "Your answering machine said Hewes' residence?"

"I live with my maiden aunt. Of course you're not familiar with the Hewes Mansion or our history in the city?"

"Sorry."

She chuckled. "Since you claim to like history, perhaps you'd like to hear some of the Gulf Coast Hewes Family history. Give us something to talk about on this date you want."

I felt my cheeks crinkle in a smile. "You bet, Sylvia. How about next week?"

"My, my, Rick. You Yankees really like to rush, now don't y'all? Southerners like to take their time, get to know each other."

"Good. We can do that over dinner. Are you free Saturday night?"

She laughed. "Perhaps the next time you want to discuss Andy's schoolwork, I'll be available. Bye for now, Rick."

"Sylvia, wait."

"Yes?"

"Um." I couldn't think of anything else to say. "Okay then. I'll call you again soon."

"I'm expecting you to." She clicked off.

I held the phone loosely by my side and stared out to the lightning far at sea. It seemed friendlier now, as if the storm came in on winds of hope.

Saturday, November 1st

The scattered showers that had ruined last night's trick and treating had left this morning's air clean. Dozens of athletic boys dressed in outfits of bright school colors loitered around the track. As I held Andrew's feet during his stretches, I scanned the crowd.

"How many kids do you think are here?"

Andrew gave the crowd a quick survey. "Six schools."

"How many runners does Gulfport High have?"

"Nine. Only top five finishers count." He stood and began twisting back and forth at the waist.

I studied the Gulfport runners, all but Andrew gathered with their coach. As he had said, each was African-American, five boys and three girls. I noticed one boy had a bandage and a limp. "Who's that boy with the knee brace? Is he going to run?"

"That's Jamerion. He's just going to walk. You gotta finish two races during the year to qualify for Regionals77. Doesn't matter how bad you do, as long as you finish two."

He pointed across the track to another group. "See those guys in the green and white shorts? That's Harrison Central. They've won every meet this year."

I looked. Harrison's team had many more runners. "You said you have to finish two races before Regionals?"

"Yeah." He stretched out, one leg at a time. "The Bay's in two weeks; Regionals three weeks later in Hattiesburg."

In Chicago I'd been to a few of his races. They'd been much smaller events, with only three or four teams, and usually held in a city park. "What's the race like? Just around the track?"

Andrew snorted. "What kind of cross country race would that be?" I followed his finger, seeing a dirt path take off along a creek, shaded by an old oak canopy. "Around the track and into the woods."

I looked across the track to the Gulfport boys. "Which is the new friend you've been telling me about?"

He stopped stretching to look. "Devonne. He's the tall guy, number six. He gets starting spot, followed by his cousin Lebron, and then me."

Andrew pointed to lane four where the coach of Harrison Central was carefully arranging his runners in place. "See that guy at the start of the Harrison line and the girl right behind him with the French knot?"

I nodded. "The boy wearing number twenty-three?"

"Yeah. They call him Flash. Came in first every meet so far. The girl's name is Judy Jones. Holds some kind of record in the four-forty. At the meet two weeks ago in Slidell, Devonne split them. First time he's beat her this year."

"Coach Dalton is waving for you," I noted.

"Yeah. I'll see you after the race." He trotted a few yards and stopped. Pointing at a small group of adults, he called to me, "Why don't you go talk with Devonne's parents? Last name's Barnes."

I observed the animated couple laughing as they set up a pitcher and some glasses on a small table between some lounge chairs. She poured a bag of pretzels into a bowl as another fellow joined them. I realized this was the first time I'd been to a social function since I'd moved South. As Andrew had said, I certainly wasn't hitting the bars at night. I still didn't feel ready.

"I guess I'll just sit and read 'til you get back," I called. "Good luck."

Andrew flashed a thumb's up and ran across to slip into his spot in line. A man with a bullhorn standing just off the track called out, "On your marks."

The runners quieted, determined looks fixing their features. They bent forward at the words, "Get set."

With a siren blast from the horn, the racers were off. I watched them string out a bit during the first lap. Devonne Barnes, Andrew's friend, ran in the top four, with Andrew striding near the pack middle. They disappeared into the woods.

I looked over at the Barnes family. Several others gathered around them, and they laughed and talked as they passed around lemonade. The woman who had poured the pretzels saw me looking and waved for me to come over. I waved back but shook my head, pointing to my book. Placing my lawn chair under a tree, I settled down and opened the biography I'd brought.

I tore myself away from the story when I noticed spectators standing and peering into the woods. The Barnes crowd and a group from Harrison Central began cheering, shouting encouragement as the first two runners broke out of the trees and hit the track. Flash ran in first, with Devonne pulling hard at his heels. They made a quarter of the way around when a second couple broke from the woods. It was Andrew in front, with Judy Jones barely ten feet behind.

I jumped to my feet as cheers broke out from the families.

At the halfway point of this last lap, Devonne caught up to Flash, but had to drop behind him on the two final curves. Andrew kept a steady pace, the distance between him and the Harrison Central runner slowly narrowing as she strained to catch up. She seemed to be pumping her legs nearly twice as fast as Andrew's longer stride.

Once past the final curve, with less than ten yards of straight away left, Devonne put on a determined sprint. At the finish line he slipped in ahead by half a foot. The Barnes crowd hooted and cheered, quieting again as Andrew neared the finish.

Judy Jones had almost caught up to Andrew coming into the final curve. I had been watching the girl make up the distance on this last lap, and worried that Andrew had given all he had. Not that it would bother me if she did pass him. Fourth place would be a fabulous finish.

I saw Andrew's eyes narrow, his mouth set. My son began pumping his legs like a locomotive, and within seconds he left his competitor far behind. When he crossed, he raised both his fists in triumph. I gave a whoop and he turned to me, rewarding me with the biggest smile I'd seen on that face in twenty-three months.

He ran across the field to a spot where Coach Dalton and the other Gulfport High parents gathered. When the other racers finished and joined the group they all gave each other "high fives." Eventually he came over.

"Third place! Did you see that, Dad? Third place!"

I pulled my son into a big hug, feeling his sweat rub onto my own skin and clothes. It was a fabulous hug, a celebration not just of this astounding victory, but more, an affirmation that finally the worst was past for Andrew.

"So how did your team do overall?"

"Scorer still calculating," he said. "Come on over to the picnic, Dad. We're going to celebrate. Maybe go for ice cream."

I looked over at the group, the parents slapping each other on the back, the kids laughing and punching each other. It reminded me of the Riverside parties, of when Jenny and her team were winning tennis trophies. The image of my daughter made me shudder and I grabbed onto my chair with both hands.

"Dad? You okay?"

I collapsed into the chair and put my head below my knees. Andrew came up and put his hand on my shoulder. "Dad?"

"Yeah, give me a minute." I took a couple of deep breaths. "You go be with your friends. Tell them I'll make it next time."

He looked at me warily. "You sure?"

I nodded. "Yeah. Just going to sit here a moment more."

He looked behind him at the group, and hesitated.

"I'll be fine; go enjoy yourself," I said, taking a ten from my wallet and handing it over. "I've got a big project I need to work on. You think one of them will give you a ride home?"

"Sure." He scampered back to his friends. I closed my eyes, resting a moment more before grabbing my chair and heading to the car.

Sunday, November 2nd

The Barnes family dropped Andrew off in the early afternoon and he showered, afterwards going over the race with me practically step by step, talking about all the runners and how he'd planned out every sprint. Late that evening we went out for a casino buffet dinner where we talked and laughed, happiness blowing away the black clouds that had taken up such an unshakeable residence.

By the time I got out of bed the next morning, Andrew had already left for his run. I cooked breakfast and we hung around the condo, enjoying the relaxation inherent in a Sunday morning. When lunchtime approached I suggested we take a walk along the beach to the mall.

The cool front still hung about, yet the beaches had a good share of weekend bathers. As we passed one set of teenagers, Andrew gave a wave to a short fellow leaning on a Chevy.

"Hey Andy," the boy called back.

Once we'd walked well past him, I asked, "Who's that?"

Andrew shrugged. "A kid from chemistry class."

"Oh? Someone you hang around with?"

"Just a kid."

His casual smile reassured me, and I pulled off my jacket, enjoying the sun on my bare arms. Soon we were eating Chinese in the food court. "Let's buy you a prize for having placed third," I suggested. "What appeals to you? A couple of CDs? Maybe some posters for your room?"

"Actually …" he hesitated. "Nah, probably too expensive."

"What?"

"How 'bout backup shoes, would ya? In case my feet keep growing."

"Are you sure? They're only a month old." I looked down at his feet. The Brooks were size thirteen, a half size bigger than my shoes. "Sure. Let's see if we can find something you like." At the Shoe Locker I watched Andrew try on two dozen pairs before finally selecting some Nikes, a full size bigger than the Brooks.

We enjoyed our walk home and an afternoon nap. That evening I cooked a frozen pizza. Andrew brought out his calculus book and I helped him understand the concept of differentials, working through three pages of sample problems until he felt confident.

Andrew put down his pencil. "I still can't believe I got third place," he said for the twentieth time. "Man, did you see me blow Judy Jones away? Huh?"

My face had grinned so much my cheeks were starting to hurt. "Great job!

You sure proved yourself! What'd your teammates say?"

His face glowed. "Should qualify us for Regionals."

"So you said the next race is in Bay St. Louis?"

"Yeah. Two weeks. Gonna be a smaller meet." He closed his calculus book. "You see the guys high-five me?"

"Yes, I saw."

He pulled out his Mississippi History book, shuffled a couple of pages, and closed it again, clearly too distracted to study. "Man, it feels great, back on a team. Tomorrow morning my name'll be posted on the winner's list on the gym bulletin board."

I leaned back in my chair and nodded. "Take a photo of it on your cell phone. Maybe you can post it on your Facebook." The kitchen phone rang. "I'll get it," I said.

I picked up the portable piece and leaned against the wall, watching Andrew work as I talked. "Hello?"

"Rick, it's Peter."

My brother-in-law's familiar voice sounded strangely raw. Though I hadn't talked to him since the separation, I was glad to hear from him.

"Hi Peter. What's up? ... Hello? ... Hello?"

I could hear his breathing, a somber rhythm that brought up memories of that prior phone call, the one telling of Jenny's death. "Peter! What happened?"

I must have shouted, because I saw Andrew sit upright in his chair. "What?" he demanded. I brought the phone and settled into the chair across the table from him.

Peter choked out his words. "The boys were out drunk driving last night, flipped the car and slammed into a tree. Travis broke his leg and some ribs."

Car accident I mouthed to Andrew, as Peter continued. "Calvin's in the ICU with brain damage. Billy ...." He choked up again. After a couple of coughs that were half sobs he said, "Billy's dead."

Little Billy? Dead? Good Lord.

"Rick? You there?"

I forced my tongue to work. "I am so sorry, Peter. I don't know what to say. I can't even think."

I could hear him sobbing on the other end. For some reason images of happier times flashed into my mind, an evening at the exclusive nightclub Buzz, oh, maybe twenty years before. Peter had just landed an important client and his law firm had given him a big bonus. The women, sleek in their cocktail dresses, wore jewelry dripping like rainwater. We thought life held nothing but glory.

Peter spoke. "How's Andy doing?"

My heart melted for this father, grieving his son's injury, and the death and injury of the other boys as well, yet still concerned enough to inquire about Andy. *Well, he is his uncle after all.*

"He finally seems to be adjusting to Mississippi. This is going to be hard on him." I glanced at Andrew. I could read the paralysis in his eyes, his need to know fighting his fear of knowing.

"The funeral's in two days," Peter said. "If Andy wants to stay with us, he can bunk with Travis in the pullout bed."

"Peter, your family, and all of the others too, will be in my prayers." I clicked off. "I think we better go out on the balcony."

Andrew nodded, stood, and ambled out. I followed slowly. At the rail Andrew pointed out the distant lights of a tanker bobbing along on its perpetual journey.

"I wonder what it would be like to live out on the ocean?" he asked.

I considered the question, trying to picture myself spending day after day at sea. "I'd probably get bored."

"Bored?" Andrew mused. "Could stand a little peace. Something's happened to Travis, huh?"

"Yes. And to your other friends."

I studied his face, features accented by strange shadows from a cloud passing over the moon.

"They all dead?"

"Billy is. Your cousin broke his leg and Calvin's in the ICU."

Andrew reached for me and we hugged tightly, his body trembling. A low mournful wail introduced his sobbing. I held him for a short eternity. When he pushed away we stared out to the enveloping night. The moon, nearly full, bathed the shore in stark white, giving the palm trees a zombie glow.

"Little Billy's dead, huh? Always the unlucky one. Who was driving?"

"I didn't ask."

Andrew leaned over the railing and let out one of his spit bombs. It shimmered in the moonlight on its way to a barely heard *thunk*.

"I've got to go up there," he said.

I shivered. Chicago had become a foreign land: a place of crime, fear, and tragedy. Now my son wanted to go into the fire. "Do you have to?" I asked.

Andrew stared out at the ocean, as if hoping the answer might come to him on the southern breezes. "My friends need me. Gotta see Calvin; stand by my cuz Travis. Why wouldn't I?"

"Chicago has a lot of temptations. Your last few months you were making bad choices. Alcohol. Drugs. Wild car rides. Chicago isn't a good place for you, Andy. What if something happens?"

He left the rail and settled onto one of the deck chairs, bending down and retying his shoes. He spent forever on each one. When he looked up he gave me a smile. "Life's funny. I've wanted to get back to Chicago since I got here. But now I wanna stay in Mississippi. This'll only be a visit."

I leaned back against the rail watching him, studying the confidence that shines in the face of a seventeen-year-old. He thought he was invincible, could resist any temptation. But I'd been seventeen once, and I knew what could happen. "What if someone offers you drugs?"

Andrew settled back against the chair, his eyes closed. "I can handle myself."

It was an answer, but it wasn't one. I sat down on the other chair. "If something were to happen ..."

"Nothin's gonna happen."

"Yeah. But if something were ..."

Andrew waited. A shiver passed through me like the chill of a sudden rainstorm. I forced my heart to quiet. "If I lost you too, I'd kill myself."

He stood, came to my side of the table, and hugged me around the neck from behind. I grabbed his arms, forcing them snug against my breast, and leaned my head back against his chest. I looked up into his face, into that blue-eyed stare that had matured so much in the past six months. He was a different boy than when he'd arrived, more confident, more stable.

"When are you thinking of leaving?"

He stepped back, leaning against the patio door. "First thing tomorrow I guess. Can I put the plane ticket on your card?"

"Of course, but can't you wait a few days? I'm in the middle of a project at work right now, giving a presentation Wednesday morning. Give me a few days and I can come with you."

Andrew stared at the stars as he considered. "Look, there's Aquarius – always reminds me of a cursive M."

I waited for him to come back to earth.

"Nah. Best leave tomorrow."

I rubbed my forehead, trying to release the tension. "How long do you think you'll be gone?"

"I guess 'til Saturday. Can you call Mrs. Perkins and have her get my classwork?"

"Sure."

The sound of a jet intruded on our world, and I looked up, picking out its shadow weaving between the stars. Its rumble slowly faded, leaving us listening to the chimes dancing with the wind.

"What do you think happens to us after death?" Andrew asked.

I looked down at my hands, clasped now, as if I were trying to hold myself together. "That's an age old question, Andy. I remember my father always believed in a soul, a spirit that would go up to heaven after death. I know that concept brought him comfort. I guess I used to believe in a soul, too."

I stopped to choke down a sob. "But after Jenny's death I stopped believing in souls. If there were souls, then there'd have to be a heaven; and if there's a heaven, there would have to be a God. And I know damned well there can't be a God."

I pounded on the table, the glass shuddering under the blow. "No God in heaven would create such pain! There's nothing left of your sister now but memories. Nothing, I tell you. Not a soul, not a spirit, not a damn thing to show for the wonderful woman she was about to become."

Andrew waited for me to calm before he answered, his voice soft and soothing. "That's pretty harsh, Dad."

I walked inside and over to the bookshelf where I pulled out one of my engineering books and held it up to Andrew who had followed. "This book and the others like it describe the world as it is. I can measure the height of a balcony. I can calculate the speed of a dropped spit-bomb."

Andrew tilted his head. "You don't believe in stuff you can't measure?"

"Right!"

"Then how many grains of sand on that beach, Dad?"

I grinned in spite of myself, turning to replace the book. Stroking the various volumes, I spoke into them, as if they were my children instead of Andrew. "Sand is real. I can't count all of it, but I can touch it."

He came up beside me, reaching over my shoulder to pull out my father's bible. "You can't touch prayers. Didn't you just say somethin' about prayers to Uncle Peter?"

I smelled the oil wafting from the bible's leather cover. I still coated it once a week with Pecard Conditioner, the same way I had watched my father love this family heirloom. I remembered when he had read it to me, using bible stories to illustrate the difference between good and evil. I remembered the Sunday services we had shared, with the comfort I felt from the traditional recitations.

"A prayer is real, something I can read and share. The concept of a soul is purely abstract, something made up to pacify the fearful."

Andrew shook his head and walked back out on the balcony. I followed, finding him pointing to the beach. "Look, see that dead fish? Why ain't that fish still swimming?"

He leaned back against the rail and I settled into the deck chair.

"Somethin' is lost when things die. Somethin' real." He pointed at a couple of beach walkers holding hands in the moonlight. "Can you measure love?"

I shook my head. "No. Sometimes you can't even recognize it."

"So maybe the soul is like love."

I pictured my father after his stroke. He lived another two months, but his life-force had disappeared. I watched the two lovers disappear into the shadows, and thought of love, and life, and death.

Andrew's voice broke my reverie. "Where's your credit card?"

"In my wallet on my dresser," I said. "Uncle Peter says you can stay with them."

"Great."

He started to leave but I stood and grabbed his arm, pulling him tightly against my chest. I whispered in his ear, "Andy, I love you. Please come back safely."

"You can count on me, Dad." He pushed away and paused by the door.

"Take your heavy coat; it's going to dip below freezing at night."

"'Kay."

"Don't forget to call every day."

"Dad!"

I nodded and smiled weakly. "Right. Well. Have a good trip."

Andrew gave thumbs up and walked back through the living room. I stood staring, unseeing, long after he was gone. Finally turning back to the railing, I watched the moon shadows dance on the ripples. Andrew's happy world had once more been thrown into turmoil. *Still, it was only for a week. There shouldn't be a problem. Right?*

I meandered back into the condo, stopping to give it the once over. Everything seemed perfect; the Ella Fitzgerald on the stereo, the track lighting on the pale blue walls, the blue and white Oriental rug setting an austere but cultured feel. It'd been years since I had my own place to decorate. Its serenity calmed me.

Returning to the kitchen, I read Sylvia's number off the note I'd taped on the refrigerator and punched it in. It rang three times before she answered.

"Hello?"

I loved the sound of her voice, its long honey-dripping syllables reminding me of the sweetness of the South. "Hi Sylvia. It's Rick Lewis. You got a minute?"

"Certainly. Is this about Andy ... or something personal?"

I paused, wondering if maybe she was hoping for the second. She was so hard to read, sometimes seeming so interested in me, and then following up with a door slam in my face. I never will understand women.

"Something's come up and Andy's going to have to miss a week of school."

I heard her catch her breath. Was she remembering how Andrew had looked when she had first seen him, his unkempt appearance and downward cast eyes? She'd been wonderful for him; of course she'd be concerned. "Is he ill?" she asked.

"One of his friends died in a car accident in Chicago. He's going to fly up for the funeral."

"Oh my. Young lives snuffed out! I've seen it all too often. I'm sure Andy's devastated."

I realized that he hadn't been devastated, sad, yes, but not hysterical. I was proud of him, my confidence a bit restored. "He's taking it pretty well. He asked if you could gather up his assignments for the week."

I listened to her breathe; sweet, almost song-like whispers echoed through the earpiece. "Rick?"

"What?"

"Are you worried about Andy going back to Chicago?"

I carried the phone back out to the balcony, letting the silence lengthen. Something about staring out over the waters brought comfort. Perhaps the immensity helped put my own problems into perspective.

"Rick?"

"I'm sure he'll be all right."

"You don't sound sure."

The moon had arced a few degrees in the ten minutes I'd been inside. It wasn't much, but it reminded me that the earth would turn, my child would get older. I had to let him go.

"Rick?"

"Nothing. He'll be fine. Say, how about I take you out for dinner Friday night and you can give me Andy's classwork then?"

It was her turn to hesitate, and when she spoke her refusal sounded halfhearted. "I told you I don't usually date parents."

"You ever eaten at Portofino's? Nice view of the beach. How does seven o'clock sound? I can pick you up or we can meet there. Your choice."

She laughed. "You're quite the persistent Yankee, you know that?"

"So that means yes?"

"Call me back Thursday evening." She clicked off.

I dropped the phone on the table behind me, and turned my attention to the moon. She smiled back at me, throwing a little wink I think, like Sylvia had given me. Yes, she was a cute one.

Tuesday, November 4th

I checked my watch for the twentieth time. The funeral had been at four, and now, nearing ten o'clock, I still hadn't heard from Andrew. Not a word since his call when he arrived at the airport yesterday. I'd considered phoning him, but decided to let him grieve in peace.

Closing my laptop, I stood and walked out to the balcony. The early November night temperature had dropped down into the forties and I shivered, reaching up to rebutton the collared shirt I still wore from work. I'd only had coffee and buttered toast when I got home, my stomach upset by my anxieties about both Andrew and my presentation planned for the next morning.

I picked up the phone and dialed Peter. He sounded glum.

"It's been a rough day, Rick. Everyone was bawling at the funeral. Mrs. Jackson was in shock."

"I can imagine." I had never known Little Billy's parents well. She did something with the American Heart Association, and the father seemed to be out of town all the time. But, of course, I knew too well how they must be feeling.

"And the boys?" I asked. I wondered how Andrew was reacting, now back with the school chums he and his sister had known all their lives. Would he see Jenny around every corner like I had?

Peter sounded hopeful. "Andy's been great for Travis; inseparable from the moment he stepped off the plane. They went together to see Calvin this morning, the first time Travis has been able to face the trip."

"Wow. How'd that go?"

"Pretty hard on them both from what I could tell. It's tough when you lose a buddy. Speaking of which, I feel like I've lost one too."

"Who?"

"You! I'm talking about you, Buddy. Aren't you tired of this hermit thing yet?"

I remembered how good it was to have Peter to confide in. We had been best friends since childhood, setting role models for Travis and Andrew. The Adams sisters had been that way, too, inseparable from birth, though, of course Mallory was a year younger.

"So how's it going with Celine these days?"

There was no hesitation in his voice. "Fabulous! She's got an art show opening in one week at a cute little gallery near the Uptown Theatre on Broadway. You remember that area? There used to be that sweet Greek restaurant."

"And Rebecca?"

This time the answer didn't come as quickly. "She's, um, doing well she tells me. Enjoying her classes."

I waited, but when he didn't continue, I prompted. "What's wrong, Pete?"

When he answered, it was almost a prayer. "Jenny was Rebecca's best friend. When Jenny died, it destroyed Rebecca too. I don't know if she's even going to classes. I keep urging her to come back home, but she says she can't face the memories."

Jenny's murder had destroyed so many lives. And for all this grief, Rod-rod only got seven months! Well, that was all the justice system had given him, anyway. I forced my mind not to go down that path, quickly changing the subject. "So what's the word on Calvin?"

"Still in a coma. The Smiths were at the funeral with their other three kids. Ed came up and we hugged."

"Any word on who was driving?" I asked.

There was a long pause. "Why stir up trouble, Rick? Let's just let it be."

I wondered if he were trying to protect Travis, but shrugged it off. Really it wasn't any of my business. Whoever it was, forgiveness was called for. Thinking of forgiveness led me to how I could never forgive Rod-rod, which led me to Jenny's death, and that brought me full circle back to Little Billy. The slaughter of our youth was all the proof a budding atheist needed.

"So big funeral, I'm guessing," I said. "Everyone from the school there?"

"Everyone and their third cousin. Lakeview had their largest viewing room open and they still had people standing along the sides and back."

All those people … I remembered the school events, the huge crowds in the auditorium and on fieldtrips. All the kids would gather in their cliques, with Andrew it was mostly the four boys. Sometimes Sarah and her gaggle of girls would join them, the boys and girls teasing each other mercilessly. "How's Sarah doing? I bet she and Andy were happy to get back together."

He hesitated.

"Don't tell me she prefers that Chris Bradshaw?" I demanded.

"Looked to me like she was avoiding Andy."

"Damn. For that stuck up little snot? I never would have thought. How about letting me talk to him, okay?"

"The boys said they wanted to go get some air. I think they took a walk to the park."

Images of the neighborhood park flashed in my mind, when the kids were little ones, pushing them in the swings, the occasional lunch picnic. "Well, they won't be out there long I would think. What's the temperature?"

He paused, and I imagined he was probably looking it up somewhere. "Four below. I'm sure you're right. You want me to have him call you when he gets in?"

I checked my watch yet again. "I guess not. It's getting late and I have a big presentation in the morning. Tell him to call me tomorrow evening."

"Sure thing. By the way, how are you doing?"

I considered. I had a good home, a decent job, and the love of my son. There'd been some rough times, but maybe life was coming along. I even had a date. "I think I may have turned a corner here, Pete. Andy's adjusted to school and making a few friends. I got these fools at work to listen to my ideas, and, well, I'm finally sleeping through the night. At least sometimes."

"Glad to hear it, buddy. So does this mean we can start talking again?"

I wondered why I had felt such a need to tune out even my best friend. Whatever that wound had been, it was finally healing. "Yeah. I tell you what. After I talk to Andy tomorrow evening, let's you and I chat it up. I'll let you know how my presentation went if you've got time to listen?"

"Always time for you, good buddy. Say about eight? Hold on a second. Yeah, it's on my Blackberry."

He paused and I began stacking the papers on my desk.

"There's one more thing," Peter said.

"Yeah?"

"Mallory. She's back in the hospital."

I didn't respond. What could I say?

"Rick?"

"I'm not surprised. I mean, thanks for telling me. But I'm here, you know, and she's there."

"That's definitely part of the problem, Rick. She needs you. You know, we were just talking about how Travis and Andy had each other for support. Don't you think you and Mallory might be good for each other? Why don't you fly up here and visit?"

I took a deep breath. "I'm not coming back to Chicago, and that's final. Hey, it's late, and I've got this meeting I gotta do in the morning. Okay? Been great talking with you."

"Whoa. Sorry I punched your button there."

I fidgeted. "No, I'm just tired, that's all. Give Andy my love … oh, and Travis and Celine too, of course. Remember to tell Andy to call me, okay?"

After disconnecting I spent another couple of hours trying to concentrate on my presentation, but my mind was too distracted. Why hadn't Andy called me? Was it really my fault Mallory kept bouncing back into the hospital? What was I doing in Mississippi, anyway? I gave it up, poured myself a stiff drink and headed to bed.

Andrew: Tuesday, November 4th

During the day homebound mothers and their toddlers kept the neighborhood park alive with laughter. Now, in the deep dark and cold, the boys had the park to themselves. Andrew pulled his coat tighter as a bitter wind whistled through the icicles in the overhanging branches.

He sat on a swing, fingering the ice-coated chains through his gloves. He watched Travis settle onto the ground, propping up his casted leg on some rocks. The park's stark lighting gave his cousin's face a cachectic look.

"Heck of a funeral," Andrew said. "Sort of good to see everyone again, though wish it could have been at a party instead."

"Yeah. Hate it we had to kill someone to get you to come home."

Andrew had noticed Travis's jokes seemed forced, the humor dark. "Not funny, Cuz. Not with Jenny's funeral less than two years ago."

Travis waved. "Sorry. Not myself." He struggled back up on his crutches and held onto the other swing, propping his leg on its seat. "I can't believe Billy's really dead."

"And Calvin's so sedated, he didn't even open his eyes when you poked him. Man, if it wasn't so good to see you, I'd hate this visit!"

Travis laughed. "Ha. Well, I sure appreciate you coming up, Andy."

"You knew I'd come."

Travis spat, the droplet pooling out on the ground where he twirled it in the dirt with his crutch. "Didn't know if you'd come or not. Last we talked seemed like you'd turned away from all of us." Travis pulled his leg off the swing and hobbled in a small circle. "Damn it's cold out here. Too cold to sit still, but my leg hurts to have it down."

Andrew thought back to the day he'd been dragged down to Mississippi. He remembered when his father had predicted that if he'd stayed in Chicago, he'd have died. His father had been right. If he'd been in that car it might just as easily have been him instead of Billy in that coffin. "I've picked a different path, that's all." He pointed at Travis's cast. "Maybe you should think about changing too."

Andrew smelled the once familiar fern-laden boggy creek, listened to the crickets serenading, and felt the cold metal rings, smooth in his hands. "Hey, remember when we used to sneak out here and down a couple of doobies? Man, those were great nights."

Travis laughed lightly. "Oh yeah! You were so funny when you were stoned, talking about the white vans spying on you."

Andrew shivered, blaming the cold Chicago weather. "That's what they tell me. I don't remember."

"What do you remember?"

Andrew started swinging, pumping his legs and pulling the chains in tandem. Soon he was arcing high, back and forth, bringing forth a rhythm of creaky metal. He wondered if he let go at the top of the arc whether he'd soar straight up to heaven.

He called out his answer as he swung, hearing the words whistle past his ears. "I remember the fun. I remember the four of us kicking back, meeting with the girls, talking about the great things we would do. I remember the joy rides and the great nights playing billiards in my basement. I remember feeling carefree and being the happiest I'd ever been in my life."

"And you're not that happy now?"

Andrew allowed the swing to slow again, and stopped with his feet. He walked to the end of the playground and back as he considered.

"No, not really. I mean, it's not as bad as when I first got there. I've met a couple of guys, but you'll always be my best friend, Cuz. You and Calvin and Little Billy were my homeboys. I'll never have anything like that again. Everything's messed up now, and even Sarah's got another boyfriend. That really hurt seeing them hanging on to each other."

Travis lowered himself onto the swing and crossed his crutches to form an elevated rest for his casted leg. "Funny, you're both my cousins, yet we're all so freakin' different. Sarah's a straight edge, and now she's got a boyfriend to match."

"Did you see how she turned her back on me?"

Travis guffawed. "Yep, that was hilarious! You dropped your jaw to your knees! She's pretty pissed you never called."

Andrew hugged himself. "Yeah, should've. But we were already on the outs. She kept bugging me about my booze and pot. 'Course, turns out she was right."

"Ah, don't go moralistic, Buddy. She's just missing out on all the fun. Hey, remember when she and our sisters had that make-up party up at your Dad's place in Wisconsin? Thirteen years old, she looked like a whore with all that crap on her face. I was ROFLin'."

"Yeah, a riot." Andrew reached up and picked a couple of icicles off a branch, handing one to Travis and putting the other in his own mouth. The coldness set his teeth to chattering. "Now Jenny's dead and Sarah hates me. At least Rebecca's doing okay, huh?"

Travis poked at a pile of dead leaves with his crutch. "Maybe. She's off in Stanford, prelaw of course. She says she may not make it home for Christmas this year."

"These are really sad times, Travis."

He nodded. "The pits. Hell. I know what always makes me feel better." Travis pulled out a joint and lit it, taking a long hard draw. He held it out. "You want some?"

Andrew shook his head. "Shouldn't."

"Come on. What's one little hit gonna do?"

The sweet aroma tickled Andrew's nose, reminding him of the good times he used to have. Taking the joint from Travis he took a deep inhalation. As he held in the smoke he felt the pleasant sensations, the magnificent images and strange feelings the drug unleashed. "I had forgotten how much I liked this," he said. "You have any more?"

"Hey, Buddy, I've got all you can smoke. I say we get so stoned that we can't even remember this awful mess."

Wednesday November 5th

After a few hours of fitful tossing I'd given up on sleep. Sitting at the breakfast table, I finished my second cup of coffee as I studied again the PowerPoint slide showing the estimated improvement in turnaround time with my proposed changes. Once I made my presentation, I was certain they'd jump at the chance to make the company more productive and profitable.

When the phone rang I glanced at the clock in surprise, reading a few minutes after five. The caller ID showed the call came from Peter's cell phone.

"Hey Pete, it's awfully early. What's up?"

His voice sounded hoarse. "Bad news, Rick. I'm here with Andy in the E.R."

The pencil snapped in my hand. "What are you talking about? What happened? Not another car accident?"

"No. He's hallucinating again. Started last night. Travis drove him around for awhile, thinking he'd fall asleep or get over it. Travis finally brought him home an hour ago and woke me up. Andy's totally out of control."

"Jesus Christ! Can't you keep an eye on your nephew? You know how vulnerable he is." I stood, carrying the phone into the bedroom where I threw off my robe and began pulling on clothes.

Peter's voice had a touch of anger. "Hey, it's not my fault. Andy's got a problem, and casting accusations isn't going to help."

I pulled the phone through my shirtsleeve. "Sorry, Pete. So what's going to happen next?"

"I guess they'll be putting him back in the psych hospital."

"No they're not!" I shouted. "Don't let them! Can't they just sedate him and let it wear off?"

"I don't think so. Anyway, with Mallory in the hospital, I don't see there's an alternative."

I pulled on my pants and reached for my socks. "I'll hop a plane there this morning. Don't let them admit him. You can do that, Pete. I know you can. Please. I'm begging you."

He hesitated only a moment, but his answer sounded sincere. "I'll do my best, Rick. It'll be good to see you."

"Hold on a moment." I ran back to the computer and pulled up the airline reservation website. Peter maintained silence at his end, though I could hear the echoes of voices in the background. "You with him now?" I asked.

"Nope, coffee shop. I'm on my laptop canceling my morning meetings."

"Yeah, I gotta do that too." With a couple more clicks I finished making the reservations, round trip for me and one way return for Andrew. "Okay, I'm booked on Continental, six o'clock out of Gulfport, changes in Houston. Lands in Chicago at ten-thirty-three."

"You want me to pick you up at the airport?"

"If you can pick me up and drive me to the hospital that'd be great," I said. "I've got to get off the phone to make a few more calls."

"Fine. I'll see you at the Continental arrival hall quarter of eleven."

"Thanks, Pete."

I clicked off the phone and called my secretary's home.

"Mr. Lewis? Why are you calling me so early? Something you need me to get ready for the meeting?"

"Did I wake you?" I pictured Mary's face, always happy, one of those people who carried a smile no matter what was going on around her. Not particularly bright though.

"Nope. Getting my kids ready for school. We're all set for your eight o'clock meeting. Everyone's going to have a lot of questions about that new method you want to institute. Lots of buzz going around. Martha says ... you know Martha? The blonde who always wears those dangling earrings? Well, she says that Mr. Cuevas has no idea what you're talking about, doesn't think you do either. But I stood up for you. Said you'd make it all clear at the meeting today."

I pushed in at the pause. "Mary, listen. Reschedule the meeting, okay? Something's come up and I can't make it in today."

For a moment I listened to her stunned silence, and then she laughed.

"Oh, Mr. Lewis, I never knew you were a kidder. You really had me going there."

"No, I mean it. I've got to fly to Chicago this morning. An emergency." I thought of explaining more, but I preferred keeping my son's problems private.

"Mr. Cuevas isn't going to like this. Didn't you promise him you'd be here today no matter what?"

I swallowed a lump in my throat. "I guess not all promises carry the same weight. Surely a few days isn't going to make a difference."

"I think he's going to be plenty mad. You know, he's invited those investors from Hancock Bank to be here. I sure wouldn't want to be in your shoes when he finds out you've taken off. Why, he's likely to fire you."

I hoped she was wrong. "Well, I have to go no matter what. See if you can talk some sense into him. I ... uh, probably won't be back at work until Monday."

"Oh my."

I clicked off, grabbed my heavy coat, and rushed out the door.

***

When I arrived in Chicago, Peter directed me to his car. He hummed as he drove. "You want to hear about Mallory?" he asked.

"Not really."

Peter stopped at a red light and turned to me. "You were married almost twenty-nine years, she's the mother of your children. Since you ran away to Mississippi, you won't take my calls, and you never bother to call here. Mallory's been struggling since you left, Rick. Seems to me you owe her a little more."

I turned away, my answer bouncing off the window. "I have my own problems to deal with, Pete. I can't handle Mal's too."

"I'm just saying …"

I interrupted. "I know what you're saying. Butt out, Pete. You and Celine always have had the perfect relationship, more money, better job, bigger house …"

"Rick, this isn't about me. Mallory needs you. And she needs Andy's love too."

I stared out the window in silence until we pulled into the hospital parking lot, where Peter laid his hand on my wrist. "Mallory took an overdose. Celine's been hanging near her bedside as much as they'll let her. Maybe once you get things squared away with Andy you can look in on her."

I pushed his wrist away as I unbuckled my belt. "I admit I haven't called her since I moved to Mississippi, but then again, she hasn't called me, either. Well, only once, and that was to talk to Andy on his birthday. Mallory and I are history. My job today is to take care of Andy."

"Rick."

I shook my head. "Maybe if I had the time I'd stop and see her, but I don't this trip." I got out of the car, followed by Peter, and we made our way to the hospital welcoming desk. There we were directed to the emergency waiting room where Peter settled in a chair, pulling out a magazine he had brought. A young fellow dressed in chartreuse scrubs brought me back through a locked door and into a small ward off to the side of the Emergency Department. When I entered a slim young nurse with high cheekbones looked up from her monitors.

I glanced around. Three egg-yellow walls covered with bulletins and machines surrounded a room cluttered with files and monitors, their beeps providing a muffled irregular background beat. Piles of papers filled shelves and bled onto the counters. A used plastic IV bottle lay on the edge of a soap-splashed sink, its life juices dripping slowly down the drain. Stringent alcohol smell hung heavy in the room.

"My name is Richard Lewis. The people up front told me my son, Andrew, is back here."

Below sympathetic eyes her mouth offered the hint of a smile. "I'm Tara, Mr. Lewis. Your son's in the first cubicle." She pointed to a monitor where I saw four scenes from a closed-circuit camera. On the upper left section a black and white image showed Andrew in bed, a sheet pulled up to his neck. The other three rooms were empty. Through the glass windows that made up most of the fourth wall, she indicated the cubicle on the end.

"How is he?"

"He's been resting since I medicated him an hour ago. The doctor just stepped off the unit. I'll page her."

"Thank you, Tara."

I studied Andrew on the screen, seemingly asleep. My hopes rose that perhaps this scare was for nothing. "Can I see him?"

"Of course." She took the key off a hook and opened the door into the locked unit. "You can wait for Dr. Hopkins in Andrew's room."

I stopped halfway through the portage, turning back to ask, "Dr. Hopkins is it?"

"You know her?"

I nodded, my lips squeezed tight. Images of how she had ranted at me when I had checked Andrew out against her advice in June stormed through my brain. "Yeah. We're not on the best of terms."

The door closed behind us and I scanned the featureless narrow hallway. Either end was capped with locked doors. Behind me stretched the glass observation window, and in front, four open doors. A small bathroom lurked in a corner.

"How many patients do you have?" I asked, as Tara led me to the hallway's end room.

"Only Andrew at the moment. We're often full, but Dr. Hopkins just made rounds, discharging two and sending the other patient upstairs to the psychiatric floor. I'm sure Andrew will be admitted too. His uncle asked Dr. Hopkins to wait for you to arrive before we did the paperwork."

Andrew's voice pleading with me to never allow him to be admitted to a psychiatric hospital echoed through my mind. "Doesn't Dr. Hopkins have to have permission from a parent to admit an underage child? Did she talk to his mother?"

Tara hesitated. "I understand his mother is ill as well."

"That's what I hear."

We reached the open door of cubicle one, a small bare cell, with Andrew lying on a thin mattress, unblinking eyes open. From the door I called, "Andy?" but the only motion I saw was a slight rising of the sheet with each breath, like gentle waves rolling onto the beach. He continued to stare at the ceiling.

I stood and watched, the minutes ticking away. I couldn't decide based on this; maybe he'd be fine in a bit, or maybe not. In any case, I was determined I wouldn't let them take him upstairs.

I heard the locked door click and shortly Dr. Hopkins came to stand beside me. "Hello again, Mr. Lewis." Neither of us offered to shake hands.

"Andy looks calm enough," I said. "Seems to me he doesn't need to be admitted."

Dr. Hopkins snorted. "He only looks that way because we've given him heavy sedation. When he arrived he was quite agitated. As we explained when you checked Andrew out this summer, affective disorders such as your son suffers have a tendency to recur. We presume you've scheduled periodic counseling sessions and administered the prescribed medications?"

Her use of the "royal we" irritated me, as if everything she decided had the authority of the whole medical community. She wore a smug smile, a snarl really, like a predator wolf.

"Andrew has been fine without your medications and stigmatizing headshrinkers."

Dr. Hopkins pointed at my son, who was moving his lips soundlessly. "Clearly you're mistaken, Mr. Lewis. It makes us wonder if you truly have the best interest of your child at heart."

I forced my fists to relax. What right did this woman have to tell me how to raise my boy? "He's been doing fine. Good grades, making friends, running on the track team. This is just a small setback precipitated by a personal crisis. I'm sure he'll be fine once I get him back home."

"Andrew should not be traveling in his current condition, Mr. Lewis. You don't seem to grasp that he's suffered an acute psychotic break. He's having incapacitating hallucinations and delusions. Do you understand those terms, Mr. Lewis, or must I spell them out in single syllable words?"

"Don't patronize me. You're always overblowing the circumstances, like putting Mallory on tons of drugs and sticking her in the hospital."

She glared at me. "And I suppose her attempt at taking her own life was just for show?"

Actually, I had wondered that very thing. I mean, if someone wanted to kill themselves, they probably could. Taking pills and then calling for help? Yes, "show" seemed to sum it up. I decided to let it drop. "Let's stick with Andy. He's had a little setback, no doubt upset about his friend dying. I'll take him home and in a day or two he'll be just fine."

She stared at the ceiling, feigning asking God for help. Or perhaps she thought she really was talking with God. She looked at me, down the track of her haughty nose. "Mr. Lewis, it's clear you have no respect for diseases of the mind. With my intimate knowledge of your family history, I can understand why you have built up these defenses. But denying the truth does not change the facts. Andrew has a chronic psychiatric condition that is susceptible to deteriorate under certain stresses."

"Stresses? Like having a close friend killed in an auto accident? I think that would make any of us a little crazy."

"In Andrew's case, this episode is drug induced."

Anger surged to my face. "Somebody slipped my son drugs? What kind?"

"His drug screen showed marijuana." Dr. Hopkins' voice dripped sarcasm, holder of secret knowledge that she shared condescendingly.

"Marijuana? That's all? Come on now, Doctor. A little bit of pot never hurt anybody. When I was his age I even took a toke or two. It can make people a little weird, but its effects are only temporary, right?"

Doctor Hopkins snorted, raising a finger to my face as if she were lecturing a perverse child. "Despite the popular media's misrepresentations, marijuana is not a benign intoxicant. In those susceptible, such as Andrew, it can precipitate an underlying psychosis. We've tentatively diagnosed Andrew as having latent schizo-affective disorder, what used to be known as schizophrenia."

My stomach dropped. "Schizophrenia? You mean multiple personalities?"

"That's a common misconception." She flashed her cold smile again, clearly amused by my ignorance. "Schizo-affective disorder has nothing to do with personality disorders, instead it occurs when the mind disassociates from reality. As in Andrew's case, hallucinations and paranoid delusions are common."

"But schizophrenia's a form of insanity, isn't it? Don't they institutionalize those people?" I struggled to control my fear.

"With current therapeutics, few sufferers end up in institutions. In latent schizo-affective disorder, such as Andrew's, the patient may seem completely normal until some factor induces decompensation. While there probably will be other agents, marijuana is well known as a trigger, and in Andrew's case, he will need intensive psychiatric care to recover."

I studied my son's expression, twisting bizarrely from inner demons. "He looks tortured." I held my hand against my chest, trying to still my pounding heart.

"Yes. Once we have your permission, we'll transfer him to the adolescent psychiatric unit. We've already reserved a bed."

Andrew lifted one hand in front of his face and stared at his fingers. He began to mumble, the jumbled syllables low pitched and confused.

"No," I said. "He's not going back to the psych unit."

The doctor bent her head forward, twisted a bit, scrutinizing me from under one arched eyebrow. "Mr. Lewis, perhaps you're being fooled by Andrew's seemingly calm appearance. When the sedation wears off he will be quite agitated. His condition under this relapse is worse than last time. The first week will require intensive supervision as we adjust his anti-psychotic medications. Depending on the severity of any lingering hallucinations, we anticipate about a month of inpatient care to insure complete rehabilitation."

I glared back at her. "No, I won't let you put him on the psych unit. I'm taking him home with me."

She snorted again, apparently unperturbed in her perception of the power the M.D. provided. "We don't think that's a wise decision, Mr. Lewis. Where is your home?"

"Gulfport, Mississippi."

I could see the disgust in her face, as if I had said we lived in the sewer.

"We're not familiar with the psychiatric units in Mississippi." She dragged out the word Mississippi, embellishing each syllable with extra hiss. "Mr. Lewis, we operate under the highest standards in Chicago. I won't authorize a transfer."

"I'm not transferring him to another facility. I'm bringing him home."

Dr. Hopkins narrowed her eyes, her lips tight. I felt I was being analyzed and found wanting. "You clearly don't understand the seriousness of this illness. If you take him home, who is going to care for him? Who will give him his medicine and watch him around the clock?"

"I will. I gladly accept that responsibility. No matter what you say, I'm taking him with me. Give me the prescriptions and I'll make sure he takes them."

Dr. Hopkins raised her finger in my face, but when I stuck out my jaw in defiance, she dropped it again. "The treatment phase of acute psychosis requires constant reassessment. Although we can provide our standard sedative protocol, the individual patient may need emergency intervention. Have you ever cared for an acutely psychotic patient, Mr. Lewis?"

I remembered Andrew's story about the girl running down the hallway at three a.m., being tackled by multiple orderlies for a sedating injection. "Not yet. I plan to learn quickly."

Her lips pursed in disapproval. "Consider the dangers to your son. Just look at him."

I watched as Andrew picked at imaginary gnats. He seemed so helpless, a victim of forces beyond his control. "You have the education, Dr. Hopkins. I'm sure you think you know what's best for him. But I have the devotion your facilities will never be able to provide. I understand what you're saying. I recognize it might be dangerous to take him with me. But I'm certain it would be worse to allow you to lock him away. I will not be thwarted in this decision."

"You're willing to sign another AMA form stating you're taking Andrew out against my advice? I'm going to list dangers of mental derangement, bodily harm, and even possible death."

Her threats made me even more certain of my decision. "I'll sign whatever you provide. You just give me the prescriptions and we'll be on our way. Our plane leaves at three PM and Andrew and I will be on it."

Dr. Hopkins and I faced off, her expression disapproving, mine determined. Turning her back on me, she strode to the door leading back to the monitor station. I followed her through just in time to avoid being locked inside.

Turning to the nurse, Dr. Hopkins flashed one of her sardonic grins. "Tara, give Andrew Lewis another ten milligrams of Zyprexia I.M. and prepare the AMA forms. Mr. Lewis is checking his son out."

I watched as Dr. Hopkins snatched the chart and papers from the nurse and began scribbling on them in large dark letters, including many exclamation points. I had heard the psychiatric branch of medicine attracted those who were mentally unbalanced. Dr. Hopkins handed the papers to Tara and stomped out the door, shutting it firmly. Tara put the papers down and shook her head sadly.

"I'm sorry about that, Mr. Lewis. Dr. Hopkins can be a bit moody."

I smiled, warming to this nurse who had to spend all day watching crazy patients, and also take abuse from a conceited physician. "It's not your fault, Miss."

She smiled sweetly, "Please call me Tara." A frown crept across her features. "Look, Mr. Lewis. Andrew truly is quite ill. I know you had a falling out with Dr. Hopkins, but I don't think your son should be going home in this condition."

I looked at him on the monitor. He'd relaxed again, his only motion barely perceptible breathing. What if …

"Do you really think there's a danger of him dying, like Dr. Hopkins said?"

"I don't have any way to judge, Mr. Lewis. I've never seen a parent take a child this sick home."

A chill ran through my chest. Settling quickly onto the stool in front of me, I leaned forward onto the counter, lowering my head, fighting off the faintness. Tara came up and laid her hand on my shoulder. "Mr. Lewis? Are you all right?"

I forced myself to sit up and smile reassuringly. "I'll be okay. Here, Tara, please sit down next to me and let's talk. I have about an hour before I have to leave to make that plane. Even though I've never had medical training, I'm certain I can take care of his physical needs. I just need some advice on how to handle his illness. What do you think I need to know?"

"There's so much!" She shrugged, palms upward. "There's no way I can tell you everything."

"Give me a chance, that's all I'm asking for, just a chance to take care of my son myself."

Tara studied Andrew on the monitor. She bit her lip, clearly ambivalent about participating in my foolish escapade. I reached out and touched her shoulder, and she turned to look at me. "Please help me, Tara. This is my son. I love him more than anything else in the world. I honestly believe this is what's best for him."

Her eyes softened and she nodded. "Well. I still don't think it's a good idea, but I'm willing to give you advice. The first problem you'll run into is dehydration. Patients in psychosis often forget to eat or drink. Be gentle yet persistent with the fluids. Water is primary, but shouldn't be exclusive. Juices and power drinks are good supplements. Keep the foods light and easy, like orange slices and peanut butter crackers. Small amounts of chocolate are acceptable, but don't overload him with sweets."

"That's good news. Chocolate's one of his favorite foods." Her practical advice brought hope.

"Some patients have problems with vomiting. Dr. Hopkins wrote a prescription you can give Andrew if he does, though the vomiting will be more of a nuisance than dangerous to his health. It may be tough to keep him hydrated and clean. In his confusion he's likely to use the floor or his bed as his toilet."

I remembered taking care of my father; care of the bedridden wasn't hard, but did require constant attention. "I'm not afraid of cleaning up."

Tara smiled. "Good attitude. Let's see, what else? Oh yeah, Andrew's likely to run a low grade fever, so check his temperature often. Here." She reached into a file cabinet and began shuffling through folders. Pulling out brightly colored pages, she explained each one's contents as she handed them to me.

"This one tells you how to treat a fever and when to seek medical care. These discuss the medicines that Dr. Hopkins prescribed and their more common side effects. This one suggests ways to patient-proof your home. You know, sort of like childproofing, only designed for the patient with dementia."

"Is that what Andrew has? Dementia?"

The nurse nodded. "Actually only delirium, but close enough. That'll be the biggest problem during the acute recovery phase. There'll be times when he'll be hallucinating, and those times can be dangerous."

"Like what?"

She bit her lower lip. "Hard to predict. On the ward we give shots when the patients get out of control. All you'll have is this prescription here, Ativan. If he's getting wild and you can get him to swallow one or two of those, he'll calm down."

I scanned the information on the pages. One paragraph advised to screw shut all windows and replace all glass with Plexiglas. "You make it sound so scary."

Tara's face remained solemn. "It would scare me, and I know what to do for a hundred possibilities we haven't discussed. Why are you so determined to do this yourself?"

I looked at Andrew on the monitor, now more restless as he tossed about on the flat mattress. "Tara, did you know that my son was a patient here a few months ago?"

"Yes sir, Mr. Lewis. I've read the information from his chart."

"When his mother left him here last time, he felt abandoned and betrayed. I swore I would never let anyone put him back into a psychiatric hospital. It's a promise I plan to keep."

She joined me in staring at the monitor. "Good luck Mr. Lewis. Maybe Andrew is fortunate in having a father who cares so much. I hope so."

I watched as Tara administered the shot Dr. Hopkins had ordered, and she helped me get him into a wheelchair. I thought about Peter sitting in the waiting room, and, worried he might try to stop me, I had Tara take us out a different way. At the front entrance she helped me get Andrew into a taxi, and soon we were on the way to the airport.

***

Andrew slept through the plane ride, stirring enough for the plane change in

Houston, and falling asleep again for the next short hop. I let him sleep in the back of my Camry, and on the drive back to the condo I picked up the prescriptions. After tucking Andrew into bed, I administered his bedtime medications, and then stood and studied him. He seemed peaceful. I wondered what monsters gnawed on his brain?

I set to work getting his sickroom ready. Pulling out my toolbox I screwed shut Andrew's windows and took the lock off the inside of his door, a lock I had just recently reinstalled. I pulled the recliner from the living room and settled it in the hallway just in front of his door.

The hours stretched out, exhausting hours, for I'd barely slept the night before, and now I wanted to get up every hour or so to encourage Andrew to take water. At midnight I stripped off Andrew's soiled clothes and sheets, and hand-bathed him.

About three a.m. I startled awake to find Andrew tugging at his window.

"They're out there," he murmured. "Watchin'."

I approached him cautiously from behind, gently placing my hand on his shoulder. Andrew leaped against the wall, looking at me wide-eyed. "Who?"

"Andy, I'm your dad. It's okay."

He cowered against the wall, whimpering; his eyes white targets with dilated black centers. I took the Ativan bottle out of my pocket and took out two of the capsules.

"Take these pills, Andy. They'll keep you safe."

Andrew studied the two tablets in his open palm, his eyes narrowing and widening in rhythmic fashion. He abruptly popped them in his mouth and grinned. "Got 'em. Mine! All mine!" He crawled onto the bed, wrapped himself into a little ball, and started rocking. In a short time he dropped off to sleep.

Thursday, November 6th

Through the rest of the night, morning, and afternoon, I struggled to stay awake, thumbing through old magazines or just staring. I considered calling into work, but didn't feel I could face that argument in my current condition. Andrew slept fitfully, usually tossing and moaning, and occasionally jumping up wide-eyed and confused. At times he shivered, and sometimes vomited into the plastic bucket I kept cleaned out by his bedside.

When I was a student I sometimes pulled all-nighters. Thirty years makes a big difference in a man's ability to concentrate, or maybe I was just asking too much of myself. Three hours sleep Tuesday night, added to a few catnaps through Wednesday night, and by Thursday evening I wasn't just exhausted, I was actively hallucinating. Familiar objects took on bizarre shapes; faces or weapons. Sounds, such as the wind beating against the window, seemed like ghosts moaning words I could almost hear. When the phone rang I was so confused it took five rings before I figured out what it was.

"Hello?"

"Hi Rick. Sylvia."

Ah, Sylvia. I had so wanted to hear her voice, yet I was afraid of speaking with her. I felt like an adolescent, clumsy of tongue, with desire battling hesitancy. The image of her cute smile wavered in my befuddled mind. I stopped by the kitchen to pour another cup of coffee.

"Rick? You there?"

"Yes, yes of course. What's up?"

"I thought we agreed you were going to call this evening? I have Andy's assignments for the week."

I picked up the mug and carried it out to the patio. An incredible sunset greeted me, the oranges and pinks dancing like psychedelic paisleys. "Andy's assignments? Oh, yeah. For school. Right."

I could hear hesitation in her voice. "You had said … you mentioned meeting for dinner tomorrow night. Did you still want to do that?"

"Tomorrow?" I had been wanting this woman for months, and finally she'd agreed to go out with me. How ironic I now knew I couldn't. "Maybe it wouldn't be a good idea for us to meet tomorrow."

"Really?"

I heard the disappointment in her voice. She must feel I was toying with her, but what could I do? "Sylvia, I'm sorry. Actually, Andy's back home."

"Oh? Is he coming to class tomorrow?"

"No, I don't think so." I took a minute to breathe deeply, trying to get my mind to function. "He had a hard time at the funeral. I guess he will need his assignments."

"Perhaps y'all'd like a visitor then. I could bring his assignments by?"

"No!" I barked.

When she spoke her tone was cold, perhaps angry, or, no, hurt by my rejection. "I didn't mean to intrude. I'll … I'll just wait 'til I see him back in school then."

Gripping the phone tightly I spoke quickly. "Wait. Please."

The silence stretched, and I tried to suppress sobs. "I … I need you. I really, really need some help."

She didn't respond and I was afraid she'd hung up. "Sylvia?"

Her response sounded hesitant. "What's going on?"

"Andy needs to be watched and I'm exhausted. Could you … do you think you could help?"

Again she hesitated, and I wasn't sure whether it was because I'd been rude to her, or whether this was her Southern morals showing up again. She asked, "Watched?"

"I'll explain when you get here. I know this sounds crazy, but I need you to watch Andy so I can get some sleep. Maybe three or four hours?"

"I have class tomorrow, but I suppose I could come by now. Andy mentioned y'all live in Legacy Tower."

"Suite 1001."

This time when she responded her voice sounded confident, the cheerfulness I enjoyed. "I'll be there by eight. Can I bring anything?"

"God, yes. Could you pick up some oranges and peanut butter and … maybe a candy bar or two?"

"Have y'all eaten?" she asked.

"No. Could you bring something?"

"Not a problem."

She hung up and I sighed with relief. She'd be here in an hour, and I'd be able to get some sleep. But what would she think? She'd see Andrew at his worst, and maybe even insist on him going to the hospital. Should I tell her I pulled him out against the doctor's advice? Should I tell her the doctor said he might die?

I went back to Andrew's room and slumped down in the recliner. Struggling to keep my eyes open, devilish images began dancing in my brain, and slowly my lids closed. It seemed like less than a minute when the doorbell woke me.

Sylvia bustled in, a small carry-bag slung over one shoulder and plastic grocery bags in her hands. She presented her cheek for a kiss, a Southern gesture I hadn't quite gotten used to. I leaned forward, planted the expected smooch, and reached to take the bundles.

"Thank you for coming, Sylvia." I saw her smile tighten.

"What in the world is going on here? You look like you haven't slept in three days."

I smiled weakly. "Pretty much. I haven't been able to take my eyes off of Andy for more than a few minutes at a time."

I placed the bags on the counter and watched Sylvia walk into the living room, looking around.

"I like your abstract art. Wouldn't fit in my house; we specialize in dusty antiques and faded portraits. Oh, and books! Lots of histories, of course, just what I expected."

I watched her turn and inspect, enjoying the pride created by her compliments.

She pointed to the couch. "Red leather? Clearly the home of bachelors."

I watched her walk over to the dining table, full of my stacks of papers and books. She pointed at it and asked, "You want to clear a place so y'all can eat?"

"How about on the balcony instead? You just missed a spectacular sunset." I peeked in the bags. "What's for dinner?"

She returned to the kitchenette. "Leftovers; pork chops, greens, and cornbread. Sound good?"

I smiled weakly. "Not what I'm used to, but I'm sure it will be delicious."

Sylvia laughed, and I felt myself grinning, admiring her cute face crinkling in happiness. She began pulling the fruit and supplies out of the bags. "So where's Andy? I've already eaten, but I'll sit with y'all."

I shook my head. "He's not well enough for this kind of food. The orange slices and chocolate are for him."

"Really?" She tucked a loose lock behind her ear. "A boy can't live on that. What has he eaten today?"

I bit my lip. "Actually, he hasn't had anything to eat all day."

"Andy's that sick? I better check on him."

I led her down the hallway where we stopped at Andrew's bedroom door. His breathing heavy, his eyes fluttering, he groaned and flipped onto his side.

"Andy?" Sylvia called tentatively.

Andrew's eyes snapped open, though they remained glassy, unfocused. "Look out!" he shouted. Jumping out of bed, he ran across the room, tugging at the window, and when it resisted his efforts, slamming his fist into it, creating a huge starburst. He stumbled back a few steps, staring at his hand.

I pushed past Sylvia and grabbed Andrew's hand, pulling out my T-shirt and holding it against blood flowing from a small gash. I eased him to the bed and called to Sylvia, "Bring me a wet towel or a washrag." I turned and saw her staring. "Please," I pleaded.

She snapped her mouth shut and hurried down the hall to the bathroom.

"There're some Band-Aids in the medicine cabinet," I called, and she returned with the needed medical supplies. I held Andrew's arm still as she cleaned the cut and applied the bandages. He sat frozen, staring at his hand as if it were an alien artifact. I picked up the plastic drinking glass with straw and put it to Andrew's lips. He sucked reflexively, the rest of his body not moving.

"Andy?" I asked. "Andy, can you hear me? Are you hungry?"

He didn't move.

"Sylvia, would you mind slicing up one of those oranges you brought?"

"Of course," she said and hurried down the hallway.

She returned with six bright slices, peeled and juicy. I tore one in half and held it under Andrew's nose, waiting for him to open his mouth. When he didn't, I squeezed his cheeks firmly until his jaw loosened, and then forced the piece into his mouth.

"Sylvia," I said, not taking my eyes off Andrew. "There are three pill bottles next to the kitchen sink. Would you mind getting one pill from each of them?"

"Certainly."

She returned with the pills and I forced them into Andrew's mouth, holding the water bottle's straw up to his lips again. He reflexively swallowed the pills, still frozen in the same position. Gently I lifted my son's legs and laid him back onto the bed, reaching up and closing his eyes. I stood and studied him, his skin pale, his breathing fast. Touching his forehead, I found it cool.

I walked down to the kitchen where I grabbed a plate, fork, and a lemon soda, and led Sylvia to the balcony table. The evening breeze had died down, the first stars twinkling in the cloudless November sky. I served myself a chop, some greens, and a hunk of cornbread. As I ate, voraciously, for it was my first full meal in three days, the calories helped clear my head. Sylvia sat watching me.

"You want to tell me what's going on, Rick?" she asked.

I stopped in mid-bite, lowering my fork back to the plate. "The doctor called it an acute psychotic break."

"And what does that mean?"

"The doctor says he has some form of schizophrenia. Apparently he got into some drugs in Chicago and had a relapse."

"I can't believe they sent y'all home with Andy in this condition."

I stared out across the dark waters where the lights from a half-dozen boats bobbed with the gentle gulf waves. I imagined their occupants; fishermen resting for the night, or perhaps lovers whose world consisted of nothing but joy. I thought of how I'd expressed disdain for a life on the seas only four days ago. Now I longed for that simpler world, relaxed and carefree.

"I checked him out against the doctor's advice."

Sylvia reached across the table and took my hand. "Tell me why."

I stared at her, wondering if she would understand. "Six months ago he had a similar episode. His mother committed him to a psychiatric hospital. He had such a frightening experience he made me promise I would never again let anyone lock him up in such a place."

Sylvia shook her head. "You can't stick with that kind of promise. After all, if the doctor thinks he needs to be hospit –"

"No!" I shouted, banging my fist on the table. "That doctor doesn't understand Andy. This is where my son needs to be. If you don't want to help, I'll do it by myself. I couldn't save my daughter, but I'll be damned if I'll lose my son, too."

Sylvia put her hand to her mouth. "Your daughter? You lost a daughter? Andy never said …"

A wail built deep in my heart, and I began sobbing, covering my face with my hands. I dropped my head onto the table. Sylvia rose and walked around the table, laying her head against my back and wrapping her arms around my chest. Taking her hand, I held it against my heart.

"I never got to say goodbye to Jenny, my sweet baby. The last time I ever saw her was the night before, when she headed up to her room. By the time I came back from work she was already out on her date. Then the police called …"

Sylvia rubbed her cheek against my back. "I'm so sorry, dear Rick."

I stood and walked over to the rail, staring out to the uncaring stars. I inhaled the sea breeze, listened to the quiet, and scanned the empty landscape. Chicago, with its crowds, noise, and violence, was a different planet.

"Seventeen years old, she was an innocent victim of a drive-by shooting. Wrong place – wrong time. One stray bullet killed my baby, and destroyed my life."

Sylvia came up and leaned against me, reaching around my waist and hugging tight. "I'm so sorry."

A night bird called a solemn dirge to accompany the quiet monotony of the surf. Sylvia reached up and traced a tear down to my lips. She ran her finger around those lips and brought it to her own mouth, kissing it. I bent and kissed her gently. She held still for me, but when I was done, she backed away.

"I can't imagine going through that," she murmured. "How could one ever recover from such a thing? When did this happen?"

I stared out to the emptiness, my voice quiet in the dark. "December second, almost two years ago. Sure didn't take long for my life to go to hell." Hazy memories flashed through my mind: the funeral, Mallory in the hospital, and then, that boy. Oh, that flippant boy. How he sat on the stand, smirking at the prosecutors, knowing, as a juvenile, he'd get minimal sentencing. "The kid who shot her was only sixteen."

I felt Sylvia's presence rather than saw her, her voice like a sea breeze. "What happened to him?"

"Served less than a year." The ugly images tortured me again, the boy in the bar after his release, laughing with his friends, enjoying life while his victim lay buried, never to sing, never to smile, never to love again. "No damn justice in the law. No damn justice."

I looked down to Sylvia, took a deep breath, and smiled. "Anyway, that's water under the bridge."

She gripped my hand. "I can imagine the grief your whole family must have suffered. No wonder Andy had such a rough time. Do you think this relapse is related?"

I thought about Jenny's funeral, how Andrew had been so shocked, he was practically a zombie. And now, another funeral had been the prelude to this. "Maybe. But I think it's just Chicago. Bad for him." I turned and stared again out over the water until I felt her tug at my sleeve.

"You still hungry?" she asked.

We returned to the deck chairs, where I took a cut off the pork chop and stared at it listlessly. "Really, I'm too exhausted to eat."

"Is that what happened to your marriage?" Sylvia asked gently.

I felt vulnerable, exposing my soul to this woman, practically a stranger. Yet there was something special about Sylvia, something that called to me, inviting trust. I slumped into my chair. "Probably. I mean, we had the arguments most couples have, but in our case it was particularly hard 'cause of her sister and Peter."

"Hmm?"

"My best friend Peter married my wife's older sister the same time I married Mallory. Seemed like a great idea at the time, but, in retrospect, it invited comparisons for the rest of our lives. Peter's a successful corporate lawyer, always making the big bucks. I suppose it's inevitable that Mallory would be envious of her sister, and take it out on me." I looked up at her. "Not that we were poor, did pretty well as an engineer up there, but nothing on Peter's scale."

I took the last sip from my soda. "Anyway, after the tragedy, she completely fell apart. Heck, she's in the psych hospital as we speak."

I studied the empty drink bottle, so lost in my thoughts that when she spoke I was startled. "Poor woman. I can't imagine what she's gone through. So how is it that she's still up there but you and Andy are here in Mississippi?"

I had been asked often by Mississippians why I moved down, as if one had to have a reason to come to the South. If someone moved the other way, from the South to Chicago, no one would have asked why. Strange. "Looking for peace, I guess." I looked at her, though unable to see her eyes in the night shadows. "Does it sound like I'm a coward, I mean, running away like that?"

"A coward?" She turned to stare out at the waters. "I'm certainly not in position to cast aspersions."

"Oh?"

I saw her glance at her bare ring finger. "My parents were a bit horrified when I chose to go to New York for college. Columbia University. You've heard of it?"

"Yes, of course."

"Majored in history, fell in love with the city. You know what they say? Nice place to visit, and it certainly was! Ah, for lost youth."

I laughed. "You're not that old. What are you, forty?"

"How old are you?"

"Fifty, last June."

"You look younger. Let's just say I'm a little younger than you. You want some wine?"

I nodded and started to get up. She held up her hand. "I'll get it. I brought a bottle of my favorite, a brand I have shipped over from a friend's vineyard in France."

"France?"

She laughed lightly, adding in a French accent. "*Certainement.* I visit yearly. Do you like to travel?"

I shook my head. "Well, not abroad. I own a dozen acres on a lake in Wisconsin that the family used to visit in the summers. Been to Myrtle Beach and Disney, too, but never Europe. While you're getting the wine, I'll check on Andy."

I found him resting quietly, watched him for a minute, and then returned to the balcony where Sylvia joined me, carrying an open bottle of Bordeaux and two glasses. She poured full portions into each.

We clinked glasses. "To Andy's health," Sylvia said.

"Thanks." We drank, and I said, "So you were going to tell me about your marriage?"

Sylvia's eyelashes fluttered. "I met Gus the end of my junior year at college. He was so handsome and full of life. Loved to travel; I hardly knew him two months and he took me off for my first visit to France. Oh, my goodness. Sitting on the banks of the Seine under the shadow of the Eiffel Tower, eating fresh French bread and being in love." She sighed, her eyes closed, her smile beatific.

I took another sip, feeling the wine's effect on my already battered concentration. "Happiness didn't last?"

Sylvia's smile faded. "Gus didn't love me; he loved an image of a Southern Belle he had created. He wanted his 'woman' to stay at home, pretty and stupid. For nine years I pretended to be what he wanted. When I came home to take care of my mother, I realized how much I had been giving up, and told him the pretense was over. I told him I was fixin' to stay in Mississippi and if he loved me he could join me. A month later I received the divorce papers from his lawyer."

She set her half empty wineglass on the table. "That marriage sucked away my soul."

"And you've never been involved with a man since?"

"I didn't say that." A dreamy looked flashed across her face, and disappeared, some memory she chose not to share.

"So maybe I still have a chance?"

A quixotic smile appeared across her face, but she didn't answer, instead looking out on the waters. I followed her gaze to the dark beach, for the moon had yet to appear. A burst of stars covered the clear skies, the November night air cool and crisp. I turned my attention back to Sylvia, watching her play with her wineglass stem.

"I've got to get some rest," I said. "Would you watch Andy for a couple of hours? Could you do that?"

Sylvia glanced back inside, her eyes sparkling from the living room lamps. "Rick, Andy's clearly quite ill. Even if y'all didn't like the doctor in Chicago, shouldn't you take him to the hospital here?"

I reached out to take Sylvia's hands, staring into her face. "Have you ever been in a psych hospital?"

She shook her head.

"Me neither. But Andy told me terrifying stories. He swore if he was locked up in a psych unit again he'd die."

"You know they wouldn't let him die."

"If they lock him up again, he'll go crazy. Either dead or insane, there's not much difference." I squeezed her hands, hoping to transmit understanding through her skin.

A night breeze stirred the wind chimes, and Sylvia turned to look out to the stars. I watched her face and waited for some indication of her thoughts.

"I once promised Gus that I'd stick with him no matter what," she murmured, her voice barely audible. "I tried for years. Eventually I had to admit defeat. I lost my respect for myself, and without that, I couldn't make the marriage work. Even now the failure haunts me."

I nodded sympathetically. "Some promises you can't keep, I know that. I'm going to try my hardest to keep this one. Will you help?"

I ran a finger along her palm, enjoying its softness, and saw her shiver. "Please."

She sighed. "I'm not sure you're doing the right thing. I'm not even sure I should be in this house. But I can tell Andy needs me. You go lie down and I'll wake you in a bit."

I gave Sylvia's hand a grateful squeeze. "Thank you."

She stood and shifted into bustle mode. "Go on now," she ordered. "I'll clean up and check on Andy. After I wake you I'll head home and return in the early morning to give you another round off. I'll call the school 'fore I come so they can arrange a substitute. Scoot." She raised one hand, pointing back towards the hallway.

I rose wearily and headed across the living room. Just a step inside the hallway I turned to watch Sylvia clear the dishes. So lithe, she looked sexy, like a dancer. Was she even a tiny bit interested in me? My mind was too befuddled to consider the issue seriously, and I headed to the bedroom.

Friday, November 7th

It seemed I'd barely put my head down when I felt a nudge on my shoulder.

I forced my mind into gear, remembering where I was and what had happened. I cracked my eyelids and saw Sylvia standing over me, staring down at my bare chest in a peculiar, dreamy way. I felt myself growing hard under the sheets and I couldn't help but smile.

"Rick?"

"Um," I muttered, mostly a groan. "How long have I been asleep?"

"It's half past one."

I slung my legs out from below the sheets, realizing I wore only my briefs. Glancing up at Sylvia I saw her stare, blush slightly, and turn away. But she glanced back before covering her eyes. I pulled on my robe, stood, and stretched. "Thanks, Sylvia. That helped. Wasn't enough, but it helped. Andy needs his medicines."

"I'll bring them and meet you in his bedroom. He's done fine. I just gave him some water." She smiled at me, and it seemed more than the cute flash I'd seen before, more committed, more alluring, more demanding. I headed into his bedroom and found Andy sleeping comfortably. In a couple of minutes Sylvia joined me, bringing the medicine bottles and a crustless and quartered peanut butter and jelly sandwich. She held them out to me, but with her hands full I leaned past them and kissed her on the lips. She kissed back, a little.

"Don't be naughty," she admonished.

I helped Andrew sit up, and together Sylvia and I gave him his medicines and fed him. He took water, too, and lay back down. I led Sylvia out to the living room where I collapsed onto the couch. "Damn, I'm tired."

"Coffee's about five hours old. You want me to brew some fresh?"

I shook my head. "Nah. Five hours is fresh enough for me. Could you get me a cup?"

"Milk?"

"Black."

She bounced to the kitchen and back with the mug. I took it from her, thanked her with a smile, and drank a gulp. "Better." I stretched. "Yeah, I guess I'm good for a round. You're an angel, Sylvia."

"Not a problem. I'm pretty beat myself, though. Guess I'll head home and take a few hours nap. I'll be back at sixish, okay?"

"Silly to drive all the way home and have to come back. Why don't you sleep here?" Her mouth looked grim, about to say "No," but I smiled at her and I saw her resolve melt away.

"I suppose I should be here in case there's an emergency."

"Great! You want me to change the sheets?"

She shook her head. "I'll be fine." She yawned and blew me a kiss. "I can find my way."

I stood and watched her go around the corner, and followed her, standing just outside and listening intently as she closed the door. The telltale click of the lock being engaged didn't occur, and I smiled. After using the hall toilet, I went back to the living room to pick up my coffee. Sylvia had left out a book, about a quarter finished, a biography on Theodore Roosevelt.

Marking her page with a turned corner, I picked it up and carried it into Andrew's room where I settled into the lounge chair. I opened the book to page one and began rereading this, one of my favorite books. It felt good, almost amazing, to be reading something just a few hours after Sylvia. Perhaps when she got up we could discuss it. I closed my eyes, and licked my lips, enjoying the slight taste of her kiss.

I settled into the book, and about an hour or two later I looked up at the sound of Andrew stirring. He sat on the side of the bed, facing the window and tilting his head, looking intently. I rose and walked slowly to stand in his line of vision. His eyes were dilated, though the color held the same deep blue as mine. People said we looked alike and he did have my cheek structure and high forehead, but I always thought of Mallory when I looked at his face.

"Andy?"

For just a moment he seemed to focus on me, his eyebrows raised in puzzlement. He stood and I hesitated, unsure if I should step forward. He pulled down his pants and began urinating on the floor in front of him. My initial surprise turned into amusement. I made a grab for the urinal, but by the time I retrieved it he was done, and he lay back down. I gave him some water and he settled into sleep. Pulling some towels and rug cleaner from the closet, I scrubbed up the spot, and threw the towels in the washing machine, where I found soiled bed linen that Sylvia must have put in. I added detergent and started the load.

Instead of returning to Andrew's bedroom, I went out on the balcony. Four in the morning, there was no traffic on the beach road. The just-past-full moon gave a ghostly shine to the deserted beach, creating a landscape that befit my mood. Andrew seemed much calmer; except for that outburst the first night, and the one on Sylvia's arrival, he'd been mostly sleeping. But ... would he recover? Tara had said he would, hadn't she? I tried to remember, but wasn't certain.

At six I woke Andrew for his morning medicines. He took them easily and squinted at me. "Andy? Do you know who I am?"

He stared at me, and then turned to the window. "They're out there," he murmured. He stood and went to the window, and I followed.

"No one's out there, Andy," I insisted. I turned his head so he was staring into my face. For a moment he seemed to recognize me.

"Dad?" he whispered.

"Yes!" I practically shouted. But his eyes glazed over and he gave me a push, trying to get past me to the door. I grabbed him and held him in a tight hug until I felt him calm down. He collapsed into my arms and I carried him back to the bed. Putting one of the Ativan tablets into an orange slice I forced it into his mouth and he swallowed it. I stood watching him and was rewarded by the sounds of his sleep breathing.

I tucked him in and crossed the hall to my bedroom, turning the knob to discover I'd been right about Sylvia not locking the door. She lay facing the wall on the far side of the bed, the sheets down to her waist, her upper body clothed in a bra. Her skin looked lovely, so alluring, and once again I felt a sexual stirring. I dropped my robe back onto my chair and climbed into the bed.

She didn't move and I rolled up against her, draping my arm across her front, and snuggling up against her neck. Her delicious smell stroked my desires, and here she lay in my bed, vulnerable, begging to be kissed, to be stroked, to be loved. I pushed my bare chest up against her back, rubbing it ever so softly.

I kissed her neck before allowing my head to rest back on the pillow. If she turned over I would kiss her, would take that as a sign she wanted me.

I closed my eyes.

And fell asleep.

***

I rose just before noon, changing places in the bed with Sylvia again, and took my turn back to the bed at three. Sylvia woke me at seven, telling me to get ready while she cooked dinner. When I asked, she said she hadn't given Andrew his medications yet.

After cleaning up in the bathroom, including a shower and shave, I dressed in casual clothes and went across the hallway to check on Andrew. I found him sleeping comfortably on fresh sheets. I aroused him to give him his medicines, and, stepping into the hallway, followed the smells of frying onions into the kitchen.

Sylvia stood at the stove and I came up behind her, kissing her on the neck. She stepped back and shook her finger in my face. "That's not why I'm here!" she said. But her smile indicated she didn't really hate it. "I've got mushrooms and onions sautéing; how do you like your steak?"

"Medium rare." I peeked into the pot on the burner and saw mashed potatoes. A bowl with a tossed salad sat on the counter. "Yummy! Now this is what I call a meal!"

Sylvia laughed. "More to your Yankee tastes than pork chops and greens?" She pointed to a bottle by the refrigerator. "We only did half the wine last night. Would you like a glass now?"

"*Certainement,*" I replied, copying the accent she had used. She chuckled and handed me the salad, which I took over to the table. I returned, poured us wine, and we clinked glasses. "To Andy's health," she said.

"To our friendship," I replied, "and may it blossom into more."

I watched her put the steaks on the broiler. "Andy give you any trouble?"

"He mostly slept. I was able to get him to use the urinal this morning, which I take as a positive step. You'll have to rent a carpet cleaner I suspect."

"Yes, a good sign indeed. I'll tell you the truth, that nurse in the E.R. sure scared me, but this hasn't been so bad ... or, at least, not now that you're here to help."

She smiled at me again, and I felt my heart melt. I was falling in love, I knew that, but I wondered if this was just because I was so grateful for her help, or because she really was the woman I had dreamed about all my life. I watched as she bent into the oven and flipped the steaks, rubbing sauce onto the new top surface. Her muscular legs looked incredibly sexy below her sundress and I had to resist the urge to touch her butt. Damn she looked good.

"Sleep well?" she asked, straightening up.

"Great! I'm ready to go another round, though I'm hoping Andy will be well enough soon to not need such close supervision."

She bent again and pulled out the steaks, plopping one onto each plate, and handing them to me. She ladled the mushrooms and onions on top, adding a dollop of potatoes on the side. I followed her out to the balcony where she had set the table. The clear skies held an incredible blanket of stars, their sparkles dancing off the waters below.

"This is fabulous!" I exclaimed, savored the juices of the sweet tastes. "What'd you use for flavoring?"

"Secret ingredients; can't tell you or I'd lose my membership in the Daughters of the Confederacy."

I laughed and continued eating.

"Did that nurse tell you how long before Andy recovered?" Sylvia asked.

"A few days. We've only got about five of the Ativan pills left, so I guess not much longer. There's lots of the other ones, but the doctor expected me to keep him on those for a long time, I think. She says he should get long term counseling."

"And will you?"

I put down my fork and looked down onto Beach Boulevard. Eight p.m. on a Friday night, the traffic was fairly heavy. A sports car whizzed past, weaving in and out of the slower traffic, giving an occasional honk as it passed. Every car was different, just like every person. Just because one occasionally needed repair didn't mean it needed constant maintenance, did it? "What do you think?"

She pursed her lips. "You really want my opinion?"

"Yes, of course. You know him better than anyone else besides me. Frankly, I don't trust the doctor, and, well, I don't believe in giving medicines unless they're absolutely necessary."

Sylvia raised her eyebrows, studying me. "Let's review, okay? Andy's only sibling is murdered. His mother goes in the hospital. His father moves a thousand miles away, seemingly abandoning him. He gets into drugs and ends up in the hospital himself. His father pulls him away from all his friends and everyone he knows. One of his best friends dies. On a return visit to his hometown, he ends up back in the hospital with a diagnosis of a severe mental illness. Frankly, Rick, to me the answer is obvious. Now, that's my viewpoint. What's yours?"

I shook my head. "You have to admit that until he returned to Chicago he was doing great: good grades, new friends, a happy kid. While I can't argue with what you've said, maybe it applies to other boys, and not necessarily Andy."

"Do you really think that?"

I grimaced. "I honestly don't know, Sylvia. I tell you what, let's wait until he recovers and let Andy decide. After all, we'll need his cooperation."

She didn't look very happy about my proposal. "Andy's quite bright, but he's only seventeen years old. I'm not sure he has the perspective to make this decision."

I shrugged. "I guess we'll see." I turned back to my eating, mulling over how well Andrew had been doing before this trip to Chicago. It really was all Chicago's fault. If I could only keep him away from Chicago, surely things would be all right.

"Rick?"

I looked up. Her face seemed troubled. "Yeah?"

"You had a phone call this afternoon."

I wondered if it had been Mallory. That certainly would have surprised her to have a woman answer my phone. "Oh? Who was it?"

"He said he was your brother-in-law."

"Peter?" I felt ashamed. After all, I had run off, abandoning him in the hospital without a word. "Was he angry?"

She shook her head. "Actually, seemed glad to hear that Andy was here and doing okay." Her voice trailed off and she hid her face.

"But?" I asked.

She looked up. "But he didn't seem too happy about my being here; wanted to know who I was and what I was doing." She turned back to her plate. "Tell you the truth, I'm not so sure I know the answers."

I watched her eat as I swallowed my own mouthful. "You know why you're here. Because Andy needs you. Because I need you."

She looked up and gave me a half smile. "I suppose. But I did sleep here last night. When I went home I had to try to explain to Aunt Frances where I'd spent the night."

"None of her business," I said.

Sylvia laughed. "That's what she said too, but I'm not so sure. I probably shouldn't have slept here."

I finished eating and pushed the plate aside, taking the last sip of my wine as well. "So? You went home?"

"Yes. Called in to school and packed up a little bag so I can stay the duration. Bought the salad and steaks on the way back. In for an inch, in for a mile I suppose."

I reached across and gave her hand a squeeze. "Thanks. Let's see, this is Friday evening, and his symptoms started Tuesday night, so it's been three days.

Wow. Feels like a week."

"Surely this can't last much longer?"

"He seems much better to me already. Early this morning he recognized me. I'm guessing he'll come around right soon."

We picked up the dishes and took them into the kitchen where we cleaned them together. Afterwards we settled into the living room, drinking wine, and discussing Theodore Roosevelt, and our lives, and so many other things. The night air was so lovely we left the patio door open. We looked up when Andrew wandered into the room.

"Andy?" I stood and started towards him.

Andrew's eyes grew wide and he shouted, "The vans!" He ran towards me and I reached out to grab him, but he dodged and ran past. "They're out there! I've got to get away!"

Sylvia jumped up, but he stiff-armed her, knocking her aside. He ran out onto the balcony and began climbing on the rail. I rushed after him, managing to clutch him by the waist and holding on tight. I pulled hard, trying to drag him back into the living room, but he held onto the rail with both hands. Rushing up, Sylvia carefully pried his fingers away, one by one, and I was able to stumble with him back into the living room. Sylvia came in too, closing and locking the patio door. She pulled the shades closed.

"Now what?" Sylvia asked, looking down us. "Give him more medicine?"

"It's not time for more. Ouch! He kicked me!"

"Tie him up?"

"I don't know." I struggled with holding Andrew who was kicking and hitting me with his fists. "Damn, he's strong."

Sylvia squatted next to his head and spoke in a calm quiet voice. "Andy, listen to me. We need you to be still."

Andrew's actions slowed, his arms falling to the floor.

I let go of his legs but stayed squatting next to him. My son's eyes remained wide, and his head twitched back and forth. He mumbled incomprehensible sounds. I looked up to the table. "Bring me my wine glass."

"What?" She glanced at the table and back at me. "Your wine?"

I nodded and watched her refill my glass and bring it over. I held it to Andrew's lips and encouraged him to drink.

"Are you sure?" Sylvia whispered. "What if the wine reacts with the pills you just gave him?"

I hesitated, but continued. "Sometimes you have to take chances in life."

Andrew drank the wine in sips, finishing the glass in a matter of minutes.

He slumped, and then fell flat against the floor.

I picked him up under his arms and dragged him back to bed. I was tucking him in when Sylvia brought a couple of pillowcases from the linen closet.

"What are those for?"

"I was just thinking, you know, maybe tie him to the bed? Just in case? At least that way we'd hear him if he tried to get up."

I looked at Andrew and nodded. "Good idea. Heck. I was just saying how I thought he was doing better. Guess I jinxed it." I tied one end of a pillowcase around Andrew's ankle and the other to the bedpost, tugging it a few times to make sure it was secure.

We returned to the living room where I handed her a refilled wine glass. She drank it down and placed the empty on the table. She stared down into it as she said, "You sure you don't want to take him to the hospital?"

I shook my head. "It was just a relapse. Gotta be the last one."

She sat in silence, thumbing her fingers on the table. I wondered if she'd finally had enough. Without looking up she murmured, "I should be going home."

I picked up her hand and kissed it, gently nipping at her fingers. "You've had so much to drink, and it's almost midnight. You said you were planning on staying for the duration."

She looked at me, her eyes yearning, her mouth unsure. "I ... I don't know, Rick. Our timing is off."

"Meaning what?"

"Up 'til now we've been taking shifts in your comfy old bed. Now we're both ready to sleep."

I didn't take my eyes away from hers. "It's big enough for two." I leaned forward and she didn't back away. I kissed her, and she responded, taking in my tongue and grabbing me, pulling me tightly towards her. She grabbed my hand and led me to the bedroom, where we closed and locked the door. I pulled her close and began covering her with kisses, and unbuttoning her blouse. She shrugged it off, followed by her skirt. Underneath she wore a red teddy, lace barely covering her nipples, the material so short I could almost see the juncture of her thighs.

"Wow! Is that your usual underwear?"

Sylvia gave me a come-hither look. "Something special – for your eyes only. You like?" She turned and lifted up the hem, exposing her gorgeous bare butt.

I whistled. "Yeah! I like it a lot!" I reached forward to touch her bottom and she stepped back.

"You know this is one time only."

"What do you mean?"

She tilted her head and gave me a wistful smile. "Do you think I sleep with anyone ... that I'm a sleep-around?"

"Of course not. I'd never think that."

"Well, I don't. And I don't date parents." She sat down on the bed, holding her thighs close together. "I want you, Rick. I want to feel your touch, your kiss, your loving."

"I want you too, Sylvia. So what's the problem?"

"The problem is that what we're fixin' to do isn't proper. It's wrong on so many levels, that you're a parent, that I've been sleeping here, and ... well, that we're not married. If we do this, if we make love, we must never see each other again. Except if we have to see each other at school, or maybe accidental encounters, we will be as strangers."

Her terms seemed absurd, and, frankly, unbelievable. I stripped off my clothes, and stepped forward wearing only my briefs. I could feel my manhood straining against the fabric. "If you think it's wrong, then let's wait until it's right. We can just hold each other. We don't have to make love, just cuddle."

She stared at my pants, licked her lips, and reached out to touch me there, rubbing against the cloth.

"I want you, Blue Eyes," she murmured. She pulled him out, kissing me there, and more. I gasped, allowing her to please me. I pushed her back onto the bed, and we made love, sweet, sweet love. The springs squealed. The air grew hot with our gasps. Our sweat and love fluids soaked the sheets.

Afterwards we lay intertwined, looking into each other's eyes. Despite all the resistance she had feigned over the past four months, I had known from the first time we met she wanted me. I'm no Don Juan, certainly not experienced in the ways of women, but this one – I mean, it was clear all along she'd been suppressing her desires.

And now what, I wondered, looking into her eyes. She had said this was for one time only. Surely it was just another of her false threats, her Southern way of pretending chastity while giving in to her human needs. It was all so complicated.

"What are you thinking?" I asked.

She smiled, pressing her finger to my lips. "Shh, Mr. Engineer. We'll talk about it tomorrow."

I closed my eyes and fell right asleep, dreaming of the delicious lovemaking we'd shared.

I awoke about four and checked on Andrew, untying the ankle binder. When I directed him to stand, he followed me to the toilet, which he was able to use, and I cleaned him afterwards. He definitely was getting better.

When I returned to my bedroom I paused to admire Sylvia. She lay naked, her sculptured buttocks like the rolling hills of Wisconsin. I went into my bathroom and cleaned up, crawling back into the bed and spooning up against her. She smelled so lovely I could feel myself stirring again. I hadn't been able to make love twice in a night since the first year of my marriage. Now I was fifty-years-old, eager to repeat that joy with Sylvia.

I licked her neck and she sighed, flipping over to face me. We kissed, and she took him in one hand, guiding me into her, and we made love again, an encore of delight. She cried out in passion as she climaxed, and smothered me with kisses. I held her tightly and in the warmth of her embrace, fell into a deep sleep.

Saturday, November 8th

When I awoke again, the light of dawn had come kissing through the shades. I felt the sheets beside me. The wet spots had dried, leaving a coldness that penetrated my heart. I looked over to the empty space that had held Sylvia's bag last night, and I knew she was gone.

Around the sink only rings remained from the lotions, creams, and powders that had looked so feminine, so foreign on my vanity. In the sink a single long brown hair had been left behind, solitary proof that it hadn't all been a dream.

I dressed and took Andrew his medicines. He seemed more alert, following me readily to the toilet, and looking at me with some comprehension, but not speaking, not responding to my questions. I took him back to bed, for a few minutes standing at the door watching him stare up at the ceiling, pleased at his relative calm, but wondering when he'd be normal again.

Taking fresh coffee to the balcony I looked out across the waters. The Saturday morning air felt cool, maybe the low forties. On the beach a jogger came by dressed in a sweat suit, her breath making clouds. I watched her until she shrank out of sight.

Inside I made myself a peanut butter sandwich, and another one for Andrew, adding a sliced orange and a candy bar to his portion. I thought about last night, on how I'd been fooled into thinking Andrew was better, how he'd almost jumped to his death. What if Sylvia hadn't been there to help? What if he tried again? I brought him his breakfast, handfeeding him.

Back on the balcony the day's warmth had settled in, and I watched a woman spread out her beach towel, lather with lotion, and lie out in the sun. I picked up my binoculars and looked her over. She was a little plump for my tastes, and I put the glasses back down. Out in the water a shrimp boat tooled by, sea gulls dancing in its wake.

A silver car approached the condo on the beach road, but it wasn't Sylvia's, and it drove on past. She had warned me if we made love she'd never want to see me again. I sighed and finished my coffee. Carrying it back into the kitchen, I rinsed the cup and left it on the sideboard. Back in my bedroom I pulled out my exercise bike and propped up my book as I worked out.

***

Late that afternoon the doorbell rang. I threw it open, reaching out to grab Sylvia in a hug, but she backed away.

"You came back!"

Her eyes were red, and her voice cold. "I've come back because Andy still needs me. You have to understand that."

I nodded and got out of the way, following her down the hallway. She examined Andrew from the bedroom door. "Still sleeping?' she asked.

"I just gave him his evening pills. He's seemed much better today, mostly aware of me and his surroundings, but not speaking and not acknowledging my questions."

She nodded, but didn't turn to look at me. I reached out and turned her to face me. "Sylvia, why are you here?"

She pursed her lips. "I told you. To help watch Andy."

I shook my head. "No. You don't make love like you did last night and not mean it."

She walked past me and I followed her into the living room. She picked up the Roosevelt book I'd left on the coffee table, settled onto the couch, and pretended to be reading. "I don't think we should talk about it."

I grabbed the book from her hands and threw it across the room. "You came back because you love me. You know you do. Why are you denying it?"

She continued staring into her empty hands, as if still reading the phantom book. I bent down, reached around her, and pulled her into a hug. She laid her head on my shoulder. Her breath came ragged against my neck, her tears wet on my shoulders.

"Sylvia. We're adults. We're allowed to love each other."

Her voice struggled, raspy in its sobs. "You don't love me. You're just grateful I'm here to help. When this is over, what will there be? I'll just be Andy's teacher, and you'll still be a Yankee. No, Rick, it'll never work."

"That's not true!" I leaned back and lifted her head, kissing her tears, and then her lips. She kissed me back, tenderly, not with the passion of the previous night. I took her hand and led her down the hallway to my bedroom. Once again I took off her clothing, and my own, and crawled in with her between the sheets. We held each other tightly.

"I don't know what I'm doing here," she whispered. "This is so wrong. It's not going to work. It can't work."

I tried desperately to kiss away her doubts. At first she resisted, but then she responded, and we made love again. Slowly. Gently. Lovingly.

Sunday, November 9th

Through the night and the next morning we took care of Andrew. Sylvia would talk about distant topics, Andrew's schoolwork, stories about her Aunt Frances and other relatives, but every time I brought up something personal, she'd change the subject. We had a light lunch on the balcony.

When I brought in Sunday's afternoon dose of medication, Andrew was sitting up in bed, looking around. "Welcome home, Andy," I said.

He stared at the window, half covered in cardboard. "Home?"

I nodded. "Yep, home. How are you feeling?"

Andrew held his head. "Lousy. How'd I get here?"

"You had a relapse in Chicago. I brought you back home and we've been taking care of you, Mrs. Perkins and me." I pointed behind me to the door.

Andrew looked over at Sylvia, who smiled and waved. He lay back, dropping his head back to the bed. "Jeez," he whispered. "Now everyone'll know I'm loony." He stared at the ceiling. "What happened?"

I placed my hand gently on his shoulder. "Turns out your brain is allergic to marijuana. Do you remember smoking some after the funeral?"

Andrew's brow furrowed, apparently trying to bring back memories long washed away by monstrous hallucinations. He lay with his head back, crossing his arms tight across his chest. An image of a corpse dressed for burial flashed into my mind.

"The night before you left you said you wouldn't be using drugs while you were gone. Do you remember that?"

For a moment Andrew lay still; then he let out a curse. He swung his legs over the edge of the bed and staggered the few steps to the window. Holding on to its rim he stared out over the beach.

"Can't be trusted? Is that it?" He lifted one hand and pushed on the cardboard. The sound of breaking glass echoed into the room.

Sylvia spoke up. "Andy, what are you thinking?"

He glanced at her and returned his gaze out the window. "Butt out."

She advanced up to him. "I don't think so, Mister. After all I just went through to keep you alive, I have every right to step into your face. Look at me."

Andrew sighed, but didn't turn.

She stomped her foot. "I said 'look at me,' Andrew P. Lewis. And I mean NOW!"

Slowly he turned. The defiant look chiseled hard on his shrunken features melted slowly, replaced by hopelessness.

Andrew's voice came low and plaintive. "I'm just a stupid schizo who's always gonna be a loser. Is that what you want me to say?"

Sylvia shook her head. "No. What I want you to say is you're determined to be the best you can be. That you'll get back to your books. That you'll continue on the running team. That you'll graduate with honors and prove to the world that you're a damn bright kid who can be someone special."

"Me?" He stared at her, his brows tented in doubt.

She lifted both her hands. "Oh My Heavens. You're the brightest, most determined kid I've met in my entire teaching career. I foresee you winning a full college scholarship to the school of your choice. With your running and your brains, you'll be able to write your own ticket. And you know what you have to do to achieve all this, Andy Lewis?"

He looked at her, only a slight lift of an eyebrow showing his hope.

"You just have to try," she said. "We all fall down. We all make mistakes. We all fail. But the winners are the ones who pick themselves back up. You're that kind of boy, Andy. I know you are."

He looked at her for a good fifteen seconds before dropping his eyes. "What makes you so sure?" he asked the floor.

She leaned forward and gave him a gentle kiss on the cheek. "Because I've come to know your father."

She glanced at me and I smiled encouragingly. "He promised to keep you out of the psychiatric hospital, and by determination and hard work, he did it. I know those traits are in you too."

Andrew turned to me, a comfortable acceptance forming on his face. We hugged, his heart pounding against my chest. "Thanks, Dad."

I tussled his hair. "You can count on me, Son."

We broke apart and Andrew sat on the bed, resting his face in his hands. "I'm beat."

"You hungry? You want me to order a pizza?"

Andrew looked up, and I saw light in his eyes, a naturalness distinguishing a real boy from the Pinocchio he had been. "Double pepperoni?"

I gave him the "okay" symbol. As I stepped out into the hallway Sylvia came out of the bedroom carrying her bag. I tried to stand in her way, but she waved me aside and walked down the hallway to the condo's front door.

Following her, I called out, "I'm just about to order pizza. Surely you don't want to leave now?"

She held her lips taut. "My job here is done. Tomorrow I need to be back at school."

I leaned forward, reaching out with both arms.

Sylvia backed away. "You do remember what we said? Only for the moment? That we'd never see each other again?"

"Sylvia, we can't go back to the way we were."

Looking down to where she had set her bag, she squatted, grabbed its handle, but stayed there, staring at it. "I can't get involved with another damn Yankee," she murmured.

I stooped next to her. "You can. You will." I whispered into her ear, "Next Saturday. Dinner. A walk on the beach."

She stood, clutching the bag to her chest. "I mustn't."

I straightened. "This started off about Andy, but now it's about you and me."

She stood still, barely breathing.

"Sylvia, I love you!" I reached out and placed my hand on hers. With my other I lifted her chin, gently forcing our eyes to meet. "Look into your heart. What does it say?"

She stared back, her gaze soft, her lips pushing out in yearning. "Saturday." She breathed. "Pick me up at six."

I leaned forward and we kissed. She tasted delicious.

Tuesday, November 11th

Andrew stayed home Monday, resting and catching up on his studies. I offered to continue him on his medicines, and he tried one, but he said it made him feel weird, so we agreed not to give him any more unless he had symptoms. After all, Dr. Hopkins had said the problem was caused by marijuana, so we figured if he avoided that, he'd be fine.

On Tuesday morning he attempted his morning run. From my perch on the balcony I watched him returning on the beach, walking, his breath coming out in clouds beneath his hoody. In a few minutes I heard him rummaging in the kitchen, followed by his appearance on the balcony with a large glass of orange juice and a bowl of cereal.

"How was your run?" I asked.

Andrew settled into the other deck chair and finished off the juice before answering. "Not so good. I missed nine days, but more than being out of shape, I feel weak. I jogged a bit, but mostly walked. Even at that, I only did a couple of miles."

"Maybe you should lay off for a few days. Did you weigh yourself?"

"Yeah. Lost six pounds. The Bay meet is in five days. Don't see how I can do it."

I watched him eat half the cereal and push the bowl away. "No appetite?" I asked.

Andrew shrugged. "What's the point?" He got up and hung onto the rail, staring out at the empty beach.

Indicating the paper, I said, "I'm sort of feeling the same way."

Andrew turned to look. "What are you doing with the want-ads?"

I closed the paper and drummed my fingers on top of it. "I got fired. I knew that Henry Cuevas was a jerk the first time I met him. Probably never should have taken the job in the first place."

"You got fired 'cause of me?"

I shook my head. "Nah. It had nothing to do with you."

Andrew was staring into my eyes so I hid them in the paper.

"Dad, tell the truth."

"The guy's a jerk. That's the way it goes. If they can't see how valuable I am to the company, then to hell with them."

Andrew sat back at the table and stirred the cereal. "Now what?" he asked.

I indicated the paper. "Don't know. The economy's bad and the pickings are slim."

He stood, picking up the dirty dishes. "I'm going to the kitchen for some more juice, you want anything?"

I held out my cup. "More coffee, please. Thanks."

I skimmed the want ads again, rereading the two circled ads. They didn't seem good, but nothing else seemed even close. Andrew returned with the juice, coffee, and his history book. He opened it on the table before him, but looked over at my paper instead of reading.

"Not many circles there, Dad."

"No, not around here. But I've got good experience. I can probably find something on the Internet. How do you feel about moving?"

"Back to Chicago?" Andrew's eyes shot open. "You mean it?"

I shook my head. "Not there, Andy. Not after what just happened."

Andrew stared out over the horizon. The pinks and oranges of dawn created a surreal sky. "Then let's stay here. At least finish my senior year."

"Sounds fair. I've got enough savings to last a few months anyway." I thought about Sylvia, how sweet she smelled, how wonderful had been our lovemaking. I couldn't believe she'd not want to see me again. I had to stay around and give this relationship a chance. I pushed the paper away.

"I'm sure I'll find something soon enough. If I have to I can commute to Mobile or Hattiesburg, or even New Orleans. Something'll turn up."

Andrew bent down to fool with his shoelaces. Talking to the ground he said, "I guess you and Mrs. Perkins are a number now, huh?"

I waited until he looked up. "How do you feel about that?"

He stood and went to the rail. I noted his sweats didn't quite reach the top of his shoes. He'd passed my six-two height, and I wondered how tall he'd get.

His answer took a long time coming. "Suppose it's okay." He turned to face me. "Mrs. Perkins's been good to me, and you sure as heck need someone."

He scuffed his Brooks together. For shoes barely a month old, they already looked pretty worn. One lace was shredded and the plastic of a toe had a small chunk missing. He settled into the deck chair. "Dad?"

"Yeah?"

"You ever think about going back with Mom?"

Memories of the fights rushed to my mind. "I don't think that's in the cards, Andy."

He stretched, twisting his body hard in several directions. "S'pose not. Lost my sister. Lost my friends. Lost my mom. Guess I gotta start all over." He disappeared back into the condo and I sat staring after him, just sitting, and wondering as I had so often recently if I really belonged in Mississippi.

Andrew: Friday, November 14th

Andrew studied the new photos from this year's Halloween party Travis had posted on his Facebook. Some were of Billy, dressed as a karate kid, complete with white outfit, green belt, and a colorful headband. Andrew guessed they were the last photos of him ever. Travis wore a superman outfit. "Typical," he muttered. Calvin was notably absent.

And then there was Sarah. Dressed as a princess, she looked especially cute with sparkles in her hair and on her face. He thought of how she had turned her back on him at the funeral. Well, he deserved it, he thought. Hadn't called her once. Now it was too late.

Or was it? Heck, nothing lost by trying.

He pushed the speed button for her number, and she answered on the fourth ring.

"Andy? Is this really you?"

He swallowed hard. *Was she going to be pissed?* "Yes! I'm sorry I haven't called before this."

Her anger rocketed through the phone. "Sorry? You're sorry? Andrew P. Lewis, you have a lot of nerve ignoring me for so long. And now you just pick up the phone and say you're sorry? What do you expect me to say?"

"I don't know. I was afraid you wouldn't want to hear from me."

"Why wouldn't I want to hear from you?"

Andrew felt hope rising in his heart. "I thought you must be angry with me. Or maybe I was ashamed for having run away. Not that it was my fault, you know. Mom made me miss the prom, and then Dad dragged me down here against my will. But ... I could have called you. I should have called you. I kept *meaning* to call you. I just never did."

"Oh, Andy, you really should have. I needed you so much. I missed you so much."

"Really? That's great! I mean ... I'm sorry I didn't call. Jeez. Now I'm REALLY sorry I didn't call. You don't know how much it would have meant to have you to talk with."

"So why didn't you call?"

Andrew felt his face flush. He took his cell phone with him as he headed into the hallway. As he passed the living room he called to his father. "Going to the beach." To Sarah he said, "Did you know what happened?"

"Of course I knew. Everyone knew. Your mom put you in rehab."

He decided to climb down the stairs instead of waiting for the elevator. At the fifth landing he stopped to catch his breath, still weak from his illness. "You knew? How come you didn't come visit me there?"

"I tried, but they didn't allow visitors."

"What? They wouldn't even let you see me? That's crazy."

"You don't believe me?"

"Oh, yeah, I believe you. I just meant it's a crazy place. Everyone there was crazy; nurses and doctors too! If my dad hadn't rescued me I would have gone crazy myself."

"It must have been horrible for you."

"I'd rather not think about it."

He came out on the ground floor and started across to the beach. Though the sun had set, the sands radiated the day's heat. He left his shoes at the curb and began walking barefoot, enjoying the feel of the sand between his toes.

"So, I saw you with Chris at the funeral. You two looked comfortable together."

"Yeah, right."

"What does that mean?"

"You think I'd rather be with Chris than you, Andy?"

"It sort of looked that way, especially when you turned your back on me." He picked up a plastic bottle someone had left on the beach and detoured to the trash barrel, tossing it from a dozen yards away. It bounced off the rim and he retrieved it, and tried again from eight feet. This time it went in.

"Sometimes you are so stupid!" Sarah lectured. "I turned my back to hide my tears. You're the only boy I've ever kissed. How could you possibly think I'd rather be with Chris than with you?"

"But … I saw you guys holding hands."

He heard her sigh through the phone. "Andy, I need a friend. Yes, he'll hold my hand, but that's all I'd let him do. He's a dork."

Andrew laughed. "Oh that is SO true. He's as dorky as they come. And pimply."

"And pimply," Sarah laughed with him.

Andrew walked along the wet sands where the waves came up and washed his feet. His foot sunk in to the ankle, and he pulled it out with a resounding plop. "So how the heck have you been?" he asked.

"Lonely! First Jenny was killed, and then Rebecca went all the way out to San Francisco for college. I don't get along with the girls my age in the school, they're into Goth for gosh sakes, black clothes, piercing. Weird stuff. And now you're gone and Travis and his gang are so wild! I really miss you! It's been over a year now."

"A year? It hasn't even been six months. I left in June and this is November."

"Andy. I lost you a year ago. Once you started smoking pot and drinking alcohol you turned your back on me."

"Did I? I'm sorry, Sarah. I guess I went crazy."

"Eventually. But at first you were just mean. That stuff is not good for you, Andy. Do you realize that now?"

"Boy, do I ever. I've sworn off all that stuff for good!"

"Do you mean that, Andy? Do you *really* mean that?"

"Absolutely! I made a mistake this time, but I really learned my lesson. I'm done!"

"You can't imagine how happy those words make me."

Andrew sat down on the sands and looked out over the water. In the stillness he saw the sand crabs scurrying across the beach, dipping in and out of their entry holes.

"Andy?"

"What?"

"Do you remember two and a half years ago when we all went to your dad's lake house?"

"Sure I remember. That was a blast!"

"It really was. Do you remember when Travis put molasses on the doorknob?"

"Hah! Uncle Peter grabbed the knob, his expression was priceless! I haven't laughed like that since."

"No. Life really hasn't been that good since. That was the summer before …"

"Go ahead. You can say it. That was the summer before Jenny was killed. Yeah. Everything went to hell after that. I …"

Andrew couldn't hold back the sob.

"I'm sorry, Andy."

"I'll be okay. Give me a moment."

He stood up and kicked the sand, creating a shower of white crystals reflecting the moonlight. Loneliness seeped into his soul. He turned and glanced back at the condo. His father had come out on the balcony and when Andrew waved, his dad waved back at him.

"Sometimes I think I'll never be happy again."

"We can't go back, Andy. We gotta take life as it is now."

"What about you, Sarah? How are things living with your new stepmother?"

Sarah sighed. "She's okay. She really is. She tries awfully hard to be nice."

"But?"

"She's just not my mom. You know better than anyone, Andy. Someone you love is gone, and it's like your heart's been ripped out."

"It's okay to miss your mom; you always will. Nothing wrong with that."

"You're right, Andy. See? I could always talk to you. You're so smart and calm."

Andrew continued walking down the beach, watching the crabs scurry away from him. "I sure miss you too. Wish we could get together."

"That'd be awesome! Can you come up for Thanksgiving or maybe Christmas break?"

"I don't think that's going to happen. With the disaster this last trip turned into, I better plan on staying in Mississippi for a little while."

"You scared the beejeezes out of all of us. You were screaming and throwing rocks at white vans. Travis was afraid to bring you home so he called me to meet you guys out at the park. It was cold as could be out there! We drove around with you 'til almost three in the morning before I could finally talk him into taking you back to Uncle Peter's house. Once he saw you, he called 911."

"I wonder what it is I got against white vans?"

"You don't remember?"

"What?"

"The fellows who killed Jenny were in a white van."

Andrew stopped abruptly. "I had totally forgotten that. See? I told you those white vans are evil!"

Sarah laughed. "I guess you're right. Say, I've got an idea."

"What?"

"If you can't come up, maybe I can come down there. How about we see if Travis and his family want to come down there for the holidays?"

"You mean like the summers in Wisconsin?"

"Exactly! I bet Uncle Peter would love to get Travis out of town for awhile. I'm sure my dad would let me come too."

"I would so much love to see you, Sarah." Andrew started walking back to the condo, his feet covered in stockings of sticky sand. When he reached his shoes he picked them up and carried them the rest of the way.

"I've missed you so much, Andy. Please stay sweet for me."

"By that you mean clean, don't you?"

"Yes."

"Then you can count on me being sweet."

"You promise?"

"Yep. I promise."

"Good night, Andy."

"Later."

He closed his phone and threw his shoes in the air, catching them and twirling them around like bolas. Washing his feet off at the ground floor faucet he raced up the stairs. Once in his room he popped open his computer and began messaging Travis.

Saturday, November 15th

A strong morning sun burned away the night fog, its unseasonable heat blasting the beach. I watched Andrew go through his stretching routine. He seemed pale and sluggish. On his hundred-and-thirty-pound frame, the recent weight loss showed.

"How you doing champ?" I asked.

He stopped stretching long enough to look at me. "I'm going to try, Dad. That's all I can say."

"Andy, you don't have to race. Just tell the coach you've been sick. He'll understand."

Andrew looked over to where the Gulfport boys were lined up, waiting on the starting gun. "No."

"Just do whatever you feel up to. Take it easy and pace yourself. You're good at that."

Andrew finished his stretches and stood to jog in place. "Sure, Dad."

I looked down the road, lined with broken electric poles; a picket fence for a malignant giant. Bay St. Louis had been hit hard by Hurricane Katrina three years ago, and brushed again earlier this year by Gustav. Much of the debris had been cleaned up, but empty foundations and blown out houses were nearly as common as rebuilt ones. "What is the race course this time?"

"Out the beach road here, around the bend, and across the bridge. Another half mile, and double back. The bridge is gonna be a killer."

I surveyed the other kids on the road and their parents setting up on the side. "Smaller meet than last time."

"Yeah, only four schools; Waveland, the Bay, Harrison Central, and us. And Waveland's only got five kids, barely even a full team."

"Waveland and Bay St. Louis only have one girl each."

"Not that many girls run cross country. That Judy from Harrison sure is tough."

"I suppose you need to do well today?"

Andrew had stood and was jogging lightly in place. "It'd be good. But even if we blow it today we'll probably get to go to Regionals."

"I'm sure you're going to win."

His mouth turned down and he pointed towards the sidelines. "Why not hang out with the Gulfport people?"

I glanced over to where the Barnes and some of the other parents were set up. "I'd feel like I was intruding."

Andrew shrugged and walked off, leaving me to head back to where I'd left my chair. I watched him join the column of Gulfport runners in blue and orange. Their line of eight was dwarfed by the Harrison Central squad, Flash and Judy in front. She had war paint on her cheeks and brow.

The starter buzz sounded and the lines surged forward, disappearing around the curve in a couple of minutes. I carried my chair up the hill and set it up under a shade tree. I had barely settled down when I heard someone shout, "Look, you can see them on the bridge!"

Maybe a half-mile away the kids were running up the pedestrian walkway to the big bridge. They looked like specks charging through the shimmering white stones. Opening an engineering magazine I had brought, I turned to the want ads. It didn't take long to find nothing, so I thumbed through the rest of the journal and soon became caught up in a fascinating article discussing gear ratio reduction equations.

In twenty minutes the parents cheered again as the runners returned back along the curve. Of the lead pack of four, three of them wore Harrison Central green, the exception being Devonne in second place. As I watched, Judy Jones passed him, her French knot bouncing across her back. The cheering got louder from the Harrison crowd. Just before the finish line another Harrison Central boy surged past as well.

Devonne stumbled across the line. After he caught his breath, he walked back to the Barnes blanket with head held down. Three, four, five more runners came into sight. *Where was Andy?*

Finally I spotted him as he rounded the bend. He jogged persistently, as one after another of the runners pulled past him. I watched in dismay when Andrew staggered across the finish line, managed a few steps, and collapsed onto the grass. Coach Dalton rushed over and began fanning him, ordering someone to bring water. I hurried up.

"What's happening?" I demanded.

"Heat exhaustion," Coach Dalton replied. "He's dehydrated." The coach reached down to prop up Andrew's head long enough to sip the water. "Take it slowly now, Son. You don't want to start heaving."

I looked down on my son's glazed eyes and bleached face. His tee shirt dripped sweat. I sat down hard on the ground next to him.

Devonne ran up and began fanning Andrew with a towel. "Don't you pass out now, Andy. Drink some water." He turned to me. "You okay Mr. Lewis?" He stopped fanning Andrew to hover next to me. "You're lookin' 'bout as white as Andy there. You need some water, too?"

I stared up at the tall boy squatting in front of me, his eyes radiating concern. The blood returned to my legs. "I'll be okay. How's Andy?"

"Heat exhaustion," Coach Dalton said again. "He'll need to get into air conditioning, rest, and fluids the rest of the day." He looked at Andrew. "You doing better, Son?"

His face slowly regaining color, Andrew said, "I'll be okay." He sat up. "Maybe feeling a little dizzy." He lay back down.

Coach Dalton turned to me. "Look after your boy. Have him drink more water."

The coach signaled for Devonne to join him and they went over to the somber gathering of parents. I saw him explaining and pointing.

Andrew managed to sit up and sip some water. "I'm okay. Give me a minute." I fanned him as he sat and stared out at the bridge.

"How you doing?" Devonne asked, coming up after the meeting broke up. His parents followed.

"'S'al'right. How'd we do?"

Devonne shrugged. "Who cares?"

Andrew reached out and grabbed his arm. "That bad? We came in second, right?"

Devonne shook his head. "Third. The Bay edged us out."

"Shit," Andrew murmured.

Devonne punched him lightly on the arm. "Forget it, Andy. You been sick. You ran. That's what counts.

The man I recognized as Devonne's father spoke up. "Don't fret, Andy. Just a bad day." He turned to me with outstretched hand. "Hi, I'm Erskine Barnes. This is my wife, Keisha." I enjoyed the gentle firmness of their handshakes.

"Rick Lewis. A pleasure to meet you."

"Devonne was just telling us you've been sick, Andy," Erskine said, turning to Andrew. He left it open-ended. I wondered how much Andrew had told Devonne, and how much Devonne had told his parents. Andrew's mental illness secret was getting hard to keep.

"I guess I didn't drink enough fluids. I'll be okay."

"Sure you will," Erskine insisted. "Don't worry about this race. You've still got three weeks to get ready for Regional."

"Speaking of upcoming events," Keisha said. "I wonder if you two would like to join us for Thanksgiving Dinner?"

I looked at Andrew who returned the look with uplifted eyebrow. "We'd love to come, wouldn't we, Dad?"

I nodded. "Absolutely. We appreciate the invitation."

"And bring your lady friend," Erskine said.

"Lady friend?" I asked, momentarily confused.

Keisha laid her hand on my arm. "Devonne mentioned you're seeing one of the teachers. If you feel it's appropriate, we just want you to know that she'd be welcome too."

"Thank you." I turned to Andrew and asked if he was ready. He indicated he was, and we made our good-byes.

We rode in silence on the way home. At one point I glanced over at Andrew, and saw his face turned to the window. Tears rolling down his cheeks reflected in the glass.

"Andy? Why are you crying?"

"I'm not crying."

"Oh."

I let the silence hang.

"You sure you don't want to tell me?"

"I let them down."

"Oh, Andy. You were sick. Everyone on your team had a bad day."

"My fault."

"How do you figure?"

He took his time about answering, using his T-shirt as a cloth against his face. "Before Pascagoula, the team felt second rate. When we won there, our attitude changed. We believed in ourselves, felt like winners."

"But Andy ..."

He shushed me. "See, in a team, everyone has a role. I'm the pacer. Devonne counted on me to be near his back. When I didn't show, he lost his momentum. Lebron planned to hang with me and sprint together at four kilos. I faded so early, I set off everyone's rhythm."

I drove slowly, concentrating on the road, though traffic was still light. "Andy, you're just one runner."

"I let my friends down."

We rode in silence the rest of the way home. Andrew went straight to the shower and then to his room. When he hadn't come out an hour later I brought him a tray with a bowl of vegetable soup, crackers, and a glass of milk. I found him curled up in bed.

I set the tray on his desk and pulled the chair up beside him. Pulling his sheet from his back, I began isolating muscles and massaging them.

"When I was a kid and my mom was dying," I said, "my father would bring me this very meal. The soup had pasta alphabet letters, just like this one. I'd take my spoon and fish out the letters, lining them up on the crackers as I spelled out crazy words. Look here." I waited until he looked up, his face full of pillow wrinkles. "Here's QZKM. That spells quizkum, Martian for soup."

He smiled, just a bit.

I continued, "I still remember my tray had a picture of a magician pulling a rabbit out of a black top hat. Your grandpa called it a magic potion tray." I set the tray on his lap.

"I sure could use some magic," he said with a whimper.

"It'll come, my son. The day I saw the light come back into your eyes, I became a believer in miracles."

Saturday, November 15th, Evening

I crept my car up the driveway of the redbrick Hewes Mansion, giving it the once over. It looked every bit of a hundred and fifty years, with tall white columns, sprawling side wings, and a third story widow's walk. A winding stone path leading to the front portico bisected the meticulously trimmed lawn.

Sylvia answered the ring, her smile bright and welcoming. "Good to see you, Rick." She leaned her cheek forward and I kissed it.

I followed her in past the entry hallway, parquet underfoot and antique coat racks along the walls. Beyond came a huge great-room, decorated with well-groomed bookcases, dozens of portraits, and a selection of other furniture, each piece handsome and proud. On a Queen Anne chair in the center of the room an elderly woman sat perfectly erect, stroking a Persian kitty that purred in her lap.

"Rick, allow me to introduce you to Aunt Frances. She rules this household."

Fire sparkled in her eyes. "A pleasure to meet you, Richard. Pardon me for not getting up."

"Aunt Frances had hip surgery eight weeks ago," Sylvia explained.

I approached and took her hand, bending forward and planting a kiss on its back. "A pleasure to meet you, Aunt Frances. From the wonderful stories Sylvia has told me, I've been eager to make your acquaintance."

She nodded acknowledgment. "Your Yankee has good manners after all, Sylvia. I must say I'm pleasantly surprised." She indicated I should sit in the chair on her left, and once I was settled, she asked, "What brings you to the Magnolia State, Richard?"

"I wanted to get away from the hustle-bustle of the big city I guess. I came down here for a job interview and decided it would be the perfect place to raise a family."

"Yes," Aunt Frances nodded. "It is that. Sylvia tells me your Andrew is doing quite well in his studies."

"Well, he was doing well, but he had a little setback."

"Indeed. I'm sorry to hear he's been sick." Aunt Frances smiled sympathetically. "I believe my niece helped you out, didn't she? I noticed she was gone a bit last weekend."

"Shush, Auntie. Tea, anyone?" Sylvia asked, taking a step toward the kitchen.

"You don't happen to have coffee?"

Sylvia laughed. "You're in the South now, Rick."

I shrugged. "Tea will be fine then." I watched her walk from the room, her bottom bouncing nicely. When I glanced back at Aunt Frances she gave me a wink. "You seem to favor my niece."

I blushed. "She's remarkable – and we have a lot in common."

"Oh?"

"Love of history for example." I pointed to the bookcase against the wall. "Do you mind if I look at the books?"

"Help yourself."

I ran my fingers along the polished edges of the bookcase. Clearly it had been carved by hand, each joint expertly dove-tailed. An imposing headpiece displayed angels reading Holy Scriptures. Stuffed with books, mostly biographies and histories, half of one shelf displayed Faulkner.

"You're from Chicago?" Aunt Frances asked.

I glanced up. "Yep, lived there all my life. I'm sixth generation Chicagoan. I only moved here last February."

"Why?"

I chuckled to myself. Sylvia had thought me very direct, but I had nothing on Aunt Frances. "I needed a change, and certainly this has been a big one."

She smiled pleasantly. "Did you know that Sylvia's ex-husband was Yankee?"

"Yes, she told me."

"And yet you still think you might enjoy spending time together?"

I had to laugh. "I think we get along very well. What does she think?"

Aunt Frances smiled mysteriously and filled in the pause with another question. "So you haven't any relatives here at all?"

I shook my head. "Not a soul when I came down. Now, of course, I have my son."

Sylvia came in from the kitchen with a tray holding a pitcher and three glasses. She looked suspiciously at Aunt Frances and asked, "What have y'all been talking about?"

The older woman gave me a wink. "Oh, just the weather, that sort of thing. Extra sugar, if you please."

Sylvia poured tea into each cup and brought mine across to the room to hand to me. Running her hand gently along the edge of a shelf, she said, "My great-grandfather carved this bookshelf 'round 'bout the beginning of the twentieth century."

I nodded my appreciation. "Beautiful work." Sweeping my arm out to indicate the room, I said, "Tell me about some of the other objects. This place looks like an absolute museum."

She walked around the living room, pointing out various pieces of interest. A portrait of a barrister stood over a small cabinet that held shiny leather backed law books. A cherry-wood breakfront displayed a dozen sepia family photographs. She picked up one of a dashing fellow in uniform and told about his part in the battle of Antietam.

"Most of the furniture in this house has been in my family for generations. This vase came over from Scotland with my great-great-grandmother before the War Between the States."

I scanned the room, enjoying the honor glowing from every nook. "I bet there's a story for every item." I pulled out a volume and blew off the dust, opening it to find it to be a first edition of Shelby Foote's Civil War book, *Fredel.* I read aloud the personal dedication to Bernard Hewes and asked, "Who's this?"

"My father. He passed away several years ago."

I replaced the book and looked around again. "Pretty crowded in here. Your antiques are lovely, but aren't you afraid of losing these old memories in a hurricane or a fire? I might put some of this in storage, or donate to a museum."

I glanced back to see Sylvia rushing off to the kitchen.

Turning to Aunt Frances, I asked, "What did I say?"

She pointed towards the kitchen. "Why not ask her yourself?"

In the kitchen I found Sylvia soaping and rinsing a glass vigorously, her face hung in shadows. When I turned her towards me I saw a tear track down her cheek. I placed my finger on the wet spot, brought it to my lips, and kissed, mimicking what she'd done for me. "What did I say?"

She shook her head, forcing a smile. "You're a Yankee, just like Gus. I can't expect you to understand." She finished torturing the glass, setting it on the drainboard. Soapy water ran down the plastic, looking like surf returning to the sea.

I held her face in my hands, staring down into those shining brown eyes. "Is it my funny accent?"

Her cute pout flashed for just a moment. "You're from a different culture, Rick. You dismiss my precious heirlooms as dust-collecting junk, when to me they're family. You say hurtful things out of all innocence, because it's the way you think."

"I didn't say dust collecting junk. I said they were lovely."

"But that's what you were thinking."

I looked at her sad eyes and tight lips and decided the best plan was an apology. "I'm sorry. I'll be more careful what I say."

"It's not so much what you say, it's the way you think and how you act. You don't understand or appreciate our culture, the little actions that make us proud to be Southerners. When you fail to hold a chair for a lady, everyone knows you're not from here. When you meet me and take my hand, you release a little too soon. When I present my cheek for a greeting kiss, you look confused."

I leaned against the wall and finished off my tea. Handing over the glass, I watched her scrub it slowly.

"This *is* a museum," she explained. "It's the Hewes family museum, a family with a long proud history." She paused, staring at me through the glass, lowering it slowly, leaving her eyes locked on to mine. "Tell me, Rick. If you were in my shoes, would you really pack away these family photos and old books?"

I knew there was no right answer. "Since they have no special meaning to me, I can't put myself in your place. It's not a fair question."

She shook her head sadly. "Don't you have any family heirlooms? Not even an old diary or a piece of jewelry?"

"I guess not. My mom died when I was young so I didn't have what you would call a feminine touch around the house. Dad always said 'Things aren't important.'"

"No? What was important to him?"

I pictured the hours I'd spent with my father, sitting on the porch looking at the stars, or walking through the woods. "My father was always fascinated with the spiritual aspects of life. He loved history, philosophy, and nature. Up in our camp in Wisconsin we'd sit under that endless sky and he'd teach me about constellations, tell stories about Greek mythology, and talk of the ways of the world."

"I wish I could have met him. When did he pass?"

"He had a stroke ten years ago."

"What happened to the property?" Sylvia ran a damp cloth along counters that already appeared spotless.

"I still own it. Last time I was there was three summers ago. Mallory's sister's family joined us for a big family get-together." I thought of the good times, and, inevitably, the bad that followed. Forcing a smile, I asked, "You hungry?"

She hung up the cloth and gave me a reassuring smile. "*Certainement.* Where are you fixin' to take me?"

"Vrazel's."

"Oh! I love them. Let me grab my purse."

We walked back into the living room where Aunt Frances still sat, now reading a magazine. "You young 'uns going out?"

Sylvia kissed her on the cheek. "I might be late. Don't wait up."

Aunt Frances winked at me. "Have a good time."

I held the doors for Sylvia, both her front and my car. The ride down to the beach and the three miles to the restaurant took but a few minutes, and soon enough the waitress sat us at a small table next to a window. I enjoyed the reflection of the ruby and emerald sunset on Sylvia's contented smile.

"This is so beautiful! I haven't eaten at Vrazel's since they rebuilt from Katrina. Years ago Aunt Frances used to bring me for Sunday brunch. The last time I was here was for the rehearsal dinner of my cousin Belinda's wedding."

"How long ago?"

"Let me think. Six years I guess. There must have been forty guests. Cousins came all the way from California. It seems that families only gather for weddings and funerals these days." She must have noticed my pained expression because she reached across and took my hand. "What are you thinking?"

"Jenny's funeral. All those girls, her friends, all standing around crying. Girls I'd watched grow up. They cried as if it really mattered to them. But how true can tears be when a few days later they resumed their lives as if nothing had happened?"

"They may have learned to cope, but people don't get over death easily."

"Some never will," I said.

The waitress arrived. "What can I get y'all to drink?"

"Sweet tea, please."

"Diet Coke."

We turned to our menus. "What's good?" I asked.

"Everything's good here. I'm having the trout, but it's such a big portion we could share it if you'd like."

"Sounds good to me, if we add salads." We folded the menus and pushed them to the side of the table. The waitress picked up on the signal and took our orders. For a moment we sat in companionable silence, sipping our drinks. Sylvia watched the sunset and I watched her.

Turning to me she asked, "How did Andy's race go today?"

"Awful! The whole team had a bad run, even Devonne. Andy finished fourteenth."

"Fourteenth? That must have been a disappointment for him."

"It wasn't for lack of trying. He pushed himself so hard he passed out as soon as he crossed the finish line. Scared me to death!"

Sylvia grasped my hand. "Oh my goodness. What did the doctor say?"

"I took him home." I noticed her worried expression. "The coach said he just needed some rest and fluids, and he was doing much better by the time I left tonight."

"I might have taken him to a doctor."

"And I might have donated some of your heirlooms to a museum. Just because we do things differently doesn't mean one or the other of us is wrong. I love my son. I won't let anything happen to him."

She smiled. "That's perfectly clear."

I took her hand. "Speaking of love, I've been missing you an awful lot this week. I find myself thinking about you every moment." I felt her wrist go limp in my hand. Her face grew pale and she lowered her gaze. "What's wrong?"

She shook her head.

"Come on, now. We've been lovers, Sylvia. I know you care for me. Why won't you allow yourself to love?"

She shook loose from my hand and stood, still not meeting my gaze. "I need to powder my nose." She dropped her napkin on the table and rushed off.

I looked out at the Saturday night beach traffic: convertibles stuffed with high school kids on their way to prep school games, SUVs with families from out-of-state coming to the coliseum show, and Cadillacs with high-rollers trying out the casinos. The waitress brought the food and still Sylvia didn't return. I continued to stare out the window.

When she finally showed, fresh mascara decorated her reddened eyes. She picked up her fork and took a bite of salad. I watched her, the silence heavy on the table.

"You want to talk about it?" I asked.

She shook her head. I remained silent and she put down her fork and gave me a faint smile. "Rick, I do care about you, but I'm not ready to be hurt again. I told you before, making love was not meant as a declaration of love. It was just passion. Animal passion. I guess we shouldn't even see each other, especially if you think this is going to lead somewhere."

I remembered my father saying, "If you don't like the way the conversation is going, change the subject." I pointed at the fish. "You know what's the only food that doesn't spoil?" She shook her head.

"Honey." I drew out the word, like a Southerner calling his mate.

Sylvia smiled. "Here's one for you. What do bulletproof vests, fire escapes, windshield wipers, and laser printers all have in common?"

I pondered for a moment. "All are safety devices? No, that's not right. I give up, what?"

"All invented by women."

I laughed. "Good one. Okay, my turn. Who was the first couple shown in bed together on television?"

She cocked her head in thought. "That's a tough one. Hmm. Ozzie and Harriet?"

"Nope. Give up? Fred and Wilma Flintstone."

Sylvia laughed. "Cartoon characters? Hardly fair."

"Hey, even cartoon characters have needs."

I thought she might be offended, but her eyes lit in acceptance. "I guess we all do."

We fell into an easy conversation. The waitress brought the tab and I slipped my credit card into the fold. While we waited for her to bring it back, I asked Sylvia, "You ready for that walk on the beach?"

She looked out at the night. "Looks a mite busy out there."

"Let's drive back to my condo and we can walk on one that's more deserted."

We took the short drive, parked at my condo, and walked across Beach Boulevard. At the cement walk we removed our socks and shoes, stepping onto the cool white sands. Rolling surf provided a lulling background as we walked down to the water's edge. I bent down and picked up a large snail shell, peering at the folded legs of the hermit crab hiding inside.

"Imagine how strange it would be to outgrow your home every few months." I handed the shell to Sylvia and she stuck her finger in the opening, ticking the crab's legs. She returned the shell to the beach and we stood and watched until its tiny feet came out like sunflower petals, dragging the shell slowly into the sea.

"How long have you lived in your house?" I asked.

"It's my childhood home. I moved to New York at eighteen, and returned after my divorce, sixteen years ago."

"Sixteen years, huh? The other day you alluded to another relationship. You want to talk about it?"

Sylvia glanced at me and then out to sea. "I don't think so."

I watched her, wondering what to say, considering if I'd ever get past her walls. I reached out and took her hand. "Sylvia, what will it take for you to trust me, to open your heart? Don't you feel something special towards me?" She turned to me and gave me just a hint of a smile, all the encouragement I needed. I pulled her into my arms, kissing her, gently at first, until she grabbed me and thrust her tongue into my mouth. The sea serenaded us as we enjoyed our passion.

Reluctantly we broke apart, and Sylvia stared out over the dark waters. She murmured, "I think you better take me home."

Pointing up at the stars, I said, "See Orion? He's a winter star constellation. According to Greek mythology, he's always chasing his lover, Dawn, a summer constellation. The way the stars rotate, Orion has always rotated out before his lover arrives."

I took her face in my hands. "Don't make me be another Orion, Baby. Don't run away." I leaned forward to kiss her but she stepped back.

"I'm not ready, Rick. I'm afraid if we don't stop now ... well, I think you better take me home."

We washed off our feet at the condo outdoor faucet and loaded into my car. As we drove I reached for her hand and she took it, raising it to her lips for a gentle kiss.

"Say," I asked. "Have you got plans for Thanksgiving?"

"Aunt Frances and I usually host a dinner for a few of our relatives and friends. Why?"

"Andy and I have been invited over to the Barnes' home for Thanksgiving dinner. Keisha and Erskine are their names, Devonne's parents. You know them?"

"I've met Devonne's parents several times. Devonne is a very hard working boy. Does this mean he and Andy have become friends?"

"Yep. Keisha suggested I invite you and I'd be honored if you'd join us."

Sylvia stared out the side window, away from me. I had taken the long way, up to Pass Road, and we came back to Beach Boulevard along Highway 49, with its fast foods and strip malls. One of my co-workers had remarked the only good thing Katrina did was wash out downtown Gulfport. It must have been pretty nasty for this to be an improvement.

She turned to me, a tremble on her lip. "I don't know, Rick. Going together to a Thanksgiving gathering will create gossip."

"So what?"

She shook her head. "You still don't understand our culture. Here we are, hardly even knowing each other, and you want us to go to a family gathering as a couple?"

"Well, how about we have another date first? There's one more Saturday before Thanksgiving. You busy? We can try a different restaurant. They say in Chicago you could eat three meals a day in different restaurants and never have to repeat your entire life."

She didn't answer, and we drove the last few blocks in silence. I pulled up in front of her home and got out to open her car door. Halfway through her home portal she turned, and I leaned forward for another kiss. She stopped me with her palm against my chest.

"I like you, Rick. I'm just not ready right now."

"You're not ready for *any* relationship, or you're just not ready for me?"

She stared at something beyond me, some image lurking in the dark, the bailiwick of memories. "This is too much too fast."

"What are you afraid of Sylvia? One failed marriage doesn't mean you need to give up on all men."

Her focus returned to my face. "I did try it again, Rick. It was another huge mistake. Twice burned."

I took her hands in mine and tried to pull her closer, but she shook loose and stepped further inside. She started closing the door.

"Wait. There's something you need to know."

With the door open only an inch she whispered, "What?"

I watched that crack, the sliver of light that showed she really did want to hear what I had to say.

"I'm not them."

Slowly the door opened and she signaled me. I stepped into the foyer and she grabbed me in a tight hug. I kissed her gently, and when I pulled back she stroked my face, staring into my eyes. "Rick, I know I must seem crazy to you, so unsure of where to go."

I nodded. "I figured this is just your Southern way, 'cause I know you love me and want me."

She laughed, and kissed me again. "You may be right, Mr. Engineer. Good thing you know your heart better than I know mine."

She opened the door again and I stepped out, stopping on the porch to say, "Good night, Sylvia."

"Good night, Rick. You may pick me up at six next Saturday." She shut the door.

Sunday, November 16th

The next morning I sat out on the balcony reading the paper and enjoying the gulf breeze. Every now and then I picked up the binoculars and looked down the beach, until finally I spotted Andrew jogging my way. An evening of fluids and rest seemed to have restored him. I went to the kitchen and brought back fruit, cereal, milk, and tableware. When Andrew joined me, a towel around his neck, he carried a quart of orange juice in hand. He looked pretty well.

"How was your run?" I asked.

"S'al'right. Mostly walked." Jiggling his body like a wind chime in dance, he said, "I don't have my strength back, but I feel great. Cleansed. Like I've gone through some sort of .... I don't know, a passage. Yeah, like the passages we talked about in psychology class. You ever heard of Dr. Jung, Dad?"

I smiled. "Yep."

"So maybe I just did one, huh?"

"Maybe. In any case, I'm glad you're feeling better. What are your plans for the day?"

"Homework." He slumped into the other chair, pulling one of the empty bowls towards him and filling it with cereal. "I barely get differentials and next week we're doin' integration. Sounds like a political statement to me."

I chuckled. "I use integrals pretty often at work. They don't really get hard until they start throwing in the trigonometry. How close are you to catching up?"

"Close enough." Andrew pulled the milk carton towards him and added some to his bowl. "How was your date last night?"

The memory of Sylvia's sweet kiss caused me to lick my lips, and Andrew snorted.

"That good, huh?"

"Well, we do like each other," I admitted. "But she's still sort of tentative. You like Mrs. Perkins, right?"

He picked up a banana, peeled it, and sliced it into his cereal. When he was done slicing and had stirred it all up, he took a spoonful of cereal. He chewed slowly, swallowed, and laid his spoon down. "Yeah, guess so. It just feels strange, you know. I mean, she's my teacher. And, well, not my mom."

"No, she'll never be your mom."

"Hmph," he snorted. "Good thing."

"Andy. You need to get over this thing with your mother. Have you talked to her?"

He resumed eating, taking several spoonfuls before answering. "No. Don't plan to."

This had been a sore subject since his birthday, my suggestions that he try to make up with her meeting unrelenting resistance. "I must say this last episode certainly gave *me* a different perspective. With all the hallucinations you were having, it seems likely you did need to be committed."

He put down his spoon, stood, and walked over to the rail, kicking it a few times.

"Andy, what are you thinking?"

"You promised me!"

"What?"

He turned, leaning against the railing and staring down at me. "You promised me you wouldn't put me back in the hospital. Now you're saying she was right putting me away?"

I drummed my fingers on the table, choosing my words carefully. "I did promise you I wouldn't commit you to the hospital, Andy. I said it, and I meant it. But that doesn't mean I don't understand your mother's perspective. Your mother never could have taken care of you in that condition."

He seemed to think about it, and, sighing, returned to the deck chair. He picked up his spoon and swirled it around the half-finished bowl. "It just doesn't seem right."

"Andy, you need to call her. I really think you should."

He pinged the spoon against the bowl a few times, setting up a rhythm of some sort, and then dropped it into the milk. "Yeah, maybe."

I poured my own cereal and we ate in companionable silence for a bit. When he finished he poured himself a second bowl.

"Say, Dad. Can we talk about Chicago?"

"What about it?"

"I know this visit sort of blew up, but I was enjoying seeing my friends. With the holidays coming up, I was wondering if maybe we couldn't go on up for Christmas."

I put my spoon down and grasped my hands together under the table, gripping tightly to suppress the trembling. "Go to Chicago? I don't think so."

"Well, I mean, this place sucks. It's one thing to have to stay here for the school year. At least I got something to do. But spend the holidays alone? Man, that's cruel."

I looked out to the sea where the clouds seemed like sour cream dollops, large and fluffy. From ten stories up I could identify the shadows they cast, a jigsaw pattern on water and sand.

I turned back to my son. "I don't think you should go to Chicago."

"Then, you gotta invite them here."

I stared at him, unsure of what he was trying to say.

"Sarah and I were talking."

"I thought you two had broken up."

"We made up. Anyway, we were thinking you could invite Travis and his parents down here, and then Sarah could come too. It'd be like old times, like when we all went to Wisconsin, or Disney." He threw his arm out towards the beach. "Course, this ain't no Disney."

It was such a good idea I wondered why I hadn't thought of it myself. I would love having Peter's company, that is, if he weren't furious at me for ditching him at the hospital. Celine was a bit of a bitch, but I suppose one had to make allowances.

Andrew must have thought my ruminations were the beginnings of a refusal, for he followed up plaintively. "Either they come here or I gotta go up there."

His threat scared me, and looking into his determined gaze, I decided he probably meant it. "I tell you what, Andy. Let's make a deal. If I call Peter, you agree to call your mother."

His shoulders slumped. "No fair."

"I think it's perfectly reasonable, a call for a call."

Andrew closed his eyes and leaned back in his chair. I watched him take a few deep breaths, and the resignation showed on his face. "Okay," he announced. "You call Peter and invite them down, and I'll call Mom. You go first."

Checking my watch, I said, "He won't be up this early on a Sunday morning. I'll call at nine."

"Sounds good." He stood, grabbed the cereal, milk, and juice, and stopped at the patio door to tell me, "I'm gonna go shower."

I sat a bit longer, sipping my coffee and finishing the crossword. Gathering the remaining breakfast dishes, I carried everything into the kitchen for cleaning. After my morning exercise bike, shower and dress, it was nine o'clock, time to make the call.

"Hello?" The sound of his familiar voice gave me courage.

"Hi Pete, it's Rick."

I carried the phone into the living room, settling into my armchair, running one finger along the chair's smooth leather armrests.

"Hey, great to hear from you. How's Andy?"

"Doing good, thanks." I thought of Peter's perpetual smile, part of his disarming charm. I supposed corporate lawyers are like that, making friends, trying to negotiate. Peter had a dark side, too. During our doubles tennis matches, if Peter got pissed at one of our opponents he'd "accidentally" beam 'em with a wild shot, apologize profusely, and turn and wink at me. No wonder Travis was such a card: a true chip off the old block.

"You're a crazy man, you know that, Rick? What's the idea, sneaking him out and leaving me sitting in the waiting room? It was almost five o'clock before I found out you guys had left!"

"Sorry about that. But anyway, he's better."

"Yeah? How'd he do in yesterday's race? Travis said he wasn't feeling too well."

Modern communication amazed me. I had never been on Facebook or any of those Internet chat things, but I knew the kids loved them, and recently I'd known many adults who used them too. "That's right. He finished fourteenth. He says he feels better today though."

"Glad to hear it. It's about time you checked in. Did you get the message I called last Friday?"

"Message?"

"Yeah," Peter chuckled. "Funny thing about that. A woman answered the phone."

"Oh yeah, that would be Sylvia. She did mention it. Sorry I didn't get back to you."

"Sylvia?"

The mention of her name brought a smile to my face. "She's Andy's teacher. Came over to help take care of him."

"Oh?"

"I hear that tone, Pete. And, actually, there may be something there. She's cute ... though she seems to be prejudiced against Yankees."

"You should think about that, Rick; if you're already having reservations about her, I mean. After all, you're talking about a state that still has the confederate bars on their flag."

"You got a point." I walked out to the balcony, reveling in the warm salt air. The weatherman had promised balmy temperatures through the weekend. Maybe I should talk Andrew into taking a walk with me down to the mall.

"Thanks for checking on Andy," I said. "How're the boys doing?"

Peter sighed. "It's going to be a tough road for Calvin. He's in physical and speech therapy. His dad's gone a bit crazy."

Crazy? Images of Andrew smashing his hand against the window flashed through my head. I shuddered and muttered something sympathetic.

"But Travis is coming along," Peter continued. "Getting used to his crutches. Seeing what happened to his friends hit him hard. He's sworn off all drugs and alcohol."

"Not much of a silver lining."

"Too damn high a price!"

I thought of the double tragedies we'd just been through, the car accident that had left Billy dead, and two years ago, the murder of my own daughter. My memories tumbled through the intermediate months; Mallory's fall into depression and alcoholism, Andrew's deterioration, and even my own life; out of work and out of friends. The return of Peter's voice startled me.

"Anyway, he's back in school. They'll run a drug test on him every Monday."

"How about his leg?"

"Doctor plans to put a new cast on it next week. Travis says he's glad, 'cause the current one is running out of space for his friends to sign. Love notes from all his girlfriends." Peter chuckled.

Travis sure knew how to love life. Out on the lake in Wisconsin three years ago he, Sarah, and Andrew had caught a dozen trout, and after each one he reeled in Travis whooped and shouted like he'd just shot a bear or something.

"You remember when Travis found that Girl Scout Troop?" I chuckled as I told the story. "Heh. I thought we'd never keep him in his cabin that night. Remember taking turns sitting guard?"

Peter laughed. "We really need to do that trip again, huh Rick?"

This reminded me of the purpose of my call. "Speaking of which, what are you doing for Christmas? I was wondering if maybe you guys would be able to visit down here."

"Pretty short notice, Buddy. Christmas is a busy time what with meetings and parties."

I should have known Peter would be booked solid. How was I ever going to convince a high-flying Chicago lawyer to give up his Christmas holidays? "Maybe you could fit in a week or so? Andy and I would love to have you, Celine, and Travis down here over the holidays. Maybe Sarah could come too."

"Hmm." He sounded non-committal.

"Ah come on, Pete. We'd have a great time."

Peter's hearty laugh broadcast through the phone. "We'll have a yappa-dabba-doo time! What a great idea."

"Absolutely! You think you could do it?"

"Hold on I'll check my calendar. Hmm. How does Dec 22nd through January 3rd sound?"

"Really? You think you can get away for all that time? Marvelous! Oh, you'll need a place to stay – and that may be hard to find on such short notice."

"No problem, Buddy. I already have us booked for two rooms at the Beau Rivage. Ocean view."

"You already have rooms? You were pulling my leg about your schedule, you creep. Ha, you're a card."

"You bet. Sarah told Travis, so of course I already knew about the plans. You know their casino has twenty-four hour non-stop action?"

"Sounds like we'll have some late nights testing the odds. Especially on your money."

Peter paused. "You running a little short, fellow?"

I realized I'd let out my secret. "Shouldn't be a problem. I've got a job interview lined up in the morning. Hey, don't tell Mallory I lost my job, okay?"

"Oh, I imagine I can keep it secret for a couple of days before Celine gets it out of me. Say, maybe this is a blessing in disguise. There sure are plenty of jobs in Chicago, Old Man. What are you now, fifty or fifty-one?"

"Fifty until March. So what? I have experience, and that's bound to be more important than youth, especially with the economy so tough."

Peter asked, "You want me to make a few casual inquiries? I bet I could get you something nice and cushy."

Move back to Chicago? No, never! "I'll find something down here."

"You stubborn old coot. Why don't you want to come back to your friends and neighbors? Have you made so many new friends you don't want to leave?"

"Can't say I've made any friends."

"You know, Mallory isn't dating anyone. I hate seeing you two broken up like this, Buddy. You guys were really good for each other."

I remembered the happy times; the four of us chilling at Jazz clubs, drinking the martini de jour, or together for a holiday, grilling steaks while the kids ran around the backyard. I also remembered the bad times; the screaming matches, the denigration, the resentment and the blame.

"I just don't see that in the cards, Pete. I've already moved on."

"And does that mean from everyone? You didn't call me for over a year. When I called, you brushed me off. What's that about?"

I had missed Peter, unsure now why I had cut him off. "I suppose I wasn't ready."

"Damn it, we've been best friends since grade school," Peter said. "You think you're some kind of Robinson Caruso? You don't need anybody and you think no one misses you?"

"I just needed to get away for a little while. All those memories were killing me."

"So now you've had some time away. You feeling good about it?"

I shrugged, though I knew Peter couldn't see it. "I'm okay."

"You're okay? You have no friends and no job for God's sake. Why not take this as a sign to come back to Chicago? Why not come home?"

I held the phone against my pounding chest. *This is my home now, not some ice-begotten metropolis with suicidal ex-wives and murderous teenage gangs.* "This place sort of grows on you." With my thickest Mississippi accent, I added, "Peaceful like."

Peter sighed. "Okay, Buddy. I'm clearly not going to convince you over the phone. I guess I'm going to have to come down there and see what it is about the Mississippi Coast you love so much."

"I'm sure looking forward to seeing you guys," I told him.

"Great! The five of us will see you the twenty-second. We'll have a Merry Christmas and one hell of a New Year."

I counted on my fingers. "Five? You, Celine, Travis, and Sarah makes four."

"There's Mallory of course. We can't leave her behind."

"What?" I whispered.

"She hasn't seen her son in six months. You can't say no to having Mallory come along; this way Celine will have someone to talk to. All figured out."

"No, Pete," I insisted. "I'm just not ready for her yet."

"Come on. Either she comes or none of us do. This could be a deal breaker."

I wiped my suddenly clammy hands off on my pants. I didn't want Mallory, but they weren't coming without her; and if they didn't Andrew would go up there and maybe be gone forever. "Okay, okay. But not for the whole trip. Don't forget Andy's upset with her. Let him have a few days with his friends before she arrives. How about Mallory comes down after Christmas?"

"You're going to deprive her of Christmas day with her son? What kind of cruel curmudgeon are you anyway?"

"Don't push me!"

Peter laughed, his common method of diffusing tensions. "All right, then. The day after Christmas it is. That'll still give her a week there. Hey, and soften Andy up a little toward his mom. Just because you're mad at her, you know, a mother needs the love of her son."

"Is this your wife talking, Pete?"

"Of course. Don't you think she looks after her sister?"

"As a matter of fact, Andy agreed to give her a call today. Is she home or still in the hospital?"

"Home for now. She's had a rough time, Rick, a real rough time. Having Andy call should be good for her, but you better sit in. Can you do that?"

"I'll try. And, Pete?"

"Yeah?"

"Thanks for coming down. It'll mean the world to Andy."

"Just to Andy?"

I laughed. It felt great, as if good times were not just a memory, but could somehow live again. "And for me too! Let's keep in touch."

"Hey, that's what I'm saying!"

I hung up and made my way back down the hall. Music leaked out from below Andrew's door. It wasn't ear pounding, Andrew had never been a head banger type. Still, it wasn't sweet. When I was his age I listened to the Beatles, Simon and Garfunkel, and the Moody Blues. I guess during college, Peter and I got into Led Zeplin and Pink Floyd, but those bands were at least harmonic. The music of my kids' generation seemed nasal, sarcastic, and violent. Rap. Couldn't stand it.

I knocked loudly and he turned the music down. "Come on in," he called.

Inside, as usual, his clothes were strewn haphazardly, the bed sheets crumpled against the wall, with dirty dishes and half-filled glasses creating a landscape on his dresser. The walls held a scattering of posters, bands I'd never heard of. He was settled in his desk chair, typing away at his computer and I lowered myself onto his bed.

"Yeah?"

"I talked with Uncle Peter. It's all set. They arrive the twenty-second and stay through the New Year."

He flashed me a thumbs up. "Sarah too?"

"I guess, assuming her parents agree."

"They will," Andrew assured me, and I knew he was right. After Peter's sister remarried, Sarah's father had moved out of the country. Even before Sarah's mother died, Sarah had been included in all our activities. Her stepfather provided a good enough home, but he never wanted to be included.

"This'll be great, Dad. Just like old times."

"Maybe more than you expect."

He looked up at me, his head cocked in anticipation. "What?"

"Your mother's coming too."

I saw the anger flash through his face. "Crap. She'll ruin everything."

I stood and went to the window, looking out at the Sunday morning tourists setting up their umbrellas and chairs. One family had brought a kite, the father throwing it in the air, only to watch it twist and dive, crashing back into the sand. He walked over, picked it up, ran a few steps and repeated. The child, holding the string, watched in admiration and anticipation.

Turning back to Andrew I said, "She's coming after Christmas, so you'll have a few days to be with your friends first. Meanwhile, you promised you'd call her this morning."

He turned back to his computer and began punching at the keyboard, pointedly ignoring me.

"Andy."

He kept typing. I walked over and pushed the off button on the monitor, sending it into blackness. "Why is this so hard for you?"

"Because of her locking me away," he said.

"You were out of control; I saw it. I lived with you, treated you, brought you back to health. I did it because I promised you I would. And, by golly, I'd do it again. But it wasn't easy! Seeing what you were like, from peeing on the floor to hallucinating about white vans, I can see why your mother thought it was necessary." I saw him squirm and I laid my hand on his shoulder. "I'm sorry for being so harsh, Andy. But it's reality. At least we know what causes it now."

"It's hard to believe a nug of pot makes me crazy. It sure doesn't do my friends."

"It's what Dr. Hopkins said." I thought about Dr. Hopkins, how I really didn't trust anything about her. Mallory swore by her, but, really, Dr. Hopkins stuck her in the hospital and loaded her up with drugs. What kind of care was that?

"Anyway," I continued. "It's irrelevant. The point here is that your mother needs you to love her back right now. So, here." I handed him the phone.

He took it from me and stared into it. Looking up at me he asked, "You gonna stand there while I talk to her?"

I took a step back. "What would you like me to do?"

He shrugged. "Guess I don't care. If you're gonna stay I'll put it on speaker."

"I'll stand over here." I leaned against the window.

He pushed in the numbers, the sequence he'd known all his life, and I heard the ringing buzz coming through the speaker.

"Hello?" Mallory's voice sounded tense.

"Hey Mom." His came out neutral, maybe even resigned.

"Andy? Oh my God, I'm SO happy to hear from you. How are you, Honey?"

He looked up at me and gave a half-hearted grin. For the first time they'd spoken in nearly six months it seemed to start well. I wondered what memories had been triggered; only bad ones? Or perhaps some of the happy days: when she threw him birthday parties, held him when he was hurt, and tucked him into bed?

"Okay, I guess. Still sorta weak."

"I was so worried about you! I almost hopped on a plane and came down."

He squeezed his eyes closed. "Yeah, you ALMOST did. But you know who DID? Dad, that's who."

"Oh, Baby, don't be mean. I love you and I miss you SO much. Don't you know I only want what's best for you?"

Andrew got up from the desk and flopped down on the bed backwards, his long legs resting on top of the two pillows, his eyes fixed on the ceiling. "As long as it doesn't mess up YOUR life, huh?"

"Andy, Andy. Please. I've been sick too. I just got out of the hospital."

"Yeah. Me too."

"See, Andy? Everyone gets sick. We need each other. I'm coming down there next month. Did your dad tell you?"

"Yeah."

"I can hardly wait. It'll be just like old times. I'll cook for you, and we'll go out on the beach. Won't it be fun?"

I watched him hug himself, a shudder seeming to pass through. "Sure. Just like old times. I gotta go."

"Okay, Baby. Call me again soon?"

"Later." He disconnected.

I stood, watching him. "So that wasn't so bad?"

"Can we talk later, Dad? I'd like alone time." He continued to stare at the ceiling.

I walked across the room, pausing with my hand on the doorknob. "If you decide you want some help with those integrals, I'll be out on the balcony reading."

"Thanks."

I left him and walked back to the living room, where I picked up a biography of Nixon I had recently started. Carrying it out to the balcony I settled on a deck chair, staring out over the waters. Hours passed, and I never did open the book.

Monday, November 17th

Checking my watch for the twentieth time, I closed the résumé package I held on my lap. Blaring fluorescent lights baked the cracked-tile floor and threadbare chairs of the reception room. A plastic palm broke the yellow color monotony, its pot soiled with cigarette butts.

I stood up and returned to the receptionist's window, staring at the youngish typist until she turned to me, exasperation creasing her face. She wore no makeup and clearly had been enjoying her sedentary job for many years.

"Check on Mr. Summerlin again, would you?"

The woman looked back at the computer screen, resuming her work as she answered. "I'm sure he knows. Look, I'm kind of busy. Did you want to leave a message or keep waiting?"

I gripped my folder harder. "Look, Miss. I had a nine o'clock appointment with Mr. Summerlin. It's now a quarter past ten. He told me your company needs an engineer and I'm sure he'd like to know I'm here. I imagine someone would be embarrassed if I were to walk out because he didn't know I was waiting."

She sighed, turned off her monitor and slid out of her chair. "Okay, Mr. Lewis. I'll tell him again." She looked at me, shook her head slightly, and left out the back door of her cubicle.

In a few minutes she returned and motioned for me to follow her. "You can wait in his office. Mr. Summerlin will be right with you."

I smiled. "Thank you, Miss." I made a mental note to mention the woman's rudeness to Mr. Summerlin. I had read somewhere a lot of bosses had no idea what kind of impression their greeting staff made on visitors.

I settled into one of the two plastic armchairs in his office and forced myself to calm. Being kept waiting over an hour for a job interview was ridiculous! An air conditioner badly in need of a coil job began banging just outside his office, choking itself back into action.

I was just about to get up to look at the dusty books stacked on one shelf when a balding man with a huge belly sauntered in, shutting the door behind him. I stood and offered my hand.

"I'm Richard Lewis, the chemical engineer. You must be Mr. Summerlin."

The fellow's maw enveloped mine. "Billy Summerlin."

"My pleasure," I replied, waiting until Billy settled into the oversize armchair on the far side of the desk before taking my own seat. "I guess there was some misunderstanding about the time? I thought we agreed to meet at nine."

He glanced at his watch. "Apologies, Mr. Lewis. We run on Southern time around here. Would you like some iced tea?"

"How about some coffee, if it wouldn't be any trouble?"

Mr. Summerlin pushed a button on his intercom. "Sally Jane. Could you bring a glass of tea and a cup of coffee please." He looked at me, "Leaded or unleaded?"

I shrugged. "Doesn't matter. Whatever you have."

"Whatever Bobby's got made up, okay Honey?"

I startled at Mr. Summerlin's word. "Honey? Does your wife work here?" I made a mental note to not mention how rude the receptionist was.

The fat man laughed. "Nah. Where y'all from, Rick? Not around here, um?"

"No. Did you get my résumé I e-mailed? I brought another one along, just in case." I started thumbing through the package I'd brought.

Mr. Summerlin picked up some papers from one of the piles on his desk. "Yep. Got it right here. Chicago, huh? What brings you down to these parts? You have kin?"

I shook my head, noting the disappointment on Mr. Summerlin's face. "I came here to enjoy the gorgeous scenery," I said. "My son and I live in a condominium on the beach." I glanced at the family photos on the desk. "He's on the Gulfport High School track team."

The frown on Mr. Summerlin's face softened. "Well, that's real nice. Doing any good?"

"He got third place three weeks ago."

The man smiled briefly and started looking through my papers. I noticed he'd drawn a few circles across the pages, with red marks in the margins. "It seems like you've looked over my papers."

Mr. Summerlin glanced up, but his smile seemed forced. "You sure got yourself a bunch of experience. Not exactly in our field, but heck, some old dogs can learn new tricks. You know that phrase?"

I nodded. "Of course. I'm quite willing to learn. I read a bit about your company and your products on the Internet. You work mostly with ethers and esters, right?"

"That's right. You ever worked with them chemicals before? You know how to hydrolyze esters?"

I sat up, ready for this one. "Like most hydrolyzing processes, one adds water to break up the double oh bonds. But in reality, the reaction with pure water is so slow that it's never used. Instead, the reaction is catalyzed by mild acid, so the ester is heated under reflux with either dilute hydrochloric or sulfuric acids."

Mr. Summerlin chuckled. "You sure done your homework, Rick. Yep, I could tell right off you're a damn good engineer. All your references testified to that. Even old Henry Cuevas."

"You ... you know Henry Cuevas?" I faltered.

"Course I do. His brother married my cousin Tammy Sue. But that don't mean I believe everything he says. That boy's been hard to get along with since he was knee high to a grasshopper. I tried to bash some sense into him a couple of times, but didn't do no good. Couldn't ever get the meanness out of him."

I wasn't sure whether to laugh, so gave a polite chuckle. Mr. Summerlin picked up the application again and popped it straight a few times on his desk. "Yep, I've got no doubt you're a fine engineer. But, I'm afraid I'm going to have to disappoint you, Rick."

I felt my feet freeze to the floor. "What? You're ... you're not offering me a job?" The slow shake of the head gave the answer. "But ... but why? You just said I'm a great engineer. And that's what you need right now. At least, that's what you said over the phone."

Mr. Summerlin sighed. "I'm sorry, Rick. As I said, I don't believe half of what old Henry has to say. But he sounded pretty convincing when he told me you ran out on him when he really needed you. I asked a couple of other people I know over there too. You want to give me your side of the story?"

I considered. This fellow had already decided he wasn't going to hire me, so it probably wouldn't make a bit of difference what I said. Besides, I'd have to reveal what had happened to Andrew. The way this town gossiped it would be no time before everyone knew about the schizophrenia. "I can't deny it, Mr. Summerlin. I left Mr. Cuevas when he needed me. I had a personal emergency."

He nodded solemnly. "Well, that's a shame. We're fixin' to start a big project ourselves, and I sure could have used the help of a fellow with your experience. But here in the South, loyalty is righteous. Unless you got a good story, I'm going to have to take a pass. Sorry Rick."

I sat stunned. "You ... you mean I'm not going to get a job anywhere in this town? Is that what you're saying?"

Mr. Summerlin shrugged. "Maybe you should consider headin' back up to Chicago. Maybe people act differently up there, more to your liking." He struggled to his feet and offered his hand. "Good luck to you, Rick. And to that boy of yours. Hope he goes all the way to state."

I rose slowly, dazed. Taking the offered handshake, I turned to the door, just as the receptionist I'd seen earlier came in with coffee and tea.

"Turns out we didn't need 'em after all, Sally Jane. Thanks a heap, though."

I nodded at her as I started to walk by, but she didn't look at me. I stopped abruptly and stared at her until she returned my gaze.

"What's your problem?" I asked.

Her gaze cool, she replied, "Henry Cuevas is my uncle."

Tuesday, November 18th

I was deep into a chapter about the Nixon-Kennedy debate when the phone rang. I contemplated ignoring it, enjoying the morning sun bathing me with its soothing warmth. Sighing, I went into the kitchen and grabbed the carry-around.

"Hello?"

"Ricky, it's Mallory. I'm so sorry to hear you lost your job. You must be devastated!"

Glancing at my watch, I read 9:30. Peter had just barely held out the promised forty-eight hours. Well, it didn't really matter. She was bound to find out eventually anyway. "Yeah," I replied. "It's a tough break. But I'll be okay."

"Peter said you had an interview yesterday?"

"It ... didn't go too well."

"Oh! I'm so sorry, Ricky. Peter said he could get you a job. Now you and Andy can come home."

I closed my eyes, holding the phone away from my ear. Not two years ago the concept of ever leaving Chicago would have seemed absurd. Now even the thought of visiting caused shudders. "I'll find a job here."

The silence from the other end of the phone stretched, and I thought I heard a suppressed sob. When Mallory spoke again her voice had softened. "You could try, Ricky. You could give us one more chance."

I took a deep breath, hoping to calm the pounding in my heart. "You're coming down in a month, Mallory. Let's take one step at a time, okay?" I carried the phone out to the balcony, standing up against the back wall to avoid the sun, now beginning to bake the air. *So strange to have eighty degree temperatures in mid-November.*

"And how's Andy doing?" she asked. "Peter said he didn't do well in his race?"

"He's much better now. He seemed pleased with this morning's run."

"I'm glad he's better. Dr. Hopkins scared me to death when she told me. She had me in the hospital at the time. You know, after Billy's death."

I almost said something nasty, something about her overdosing. But I decided to let it pass. "I'm sorry you were sick, Mallory."

"Thank you, Ricky. I sure wish you could be here; I need your help, just like I always have. And I need Andy, too. Did you know he called Sunday? I didn't get a chance to ask him how he's doing with his counselor. What medications did they start him on?"

I gritted my teeth. "Andy's fine now. He tried the medications but didn't like them. He knows all he needs to do is stay away from pot and alcohol."

"Oh, good God, Ricky. He's a time bomb ready to explode. Kids nowadays are exposed to drugs in the schools all the time. I could quote you a hundred statistics. It's not a matter of 'if.' It's merely a matter of 'when.'"

"Not Andy. He knows what he needs to do and he's got the will power to do it. I've got complete confidence in him."

"You've got no right to take that risk. What if the next time he kills himself?"

I dropped the phone as I crumpled, putting my head between my knees to avoid fainting. Regaining my poise, I picked up the phone. "Jesus Christ, Mallory. Don't ever say that. Look. He knows what he needs to do. Let's give him a chance."

She hesitated. "Does that mean you'll give me a chance, too, Ricky? We all make mistakes. We can all get better."

I thought about Mr. Summerlin's advice. *What am I doing down here? Am I trying to prove something?* "I don't know, Mallory."

I saw a young woman in an oversize T-shirt carry her chair out to the beach. She stripped off the shirt, revealing a scrumptious body barely concealed by strips of bikini. I picked up the binoculars for a closer look. Nice.

"I've been so good about keeping your secret, Ricky. You have to admit that."

I carefully replaced the glasses on the table. "What are you talking about Mallory?"

"Oh, you know. About your chemicals in the basement. But don't worry, Sweetheart. I promise I won't EVER say a word. I'm not like Peter. I can keep a secret."

I felt my stomach sink. "I have no idea what you're talking about."

"I get it. Not another word spoken. Just thought you might want to know that I knew."

"Mallory, don't go spouting off your mouth and causing problems."

"Of course not, Dear. I'll see you in a month. But if you feel like calling me sooner, I'd love to hear from you. Give Andy my love, and please ask him to give me a call."

She clicked off and I set the phone down. Damn it. Despite what she claimed, Mallory wasn't any better than Peter at keeping a secret, especially from Celine. I supposed, thinking she had something important here, a bargaining chip, she might try to keep it to herself. I wondered if I could convince her she was mistaken before she started causing problems. It'd be hard, considering all the circumstantial evidence.

Picking up the binoculars I focused on the woman on the beach. She had removed her top; after all, no one could see her there. That is, no one without binoculars and a bird's eye view. I put the glasses away and settled into the deckchair. Thoughts of the night with Sylvia danced back into my brain and I smiled. We had another date coming up in five days. To hell with Mallory and the dead past.

Saturday, November 22nd

I picked up Sylvia for our "second date" at six, and she gave me the traditional peck on the cheek. I suppose it was better than a handshake. Dating at fifty. Gads. It had been hard enough at twenty, and now I was totally out of practice. I had brought her some flowers, which she put in a vase that sat next to Aunt Frances. The old lady gave me a wink.

As Sylvia and I drove down Beach Boulevard, Sylvia pointed out landmarks, some rebuilt, though many just empty lots, telling me what had been there before the storm. The conversation was spiked with local history, and once we passed Beauvoir we became so engrossed with our discussion about the Civil War, we sat in the car in Mary Mahoney's parking lot for twenty minutes before agreeing to continue our talk inside.

We had to force ourselves to break to study the menu. When the waitress brought our drinks, a glass of Riesling for Sylvia and my Diet Coke, we were deep into the reconstruction period, discussing whether carpetbaggers had destroyed the South or rescued it.

Sylvia asked the waitress "Is the bass good tonight?"

"People love our seafood," she assured Sylvia. I noticed that the waitress hadn't answered the question, but Sylvia seemed satisfied. "I'll have that, with the creamed spinach on the side."

I asked, "How's the gumbo?"

"Mary Mahoney is famous for our gumbo," she replied, and, again, I noted she hadn't said whether it was good or not, just that it was renowned. I ordered a bowl of the famous. She didn't write the orders down, just gave us a reassuring nod and headed away.

"You certainly know your history," Sylvia noted. "I can't think when I've had such an interesting conversation."

I smiled broadly. "Agree totally! You and I seem to have so much in common, besides the history, similar tastes in food and music."

The waitress came with a fresh glass of wine and Sylvia took a small sip. "Yummy! Sure you won't have any?"

I shook my head. "Driving, you know. I'm more of a beer drinker anyway. You seem to know your wines."

"I belong to a local wine club. Somewhere in a Bordeaux vineyard there's a patch of vines named after *moi*."

I laughed. "You continue to surprise me."

"And you surprise me." Sylvia replied. "I'm amazed that you hold so many patents. I'd think you'd be rich!"

"Sadly, though I hold the patents, the rights to use them belong to my former company in Chicago." My mind drifted back to a party the company had thrown for my first patent. I must have been twenty-five or six, and such a rising star. "I never would have predicted I'd end up unemployed in South Mississippi."

Sylvia laid her hand over mine. "You're not in Chicago any longer."

I gently flipped my hand over to hold hers in embrace. "I might just end up moving back, at least, that's what everyone's suggesting."

"Really? Which people are those?"

"My brother-in-law Peter for one. He said he'd get me a job."

"Oh?" I felt her hand stiffen in mine. "And are you considering it?"

I closed my eyes, weighing all the pros and cons, as if this were some damn engineering equation. Looking to Sylvia I sighed. "I really don't know. What do you think?"

I watched her hesitate, her mouth drawn-in tightly. "I think I shouldn't be commenting."

Squeezing her hand warmly I gazed into her eyes. "No, really," I insisted.

Her cheeks crinkled with that hint of a smile, the little mischievous look that had captured my heart the first moment I'd seen her. "Well, I'm honor-bound to represent the student's interest here. So I have to ask, 'What would be best for Andy?'"

I remembered what we had just gone through, and after Andrew had been in Chicago for only two days. How could he possibly survive if we moved back? "I think it would be better if he stayed here."

"So ... is there anything else to even consider?" Leaning back, she took her wineglass and swirled it in front of her face. A drop or two slipped over the top, leaving a trail of red tears down the side. The waitress arrived with our food and we dug in.

After a few bites Sylvia put down her fork. "Rick, about Andy."

I stopped eating and sat back. "Yes?"

"Well, he certainly seems to have recovered."

"I think so too. But?"

She took a sip from her wine, watching me closely, her eyebrows knitted in concern. "Andy's been through a lot; his sister's death, his parents' divorce, leaving behind all his friends. While he has great emotional strength, it's clear Andy needs counseling."

I rubbed my hands in the napkin. "You sound pretty sure."

"Rick, it's what I do."

I stirred my soup, scooping up a shrimp in a tablespoon of thick brown broth. I let the tangy juice swish in my mouth before swallowing. "Something you want to do?"

"No, I can make some recommendations though. You want some names?"

I shrugged. "I guess so." I went back to my soup but looked up and saw she was staring at me. "What?"

"I'm serious about this. It's not just Andy. You should consider counseling too."

I picked up the paper she pushed across to me and read the list: counselors, advisors, psychologists. Jesus. "You think I'm crazy?"

"No, Rick, not at all. Getting counseling doesn't mean you're weak or crazy. It's to help you get on a more even keel. You've been through the same trauma Andy has, and no doubt much more I don't even know about."

I shuddered. "Way too much."

"There's a group counseling session for parents who have lost a child. They meet second and fourth Thursday nights."

This wasn't how I had expected the dinner conversation to go. "I'll think about it, okay? But right now I'm trying to budget as I look for another job. As far as Andy, hey, you said yourself it seemed like he'd made a complete recovery."

"Not complete, Rick." She took another bite of her fish and pushed back that errant hair lock of hers. "Andy is a special boy. Determined, yes, that's the word. He's the most determined student I've ever known. I gave him an assignment yesterday 'bout the pestilences of the dust bowl. This morning he laid the first draft on my desk. Why, he'd earn an A if he never even showed up for the final."

I chuckled. "Yep, he's a good kid. Does his schoolwork and always makes time to run every day."

"I'm sure the running is good for him. Y'all think he'll be ready for Regionals?"

"He's convinced he'll be ready. Still, I can't help but worry." I looked at her, that cute buttoned collar highlighting her pretty neck and face. "Say, you want to come to Hattiesburg with us? The race is two weeks from today."

Her face lit up. "Why I'd love that Rick. You sure Andy wouldn't mind?"

"I'm certain he'd love it. He's always telling me you're his favorite teacher." Well, not always, but close enough to the truth.

"How sweet." Sylvia pulled a small pocket calendar out of her purse. "December sixth? I'll pencil it in. Check with Andy and give me a call after y'all have talked it over."

The waitress came by and took my empty soup bowl, and Sylvia asked for her leftovers to be boxed up. I refused the waitress' offer of a Diet Coke refill, requesting coffee instead. Trying to persuade us of their cheesecakes, the waitress promised that they were known throughout the region. I decided to see how they stacked up against Sammy's, Peter's favorite corner deli, ordering slices for both of us. When they came, they were as rich and creamy as the best you could get in the finest Chicago restaurant. Nice!

"Food was good," I said, a bit of dessert melting in my mouth. "You mentioned Andy's been happier this week and I bet I know why."

"Oh?"

"You remember when I told you my childhood best friend, Peter Wilburn, married my wife's sister? Well, he's coming down with Andy's cousin, Travis, who also happens to be Andy's best friend."

"Isn't Travis the boy who got Andrew into trouble two weeks ago?"

I nodded. "Yeah, but Peter assures me that Travis has reformed. Besides, Travis's mother will be here to watch him too."

"Your ex-wife's sister is fixing to visit? That seems a little strange." Her voice sounded colder than a Chicago winter.

"What seems strange about it?"

"I'm thinking you'll have Peter to talk with, and Travis will have Andy. So who will be there for … what's her name?"

"Celine."

The waitress came with my coffee and Sylvia ordered another wine. Smiling sweetly, Sylvia tucked her hands under her chin. "You were saying, Rick?"

"Well. Actually there are others."

"Really?"

"Yeah, they're bringing Sarah Ryan. See that's Travis's cousin too, on his father's side. Sarah and Andy aren't related, but being the same ages, they've hung together all their lives."

"Uh-huh. And who else? You said 'others,' in the plural."

I took a sip of the coffee, setting the cup down carefully on the saucer. "Well, Mallory is coming too."

"Andy's mother?"

"Yes, that one."

The waitress came with Sylvia's new wine. Sylvia saluted me and gave it a long taste. "And she's coming down to stay with you?"

I held up my hands. "No, no. She'll stay at the Beau with them. That's all arranged."

"Right," She muttered. She set her glass down and ran her finger along the rim. "All arranged is it? What else is involved in this little arrangement?"

That came so fast. "Now don't go getting all upset. I only agreed to this because if I didn't let Andy's friends come down, he was threatening to go back up to Chicago, and you know better than anyone else what happened last time. Anyway, don't you think it's important for Andy to get to see his mother? It's been six months."

Sylvia's hand retreated below the table. "Does this mean I won't be seeing y'all the whole holidays?" She had looked away, and I waited until she turned back before answering. Her eyebrows drooped in sadness.

"No, of course not. I'd love to have you meet my friends. Mallory's not even showing up until after Christmas. Why don't you be there when Peter and his family arrive? We can start right off making friends."

Silence hung and we gazed into each other's eyes.

"Are you upset?" I asked.

She flashed me a cryptic smile, a bit colder than I had hoped for, and way too brief. "No, of course not. I'm just wondering if your friends would really want to meet me. It's probably best if I stay out of the way."

"Well, it's more than a month off. It'll give us time to talk about it. By then I'm thinking you'll have more confidence in how much I care for you."

That cryptic smile returned, and this time it had warmth to it. "I have enjoyed my time with you, Mr. Engineer."

"It's a time that hasn't come to an end. This is only the second part of the three-part deal, you know. Thursday will be our third. You are going to come with me to the Barnes' house for Thanksgiving, aren't you? They seem like such a nice family."

Sylvia turned her attention to her food, taking another bite of her cheesecake, chewing it carefully, and pushing her plate aside. She leaned back in her chair. "I don't know, Rick. With your wife coming down, maybe we shouldn't."

"Ex-wife." I reached across and took her hand. "Sylvia, the first time I saw you I felt something special. Let's give this a try."

She seemed lost, looking into our hands. Her words drifted softly across the table, musings meant to be unheard. "Should I live the rest of my life alone?" Lifting up her wine glass she took another sip, the slightest flutter to her eyelids. She ran her tongue along the edge of the glass rim, and I wondered if she were being purposely provocative, or just absent mindedly playing with my emotions.

"Sylvia, may I ask you a personal question."

She set the glass down, looking at me below one raised eyebrow. "What?"

I took another swig from my coffee. I didn't care much how coffee tasted, usually didn't notice, but this one had a strange quality. Sort of woody. "Would you mind telling me about the other time?"

"The other time?"

"Just at the end of our date a week ago, you said 'Twice burned.' You've alluded to another relationship since your divorce before."

Sylvia slipped her hand from mine. Picking up her wineglass, she drained it, set it gently on the table, and stared into its empty shell. "I don't know if this is a good time," she murmured. Her gaze rose slowly until it entranced me. "It's a matter of trust."

I brought her hand to my lips, gracing it with a kiss. "Then trust me."

She tucked that loose hair-lock behind her left ear and looked away. The silence lengthened, the gentle hum of the crowd providing a lengthened time of reflection, broken by the return of the waitress.

"Would you like another drink, Hon?"

Sylvia began shaking her head, but paused, and nodded. "Yes ma'am, I do believe I'll have another."

Once the waitress had left, Sylvia turned to me. "You have to promise not to condemn me; no matter how heinous you find my action."

I reached to the back of my neck, giving it a good scratch. "I'm not one to be passing judgment." In a voice just drifting over the hum of the restaurant, I whispered. "Someday I'll need your forgiveness, too."

She looked at me sternly. "Maybe I shouldn't share."

I opened up my hands to her, raising them in a gesture halfway between a shrug and a benediction. "Sylvia, you're going to have to make that decision. If you feel like it's something I should know, tell me. I promise to honor your trust."

She turned away to stare out into the darkness. I studied her wavering reflection, wondering if she were still aware of my presence. Her voice echoed off the glass.

"I came back home after the divorce; the old mansion needed me, and certainly Aunt Frances did. I realized my destiny was to end up a bookish Southern Lady living with her old maiden aunt. I had my tennis, my social clubs, and my teaching. Even wrote a novel." She flushed a little and glanced my way. "Never finished it, but someday."

She picked up a little paper napkin and began tearing it into a daisy.

"I met Michael at a charity function, the Blessing of the Fleet Ball. Black tie. Red formals." She sighed. "Before Katrina we used to have those all the time. The orchestra was magical. People danced and drank and laughed. Oh how we laughed."

She paused, pointing a finger at the table for emphasis. "Michael's old money – railroad and oyster factory. He wore a tailor-made tuxedo and a cocky smile, the absolute epitome of Rhett Butler. Can you imagine?" Her eyes drifted closed.

"And so you and this Michael fellow became involved?" I prompted.

"I knew it was wrong, but I just kept trying to convince myself otherwise. He was so handsome and debonair. He took me places, like a week in Hawaii. Of course, he had to spend half the trip working, but at least we were together."

The waitress returned with her wine, and Sylvia took another shot of liquid fortification, setting it down half emptied.

"You said 'at least we were together.' What does that mean?"

She looked mildly offended. "I don't know about Chicago, Rick, but here in the South people don't make public displays of affection unless they're married to each other."

I smiled. "So this is the whole thing? You had a relationship with this guy and now you want me to forgive you for it? How long did it last? A couple of months?"

"Three years."

"Three years is a long time," I admitted. "That must have hurt terribly when you broke up."

She nodded, lifted the wineglass, and nearly finished it off. "Oh, Honey. Breakin' up with Gus was a cinch compared to Michael. Because, you know, with Gus, I could blame him. With Michael there's no one to blame but myself."

She stared into her nearly empty glass, twisting the stem; no doubt seeing images of the short joy she'd experienced.

The waitress came back and I refused her refill offer. "Y'all ready for your check?" she asked. I handed her my credit card. "Go ahead and add 20% tip and ring it up." She took it and left.

"Sylvia, it's not unusual for a young woman who's divorced to have a relationship. Are you this upset because you two had sex out of wedlock?"

Not looking up, she shook her head. "Well, of course, that was part of the problem." She drummed her fingers on the table before continuing. "Michael had something I knew about, something that should have kept me miles away. But I loved him anyway."

A trickle of mascara ran down one cheek. "Can you possibly guess what that thing was?"

Horrible thoughts flashed through my mind. *Venereal disease? A mafia connection?*

She picked up her wine glass and began toying with it. She raised it slowly and took the last sip, a single drop straying down her cheek.

The waitress brought the check and I signed it. Placing my card back in my wallet, I kept my gaze on Sylvia, waiting for her to solve her own riddle. A sly smile came to her lips. "You going to take a guess?"

I realized I didn't care what it was. I wanted this woman, this history teaching, tennis playing, child rescuing, sexy marvel. I needed to know her secret so I could prove my worthiness by forgiving her.

"Please, Sylvia. What was it?"

She placed the empty glass on the edge of a fork and the glass tipped over, tumbling off the table. She didn't even glance its way.

"What he already had," she said slowly, her voice soft and luxurious. "What he already had ..." Her voice faded away.

Forcing a breath, I whispered, "Go on."

She leaned forward, putting her hand behind my neck and pulling my ear close to her mouth. In a whisper that percolated into my brain, she said, "A wife and two young'uns at home."

I took both her hands and held them, waiting until our eyes were well locked. "Baby!"

She closed her eyes, breathing slowly, deeply. "Yes sir. Babies."

"No, I meant, I forgive you, Baby." I loosened one hand and placed it under her chin, gently stroking. "Sylvia, we all make mistakes. I've never been in that situation, but I can still forgive you. We're only human, after all. Victims of our circumstances, susceptible to lapses in moral judgment. But you recognize your mistake and you go on. You can't live your life in regret."

She pushed my hand away and leaned back in her chair. "I don't know if I can ever forgive myself."

"You have to. Look, the situation is different here. I'm divorced."

She sighed. "I suppose. So what did you do?"

"What?"

"You said I would have to forgive you for something, too. Tell me about it."

I shook my head. "Now's not the time. But, yes, I did go on with my life. It meant leaving everything I knew and loved behind, but I went on. That's why I'm here, of course." I glanced at my watch. "You ready to go?"

She nodded. "I guess so."

I held her chair, and the doors, and we drove in silence the mile to her house. Well, I was silent. She gabbed about her aunt and long history of the Hewes family. I'd noticed that Southerners tended to talk more freely about themselves than I was used to, but it made a pleasant background and I sort of zoned out.

When we reached her home I got out and held her car door open, offering my hand and helping her out.

"You want me to come in for some coffee?"

She looked me over once. I mean, REALLY looked me over. I watched her hesitate, but she ended up in a headshake. "No, better not."

"So … Thanksgiving is a go, huh?"

She nodded and offered her cheek for a kiss. I lingered on it, until she stepped back and curtsied ever so slightly. "Good night, Sweet Prince. Pleasant dreams."

I watched her stroll up the walk, enter, and before closing the door, blow me a kiss. I settled back into the driver's seat and drove down to the beach. Even on a Saturday night traffic was light, nothing compared to what such a beautiful beach road in any other part of the country would host. Of course, there wasn't much on the road to see besides the beach. Hardly any of the houses had been rebuilt. The old library remained a blown-out shell, a six-foot fence warning off strangers. The old oaks stood bare of leaves. Mississippi seemed empty and desolate, but hope and warmth lay here, hidden, found only by those determined to search below the surface.

Thursday, November 27th

I maneuvered the car into a small gap left open among the score of vehicles crowding the front of the Barnes' homestead. We made our way around to the side of the farmhouse where we found a few dozen people milling about, the adults drinking beer or overseeing the food, and the children chasing chickens, playing T-ball, or otherwise underfoot. Aroma of smoked turkey tickled my nose.

Keisha came up and leaned forward for a peck on the cheek. "Welcome Rick. Andy. Good to see you again." She offered her hand to Sylvia. "Mrs. Perkins, glad you could join us."

Sylvia took the hand, and pulled her forward for a hug. "Call me Sylvia."

"Please, everyone, make yourselves at home." Keisha pointed across the yard. "Rick, Erskine's under that tree with my brother Fred – that's Lebron's father."

I held my hand up to shade my eyes and spotted the two. "He looks familiar."

"Lebron's on the track team. You've seen Fred with us at the meets."

"Where are the guys?" Andrew asked.

Keisha pointed vaguely to a backyard that seemed to go on forever. "There are several your age, but you'll have to go looking for them."

He nodded and sauntered off. I looked beyond him to the various outbuildings stuck up in the fields. In the distance an ancient pine forest loomed.

Sylvia indicated the foil-covered dish she was carrying. "I brought a squash casserole."

"Wonderful! Let's take it to the food table."

Keisha and Sylvia walked away, deep in conversation, and I turned my attention to the rambling red brick home. Haphazardly added additions stretched out on each side of an antebellum farmhouse. The original bricks looked handmade, and the windowpanes had the wavy look of century-old glass.

I walked over to where Erskine stood talking with a group of men where he introduced me around. Fred flashed me a smile and I could tell instantly he was one of those guys like Peter, never met a man he didn't like, could wheel and deal and make things happen – a good man to have on your side.

We talked for a bit, and we left him as Erskine led me around the yard. He knew volumes about the farm's history, and I barraged him with question after question, learning fascinating local tidbits that even Sylvia probably didn't know. At the grill I loaded up a plate with turkey, and at the food table spooned on potato salad, corn, and some of Sylvia's casserole. At the keg I filled up the first of what was to be a long succession of afternoon beers.

We settled at a picnic table built onto the stump of what must have been a two-hundred-year-old oak. The beer, the pleasant conversation with new friends, and the gorgeous fall weather added up to a picturesque Thanksgiving holiday. Keisha and Sylvia joined us, and I reached above the table for her hand. After a moment of hesitation, she smiled and gave it.

"That boy of yours sure scared us last weekend," Erskine said. "How's he doing?"

"Better, thanks. He says his times are back where he wants them. Even if he doesn't place in regionals, I'll still be proud of all he's accomplished."

"Place in regionals?" Erskine's face grew contemplative. "Place in regionals, huh? Like maybe if Andrew and Devone and Lebron are all at their peaks? And even Jamerion can run? We just might have a chance to go to state!"

It was a nice dream and for a moment we both reveled in it.

He turned to me. "Say, maybe you and Andy would want to ride with us up to Hattiesburg for the race?"

The buzz from the beer and the pleasant company reminded me of the summer picnics we used to have in Chicago. I felt like I'd finally found a niche. "That'd be great, Erskine."

Keisha asked, "You'll join us too, won't you Sylvia?"

Sylvia's face lit up. "If I wouldn't be in the way. I count seven already with Fred, Rick, Erskine, the three boys, and you."

"Our van fits eight," Keisha assured her. "I can definitely use some female help taking care of six men. We'll leave early in the morning and return here early afternoon. Your squash casserole is delicious. Perhaps you'd help me prepare a picnic lunch?"

"My chicken salad won second place at the county fair."

"Then it's a date!" Keisha stood and stretched. "Seems like the mosquitoes have discovered our picnic. Feel like giving me a hand with the food?" Keisha asked Sylvia.

"*Certainement*," she said, in that cute French accent.

Keisha looked up in surprise. "*Parlez-vous français?*" Babbling in tongues the two walked off carrying the extra food off to the house.

As the evening stretched into dusk the party thinned. Erskine led me inside where we settled into comfortable armchairs in the den. Floor to ceiling bookshelves took up one wall, and the others held a scattering of framed photos, mostly people in small groups, weddings and graduations it looked like. All homes have their own character, showcasing the soul of their owners. This one was warm and welcoming, relaxed and understated.

A young man joined us, introduced as Devonne's older brother, Rashad. He told me he was a senior at the University of Southern Mississippi.

"What are you studying?" I asked.

He looked at his father. "You haven't told him yet?"

Erskine waved his hand in my direction. "I thought I'd let you do it."

Rashad turned back to me. "Chemical engineering, like you. Right now I'm trying to do some variations on the Bernoulli principle. I'm sure you know all about that."

I loved talking shop, and it'd been a long time. "Sure! You working on incompressible flows or Mach's numbers?"

Fred walked in. "Ah, already down to business I see. So, what does Rick think?"

Erskine shook his head. "I haven't brought it up yet. I thought we'd wait for the women."

"Business?" I asked.

"We have a little proposal," Erskine admitted. "When Devonne told us you were a chemical engineer, Rashad went online and checked you out. No offense."

"Hopefully I've hidden my skeletons well."

The others laughed. "Only good things," Rashad said. "In fact, very good things. How many patents do you have anyway?"

I beamed. "Thirteen. And another one shared." I took the beer Fred offered me and popped the tab, swallowing a gulp and resting the can on the side table. "Technically, the Chicago company has the rights, but I can use the techniques. Just can't sell them. Now what's this all about? You've got my curiosity burning."

"That's good," Erskine said. He told Rashad, "Go see what's keeping your mother." Turning to me, he asked, "You want Sylvia in on this?"

"I guess."

The men stood when Sylvia and Keisha entered the room, Rashad shutting the huge pocket doors behind them. Keisha carried a tray of glasses and Sylvia a cut-glass bottle.

"Anyone for brandy?" Keisha asked. Setting the works on a side table, she poured everyone a glass. We waited until Keisha and Sylvia had settled into an oversized sofa and Erskine lifted his glass. "A toast; to successful business ventures."

"To ventures," Keisha, Fred, and Rashad echoed. We drank.

Sylvia looked at me, her face questioning. I shrugged back.

I took another gander at the bookshelves, picking out a whole row of new looking chemical engineering books. It looked like Rashad was pretty serious about his studies. "So what's this business proposal you're talking about?"

"Did Rashad tell you he's going to graduate from USM in a few months?" Keisha asked.

"Yeah. The school's got a pretty good reputation. Wasn't their past president a chemical engineer?"

Rashad answered. "Yep. One of the top ten in the country on some lists."

The brandy was going down smoothly, reigniting the fading beer buzz. "So I guess you want my help on something for school?" I ventured.

Rashad nodded. "In a way. You see, one of my classes last semester required a project; specifically to develop a plan for an independent business based on a chemical engineering process."

I nodded. "I remember having to do something like that too. Of course, a lot has changed in twenty-five years."

"But not everything. I read you've done a lot with gibbsite?"

"Gibbsite?" I finished off my brandy and allowed Erskine to refill my glass. "You mean aluminum tri-hydroxide of course. In Chicago I worked primarily with bauxite and hydrous aluminum oxides. We used to mix boehmite, diaspore, and gibbsite with the iron oxides goethite and hematite all the time."

I looked around and saw that only Rashad was following me. Everyone else's eyes glazed over, except for Fred, who smirked.

"You're the man!" Rashad exclaimed. "Okay, here's the deal. I bet you didn't know that Gulfport is the third busiest port on the Gulf of Mexico? A lot of raw bauxite comes through, gets loaded onto trains, and makes its way to smelting plants hundreds or thousands of miles away. There it's turned into aluminum sheeting and shipped to secondary markets, sometimes back here. Our plan is to set up a local smelting plant. I read that company in Chicago you used to work for was heavy into smelting."

I felt my pulse rise. "You're talking about the Hall-Héroult process, right?"

Sylvia spoke up, "Sorry to interrupt … but what on earth are y'all talking about?"

I turned to her. "Rashad is thinking about starting a boutique factory processing aluminum. It's a great idea."

Rashad nodded enthusiastically. "Dad could be our accountant and Uncle Fred would be our salesman. He has lots of business contacts on the coast. I've got the college training to run the chemical business. But you, Mr. Lewis, you have what we really need to get the business rolling. You've got the experience and expertise."

I drank some more brandy and considered. "You can call me Rick. You know, you really might be onto something here. A local plant could do well." Setting my glass down, I leaned back. "You envision a large operation?"

"Nah. We're going to work on small local orders. Lots of little companies need smelted aluminum. Heck, this is hurricane alley. Everyone needs aluminum to protect their homes and businesses. Once we have a reputation we could ship our aluminum to any destination on the planet."

Sylvia looked troubled. "Have any of y'all ever started up a business before?"

"I run my own accounting firm," Erskine said.

"Doesn't seem the same as a plant," Sylvia observed. "Do y'all already have the site?"

"Not yet, but we've got our eyes on a couple of spots," Fred reported.

"No one's ever tried it in this part of the country," Rashad said. He paused to sip his drink. "I toured a plant in Georgia. They shipped bauxite in by train and aluminum out by truck."

Erskine stood and took a wooden box off a shelf, bringing it to me before popping open the top. The alluring aroma of fine tobacco drifted up from the neat rows of cigars. I picked one, holding the tip into Erskine's offered light, puffing until it burned. I blew a ring. "My dad used to smoke these on special occasions."

I had a sudden coughing fit and the others laughed. "Guess I'm a little rusty with 'em."

"So are you interested?" Fred asked.

I nodded. "Intrigued, for sure. How much would I be paid?"

Keisha reached over and took Erskine's hand. "There's no extra money. We're putting everything we've got into this project; our savings, a second mortgage on the house … it's a big risk, but that's how one makes a success."

I sat back in my chair. No income for however long it took to get this going? "I don't know. How am I gonna pay my bills?"

"I sell at Home Depot," Fred suggested. "I can get you a job there until money starts coming in. Decent pay and benefits too."

I considered the difference in income between an engineer's pay compared to pushing plumbing at a hardware box. "Well, the Home Depot part doesn't sound so hot. But as far as the whole project …"

"What?" Rashad urged.

I gave him a half smile and a shrug. "As I said, I'm intrigued, but I'll need to think about it."

Sylvia stifled a yawn. "Oh, excuse me. It's been a wonderful party, but I'm fixin' to call it a day. Rick?"

I nodded and reached out to shake hands with the men. Keisha pulled me into a hug.

"You're part of the family now," Keisha explained. "It's the Southern way."

I felt a little woozy, probably from the alcohol and cigars. Bringing out my cell phone, I gave Andrew a call, asking him to meet us at the car. We made our goodbyes and went out the door.

The wind had picked up, brown leaves swirling in small whirlwinds of dust. As we leaned against the car, waiting, I leaned forward to kiss her, and Sylvia responded; tentatively at first, and then with enthusiasm. I placed my hand on her butt to pull her closer and she snuggled up into me. Quite delightful. We broke apart when we heard Andrew's and Devonne's voices coming.

"Hey, Mr. Lewis," Devonne greeted me. "Mrs. Perkins." He stuck out his hand and we both shook it.

"Have a good ..." I broke off, recognizing the odor of marijuana on them both. "Andy! Have you been smoking pot?"

He shook his head vigorously. "No, Dad. We were out in a barn with a couple of Devonne's cousins. Someone passed joints around, but neither of us smoked any."

I clamped him on the back. "Good job, Andy. Proud of you."

The three of us got in the car, Sylvia driving, and headed back into town. "I'm glad you had the resolve not to smoke," I said.

I heard him let out a sigh of relief. "You wanna hear something strange? I wasn't even tempted. Watching Devonne's cousins, I realized stoned kids are just silly."

Sylvia added, "And it prevents them from being successful, too! Good for you, Andy."

The rest of the way home, Sylvia chatted with Andy, but I was quiet, my thoughts taken up with the Barnes' proposal. Once at Sylvia's house, I walked her to the door while Andrew happily slid into the driver's seat.

"It's been a great day, Sylvia. Being with you was so...natural."

"I enjoyed it too, Rick. You've got a lot to mull over. Good things."

"What do you think about the job offer?" I asked her.

"I tell my students, consider the options, and do what feels right."

"What would feel right is to spend the rest of the night with you." I leaned in, hoping for another kiss.

Sylvia stopped me with a hand against my chest. "Steady boy. Your son is watching from the car."

I turned and looked at Andrew who feigned attention to the CD player.

"Okay," I agreed. "Then how about another date? You free tomorrow?"

She shook her head. "I have plans already."

"Saturday?"

She laughed. "You are one persistent Yankee!"

"You bet!"

She stepped on tiptoes and kissed me on the cheek. "You said you play tennis? You have regulation whites?"

"I can get them."

"Good. Meet me Saturday at the Gulfport Tennis Club at one o'clock in the snack area. I'm huddling with my girlfriends for lunch, and we can play afterwards." She waved at Andrew, and stepped into her house, shutting the door firmly behind her.

Saturday, November 29th

I pulled up to the Gulfport Tennis Club just before the appointed hour. A cold front had come through, though in south Mississippi that meant midday temperatures in the pleasant low-sixties. Dressed in whites as Sylvia had instructed, I pulled my tennis racket and gym bag from the trunk. After registering at the front desk as Sylvia's guest, I was directed to the luncheon area.

I spotted her at a table, sitting and talking with a pair of casually dressed women about her age. From the door, I paused to admire Sylvia's legs, tanned below the white tennis skirt. She looked my way, flashed a smile, and waved me over. After introductions, we talked as a group for another ten minutes or so before Sylvia led me out to the tennis courts.

"Those women are quite involved in community charity projects," I observed.

Sylvia nodded. "Mississippians give more to charity per capita than any other state in the nation. We're proud and generous."

"And you! I didn't know you were involved in the Pink Heart Fund. I'd noticed you've been letting your hair grow."

"Yes. The last day of school I cut it all off and donate it to be made into wigs for women undergoing chemo for breast cancer. My mother died of breast cancer, you know."

"That's what my mother died of too! I mean, it's tragic, but isn't it strange we have so much in common? It's as if fate pulled us together!"

She flashed me another one of those marvelous grins of hers. We separated to either end of the court and she began bouncing the tennis ball. "You want to warm up a bit?"

"First time I've played in two years. We better volley."

"Sure." She served an easy shot I lobbed back. After a quarter hour I felt confident and announced I was ready. Holding the ball in front of me I yelled, "Love all. Hey! Love all! That's pretty cool."

She laughed. "It's just a term; go ahead and serve."

I did, and quickly realized she was no pushover. In fact, in two sets she beat me six-three, seven-five.

"Up for another one?" she asked.

I pranced a few steps, judging my fatigue while trying to assess hers. I worked out every day on my bike, and I thought she seemed to be getting weaker during the last couple of games.

"You bet," I called. I picked up the ball and shot an ace down the side. I played hard this last set, purposely making her run, and finally broke her serve in the tenth game, winning six-four. We met at the net for the traditional handshake.

"Wow, I'm bushed!" she said.

"You won two out of three sets. How about I treat you to dinner?"

She hesitated, and when she looked up her eyes had a sly look. "How about I cook for you instead? I do a delectable French shrimp and mushrooms in garlic butter."

"Sounds yummy! I'll need to shower and change."

"Good. Meet me back at my place at seven."

We exchanged a brief kiss and I headed home. After a shower and a nap, I got up to find Andrew eating a peanut butter and jelly sandwich.

"Hey Dad. How'd the tennis go? Mrs. Perkins any good?"

"She's got a wicked serve and decent backhand, but my longer reach eventually tired her out. What're your plans for this evening? Homework?"

"Saturday night? Nah, skateboardin'. Devonne's picking me up. Can I have twenty bucks?"

I pulled the bill out of my wallet but held it out of his reach. "Remember we're on a budget these days."

He reached out and snagged it. "Thanks, Dad. How's the job search going?"

"Nothing new. I check the paper and Internet every day. I didn't mention, the Barneses made me a proposal when we there two days ago."

"Yeah?"

"Intriguing idea, but I'm hoping something more traditional turns up."

Andrew finished off his glass. "Last of the milk. You goin' shopping, soon?"

"Sure. Add it to the list on the 'fridge."

He stood and grabbed his plate and glass, taking them into the kitchen. "So what about you? Gonna stay in and read?"

"Actually, I'm having dinner with Sylvia."

"Oh?" Andrew looked up, still holding the plate on its way into the dishwasher. "Where you going?"

"Her house."

He shut the dishwasher door slowly. "Her house? Like, you're gonna spend the night?"

I felt myself flush. "I don't think so."

He started to walk past me and I put my hand on his arm. "Andy, what are you thinking?"

He shrugged and walked out to the balcony. I followed him, standing next at the rail. The pungent salt air smelled clean, freshened by last night's shower. With the early sunset the cool air reminded me of fall days in Chicago.

Staring out to the waters Andrew sighed. "I don't know, Dad. It just seems weird."

"What's weird about it?"

I watched him kick the railing a few times. With wistful voice he said, "Maybe I'm just dreaming. I mean, I know it'll never be the same, with Jenny dead and all that. But still. Seems like we were happier in Chicago. You know, a real family."

"Life goes forward, Andy, not back."

"So you don't love Mom at all?"

I stared out over the waters, memories of my twenty-nine-year marriage floating in on the sea breezes. She'd never been hateful. Demanding, yes. Whiny, yes. But never hateful. Should I forgive her, remake the family for Andrew's sake?

"There's an old cliché that applies here. 'You can't go home again.' We could go back to Chicago, sure. I could remarry your mother and find another job. You could be back with your friends. But no matter how hard we tried, it would never be the same. The ghosts would still haunt us."

I paused, watching Andrew out of the corner of my eye, wondering if he'd say anything. He kept his peace.

I settled my arm on his shoulder. "Sylvia's got a wonderful soul. You know that. Kind. Loving."

Andrew let the silence stretch before asking, "Are you gonna marry her?"

The question startled me, and I wondered if the thought had been percolating below the surface in my own brain. "We're nowhere near that."

I watched him stare into the pinks of the evening, the glow adding a ruby tinge to his sun-darkened brow. A couple of seagulls gave calls as they flew past. Finally, he looked back and smiled.

"Well, have a good time."

I rustled his hair. "Thanks, Kid. You too."

After he left I checked the weather on the computer, and decided I could get by without a jacket. I made a detour to Wal-Mart on the way, intending to pick up some flowers, but the lines were so long I gave it up and just continued on to Sylvia's house. Since my last visit a row of red-topped poinsettias now graced the walk and porch.

Sylvia greeted me with a kiss. She had donned a cute outfit; black blouse over red skirt, embroidered gold trim around neck and sleeve. Her fine legs showed below its lower-thigh length. I followed her into the dining area that she had set fancy, complete with candlelight, china, and crystal wineglasses. In the background a husky feminine voice sang "You and I."

After listening a moment, I asked, "Say, isn't that Mary Pearson?"

"Yes! Not many people would recognize her voice. You like?"

"One of my favorites. Hey, this is what I was saying earlier today. We love the same music, the same foods, the same histories. It's sort of eerie."

"Why so?"

"Just … I never had that with Mallory. Always seemed to be on a collision path instead of working together." I glanced at the table again. "Only two settings?"

"Aunt Frances retired early tonight."

I followed Sylvia into the kitchen where she had the ingredients to our feast laid out. A dozen jumbo shrimp and a bowl of peculiar looking mushrooms sat next to the stove. She cut a slab of butter into the pan and dumped in the mushrooms. In a few moments their musty aroma filled the kitchen.

"Weird looking 'rooms. Where'd they come from?"

"France. I buy them freeze dried at the country market in the village where I stay each summer."

She added the shrimp, stirring until they turned a lusty red, and then spooned the mixture onto two plates that she handed me. She grabbed the wine bottle and I followed her back to the dining room. I set the plates in their spots and she poured the wine.

After we settled into our places, I observed. "This is so lovely. I haven't had a candlelight dinner since … oh, I'm sorry."

"What?"

"Just thinking of old times."

"Mallory?" she asked.

I nodded, embarrassed that I'd brought up the subject of my ex. I glanced up and Sylvia had leaned forward. She laid her hand gently on my arm.

"You miss her, don't you?" she murmured.

"I miss what we once had."

Sylvia raised her glass. "Here's to the love we've lost."

I joined her in the toast, our eyes locked as we sipped. The flavor was superb, a Chablis, ripe with sweet grapes. After we set our glasses down, I asked, "Do you miss your husband?"

"Like you, I miss the good times."

I watched her cut a shrimp into tiny wedges, stirring it gently in the small pool of butter, picking up black flecks of pepper. It reminded me of when Peter used to take us to his club for fine dining; one of the few things I really missed about Chicago. I placed a succulent mushroom in my mouth, savoring its flavor as it melted on my tongue. After I swallowed, I asked, "How did you meet your husband?"

"I was at Columbia University studying early American history. Oh, I had such wonderful plans. I dreamt of someday becoming a professor." She turned to her salad, stabbing a tomato, and letting it dance on the end of her fork.

"And Gus changed all that?"

She lowered her gaze, one hand gripping the table edge. "I thought we understood each other. I made it clear before the marriage I intended to continue my career. Yet after the nuptials, he sure changed his tune."

I rested my hand on hers and she grasped hard. "You gave up your dreams?" I asked.

Sylvia looked down to her plate, slowly stirring the shrimp. "Let's say I put them on hold. He wanted me to spend my life being his personal cheerleader. He used to take me to office parties, big corporate affairs sometimes, where I knew no one, and could find no one to talk to. He'd just abandon me, tell me to 'mingle.' Afterwards he'd complain that I hadn't made a good impression.

"Eventually I refused to go, which he claimed embarrassed him. Well, I was in a paradox there, wasn't I? I embarrassed him when I did go and I embarrassed him when I didn't."

I served myself seconds, my appetite sharpened by all the tennis. It'd been a couple of years since I had such a hard workout. "This is delicious," I said. "Do go on with your story."

"I don't know if I would have left him or not, but for my mother's illness. This was ten years into the marriage, and I was lonely and miserable. I'd gone back to school and obtained my masters in social work, intending to take a job with the New York public school system as a counselor. And then my mother became ill and Aunt Frances called me home."

"Was it a long illness?"

"From diagnosis she lasted three months, but not a good death." Sylvia picked up her napkin, grasping it tightly in both hands. "We held her wake in the First Methodist Church, on a lovely June afternoon."

"I'm sorry I never had a chance to meet her. You must miss her deeply."

Sylvia's eyes glistened. "I mention her every night in my prayers."

"She and Aunt Frances were sisters?"

"Not just sisters, but best friends. They were practically inseparable, even after my parents married. For all practical purposes, Aunt Frances is my second mother."

I'm no connoisseur of wine, but this was a good one, and went well with the shrimp. I paused to sip a bit more before asking, "You ever go back to New York?"

She shook her head.

I watched her eat, taking carefully selected tidbits to her mouth for gentle savoring. I forced my thoughts away from her mouth. "I have the same reluctance about returning to Chicago. Fortunately, I've only had to go back twice. Well, you know about that."

I took another bite of my own meal, savoring its juicy flavors and wondering how much weight I'd gain if, well, if Sylvia was cooking for me all the time. I asked, "Do you ever regret your decision to give up your marriage?"

She looked up, past me, perhaps imagining what might-have-been. A certainty settled onto her lips. "Never have, Rick. I made the right choice."

I leaned back in my chair, pushing away my plate. "Boy, that sure was delicious! I can't eat another bite."

"I'm full as a tick myself!"

I laughed. "First time I've ever heard that one."

She smiled back at me, stood, and took the plates. "I'll clean up." Pointing to the wine glasses she said, "Why don't you give us refills and meet me in the kitchen."

I followed instructions and, once near her again, settled onto a tall stool at the bar. She bustled around the kitchen, scrubbing the food off the dishes, rinsing, and stacking them on the drain board. Glancing over at me, she said, "I just told you about my marriage and divorce. Tell me about yours."

I watched her, those strong calves dancing across the floor, and the last thing I wanted to talk about was Mallory. But I figured she'd asked, so I better start at the beginning. "I first met Mallory my senior year in high school. She was a junior at the time. I was sort of a nerd, didn't have a date for the senior prom. Peter had been dating Celine for a couple of months and he suggested I take Celine's younger sister.

"We got along all right, but I wasn't too suave, not like Peter, and Mallory broke up with me. She dated several other men over the next few years, had a real hot relationship with a business major for over a year. But just before Peter and Celine's wedding, the guy dumped her, and, well, I jumped at the opportunity to catch her on the rebound.

"It was sort of sudden and maybe it wasn't such a good idea. Anyway, we had a double wedding and tried to make the best of it. It seemed to me she maybe thought I wasn't worthy of her, she wanted someone richer and more socially able."

I took a drink from the wine glass I'd brought in with me. Sylvia picked up hers and drank most of it down. I wasn't sure, but I think this was her third, maybe her fourth.

"Mallory and Celine thought life could be all planned out," I continued. "They waited ten years, and then both sisters got pregnant within months of each other, by coincidence both having girls; Rebecca and Jenny. Two years later they repeated with the boys. We seemed to have the perfect lives."

Sylvia brought out two bowls, each with a small scoop of sherbet. She set them on the kitchen bar and we settled onto the bar stools. I tasted mine. "Yummy."

She laughed. "Goes well with this wine, don't you think?"

"Definitely."

I closed my eyes, savoring the delicate flavor and the sharp coldness that makes sorbet so great.

"So Jenny's death changed everything?" Sylvia prompted.

I put down my spoon, arranging it carefully next to my bowl. "Yeah, Jenny's death was the catalyst. Mallory and I had fights off and on throughout the marriage, I mean, maybe all couples do. But after the tragedy I was so angry at the world I lashed out everywhere. Mallory became severely depressed. Her doctor had her in and out of the hospital, but it wasn't helping. Finally, we agreed on a separation, and the divorce followed quickly."

"And now?"

I took another bite of the sorbet, watching Sylvia taste hers. A small white ice chip glistened on a corner of her lips and she reached her tongue out to lick it off. Nice looking tongue.

"What do you mean?" I asked.

"Seems to me your decision to divorce might have been based on the anger of the moment. Now that time has passed, suppose she wants to get back together? You think you might be willing to try?"

I stood and, standing behind her, hugged her against my chest and nuzzled her neck. She laid her head back, her eyes closed, her breathing heavy. I turned her around, worked my way up to her mouth, and we kissed, a comfortable gentle touching that lasted as long as our breath. Working my mouth back to her ear I whispered, "Never! Especially now that I've met you."

She held me tightly, her eyes closed.

"Listen to the jazz," I whispered. "Will you dance?"

She pushed away, just a few inches, holding my shoulder with one hand and grasping my hand. My other hand dropped to guide her along her waist. We swung softly to the compelling song, a woman singing plaintively of lost love.

We danced across the kitchen floor and into the great room. When I looked up I saw rows of ancestors frowning down on me and I came to a stop.

"What's wrong?"

I pointed. "I think they don't approve of their descendant dancing with a Yankee."

She laughed and went back to the kitchen to grab our wine glasses. She returned with them full. "To our ancestors," she said, and we clinked glasses.

After we drank, Sylvia requested I talk about my parents. I settled onto the love seat, patting the spot beside me. Sylvia sat and snuggled up.

"I don't remember my mother. She was diagnosed with breast cancer a few months after I was born. In those days there was nothing anyone could do. She died before my second birthday."

"How awful to be raised without a mother."

"It wasn't that bad. Maybe because I never knew any different, I never missed having one. My father raised me."

"He certainly did a fine job. What was he like?"

How could I describe the force that shaped my whole life? "My father was a man of faith. He believed God had a plan for all of us, and if we were good, He would reward us. My mother's death never fazed that certitude."

"While I had three parents, you only had one, yet he taught you manners, a love of history and science, and respect for God."

I looked at her, and then away.

"What?"

I squeezed her hand gently. "I used to respect God. More, I used to have a great love and fear of him. But after the tragedy I … well, I realized I couldn't believe in a God that would allow that to happen. I lost my faith."

I felt her hand squeeze back. "It doesn't seem to me like you've lost faith in God."

I thought about this a bit. "You know something? When you helped me care for Andy, when you were there to see the light come back into his eyes, I began to believe again. Just a little."

She smiled, "Sometimes a little is all you need. I see that in my students all the time. They begin to believe in themselves, and the next thing they know, their troubles are behind them."

I took her in my arms and kissed her again, enjoying the tender softness of her lips. I felt her reach up and massage my scalp with her fingertips. She urged my head deeper into her embrace. We kissed long and hard, and I felt her unbutton my shirt and rub my chest hair.

I reached around and unbuttoned the neck button on her blouse. She wiggled it off, and I unhooked her bra. It fell softly to the floor. I leaned forward, bringing my face to her chest, and slowly, luxuriantly, ran my tongue around her nipples, feeling them harden in my mouth.

She pulled my shirt off.

"Would you like to go to the bedroom?" I asked.

"It's such a lovely fire. Why don't we can settle in front of it for awhile?"

She pulled a couple of blankets out of a drawer and laying one in front of the hearth, threw some pillows from the sofa onto it. We snuggled down on them and she covered us up with the other blanket.

Once we had settled, I said, "Tell me about your father."

She picked up my hand and guided it under the blanket and onto her breast. I held it firmly, occasionally running a finger around her nipple. She reached under and rubbed my chest hair.

"Everyone loved Bernard Hewes, served in the legislature for six years. Some of my fondest childhood memories are the marvelous parties my parents threw here. Judges, doctors ... all the movers and shakers were there. After dinner the men would retire to the library for brandy and cigars."

"How did he die?"

"Heart attack at age fifty-eight on the golf course. I had just left for Colombia. Nearly a thousand people attended his funeral."

"So we both lost both our parents at fairly young ages. It's so strange, like one coincidence after another."

"I think you're right. Perhaps it is meant to be." She raised up on one elbow and kissed me again, a lingering hold, and I enjoyed the sensation of exploring; both each other's mouths with our tongues, and each other's chests with our hands. Her hand trailed down, finally resting on my pants, feeling my passion.

"I think I'm ready to move on to the bedroom," she whispered. She stood, and   I   followed   her.

Tuesday, December 2ⁿᵈ

"Dad?"

I had ignored Andrew's knock and I ignored his call as well. I hadn't locked the door, though, and I heard him push it open.

"You okay, Dad? What are you doing in bed?"

"Leave me alone."

He pulled away the pillow I had covering my head. Cracking open one eye, I saw his worried frown.

"Dad? It's seven o'clock. You okay?"

I grabbed the pillow back and buried my head. "Not today."

It took him a minute, but when he answered, I knew he understood. "Oh. Sorry, Dad. Yeah, you just stay in bed all day. Probably a good idea." I heard him shut the bedroom door on the way out. I went back to sleep.

In a few hours the phone woke me. I pulled my head out from under the pillow and saw Sylvia's name on the caller ID. I ignored it. In a few minutes she rang back and I grabbed it.

"What do you want?"

She hesitated. "Rick?"

I took a deep breath. "Yeah, what?"

"I ... I mean ... it's been three days. I thought maybe you'd want to talk?"

"Today's not good for me." I dropped the phone on the cradle and got up to answer the call of nature.

Throwing on a robe, I wandered out to the kitchen where I grabbed a bottle of whiskey and a glass. At the table I poured myself a shot, drinking it quickly. I slowed down after the second one, but kept sipping the hours away. When the doorbell rang, I ignored it. After a few more rings, I pulled myself up and staggered down to throw it open. Sylvia stepped back, no doubt alarmed by my disheveled appearance.

"Rick? Are you okay?"

I ignored her and made my way back to the couch where I stretched out flat. Sylvia followed gingerly. "Rick? Can I come in?"

I tried to raise my head, but the nausea and giddiness forced me back down. I gave her a jaundiced look.

She pointed at the nearly empty Jack Daniels on the table. "What's going on, Rick? Are you drunk?"

I struggled to a sitting position and, using both hands, managed to splash a couple of fingers worth of the Jack into a glass. Raising it in salute I said, "Best just go away."

"I rush over on my lunch hour and find this?" She reached for the bottle, but I snatched it first. "I ain't done." I drained the glass and refilled it with the rest of the whiskey. Handing her the empty, I said, "Now I'm done."

Sylvia took the bottle to the kitchen, returning with a damp cloth. As she wiped the table, she asked, "What's going on, Rick? Is this about us?"

I tried to laugh at her audacity, but settled for a smirk. "No."

"Then what? What's going on?"

"With me? No job. No life. Got nothing but regrets." I forced myself to stand, holding still until I had my balance. Staggering to the kitchen, I pulled a bottle of rum out of the cabinet.

Sylvia had followed me, and she leaned against the wall, her arms crossed. "You're just feeling sorry for yourself? You make love to me and then go on a three-day drunk? How do you think that makes me feel?"

I twisted off the top, threw it in the general direction of the sink, and lifted the bottle to my lips. After a good swig, I smacked my lips. "In the words of one of the great heroes of the South, 'Frankly, my dear, I don't give a damn.'"

Sylvia stepped forward and snatched the bottle out of my hands. I turned aside as if I didn't care, and then lunged forward and grabbed it back. "Gotta have my priorities. Right now, it's this rum."

She glared at me. "I'm very disappointed in you."

I shrugged. "You're not the first and you won't be the last." I took another swig from the bottle and pushed past Sylvia. Using the wall for support, I made my way out on the balcony where I leaned against the rail and stared across the water. She continued to follow me like some sort of lap dog; no matter how many times you kick, it keeps coming back for more.

"It ain't been three days," I told her. "Just today."

"You think you can drink your way out of your problems?"

I didn't even turn to look at her. "Not one of your students."

I could feel her glaring at me but kept my gaze on the beach. "Look, Sylvia, why don't you just leave me in my misery?"

"Is that what you really want?"

Dreary storm clouds covered the skies, and in the distance lightning flashed. The air had a muggy heaviness. I heard her sniffle, then sob. In a bit, she backed away, and I heard the door slam. One more item to add to my checklist of failures. I took the rum back to the armchair and drank until I passed out.

I had aroused again by the time Andrew came home late that evening. He joined me on the balcony, where I sat staring into the nothingness. It had rained and my pants were uncomfortably damp.

Pointing to the bottle in my hand, he asked, "You been drinkin' all day?"

"Yep." I shivered in the December chill.

"You eaten?" he asked.

I lifted the bottle and squinted at it. Vodka. Didn't know I even stocked vodka. After another hit from the bottle, I said, "I'm not hungry. Go get yourself something."

He patted me on the back and I heard him rumbling behind me. At some point I glanced inside and saw he'd set up his homework on the table. After awhile he came out to check on me.

"Maybe you should come inside."

I studied the last ounce dancing at the bottle's bottom. "Almost done."

He put his arm around my shoulders. "I miss her too. Maybe you should call Mrs. Perkins? You could stand some cheering up."

I shook my head. "She was here. Chased her off."

"Oh."

Taking the last sip from the bottle I held it out over the rail. "Dive bomb?"

Andrew took it from me. "Broken glass." He led me inside, standing by as I brushed my teeth and used the toilet, and then led me to bed, tucking me in. He leaned down and kissed my cheek, a strange role reversal that almost made me smile.

"Sleep well, Dad," he said. "Tomorrow's another day."

Saturday, December 6th

I hadn't called Sylvia back, and when Andrew and I showed up at the Barnes' home without her, Keisha gave me a questioning look. She had the courtesy not to ask and I didn't volunteer any information. During the ride up I kept my peace, mostly listening to the kids chattering in the back seat. Fred leaned against the window next to me and slept through the hour-long trip.

Hattiesburg's University of Southern Mississippi's track featured neatly chalked white lanes surrounded by landscaped grassy hills. We Gulfport High families spread our blankets in a quilt-like pattern around turn four, near a small section of stands. At the referee station a long table held dozens of trophies, the tall team ones standing above individual awards like skyscrapers above a village. I settled onto a red blanket with Keisha, Erskine, and Fred. From the rise where we sat I watched the young runners in various colored outfits wandering about, greeting old friends, or stretching and sprinting.

"Boys look eager," I said.

Fred chuckled. "Shore do. They know this is for a chance at the limelight."

"What does that mean?"

"There are four regions in the state." Erskine handed me a cup of lemonade as he explained. "Only the first place team from each region competes in two weeks at the state meet in Clinton."

I looked at the competition again. Each school only had six runners this race, Andrew had told me; their five best with one back-up. I tried to count the groups. "Are there eight teams?"

"Yep," Fred confirmed. "Invitation to Regionals is based on the number of points each team accumulates during their best five races in the regular season. Harrison Central had the most in the Southern Region with thirty-eight."

"How did Gulfport do?" I asked.

"Barely snuck in at seventh, mostly on that Pascagoula meet where Andy got third."

Erskine called, "Hey, Rick."

I had been watching the Harrison top runners stretch. They looked stronger than ever. "What?"

"You think Andy's gonna do well this time?"

The image of how he looked when he collapsed at the Bay race flashed into my mind. Suppressing it, I stood and looked over at him, stretching with the other five Gulfport boys. "You're going to do great!" I called out, though I figured he couldn't hear me. Turning to Erskine, I said, "It's been three weeks since Bay St. Louis."

Erskine rolled his bottom lip between two fingers. "I know how long it's been. I asked if you thought Andy was going to do well."

I looked back at my son, now at the starting line. Coach Dalton arranged their order; Devonne first, Lebron second, and Andrew third. Jamerion Hye, the boy with the elastic bandage on his knee, stood in fourth. Seemed like Gulfport had more than one unknown. "I guess we'll soon find out."

Still standing, I looked around the track and along the path that led out a gate. "Where to this time?" I asked.

"There's a trail out the back," Fred told me. "An old railroad track. They've paved it into a walk and bike path."

With the starter gun's bang the runners exploded, colors flashing past each other as runners jockeyed for position. The line judge watched closely to be sure shoves didn't exceed the rules. The runners circled back past us on the fourth corner, and headed out the gate. I counted Devonne in fifth place, Andrew about two thirds back in the pack. His expression seemed calm.

When the last polyester clad racer disappeared through the opening Fred tapped my shoulder. "So Rick, have you decided?"

"What?"

"The smelting plant. Surely you've given it some thought?"

I nodded. "Yeah, a lot of thought. I've gone over those plans and done some checking on the Internet. I think you could make a go of it."

I saw Erskine's and Fred's smiles disappear. "You said 'you' not 'we,' meaning what?" Erskine asked. "You don't want to be a part?"

I took a sip of my lemonade, turning to look out across the field. On the far side the trees had lost all their leaves, dormant skeletons of what had once been a full life. Turning back to my friends, I said, "It's just all so risky, so tentative."

Fred clapped me on the shoulder. "Nothing ventured, nothing gained. Here's something new; we got an option on some land. It's a perfect plot in the industrial park with railroad access. The owner's giving me until Monday to come across with the money."

I examined the land survey Erskine handed me from his briefcase while Fred pointed out the features: the building, railroad spur, and truck ramp. I visualized how the machinery would have to be laid out. "The key is the equipment," I said. "I was pricing on the Internet, and a new smelter, even a small one, is going to run about a hundred grand. And then there's the other stuff, a trough, and wiring."

Erskine pulled more papers from his briefcase. "Look, Rick. Rashad found a large plant in Oklahoma City ready to junk their twenty-year-old equipment. For five grand we can have it loaded on a rail car and shipped to our spur."

I examined the photos. The machinery looked usable; simplistic, perhaps, without all the dials and adjustments I was used to, but still. I made quick calculations as I handed the papers back to Erskine. "Five thousand for the equipment, option on the land, installation, permits, surveys, closing costs, wiring … what's the bottom line?"

Erskine handed me a spreadsheet. "We figure we can start up for fifty grand."

"And how much do you have?"

"Twenty-five," Keisha said. "And that's with a second mortgage on the house. Rick, we need your expertise, definitely. But we're also hoping you'll be able to match our investments."

I'd lost the bulk of my net worth in the divorce, giving Mallory the house and half our savings. With the expenses of the move and Mallory's and Andrew's medical expenses, my savings amounted to forty thousand. I was counting on living on that until I could get back on my feet. Also I was wondering how I was going to pay for Andrew's college next year. "I'm not rich, Keisha. What about borrowing from the banks?"

Fred sighed. "No one's willing to loan us money without more collateral. You know what the economy's like. We need at least another fifteen grand right away or we'll lose the land and the opportunity to get the equipment. We'll need the other ten in two months. You have to believe it's going to work. If you do, you gotta be willing to commit."

Once again I looked out over the field, where somewhere my son was racing his heart out, giving his all for a team. If I agreed to this project, it'd require most of my savings, and all my time. It was crazy, that's what it was. Reckless. Foolish.

For some reason I thought back thirty years to when I was considering marrying Mallory. I'd sought my father's advice, and we sat together on the porch, under the canopy of stars. I asked, "How can I tell if she's really the one?"

My father pointed to a meteor flaring in the atmosphere. "In ancient days people looked to the stars for their answers."

"Sounds like superstition to me," I had said.

"Maybe. Then again, maybe God does give us signs. You just have to have your eyes open. When a miracle happens, you'll know it's meant to be."

My musings were interrupted by someone shouting from the top of the stands, "They're coming back!"

All the parents stood, straining to see the runners as they entered the gate. The first five came in a close pack, two Harrison Central green and white, two Gulfport High blue and orange, and one Hattiesburg High purple and gold. They sprinted back onto the track for the last lap. The timekeeper called out the sixteen-thirty mark.

Places shifted back and forth as the leaders rounded the first two curves. Andrew held in fifth, pulling on the draft of the runners in front of him. On the halfway mark of this last lap he burst past the other four to take a two-to-three-yard lead. Devonne, who had been second, cracked a huge smile. Bearing down, he pulled even with Flash, the Harrison Central boy. They rounded the last corner that way, Andrew two yards ahead and seeming to get further ahead with each step, Devonne pushing himself to the limits, and Flash straining for all he was worth.

At the finish line Andrew cleared the others by three yards. From where the Gulfport parents stood, the next two seemed to be dead even. They listened to the line judge call Devonne's number first. Sixteen-fifty-three the timer announced.

"The first five all broke seventeen minutes!" Erskine shouted. "That's got to be the fastest times for top finishers this region has seen in years."

The scorekeeper scribbled furiously as racers crossed the line, the timer calling out the seconds, the line judge announcing school and jersey number. Lebron finished eighth, his arms raised high in triumph. Jamerion came in a few places later. Many of the boys who had finished were taking cool-down laps and stretching. Some lay exhausted on the ground, sipping from water bottles their coaches brought.

As Devonne, Lebron, and Andrew approached us, Keisha ran out and greeted each with a big hug. Erskine and I clapped the boys on their backs, and Fred shook their hands. The runners settled onto the quilt and wolfed down sports drinks as they wiped off their sweat with towels.

"So since we came in first and second, does that mean Gulfport gets to go to state?" I asked.

Keisha shook her head. "It's the team time that matters. Having Andrew and Devonne as the top two certainly helps, but it's a team effort. There will be a ceremony in about half an hour, after the results are tallied and rechecked. Meanwhile, anyone hungry?"

She opened the picnic basket and brought out fried chicken, biscuits, and baked beans. Though we ate well, everyone kept an eye on the scorekeepers' table where Coach Dalton and the other coaches hovered. It took forty minutes before the group broke up. Coach Dalton waved at us as he approached, his toothy smile and the huge trophy he carried telling the story. Another man walked by his side.

"We did it, boys!" the couch shouted. "It was close, but we edged out Harrison Central by three points. We're on our way to State!" He held up the big trophy with the plaque proclaiming "First Place, Mississippi Southern Region, 2008." Passing it around for everyone to hold, he also handed Devonne, Lebron, and Andrew their individual trophies.

Andrew brought his to me and we were examining it when Coach Dalton spoke again. "This is Coach Broussard," he said, indicating the stranger. "I'd like you folks to listen to what he has to say."

The new coach handed around a stack of calling cards. "I'm the track coach here at the university." He pointed at Andrew and Devonne. "You two sure ran a great race."

"Devonne Barnes," Devonne said, shaking the coach's hand. "And this here's my friend Andy Lewis. He's the one that done it. When he burst ahead, I felt right inspired to giddy up myself."

"That was quite an impressive sprint, Mr. Lewis," the coach said, shaking Andrew's hand.

"Had a good day I guess."

"Modest too? I like that. Listen fellows, and parents too. Have you thought about USM for college?"

Andrew and Devonne looked at each other and back to the coach. "Why?" Devonne asked.

"Because USM needs good runners. You two may be the best in the state, and if you come here, we can offer you some of the finest training facilities in the country. We have a state of the art gymnasium with an indoor running track. And USM isn't just about sports. A degree from this university is practically a guarantee for a job when you graduate. You men know what you want to study?"

Devonne said, "My brother Rashad is gonna graduate in chemical engineering at your school in May. I'd sort of like to go that way too, but I don't really have his smarts. I've been thinking of maybe taking a year at Jeff Davis first."

Coach Broussard nodded. "I'm familiar with the junior college, Mr. Barnes. It's a fine school, but it doesn't have a sports program. How about you, Mr. Lewis?"

"Chemical engineering too. Was hoping U. of Chicago."

"Illinois?" I managed to squeak. Of course Andrew would be thinking of returning north. Just because I didn't want to return, didn't mean he wouldn't.

Andrew glanced my way. "Though don't really know. Money's a bit tight."

Coach Broussard put one hand on each of their shoulders. "USM might be able to help you out. I'm authorized to offer a full track scholarship to a qualified and needy student. I'm talking all tuition and fees, room and board at one of the dorms, and full reimbursement for all books and supplies. In addition, we provide a stipend in exchange for a few hours a week working in the gym. Should make college completely affordable. It's guaranteed for two years, and renewable after that."

The boys broke into big smiles and punched each other on the shoulders. Erskine silenced the frivolity when he asked, "You only have one scholarship to offer?"

"That's all we have budgeted at the moment."

"How do you decide who gets it?" I asked.

"There's an application process, and a committee involved, but basically the final decision rests in my hands. I'm looking for the fellow who can offer the most to our track team. If you both apply, it's going to be a tough decision."

"Give it to Devonne," Andrew said. "He's always wanted to go to USM, and with his brother already here, seems pretty obvious to me."

"Nah. Andy deserves it," Devonne said. "He won the dang race. I'll be okay at Jeff Davis for a year."

Coach Broussard stroked his chin. "It's good to see such selfless friends. How are your grades?"

"Got a B average," Devonne said.

"Don't know," Andrew admitted. "I just moved here."

Couch Broussard handed them each a packet. "A win at state would certainly be a big plus on this application."

Keisha asked, "Are Devonne and Andy the only two in contention?"

"No. There are others, especially a fellow in Jackson who's won several races this year."

"That'd be Wolf Mueller," Devonne muttered. "I've been reading about him."

The coach shook hands with everyone and accepted a cup of lemonade and a cupcake from Keisha. In a few minutes he walked off towards the Harrison High group and we began putting away the food.

Andrew, Devonne, and Lebron climbed into the backseat of the SUV, each hugging their trophies. Erskine settled into the driver's seat with Keisha riding shotgun. Just before I started to climb into the middle seat, I felt Fred's hand on my shoulder. He pulled me back a few steps.

Looking me straight in the eyes he said, "In forty-eight hours, noon Monday, I gotta have that money. Are you in or not?"

"What would it mean to be in?" I asked.

"We'll need fifteen thousand dollars first thing Monday morning, Rick. I could pick you up and take you to your bank. That way we can transfer the funds to our business account and afterwards go by the lawyer's office and sign you into the corporation."

"And if the project falls apart?"

"We won't let it fail."

I looked in the window at the boys, Andrew hugging his first-place trophy and laughing with his friends. A man would have to be blind not to recognize this miracle. I shook Fred's hand to seal the deal. "Count me in. I'll be ready nine o'clock Monday."

Fred squeezed back firmly. "You won't regret this, Rick."

We climbed into the car and took off south, my head full of dreams of a better future.

Tuesday, December 9th

I stood marveling at the stars. How many planets had sentient beings? How many of those were standing somewhere, staring into the heavens, and wondering how to apologize to an offended lover? I could imagine infinite possibilities, and that gave me the fortitude to call.

It rang and rang, until the answering machine picked up. I disconnected.

I let the phone dangle in my hand, but I didn't put it down. *Sylvia had been wonderful to me. Would she understand my rudeness was due solely to my grief? Would she even listen? It'd been a week since my drunk, and three days since the state meet. You'd a thought I'd have found time to call before this. There was time. Plenty of time. Time is what I seemed to have most of these days. Just not the fortitude. That needed to change.*

I called again, and again was met with the answering machine. I clicked off again. This wasn't working, but I couldn't think of any other plan. After a few minutes I tried again. To my surprise I got an answer.

"Hello?" It was Aunt Frances' voice.

"Hello, Aunt Frances. This is Richard Lewis." I half expected her to hang up on me. After all, she was bound to take Sylvia's side.

"Yes, Richard. I remember you quite distinctly. You're the tall Yankee with the nice manners, the rumpled shirt, and the deepest blue eyes my niece has ever seen."

I stifled a chuckle. In the background I heard, "Give me that."

Sylvia came on the phone. "Hello?"

I fumbled for something to say, but didn't know how to start.

"Rick?"

"Yes, I'm here." The words erupted like water from a broken levee. "Look, Sylvia. I'm really sorry. I miss you. I was a jerk. I know I was. It was a bad day for me. If you never want to hear from me again, I understand. But, gosh, I love you. I need you." I let my words trail off, fearing she'd respond in anger.

I listened to her shallow breathing, as if she wasn't willing to commit to a full one. She said, "You were a jerk or you still are?"

"Please let me explain."

"No, let me explain. I believed in you, trusted you – let down all my defenses. But it seems this whole relationship is on your terms. You call me only when you want something, and when your needs are fulfilled, it's 'see you later.' That's not a relationship. That's a one-way street. I deserve better than that, Rick."

"Sylvia, please. Please see me again."

Her answer seemed to take forever. Fear clawed at my throat.

"You let loose a mouthful a moment ago. Did you mean everything you said?"

"Yes, yes of course. What?"

"Think about it, Rick. Think long and hard about every word you just said."

I strained to remember. *What? I said I was a jerk. I said I was sorry. What else?* I stared up onto the stars, spotting Orion on his endless and fruitless chase. "Sylvia, I love you."

I heard her sigh. "Okay. I'll give you one more chance. Meet me in an hour at P.J.s. You can attempt to explain why you were drunk and rude."

"Please, Sylvia. This is going to be very difficult for me to talk about."

"One more chance, Rick."

"I'll be there."

I brought the phone back into its cradle in the kitchen and hurried to my bath to freshen up. Finding Andrew working on his bedroom computer, I told him I was going out for a bit, and he grunted. I stuffed the drawings into my briefcase, clamped it closed, and carried it down to the car. Down the beach road, at one of the many dark, quiet spots, I pulled off and parked. I sat there, listening to the surf roll in, looking over the waters. In my professional career I had prepared many a talk, writing notes, considering possible questions and objections. I felt totally vulnerable now, not knowing what to say or what to expect. In a bit I pulled back onto the nearly empty road.

P.J.s Coffee had a modern feel, with cushiony chairs and expensive drinks; the latter full of additives like whipped cream. I loved it.

I found a quiet table in the corner, setting my briefcase next to me on the floor. Sylvia spotted my wave when she arrived. She wore a short blue dress again, accenting her contoured legs. She slipped in across from me and a waitress took our orders.

"Sylvia."

I waited until she looked up at me. Her eyes were heavily made up.

"Sylvia, I'm sorry. I was a jerk, I know it. Please forgive me."

She thumped her fingers across the tabletop. "Ignoring me for three days was awful, but the way you treated me when I dropped by was horrendous. You were more than a jerk, Richard Lewis. You were a drunken bastard. I swore I never wanted to see you again."

"No," I whispered.

"I gave you everything I had! You treated me like dirt!"

I glanced around. The two other patrons in the nearly empty shop were paying no attention to us.

She glanced around too, her face suggesting she was having second thoughts about even being here. With subdued tone she demaded, "Give me one good reason why I should forgive you."

I took her hand. "Sylvia, we have something here, something magical. I've never been so much in love with anyone as I am with you."

"Then how could you possibly act that way?"

I forced my heart to calm. "It was the anniversary."

She looked puzzled. "Your wedding anniversary?"

"No. Jenny's death."

Sylvia's hand flew to her mouth. "Oh God! I'm so sorry. I ... Oh my God." She rose and came to my side of the table. Leaning over, she kissed me. Gently, lovingly. I reached to pull her closer, and the waitress arrived with our order.

"Having fun, kids?" she asked. She placed our coffees and cakes before us.

We relaxed, able to enjoy the treats now that she understood. After swallowing a bite, Sylvia asked, "Is this the time?"

I stopped chewing and tried to recall if we had been talking about something this could relate to. "Time for what?"

"You know. The time for forgiveness – the one I owe you."

I realized what she was talking about. "No." Leaning forward I took her hands. "When you asked for my forgiveness it was for a perceived moral lapse in your past. I've got such an event in my recent life too. I did something horrendous, yet I'm not sure if it was good or evil. I think I need to figure that out before I ask to be pardoned."

"There is no absolute good or evil, Rick. I'm sure whatever it was, I'll forgive you. Why don't you just tell me?"

I shook my head and we sat in silence. Searching for a new topic, I remembered the pouch of drawings I'd brought. Pulling one out, I presented it across the table. "Take a gander."

Sylvia studied it as I talked. "I've signed on with Rashad and Erskine Barnes, and Fred Johnson. See? I've tried various arrangements, and I think this one works best. We'll put the smelter here, with the chipping plates on this side. Here's the land plat. See this? That's a railroad spur. We can get small loads of bauxite dumped right on the property. It's great road access too. We'll make aluminum plates and be able to deliver them locally. Heck, with time we can build our own stampers. Rashad can design the necessary equipment for us to custom mold per order. This is going to be .... Why are you looking at me like that?"

Sylvia's smile wrinkled her cheeks. "It's like you're a totally different person. You've been so discouraged, and suddenly you're glowing with hope. Congratulations." She took a sip from her coffee. "I'm so happy for y'all. Best of luck for you and your new business, and congratulations for Andy and the track team."

"Thanks! Man, I was so happy for Andy. I wish you could have been there. Say, how 'bout joining us in Clinton in two weeks for the state meet to root him on?"

"That's only two days after the end of the semester. I might have tests to grade or students who need counseling."

"Oh come on, Sylvia. It'll be Christmas break. What do you say?"

I watched her smile come, falter momentarily, but finally win out. "Okay. So we leave early that morning?"

"Yep. It's about a three-hour drive and the race starts at eleven. Keisha says we'll depart here at six just to be safe."

Sylvia looked at her watch. "Speaking of early mornings, I should be going. I have a ton of lessons to grade."

"I'll be up early too. I like to make sure Andy gets breakfast and also get my exercise bike in before I head to work."

"Work?"

I shrugged off a grimace. "Home Depot, ten 'til four, four days a week. Got to have some income."

"I approve," Sylvia said, patting me on the wrist. She stood and I did too.

"So will I see you before the state meet?" I asked. "I don't think I can stand waiting another eleven days."

She gave me a wink. "I'm awful busy at end of semester, and this coming weekend Aunt Frances and I are driving to Gulf Shores to visit our cousins." She rested her hand on my arm. "When did you say your friends and ex-wife are arriving?"

"Mallory isn't coming until after Christmas, but the rest will be here on the twenty-second, two days after the state meet."

She hesitated and I felt her hand squeezing me. "After Christmas? Well, perhaps."

"What?"

She seemed to make up her mind and gave me a smile. "Aunt Frances and I are hosting our annual Christmas Open House the twenty-fifth. Here in the South, people drop by throughout the day, sometimes staying for meals."

"Great! I'd love to come. Should I bring all my guests?"

Her smile faltered. "I'm sure Aunt Frances would love to meet Andy, considering how much I talk about him. Maybe we should wait for the others, you know, see if they like me."

"Oh, Peter likes everyone, and Andy's friends are nice too."

She looked doubtful. Lifting her coat off the hook she said, "By the way, it's polite to bring a bottle of wine or some such when you visit someone's home."

"I know that."

"Oh? I must have overlooked the gift you brought Aunt Frances last visit."

I blushed. "How about I bring two bottles next time?"

"Perfect."

I helped her on with her jacket. When she turned back to face me she showed her cheek, but I wanted more. I leaned into her, kissing her hard on the lips, forcefully, until we finally stopped to breathe.

I smiled broadly. "That was nice."

"Yes, it was. Perhaps we'll have more later." She turned and hurried out the door.

Andrew: Saturday, December 20th

In the locker room as the boys got dressed, Andrew watched Devonne place his Air Jordans on the bench. Beside them he set a roll of silver tape.

"What's that?"

Devonne pulled off a strip, wrapping it around his shoe. "Caint let that heel get loose."

Lebron glanced up from tying his own pair. "Duct taping your shoes for the state meet? Talk about ghetto."

"I told you three days ago you couldn't run in those shoes anymore," Andrew said. He pulled out a shoebox from his bag. "Here. My dad bought me an extra pair last month. Only worn 'em twice. See if they fit."

"Fine looking Nikes," Devonne said. He looked at the box again. "Fourteens? I thought them Brooks you wear was thirteens."

Andrew looked down at his shoes, wiggling his toes inside. They rubbed against the front. "Yeah. Guess my feet are still growing. What's your size?"

"Twelve and a half." Devonne examined the Nikes, weighing them in his hand. "Yep these are sweet. Shame my foot'd slip right out." He handed them back to Andrew. "'Sides, we're racin' against each other. What if I beat you while I was wearing your shoes?"

Lebron laughed. "That'd be a riot."

Andrew put his foot up on the bench, unlaced and removed his Brooks. "Here. These will fit you better. I'll wear the Nikes."

Lebron grabbed a Nike and looked it over. "You gonna give up your Brooks for these? They ain't even broke in."

Devonne had picked up the Brooks, which he now placed back on the bench. "Lebron's right. I caint wear your Nikes and you gotta wear the Brooks. I'll make with duct tape."

Andrew sat on the bench and pulled on a second pair of socks, followed by the Nikes. "The Brooks are too small; I'm wearing these. Either wear 'em or let 'em sit."

Devonne snorted, retrieved the Brooks, and proceeded to don them.

Lebron laughed. "You gonna let Devonne beat you, Andy?"

Andrew shook his head. "Not if I can help it." He stood and ran in place a moment. "Not that I'd mind if he did."

Devonne shook his head. "You thinking about that there scholarship? You the smart one, Andy. You should get the money."

"Listen at you guys," Lebron said. "That kid from Jackson is gonna whip both your tails. And I'll be comin' in behind, laughin' all the way."

"Ain't nobody gonna beat us," Devonne said, giving his cousin a little shove.

"Ha!" Lebron snorted. "You know how long it's been since a Gulfport High runner won state?"

The other two shrugged.

"Eighteen years."

"Eighteen years, huh?" Andrew asked. "I'd say it's our turn."

The boys stepped out of the locker room and scanned their competition. Tall teenagers in their brightly colored outfits stretched beside the track. Andrew spotted his father and Mrs. Perkins sitting together in the stands and gave them a wave.

"Some fast lookin' kids here," Devonne said.

"We're gonna do fine," Andrew assured him. "Come on, Coach is wavin' at us." The three went over to where Coach Dalton waited with the other three Gulfport runners, sat down, and began their stretching exercises.

"Whatcha gonna do ifen you don't get the scholarship?" Devonne asked.

Andrew glanced at his friend, and returned his concentration to his calves. "What do I wanna do or what *will* I do?"

Devonne grunted as he stretched his hamstrings. "Tell me both."

"What I wanna do is go to U of Chicago. That's always been my dream. Got a girlfriend there."

"Yeah, you said."

"But that's not gonna happen unless I get a whole bunch of scholarship money. I don't know what I'll do. Get a job? Maybe I'll be a beach bum."

The warning whistle blew and the team gathered at the starting line. Coach Dalton put Devonne first, followed by Andrew and Lebron.

Huddling next to Devonne and Andrew, the coach said, "Now listen, boys. This is it. The state championship. You boys are strong, maybe the strongest runners Gulfport High's ever seen. You can win, but it's going to take everything you've got. There're a handful of really fast boys here – rabbits. They'll be out front early, but they'll fade halfway. Happens every year. Don't let 'em throw you off the pace."

He pointed out a tall muscular boy in blue spandex standing at the head of row two. "That's Wolf Mueller. He's won four cross country races this year. From what I hear, he starts off strong and stays that way. If you don't keep up there'll be no catching up."

Andrew studied the boy, how he stood still over his starting block, breathing quietly, as if he were practicing Yoga.

The coach noticed Andrew's shoes. "What are those? Nikes? Where're your Brooks?"

Andrew shrugged. "My feet grew."

Coach Dalton looked at Devonne's feet and back to Andrew. He nodded slowly. "Okay, boys. Have a good race." He stepped down the line to talk to his other runners.

Devonne threw his chin in the direction of Wolf. "Whatcha thinkin'? Kid sounds awful quick."

Andrew nodded. "We can beat him. Like Coach said, start off fast and stay that way."

"You better not fall behind neither."

The two stared at the boy who remained focused on something beyond his surroundings.

"Don't plan to," Andrew said.

The line judge's white and black horizontal stripped shirt flowed over his bulging stomach. He took five minutes to read the rules out loud, and then to describe the course. When he was done he climbed up on his platform at the side of the starting line. Pulling out a bullhorn, he announced, "ON YOUR MARKS."

The racers bent to their positions. Quiet descended as they focused.

"GET SET!"

Jaws clenched. Muscles tightened.

"BANG!!"

Springs uncoiled. Bright nylons streaked down the track, like flags ripping in the gulf breeze. They rounded the turn and off onto the sidewalk, plunging onto the wooded hilly path.

Andrew settled into tenth place, eyeing each runner ahead of him, analyzing their pace, judging their stamina. By the second kilometer marker he had moved up to eighth. At the head of the pack ran three "rabbits," with Devonne and Wolf three meters behind them.

Andrew concentrated on his feet, wiggling his toes between strides. They felt great, as if they'd been released from a prison. *Why didn't I switch to these Nikes a month ago?* He studied Devonne's stride. As near as he could tell, his friend had happy feet too.

At the fourth kilometer the three "rabbits" had fallen behind leaving Devonne and Wolf with a ten-meter edge over Andrew and three other runners. Andrew decided it was time to make his move, and, pumping hard, he began leaving the other three behind.

At the four and a half mark Andrew ran two meters behind Devonne, who lagged about the same behind Wolf. They entered the track that way. Andrew kept pushing, concentrating on keeping his stride long and even.

When the three rounded the second of the four last curves, he gave that little extra effort he knew he had kept in reserve. He shortened his stride just a tiny bit, able to use the extra energy to increase his speed. As they came around the last curve, Andrew pulled ahead of Devonne, and then Wolf.

I'm going to do it! I'm really going to win.

A mere ten meters from the finish Andrew caught a flash of color beside him. He knew he had nothing more to give. In despair he looked to his side, expecting to see Wolf passing him for the victory.

Instead, he saw Devonne.

His friend raised his hand in a high five and Andrew grasped it, just as they crossed the finish line together.

Monday, December 22nd

I brought the three mugs to the table. "This place sure thinks highly of their brew. Twenty bucks for two cups of java and a hot chocolate. At Waffle House you can get coffee for two dollars, and free refills."

"Beau Rivage's coffee is worth it," Sylvia said, lifting her mug for a sniff and a taste. "Mmm. Much better. What did your friends say?"

"They'll be down any minute."

Sylvia looked over at Andrew and laughed. "You have whipped cream on your nose!" She reached over with her napkin but he held up his hand to stop her, instead using his finger to wipe it off and licking his finger clean.

Spotting the group approaching down the hallway, I announced, "Here they come."

We stood and walked out of the shop to meet them. As they strolled up, memories of these four poured into my brain. Peter, Celine, Travis, and Sarah, how often had I'd seen this group together, how many adventures had we shared? The older two looked unchanged: Peter's crisp suit every bit the corporate lawyer, Celine's red gown the statement of fashion. The two kids had grown in the year since I'd last seen them, their faces maturing as well. Andrew raced up to them and they began gabbing at once.

Peter grabbed my offered hand and pulled me into a solid hug accented by a pound on the back. "Great to see you again, Buddy!"

My smile stretched to my cheekbones. "I am *so* glad to see you, too! Man, it sure is good to be back together ... and not under pressure like last month! By the way, thanks again for helping out my boy."

Peter poked me in the belly. "You're looking good too. Just doing my uncle-y duty."

I turned to Peter's wife. "Hey, sis-in-law."

Celine flashed a crimson-painted smile. Both sisters enjoyed natural beauty, though I preferred Mallory's softer bone structure over Celine's lean shadowed cheeks. She bent slightly forward for a bit of a hug. "It's been too long for friends to be apart, Rick. Everyone back in Chicago is missing you. And I do mean everyone."

Ignoring Celine's pointed look, I turned to Sylvia. "Allow me to introduce my lifelong buddy Peter and his wife Celine. Guys, this is Sylvia Perkins."

Sylvia smiled cheerfully and offered her hand. "I've been so looking forward to meeting Rick's friends."

Celine gave her hand a touch and stared at Sylvia's left hand. "Is it Miss Perkins or Missus?"

Sylvia stepped back. "Mrs. Perkins, thank you. I'm divorced."

Celine smiled sweetly. "Ah. My sympathy."

Peter took Sylvia's hand and shook it warmly. "Nice to meet you. I think we've spoken on the phone once."

I saw Sylvia's cheeks flush. "Yes, when I was helping Rick take care of Andrew."

"Speaking of the boy," he said, and turned to the teens. "Hey, Andy, come over here and greet your favorite uncle."

Andrew stepped up and accepted his hug. "Hey, Uncle Peter. Sorry for all the trouble last month."

"Don't worry about it, Andy. What's important is you're recovered … and that you've learned your lesson." He gave Andrew a questioning look and my son nodded vigorously.

"You bet. Don't never want to go through that again."

"Good boy. Travis tells me you won the state championship in cross country last week. That's quite an achievement!"

Andrew smiled proudly. "Actually it was a tie."

"That still means you won. I understand this includes a scholarship."

"Maybe. After New Year's I'll check into what they're willing to offer."

"Are you still considering U of Chicago?" He indicated the other youths. "Hang out with your friends?"

Andrew glanced at me. "It's definitely on my list."

The other teens approached and I gave them each a little hug. "Hello Travis, Sarah. Good to see you two again. How was your flight?"

"Just fine," Travis answered, "but we're starved. When I asked for a second bag of pretzels the stewardess acted like I was threatening to hijack the plane."

"That's 'cause you were so obnoxious about it," Sarah said. "She gave me an extra bag."

"What? And you didn't share with me?"

I laughed. "Let's go eat. Everyone ready?"

We weaved our way through the casino to the buffet, the kids bug-eyed as we walked past row after row of slot machines. Travis put on some faces, imitating the people playing, and we laughed all the way into the dining area. There we all charged into the food area, with Peter sticking with me as we bounced around the various food islands. I enjoyed explaining to him about the foreign dishes; fried okra and cheese grits.

After we'd settled at the table, Celine said, "My studio is sponsoring an art show by a new abstractionist next month. Shawn Kennedy. He's a John Miro type, Rick. You used to love Miro, didn't you?"

"Oh, yeah. Still do." I turned to Sylvia. "Those are Miro prints in my bathroom. You know, Celine is a bit of an artist herself." Turning back to Celine, I said, "Tell Sylvia about some of your awards."

"I'm sure Mrs. Perkins wouldn't be interested," Celine answered demurely.

"Go ahead," Sylvia insisted. "Don't hold back now."

"I presumed a small-town Southern girl like you wouldn't comprehend the world of big city art. But since you asked, I own a gallery on the Magnificent Mile. Are you familiar with that part of Chicago, Mrs. Perkins?"

Sylvia shook her head. "No. I've never been to Chicago."

Celine cocked her head. "You've never been to Chicago? Really?"

I held up my hand. "Back off, Celine."

Sylvia took a sip of her tea and dabbed her lips with her napkin. When she spoke her voice dripped of honey. "Oh I enjoy travel. It's just that Chicago hasn't interested me. After all, who would want to visit the country's most corrupt city?"

Celine turned to me. "Your friend seems totally ignorant of the finer aspects of life. I'm glad Mallory will be here soon. We'll be able to have much more intelligent dinner conversations."

I cleared my throat. "How about we change the subject?" I turned to Peter and asked, "So, any good cases lately?"

Peter finished swallowing before responding. "Absolutely. Just put together a nice corporate merger. Next time you're up in Chi-town, I'll take you out to the club to celebrate. You planning on a visit any time soon?"

"Not really."

"Ah come on, Rick. You can't tell me you don't miss your friends. What about all those engineering buddies you used to talk about? Hey, I tell you what. I know someone who can get us fourth row tickets to a Bulls game. Just give me a few days' notice and I'll set us up sweet."

"Fourth row? Man, I'd love that." I glanced at Sylvia who had stopped eating. She sat quietly, staring at Celine who seemed to be enjoying her meal. I continued, "Let's not talk about me going back to Chicago, okay Pete? I'm happy with what I'm doing here."

"Glad to hear that, old friend. And what the heck *are* you doing these days?"

"I'm designing a smelting plant." I felt the familiar rush of comfort brought by talking about my work. Man, I missed these discussions. "I've been drafting designs for three weeks, searching the Internet for equipment, and researching all the safety and legal specifications. You want to see a sketch?"

I reached for a napkin and drew all over both sides as I talked, showing Peter some of my ideas.

Peter seemed impressed. "Sounds marvelous. I hope they're paying you what you're worth. A job like that in Chicago would bring in … what? Twenty grand a month?"

I grimaced, remembering when I had enjoyed a six-figure income. In those days we'd go out for a night on the town and not worry about the costs. Now even this buffet was a budget biter. "Actually I'm not pulling money out of the business yet."

Peter leaned back in his chair. "You know, Rick, the economy of Mississippi may not offer a man with your talents the best opportunities. I know some people in Chicago who'd be interested in a person with your years of experience. Would you mind if I mentioned your name? I mean, if they wanted to fly you up for an interview, do you think you'd be interested?"

I fingered my fork, flipping it over next to my plate. "A job? Doing what?"

Peter scratched his chin. "Just saying I could make some calls this week if you're willing to commit. I'm certain I could pull some strings."

I looked across the room at Andrew, who was joking with his two friends as they loaded up their plates for the second time. Or was it round three? What if we did move back to Chicago? Here, talking with his friends, he seemed the happiest I'd seen him since the tragedy.

I looked back at Peter, surveying his confidant smile and successful look. I remembered when I'd been doing well in my company, senior engineer. It'd been fun; challenging work with responsibilities to match. Maybe I should consider Peter's offer.

I glanced over to Sylvia who seemed intent on her plate, though more poking with her fork than eating.

"Well, I …"

"Seriously, Rick," Celine said, reaching across to lay her hand on my wrist. "You should listen to Peter. He can bring you back where you belong."

I looked at Sylvia again. She gave me an attempt at a smile. Her eyes seemed so sad I wanted to wrap my arms right around her.

"I don't think I'm interested, Peter. Andy wants to stay here and finish his schooling and I'm committed to this project. Chicago isn't my home any longer, though I do appreciate the offer." I heard Sylvia release her breath.

"You could have your family back together," Celine said. She turned to Sylvia and flashed a smile, just enough to bare her teeth. "Rick's wife is a fashion designer with Macy's. She's been in meetings with Ralph Lauren and Martha Stewart."

"Ex-wife," I interjected.

Celine asked Sylvia, "What is it you do here in Mississippi?"

"I'm a school counselor."

"And a history teacher," I added.

"Oh. You're a grade school teacher in a small Southern town. How quaint. Public school, I'm sure?"

Sylvia smiled sweetly. "I try to teach young people manners. Clearly they don't teach that to y'all in Chicago."

Celine opened her mouth but Peter placed his hand on her wrist and she bit back her retort. The kids came up with their food and noisy conversation, their words tumbling over each other.

"Remember that time we went skateboarding down the school's parking garage!"

"Yeah! Yeah! That security guard was running down those stairs trying to catch us!"

"But every time he got to the next level –"

"We were just racing past him down the ramp."

"He never did catch us –"

"And we were out the door –"

"And down the block."

"He stood at the entrance shaking his fist at us –"

"And puffing to catch his breath."

"That was hilarious!"

Everyone at the table but Sylvia laughed.

"You guys are certainly having a good time," I said.

Sarah leaned over and kissed Andrew on the cheek. "We're celebrating finally being together again."

"Yeah," Andrew replied. "I've missed you guys, and all that Chicago jazz." He turned to me. "Maybe we should consider moving back, huh, Dad?"

Silence descended on the table.

Sylvia stood. "Rick, I suddenly have this terrible headache."

I stood too. "You need some aspirin or something?"

"No, I think I better go home."

"Now? You want me to drive you?"

"No, no. I wouldn't hear of it. I'll catch a cab."

"A cab? No that's silly. I'll –"

Sylvia squeezed my arm. Hard. "No. Please stay with your friends. Give me a call sometime."

I watched her scurry across the room until she disappeared out the door. When I sat back down, I turned to Peter. "Jeez. That sure didn't work out well."

He shrugged. "Let her have her little tiff. She'll get over it."

"I hope you're right. I'll call her later."

"No hurry," Celine murmured.

Thursday, December 25ᵗʰ

I pulled up to the Hewes Mansion, surprised to find no cars parked on the circular driveway. Of course, it was only nine, probably too early. I hesitated, but figured she hadn't said when I should come, just that I should. After a quick walk up the laid brick path, deep chimes rewarded my ring. Sylvia flung the door open, stepping forward into my arms and giving me a deep kiss.

When we broke apart she pointed up at the mistletoe, and we came together for an encore. This time when we had enough she looked behind me. "All alone?"

"Yeah. Andy was going to come, but I couldn't wake him this morning. He and his friends were up most of the night playing video games." I followed her in and pulled out the wrapped gift from the bag I'd brought. "This is from Andy and me."

She led me into the great room where Aunt Frances sat in the easy chair. "So nice of you to drop by, Richard," she said.

"Merry Christmas, Aunt Frances. Please don't get up." I walked over and gave the back of her hand a kiss. I handed her a bag containing two bottles of wine, each with a bright bow. She pulled out each one in turn, making appropriate thanks, and returning my Christmas greeting.

"You're looking well," I said.

She acknowledged with a nod. "You as well. You'll stay for lunch, won't you? Sylvia has been basting the Christmas ham since early this morning."

I noticed the sweet aroma drifting in from the kitchen. "Smells delicious, but I can't stay quite that long." I turned to Sylvia. "Maybe you could join us after dinner?"

Sylvia shook her head, a sad smile gracing her face. "It would be better if I didn't. It's clear your friends don't want me around."

"Darlin'," Aunt Frances said. "Don't let others' opinions prevent you from doing what you want to do."

Sylvia flashed her a brief smile. "If only life were that simple."

"Well, at least open your present," I said.

Sylvia carefully loosened the tape and unwrapped the box. When she removed the lid she gasped. Gently unwrapping the old book, she held it up and, with a deep breath, blew away a history of dust.

"Oh my goodness! An autographed copy of Robert McElroy's 1937 biography of Jefferson Davis. Listen to this," she called, as she placed on her glasses to read the handwritten dedication. "'To my loving wife on our thirtieth anniversary. May your love of our Southern Heritage forever nourish our life together.'" She held the book against her chest. "This is *so* sweet."

"I ordered it online from a place that specializes in antique and rare books. Glad you like it."

Sylvia placed the book gently on the table, stepped forward and kissed me firmly on the lips.

Aunt Frances laughed. "Clearly she liked it."

"Oh, wait right here," Sylvia said. She rushed out of the room, returning in a minute dragging a large rectangular box.

I laid it on the ground and tore off the red foil wrap. "It's the 130 SLT Celestron Nexstar! Wow! I can't believe this!"

"It's the telescope Andy said you wanted, right?"

"Absolutely!" I grabbed her and gave her a smashing hug and kiss. Bending back to the box, I pulled out the instruction booklet. "Listen! Two lenses with a seventy-two power magnification and a view of six tenths degrees!"

"I don't know what you're talking about, but I'm glad you're pleased."

"I can't remember when I've gotten a better present! I'm going to start setting it up as soon as I get home. This is marvelous! Thanks so much, Sylvia."

I placed the book back in the box, carefully reclosed it, and picked it up. When I stood, I looked from one to the other. I almost choked on my next words. "I hate to run, but I've got to get back."

Sylvia's smile disappeared. "You're leaving already?"

"I mean ... you did say I could just stop by ...?"

I glanced at Aunt Frances who was watching Sylvia. "Of course," Sylvia said, "You have people waiting on you. I understand. I'll walk you to the door." She led the way, stopping to retrieve my jacket from the closet.

"You sure you won't come over?" I asked, as I slipped my coat on.

She shook her head, giving only a light peck on my offered lips. I yearned for more. "Rick?"

"What?"

"Nothing." She dropped her gaze to the floor.

"No, what?" I touched her chin, gently raising her face.

She brought her hand up and laid it gently against mine. "Do you think y'all are moving back to Chicago?"

I bent and gently kissed her forehead. "Sylvia, I love you. I'm not going to abandon you."

She grasped my hand tightly, just for a moment, before dropping it firmly and stepping back. "You say you love me ... but I wonder how much? You know your friends want you to move back. The whole reason they're here is to belittle me and convince you and Andy to return. When does your ex-wife arrive?"

"Tomorrow."

"Will she be sleeping with you?"

"Of course not! How could you ask such a thing?"

She shrugged. "Just seems like part of the grand plan to me."

I moved up to try to kiss her, but she stepped back, her arms crossed firmly across her chest. I spread mine in a wide welcoming gesture. "Sylvia, listen to me. I am not going to move back to Chicago. You ... you don't know what happened there, despite all I've told you."

Her eyebrow shot up, confusion crossing her features. "What does that mean?"

I again bent to kiss her. She tentatively offered her lips, but kept her hands pressing my chest away. When we broke, I pulled her gently to me, stroking her back. "Baby, you have nothing to worry about."

"You promise?"

I stared back into her eyes. My heart raced as I remembered how a broken promise had just cost me my job. And now I was being asked to promise I'd never move back to Chicago. "Yes, I promise."

I turned to the door, picked up my telescope, and grasped the knob. I felt her hand on my arm and turned. "What?"

"It's not easy for me to trust you."

I put the box down again, turning and taking both her hands. "Why not?"

I watched her turn her gaze out the window, and I followed it, seeing nothing beyond the bare trees and dry grass. She didn't look at me. "It's not easy to trust after being hurt. Not easy at all."

I reached for her again, but she shook me off, walking past me to hold the door open. After a step outside, I turned, and she waved. "I know you're not big for using the phone, but still, please call me if you can find the time." She shut it firmly in my face.

Friday, December 26th

Three years after Hurricane Katrina had flooded it, Gulfport International Airport finally finished its facelift, providing spacious lounges and tall glass walls. Andrew and I waited in the crowded reception area with other eager families. Actually, neither of us was eager, though I was at least ambivalent.

When I spotted Mallory, I elbowed Andrew who was engrossed in texting Travis. "Put it away. Your mom's here." Andrew ignored me, continuing to thumb the keyboard.

As Mallory approached along the corridor, I sucked in my breath, smitten, again, by her beauty. Her auburn hair bounced above chic sculptured eyebrows, penetrating green eyes, and startling red lips. Her legs took long strides in her stylish yellow pantsuit. A sparkle from her diamond earrings bounced in my eye.

"Over here, Mallory," I called.

She waved. Pulling her wheeled carry-on bag she hurried over, dropping it and her large purse at my feet as she flew into my arms. Startled, I returned the hug gingerly, and when she puckered up, almost kissed her on the lips. At the last minute I dodged and targeted her cheek.

"It's so good to see you again, Ricky," she said, holding me at arm's length, "You're looking as handsome as ever." She grabbed me for another hug. It felt strange to be hugging someone almost my height, instead of having to bend down as I did for Sylvia.

"Thanks. You look fabulous yourself. I guess you're still running?"

"Of course. Remember how we used to work out together at the gym, you on your exercise bike and me on the treadmill? I've always been so proud of how you've taken care of your body. And here's Andy! My God, you've grown another three inches!"

Andrew glanced at her. "Hello." He focused back to his phone, but she stepped up to him, wrapped her arms around and squeezed tightly. He kept his arms stiffly at his side, staring out at the coffee shop until she stepped back. He again tried to return to his texting, but she interrupted by kissing his cheek. He turned his back.

"Andy!" I chided.

He didn't respond. I started to reach for him but Mallory grabbed my arm. "It's okay," she said. "Give him some time."

I nodded and picked up the suitcase. "Is this all you have?"

Mallory laughed. "Of course not. I'm going to be here nine nights! Which way to baggage claim?"

I led the way as Mallory talked on and on about Chicago, telling me about all our friends and the many events. She told about how the city looked for the holidays, how all the stores had these wonderful sales, and about the carolers and ice skaters she'd been watching. As we waited for her luggage to arrive, she reported about the many parties she'd attended, including the school activities and Andrew's friends.

As we pulled out of the airport parking lot, I remarked, "It's about half an hour drive to the Beau. I'll point out my place as we drive past."

She looked at me in surprise. "The Beau? I can't afford the Beau Rivage. I was planning on staying with you."

"What?" Andrew shouted.

I stopped the car. "I thought you were going to stay with the Wilburns. It was all arranged."

"This is the first I've heard of it," she said.

Andrew called from the back seat. "Tell her she can't stay with us."

"Oh come on, Andy," she said, twisting to look at him over the seat. "We've lived together all your life."

I squeezed the steering wheel so hard my knuckles showed white. "What a God Damn setup. I should have known you guys were plotting something. I have half a mind to take you right back to the airport."

Mallory's eyes filled with tears. "Ricky! Please don't ruin everything." She reached over and stroked my face. "Aren't you even a little glad to see me?"

I closed my eyes, trying to ignore her touch. But it felt so nice, and she leaned over, kissing me on the cheek, lingering a bit, and nipping my ear. I felt a rush. Memories. Good ones.

I sighed and shifted the car back into gear. "I suppose there isn't much of a choice. I certainly don't want to put out a thousand dollars to stick you in a hotel."

Mallory reached over and gave my earlobe a pull. "Great! I'm eager to see your condo. I always wanted a place on the water, you know. Remember when we used to talk about getting a beach home? I guess the summers we spent up at the lake with the Wilburns were just about as good. Oh, those were wonderful days. That's what this week is going to be like, isn't it?"

When no one answered she started up again. "Guess what they've done to Riverside? They completely redid the library! You should see it." She gossiped all the way back to the condo. Once there Andrew jumped out of the car and bounded up the stairs, leaving his mother and me to drag the luggage into the elevator.

"I'm sorry about the way Andy's acting," I said in the privacy of the elevator.

Mallory gave me a wan smile. "Why is he so angry with me?"

"Resentment about being in the psych unit."

"Can't he see I did it for his own good? Can't you?"

I could, I did, I had, but I didn't want to grant that to Mallory, and I was unsure why. *Was I being selfish, hoping to keep Andrew's resentment of his mother strong so he would stay with me?*

I let her into the condo and set the bags in the foyer. Mallory walked through the living room onto the balcony, standing and gazing at the pink and purple skies. "This is incredible! I've never in my life seen such a gorgeous sunset."

I joined her to stare out over the water. "Yeah, it is special. Andy and I like to hang out here and talk, and often we eat out here. Speaking of meals, you hungry?"

"I could eat. Do you men want me to cook something?"

"How about I phone out for pizza? I'll go check and see what Andy wants on it."

I walked down the hallway and knocked on his door. "Andy? You want to talk?"

"Is she out there?"

"No, I'm alone."

Andrew let me in and locked the door behind us. He lay back on his bed, gripping his hands behind his head, and stared up at the ceiling.

"Andy. Why are you so angry?"

He glared at me. "You know exactly why. She put me in the loony bin. What kind of mother would do that?"

I walked to the window where I observed a woman and little girl walking along the shore, each with a bucket in hand. "I can't make you forgive her; I'm not even going to ask you to. But she is your mother and deserves your respect."

Andrew rolled to face the wall. "I don't wanna hear it."

"Well she's here and you're going to have to deal with it. I'm about to order a pizza. What kind would you like?"

Andrew's voice bounced off the wall. "Whatever. I'll stay in here and you can bring me some."

I sat on the bed, laying my hand on Andrew's back. "You can't run away from your problems, Son. If you have issues with your mother, you should talk to her about them."

Andrew turned and sat up. "What do you mean, you can't run away? Isn't that exactly what you did? Huh?"

"That was different," I said, standing. "Look, you're practically an adult. I'm not going to force you, but I think the sooner you deal with this the better."

He kept his head lowered and his mouth closed.

"And I'm not going to bring you supper in bed," I said on my way out.

I returned to the balcony where I found Mallory sipping on a drink. "Bourbon and soda," she said. "I brought you a bottle of Chivas Crown Royal."

"Thanks."

"Yours is on the kitchen counter."

I returned with my drink. "Ah, delicious!"

"So how's Andy?"

I shook my head. "Give him some time. What do you want on your pizza?"

Mallory smiled and I felt my heart skip. "You know what I like," she teased.

"Mushrooms and black olives?"

"I knew you knew. You also know what else I like." She winked.

I phoned in the pizza order, and we settled onto the deck chairs. She asked me how I'd lost my job, and I blamed it on the economy. She asked how my job search was going and I launched into the plans for the smelting plant. I became so involved telling my ideas I was startled when the pizza boy buzzed the door. I rode down to get them, and brought the two boxes to the table while Mallory rummaged in the kitchen for napkins and plates. I knocked on Andrew's door.

"Pizza's here."

"Bring it in to me."

"No. Come out and get it or we'll throw it out."

I returned to the table and in a few minutes Andrew joined us, his sullen face avoiding all eye contact. Mallory chatted on and, after we were done, continued as we dumped away the paper plates.

When we finished, Mallory asked, "How about a game of cards? It'd be good family time."

"We are NOT a family!" Andrew exclaimed. "I'm going out."

"Where are you going?" I asked.

Andrew's eyes flashed with anger. "Out." He slammed the door behind him.

I looked at Mallory, who stared at the closed door.

"Sorry, Mal."

She gave me a smile, though tears glistened around her eyelids. "Tomorrow's another day. You want a refill?"

I nodded. "Yeah, thanks. Just one more though. It's been a long day. I guess you can take my bed and I'll sleep on the couch."

"Oh, it's early yet. How about we watch a movie? You have a DVD player, right? Do you have anything I'd like?"

I pointed to the cabinet below the television, and Mallory selected a romance, placing it in the machine and settling on the middle of the couch. She indicated the spot next to her, but I sat on a chair instead.

After the movie I stood, stretched, and yawned pointedly. "Aren't you tired?"

Mallory shrugged. "Maybe a little. It certainly is a beautiful night." She headed out to the balcony. "Look at all the stars! Is this a new telescope?"

I stopped at the glass doors. "Yep."

"You know every star out here, don't you? Which one is the Love Star?"

I sighed. "Stop it. We're divorced."

"Oh lighten up, Ricky. How about a midnight walk on the beach? You can point out your favorite constellations."

I thought about my walk with Sylvia, only a month ago. It had ended with a redemption kiss. Now there had been so much more. "I'm tired, Mal."

"I'm not."

"Mallory. Go. To. Bed."

Mallory glared at me. "Very well. I can tell when I'm not wanted." She stomped into my bedroom and slammed the door.

I knocked on it.

"Change your mind?"

"I need my toothbrush."

Mallory thrust it through the door at me.

I settled onto the couch, but my mind kept racing. *What would Sylvia think if she knew Mallory was sleeping in my bed tonight?*

About two a.m. I heard Andrew come home, but I didn't get up or call to him. I drifted off to troubled dreams.

Andrew: Saturday, December 27th

"Hold up a moment."

Andrew glanced back at his mother, who had dropped from their run to a walk. He stopped, looking out to the water's edge as he waited for her to catch up. The tiny lesser terns skittered along the seashore, keeping several yards away. Looking up and back, as far as he could see, they had the beach to themselves.

"You okay?" he asked.

Mallory nodded. "Just need a walk break. How far have we run?"

"'Bout three miles." Andrew fell in beside her, walking east towards the rising sun. Out of the corner of his eye he saw her stop again, and he waited as she stretched, twisting back and forth.

"I never imagined this would be so beautiful," she said.

Andrew buried his hands in his pockets, his gaze down at the sand. "Suppose."

"I can see why you and your father like it down here. I can't believe we can run barefoot, wearing short sleeves at the end of December."

He didn't reply.

"I'm surprised there're so few buildings. If this was the Great Lakes' shore, there wouldn't be a single open space. Driving down the road yesterday I was astonished at all the empty slabs and blown out signs. Why are the Waffle Houses the only things built back?"

"That's Mississippi for you, Mom. We're just a bunch of lazy asses I guess."

He looked up when he felt her hand on his shoulder. "What?"

"Andy, why are you so angry?"

He didn't answer, just turned and strode away. She hurried to catch up, and they walked several more yards. "You stuck me away in a crazy house."

"Andy, you needed to be in the hospital. That's what Dr. Hopkins said."

He stopped, staring out over the water. "She was wrong."

"Was she?"

Andrew studied his mother, noticing for the first time how she'd aged, how her usually perfect makeup tried to hide the frown lines and crow's feet. He recalled pictures of the family together where she looked so much younger. Strange.

"Do you remember when we took that trip to Myrtle Beach?" she asked. "You and Travis were ten, Jenny and Rebecca twelve. The four of you built a huge sand castle. I have a picture of you planting a flag on its very top."

Andrew remembered. They'd spent hours on that castle, proud of the runs of corrugated turrets and the tall white towers. "It was magnificent!" he said. "Early the next morning Travis and I checked on it. All that was left was a mound of water-logged sand. I guess nothing's permanent."

"There are some things that never die," Mallory said softly. Andrew stiffened when she grabbed him in a hug. "Oh, Andy. I miss you so much! Please don't be angry with me. I need your forgiveness. I need my son back."

The hug felt hot and sweaty, yet somehow reassuring. He waited until she had dropped away before dropping his gaze, staring at his foot digging into the sand. "I don't know if I can, Mom."

"Why not? What did I do that was so awful? Please tell me."

He shook his head, trying to quiet his heart. Mallory reached out and grasped his arm. "Please," she pleaded.

He looked into her eyes, eyebrows tented in anguish. He stepped forward into her arms and they hugged tightly, his eyes clenched closed.

"God, Andy. I've been so lonely."

He held her so close he could feel her heart beating against his chest. The small wavelets of surf provided the only sound, until a seagull swooped by with a "caw" and landed a few feet away.

Andy stepped back and pointed at the gull. "We should bring out the leftover bread."

They watched the gull, which, deciding there were no handouts coming, flew off along the water's edge.

"Andy, please come home with me."

His eyes flashed in surprise. "What?"

"You heard me. You're a Chicago boy, not a Mississippian. Everybody you've ever known is there; your friends and neighbors, your cousins and teachers. When I told Mrs. Floyd I was coming down to visit she asked me to give you a hug from her. At the bridge party Sally Marchand went on and on about how much she missed you. Even the postman asked why he hadn't seen you around. When I walk down the street I have memories of you everywhere, playing with the kids in the skate park, rummaging through the comics at the corner grocery, or running down the street chasing the ice cream truck."

Andrew stared out across the forlorn shoreline with its solitary Waffle House. He remembered the streets of Chicago, the bustle of weekends hanging out with his buddies, and the laughter of the crowds. Like Travis said, "Always something happenin' in Chi-town." Why was he here in this desert?

"I do miss it, Mom. I've made a few friends here, though. And, like you said, it is pretty."

"Come home Andy."

They reversed direction, running a bit more before stopping at the Waffle House at Mallory's suggestion. Sitting in a booth by the window, they looked out on the sun glistening off the water. Palm tree fronds danced in the breeze over a couple of gulls scouring the parking lot for a meal.

The waitress brought Mallory's coffee and Andrew's hot chocolate and a short stack of pancakes.

"You certainly have your appetite back."

"Just a snack. If you get the waitress' attention have her bring me some milk, would ya?"

Andrew ate while Mallory watched. When he was done he turned to stare out the window. "Why wouldn't you let anyone visit me in the hospital? Sarah said they turned her away."

"Is that what you're so angry about? Dr. Hopkins makes the rules. Despite what your father thinks, she is an excellent doctor. After Jenny's murder, she saved my life. If she felt you weren't ready for visitors, I'm sure she was right."

Andrew continued staring out the window. Having his friends visit him here had brought back the great feelings of old times, the joy of camaraderie and familiarity that Mississippi would never give him. "I thought Dad has legal custody of me now."

"Nothing was ever formalized. You're seventeen years old: you can do what you want. Does this mean you're considering it?"

Andrew scuffed his feet against his seat's floor. "Maybe I have been unfair, blaming you for putting me away in that torture chamber. That don't mean I'm ready to move back in with you."

He stirred the few remaining pancake crumbs in the syrup. "Dad is my hero. He's always there for me; calm and determined. He thinks things out in a logical way. And when things go bad, like he loses his job, he just keeps going. Sure, he has his bad days. We all do. But mostly he's a rock."

Andrew watched Mallory clench her fists on the table. "Your father is no rock. He ran away, leaving me to deal with all those problems by myself."

"He moved on with his life. He had a job here 'til I messed up and caused him to lose it. Now I owe it to him to stay."

The waitress came by with Andrew's milk and refilled Mallory's coffee cup. She stirred in the creamer and sugar substitute. The silence stretched.

"What if your father came back to Chicago too?" Mallory asked tentatively. "He doesn't need to be down here. Your Uncle Peter could get him a job. We could be a family again."

Andrew looked at his mother, observing her hopeful face. "Have you talked to Dad about this?"

"Maybe he thinks he needs to be here because of you. If you were to tell him you wanted to move back it would make a big difference."

Andrew thought about his room at his mom's house with the old Star Wars posters, bookshelves stuffed with comics, and closet full of games. Life had been so happy before Jenny's death. Even during those last alcohol and drug filled months, his room had been a sanctuary where he could hide from the world's beatings.

"Things will never be the same, Mom. We'll never be a family again."

He saw his mother's eyes tear up as she grabbed a napkin and raised it to hide them. "Don't say that Andy. Don't ever believe it. We can go back. We can heal! People heal, don't they?"

Andrew thought about his stay in the psychiatric unit, about some of the kids there, how they had been through so much emotional trauma, some of them returning to the unit over and over. He thought about his father on Jenny's anniversary, and wondered if he'd ever heal. "Some people never will. As for that family thing, you get things worked out with Dad for both of us to move up there, and I'm your man. But if he ain't goin', I ain't either."

"You trust him completely don't you? You think he's some paragon of virtue? You just don't know what he did!"

Andrew eyed his mother speculatively. "Yeah? What?"

Mallory's head drooped. "I can't tell you. It's just … something you don't want to know."

He stood. "I'll wait outside."

He walked out of the Waffle House and stared down the beach towards the condo. About a mile away, it stood high above the old twisted oaks along the beach, its blue and white balconies looking like the towers of a sand castle. He wondered if his life in the condo had any permanence, or if the next wave would wash it away too.

Tuesday, December 30th

I leaned against the pantry door, watching Mallory cook, Andrew as much in the way as possible. She handed him a spoon and ordered him to blend the potatoes. Years had passed from his face, a childlike delight sparkling in his eyes.

"What was your favorite thing we did this week?" Mallory asked him.

He pulled the spoon out of the potatoes and licked it clean. "Hmm. Gotta be the trip to New Orleans. Those people on Bourbon Street were crazy! And gotta love fried oysters."

"How about you, Ricky?" Mallory asked. "What's been your favorite?"

"Lots to choose from."

Andrew shook the spoon in my direction. "Come on, Dad – gotta choose."

"Okay, then. I'll say my favorite was the walk through the Hard Rock Café. Man, Peter sure knows a lot about 70s hard rock music. He talked all evening about that Les guitar."

"I've always loved Hard Rock Cafés," Mallory agreed. "But my favorite was the Beauvoir tour."

She took the potatoes from Andrew and scraped them into a serving bowl. "Tomorrow we should sleep in because we'll want to stay up late for New Years. I'm planning supper for sevenish. Ricky, remember you have to stop by the liquor store tomorrow and pick up extra scotch and two bottles of champagne."

"I won't forget." I opened the pan lid to sniff the aroma from the asparagus. "De-lish-ee-ous!" I said, stretching out each syllable. I followed Mallory's instructions on draining and placing them in a bowl. Andrew held the plates up for Mallory to place one sizzling steak on each.

Once everything was on the table, Andrew grabbed his knife and fork, cutting off a large slab and releasing fine red juices to bubble into his potatoes. He chewed slowly, ecstasy registering on his face. After he swallowed he let out a long sigh. "Man, I've sure loved your cooking this trip. Jeez! This steak's great."

"It's important to eat right. When you two move back home ..."

"Mom!" Andrew interrupted.

She smiled at him. "Sorry, a slip of the tongue. I meant the next time either of you come visiting I'll be happy to provide a home cooked meal. Even if it's after you go away to college, Dear. You are still interested in the University of Chicago, aren't you?"

Andrew finished swallowing before answering. "I'd love to, Mom, but I gotta consider finances. I'm looking at full scholarship at Southern Miss."

I watched Mallory cut off a corner of her small steak and chew slowly. She had her eyes fixed on our son. "Your Uncle Peter told me he'd help you with the tuition. And you could save money by living at home. It wouldn't hurt to apply."

I spoke up quickly. "Whatever is best for you is definitely the right choice, Andy. Remember, though, USM is only an hour away. If you go there you could come home on weekends, meet with the friends you've made here. You wouldn't want to give up that full scholarship, would you?"

Mallory shook her finger at me. "And in Chicago he's got lots more friends and family. Think what living in Chicago would be like; so many opportunities, especially the jazz and politics you so love. Do you get to talk about politics much down here?"

"Not a bit. Travis told me he's on the Riverside debate team where they talk politics all the time. They won third place at a tournament."

"Does Gulfport High School have a debate team, Andy?" I asked.

He shrugged. "Don't think so. Travis named off the members of the Riverside High team – I knew 'em all."

"You'll be with everyone you know, Andy," Mallory said. "And once you're at U of C, we could lunch together. Now that I have my job back at Macys we'll both be downtown."

"You have your job back?" I asked in surprise. "When did that happen?"

"Just in time for Christmas rush. Oh, don't you just love the magic of Christmas; the sounds of carols and the smell of brand new merchandise? You should see the elaborate decorations this year; even with this stupid recession, it's the best ever." She put her hand on Andrew's arm. "Maybe you can set up the TV recorder for the Rose Bowl Parade New Year's morning? We'll view it later with a bowl of popcorn and some milk shakes. How does that sound?"

I watched my son, my heart aching at his joy. I had urged him to make up with his mother, but I had never thought I'd lose him to her. I wanted him to be happy ... but if he went to Chicago, would he be? Would I?

"Stop it, Mal. You know what just happened when he was up there."

Andrew snorted. "That's not fair, Dad. I know what I did wrong. And, anyway, Travis has gone straight now, so it's not going to happen again." He turned to his mother. "Not that I'm saying I'm going back."

"I was thinking of updating your room," Mallory said. "How about I replace those posters with some framed pictures? What do you think? You need a new bedspread and drapes for sure."

He grimaced. "Don't be messin' with my room."

She smiled, her eyes bright. "Okay. You should be thinking about it, anyway." She turned to me. "Don't you agree it would be better for him to stay with his mother instead of the Wilburns when he visits Chicago?"

I hesitated. "Last time …"

"Exactly! And he was with Peter and Celine." She stood. "Seems like it's about time for dessert. I have some chocolate ice cream for Andy, and for Ricky, peaches and cottage cheese."

I laughed. "I can still eat ice cream. I'm not fat."

Mallory batted her eyelashes at me. "Not a bit. You're still as sexy as the day we first made love."

"MOM!" Andrew groaned.

After dinner Andrew cleared the table and I did the dishes. When we finished, Mallory announced it was time to exchange Christmas gifts. Though it was now the day before New Year's Eve, she had insisted on waiting until Andrew and she were getting along. Clearly that time had come. I went into the bedroom where I had hidden her gift in my underwear drawer, and we gathered in the living room. Mallory handed each of us a beautifully wrapped package, each with a Macys' label. I tore off my wrappings to reveal a diamond tie pin.

"Tie pin?" I asked, sending a questioning look at Mallory. "When will I ever wear this?"

"When you come to work at the job Peter will find for you."

Andrew pulled a watch out of his package. "Wow! Look at all these dials!"

Mallory pointed to the different circles. "There's a stop watch, thermometer, barometer, and even a pedometer. You enter your stride length and it detects your arm motion to keep track of how far you've gone."

"Absolutely awesome!" He picked up the instructions and began working on the settings.

I pulled a small package from my pocket and handed it to Mallory. "Here. Merry Christmas."

She looked at it and then back in my face. "What I want for Christmas doesn't come in a box."

Indicating my tie pen, I said, "We don't have to like the gift to appreciate the intentions of the giver."

Mallory unwrapped a shapely turquoise brooch. Turning to the mirror, she held it just above her left breast. "Oh, it's gorgeous!" She turned from the mirror, her eyes glistening, and grabbed me in a big hug. She pulled back, placing her hands on either side of my head, kissing me hard on the lips.

My gift for Andrew was a $50 iTunes card. He had bought me a biography of Richard Daley, and for his mother he'd decided on a box of chocolates, perhaps a bit self-serving. She opened it and we each had a piece. Well, Andrew had four.

He stood and yawned. "I'm going to my room, maybe do some computer work."

As he walked past his mom, she grabbed him, kissing him on the cheek. "Good night, Andy. I love you."

He walked another ten feet, until he was almost out of sight behind the corner. I watched his foot half raised in preparation for another step.

Floating back to my ears like some sea gull's distant call came, "I love you too, Mom." He continued down the hallway and I heard his door click shut.

Mallory sighed. "You can't imagine how much I've longed to hear those words. Even if I get nothing else from this trip, hearing Andy say he loves me has made it all worthwhile. Thank you for inviting me, Ricky. That was *so* thoughtful."

I looked out towards the bedrooms. "You've certainly made up with Andy."

Mallory settled onto the couch and scooted to one side, indicating I could sit on the adjoining spot. I chose to settle into the armchair across from her.

"So are you seeing anyone, Ricky?"

I leaned back into the cushions. "Why do you ask?"

"Celine said you introduced her to a teacher, but you haven't mentioned her to me."

"Yes, one of Andy's teachers actually. We've been out a few times."

"Have you slept with her?"

I took a sip of my decaf. Mallory had made it from fresh ground, and it tasted delicious. "You and I are divorced. What I do in my private life is my own business."

Mallory nodded slowly. "I see. So how does she compare?"

I felt myself blush. "Really, Mallory."

She crossed and sat on my lap. She began unbuttoning my shirt, stroking my chest. "I bet she doesn't know how to please you like I do. We know each other's secrets, don't we? Really nice secrets." She finished my shirt and began with my belt buckle.

I stopped her. "Stop, Mal. This isn't right."

She leaned forward and licked my nose. "Maybe I can change your mind?"

I shook my head. "It wouldn't be a good idea."

"Are you certain?"

Once more she reached for my buckle and I grabbed her hand.

"Please," I whispered, her ear no more than six inches from my tongue.

She waited until I released her, and she stood. "Very well, Ricky." Staring at the bulge pushing against the front of my pants, she said, "You're not going to sleep very comfortably like that."

"I'll be okay."

"Missed opportunity."

I shook my head again.

"If you change your mind, the door will be unlocked." She bent down and kissed my forehead, before sashaying off to my bed. I listened carefully for the door to click. It was a long time in coming.

Wednesday, December 31st

I awoke, suffering muscles stiffened from five nights of couch sleeping. Mallory and Andrew's muffled voices penetrated the balcony's doors, and I lay still, watching them through the glass. Beyond them, menacing clouds hung heavy with promised sleet and hail.

I headed to the bedroom and did my forty-five minutes on the exercise bike. Grabbing some fresh clothes, I stripped for the shower. As I scrubbed, I reviewed the events of the previous night, proud that I'd resisted Mallory's advances. With a start I realized I hadn't talked to Sylvia since Christmas, a week ago. I finished my toilet, dressed, and grabbed my wallet and keys. In the living room, I found Andrew watching TV and Mallory in the kitchen.

"You want some breakfast?" she asked. I watched her check her watch. "Well, lunch really. It's nearly noon."

I took a sniff. "Nah, but I'll take a cup of that sweet-smelling coffee. I'm sort of eager to get to my errands."

Andrew looked up. "Can you drop me off at the Beau? I'd like to hang with Travis and Sarah."

"Sure. Mal, you want to come?"

"No, I'll stay here and prepare the food and clean the apartment. Now don't forget the liquor."

I laughed. "You've only reminded me five times."

I always enjoyed driving along the beach road, the openness of the water bringing a sense of infinite possibilities just beyond the horizon. Usually the beaches had dozens of bathers on a holiday like this, but with the temperature plummeting and the skies threatening, the sands were berefted.

I asked Andrew if he had thought more about his future.

"All the time," he assured me. Apparently he wasn't in the mood for talking because he plugged up his ears with his music earpieces. I glanced at him occasionally, but was comfortable just having him sit next to me. I dropped him off at the Biloxi casino and turned back, stopping at the grocery store, a liquor store, and then a drive-in for the ice.

When I reached the condo entrance I decided not to turn in, instead continuing on down the road towards Sylvia's house. When I pulled up into the circular drive the house had a haunted look. The tree's lights still blinked in the window, but all the colors were dulled by the gray day. As I sat in the car a drizzle began, and once out, I had to pull my jacket around me as I rushed up to the portico. No one answered my first ring.

I stamped my feet, trying to get the chill off; it seemed the temperature was dropping a degree every few minutes. The wind had picked up, and my pants' legs below my jacket were starting to get wet. I rang the bell again and tried the doorknob. It was locked.

I had just about decided to leave, figuring no one was home, when I heard Sylvia's voice penetrate from the inside. "What do you want?"

"What do you mean, what do I want? I came by to talk, of course. I miss you."

This didn't seem to bring any response. Out on the road the dust and dead leaves created small whirlwinds.

"Hey, I'm freezing out here," I called.

"I thought you damn Yankees were used to cold weather."

At least it was a response. I pressed my forehead against the door, calling loudly. "I want to talk to you. You expect me to shout through the door?"

"Six days without a word. And NOW you want to talk?"

I stepped back and leaned against one of the big white columns, trying to hide from the blowing rain. Why had I not called? Sure, this past week with Mallory and everyone had been fun. Heck, I'd been actually content for the first time since the tragedy. But I knew this pattern. Mallory would be sweet and loving and supportive, and abruptly change, becoming demanding and sarcastic. I had moved to Mississippi to get away from all the drama, and I intended to stick with that pledge.

In contrast, my two months of dating Sylvia had shown me how love could be fulfilling. With Sylvia I had a kindred soul, a woman who cherished history, one who supported me and made me feel proud. And making love, ah, that was so sweet. Not that Mallory was bad. She had been right in saying we knew each other's secrets. But for Mallory, it was often all for her, while with Sylvia, there seemed to be more sharing, more caresses than carnality.

I walked back to the door, cupped my hands against it, and shouted, "Sylvia, I love you!"

She cracked open the door, but kept the chain engaged. Eyes as stormy as the skies peered from deep shadows. Her mouth was taut, her frown tense. "Don't say it if you don't mean it," she whispered.

"Let me in, Sylvia. Please."

I watched her hesitate, and she shut the door slowly. I wondered if I'd hear the chain coming off, or the lock clicking back into place. After too many heartbeats, the chain clanked. She opened the door and retreated three feet, allowing me one step into the foyer. Handing me a towel, she shut the door softly.

A single lamp in the great room fought against the darkness. In my previous visits I had thought the minimal lighting romantic. Now it felt gloomy.

"Why should I believe you love me?" she demanded. "It seems to me you only want me on your terms. At other times I'm just in the way."

I slipped out of my jacket and scrubbed the wetness out of my hair, handing the towel back. She folded it neatly and set it on the floor beside her. I stared at it, trying to sort through my feelings, to find the right words.

"Sylvia, I'm not a poet. I can't tell you how my love is deeper than the ocean or higher than the moon. I can't promise you romantic vacations in Paris."

The hints of a grin pulled at her features. "I don't need those things, Rick. Well, maybe the trip to Paris, but I'll pay my own way."

"What the heck *do* you need?"

She pursed her lips, raising one hand to tuck that stray lock behind her ear. I'd seen her do it a dozen times, each creating an image of a young girl self-conscious at being so pretty.

"I need a man I can trust," she said. "Not some hero or poet, just a partner in life who will always have my needs foremost. I want a man who, when his friends talk me down, stands up in my defense, demands an apology, and then calls me immediately telling me that he loves me and needs to see me right away. Not days later. What do you think I've been going through these last few days, Rick? What could you possibly have been thinking?"

I hung my head. Her questions cut me with their truth. I got down on one knee before her. "Sylvia. I love you. I'm in a situation here, and I'm just trying to do my best. They'll all be gone soon, just four more days. Please. Bear with me."

"Get up," she ordered.

I rose slowly. We stood two feet apart, looking uncomfortably at each other. I stuck my index fingers in each side of my mouth and pulled my cheeks out in a silly face, giving her google eyes. She broke a tiny smile.

I stepped forward and she gave herself to my kiss, responding slowly at first, until giving into it with a passion that took my breath away. After she stopped kissing me, she grabbed me in a tight hug. Without heels her head pressed snugly against my chest.

"Oh, Rick. I needed this."

"Of course you did! We both did!" I grasped her, feeling her warmth penetrate into my heart. "Baby, I've missed you so much. It's been so strange with Mallory around."

"I can imagine! And I'm sure it's been particularly hard on Andy. He has such resentment towards his mother."

"Yeah, but he's making progress. On the way to bed last night he even told her he loved her."

Sylvia staggered back, her face blanched. "She's staying with you? You're sleeping with your ex-wife?"

"No! It's not ... I mean, she couldn't find ... I mean, it was really short notice." My tongue seemed stuck in its dry cavern. "I'm sleeping on the couch and ..."

She lifted one hand to block her view of my face. "I really don't care to discuss the details of your personal life." She yanked open the door and pointed. "Out."

I held out my hands, supplicating. "Sylvia, don't do this. I love you."

With face turned away, she commanded, "Out."

I stumbled across the doorjamb, turning when I had just barely cleared the threshold.

"You ... you're .... Maybe you might come to the New Year's Party at my house this evening? See for yourself there's nothing going on."

She glared at me. "When hell freezes over."

The door slammed, followed by the sounds of both deadbolt and chain.

***

I drove around the city a bit, not wanting to face Mallory. By the time I got back to the house it was nearly five. I parked on the third level near the elevator and grabbed the ice, taking three trips to bring everything to the landing. I loaded it all into the elevator, and at my floor, unloaded, taking another three trips to bring it all to the condo front door.

I still didn't feel up to facing Mallory so I took the ride back to ground level and walked out to the beach. The icy darkness fit my mood. Heavy winds lashed the normally placid waters into a fury. Though the rain had let off, the icy spray penetrated to my skin. I could only stand a few minutes of it.

As soon as I opened the door the sweet smell of Mallory's cooking enveloped me. I grabbed the ice and brought it with me as I followed the aromas into the kitchen. Swedish meatballs steamed in a stove pot. Dough and dogs for pigs in a blanket dotted the cutting board. Chili con queso crackled in a crock pot.

Mallory stopped stirring a fruit punch bowl to look me over. "Good God, Ricky. You look like a drowned fish!"

"I feel like one too." I stuck my finger into the crab dip, bringing it to my mouth. "Yummy. Looks like you've cooked enough for a small army."

"Just the seven of us, but that includes three teenagers." She looked at her preparations. "I bet most of this gets eaten. Did you get the liquor?"

"Of course. I left it just outside the door."

She laughed. "Celine had bet me you'd forget."

"What do you want me to do with the ice?" I held up the dripping bags.

"Stick it out on the balcony. It's practically freezing out there anyway."

I set the three bags out on the balcony, shuffling furniture to make room. A sudden gust knocked a shower of ice crystals off the railing, some of them finding my exposed neck. Chilly! Retrieving the other packages and settling onto the bar stool, I opened the first bottle of scotch. "Mal, hand me a glass and some ice, please."

She cocked her head. "How about waiting for the guests? They'll be here pretty soon."

"C'mon. A bit of bourbon will keep this cold from getting into my chest." I sneezed for emphasis. She dropped a few cubes into a glass and handed it to me, into which I poured a couple of fingers worth and slugged it down. Hit the spot. I poured a second one.

"Ricky. Really now."

I took a sip of the new drink. It felt almost as good as the first, providing a warm feeling working its way up my chest into my face. Mallory handed me a towel through the opening and I scrubbed my hair. She returned to her cooking and I watched her flit about. Throughout our marriage Mallory'd done all the cooking, except for the occasional backyard grill. Our marriage had worked well that way; division of duties. I was the repair man, she did the simple maintenance. She did the dusting and wiping, I did the vacuuming and scrubbing. But that was then, and now it was time to move on.

"It wasn't right for you to try to seduce me last night."

She glanced up at me before turning back to her work. "Honey, if I'd wanted to seduce you, you'd have been seduced. I was just teasing."

Mallory kept her back to me as she worked on the dough squares for the miniature hot dogs. I watched her buttocks dancing in the tight pants she wore. Man, I used to love that butt. That, too, was in the past. "I think it'd be better if you moved into a hotel."

She turned to me, her ruby lips upturned in perfect curves, white teeth in a fetching pattern. "Ricky, Darling. It's New Year's Eve. There aren't going to be any hotels available. Besides, this will be my sixth night here, only three to go. Seems silly to make me move now."

She came around the counter and nuzzled up to me. "Besides, Andy is enjoying having me here. Aren't you?" She started nibbling my neck, sending chills down my spine. I had to stand and back away to get her to stop.

I finished off the second drink and reached for the bottle but Mallory placed her hand on mine. "Why don't you go shower and dress? The liquor will be here when you get back."

I sneezed again and decided she was right. In the bathroom I stripped off my wet clothes, dropping them in the basket, and turned the shower knob to full heat. The steam blasted the chill away, leaving my skin luxuriously red. I stayed until the water heater ran out of hot water. Finally relinquishing the lost battle, I toweled dry. Most of the bathroom counter was covered with Mallory's potions and lotions, and I had to clear a spot to do my own toiletry.

I dressed. When I went over to the dresser to pick out my socks I spotted the photo on top. Andrew's smiling face shone bright, but this time I took out the photo and gently unfolded the crease. Jenny looked back at me, that happy innocence of two years ago frozen in time. I settled onto the bed, staring at the picture.

I don't know how long I sat. When I heard the knock on the door I stuffed the picture under the bed. "Who is it?"

Peter opened the door and came in. Indicating my bare feet he asked, "Forget how to put on socks and shoes?"

I shrugged and got up, returning to the dresser and pulling out some green ones. I settled back on the bed to pull them on.

"You okay, Buddy?"

I glanced up at him. "I suppose. Just thinking."

"Well, how about doing it out in the living room with your guests?"

"Pete, are you and Celine still as much in love as the day you met?"

He stroked his chin, looking me over before answering. "Nope."

"Nope?"

"Nope, we're much more in love than that, and it grows every day. You gotta nurture love, Rick. You and Mallory could do that."

"Pete ..."

"No, listen to me. You two have had a bad run, what with Jenny's death, and now Andy's problems. But that's all the more reason for you to come back to Chicago and give your marriage another chance. You two need each other."

I stared at myself in the mirror, patting down a half gray cowlick. It seemed only yesterday my hair was solid black. The one time I'd grown a beard Mallory had loved to stroke it. Damn, we'd been so much in love.

But that was all past. Now I had Sylvia on my mind. "I've moved on, Pete. I have a new residence and a new love interest. You know what they say? You can't go back home."

Peter leaned up against the wall, crossing his arms. "You're trying to tell me you're madly in love with a woman you've only known a few months, someone who you have nothing in common with? Rick. I met Sylvia. No offense, but she really doesn't stack up against Mallory."

I felt my face flush. "You've only met her the once, and you guys drove her off. I did love Mallory, I admit it. But now I'm in love with Sylvia and she ..." My voice trailed off and Peter looked at me quizzically.

"Trouble?" he asked, a fake innocence in his voice.

"She was pretty upset when she found out Mallory was sleeping here."

"Oh, the jealous possessive type, is she? Are you sure that's the kind of girlfriend you want? Was Mallory like that?"

"I never gave her any reason."

"So, what is it about Mallory you don't like? I'm just curious, 'cause you're certainly not giving her a chance. And meanwhile, there are lots of my friends who are interested in dating her. I've been holding off introducing her around, though she's quite a catch. Pretty, sexy, creative. Personally, I'd say if you don't grab this opportunity it's going to be lost forever."

I recalled the sixteen months between Jenny's death and my departure for Mississippi. They'd been awful, with screaming arguments, and Mallory's crying. But much of that was the grieving process. Apparently she had gotten through it.

"I can't go back to Chicago."

"Why not?"

"Well. For one thing, I don't have a job there."

"I'm pretty well sure I could help you get a job."

"You're pretty sure, but what if it doesn't happen?"

Peter flipped his hand, indicating ambivalence. "I'm fairly certain. But even if not, you'll be no worse off than you are now. I'd sure like to see you and Andy come back. Travis could use Andy's good influence, and I'd love more of those delicious steaks you grill."

I felt a joy beat in my heart. It beat once, and then, like a candle in a Gulf storm, extinguished. "I can't go back, Peter. Even if everything was perfect, even if Mallory and I were back in love, and even if you found me the perfect job, I still couldn't go back."

"And why not?"

"Because of what I did after the tragedy."

"What the hell was that?"

I looked up at him for just a moment, before burying my face in my hands. "I can't tell you Pete. Even you, my best friend of my whole life, even you I can't tell."

I took some slow deep breaths, gathering my aplomb. When ready, I reached down and picked up my shoes, holding them up for Peter to see.

"Here they are. You go on out and I'll join you in a moment."

"I think I'll just watch and make sure you haven't forgotten how to slip your foot in."

Peter supervised, I slipped and stood, and together we returned to the party where Peter poured us fresh drinks. The kids clustered around the TV playing a video game. Mallory had brought a photo album of some of the trips we'd taken as extended families, and the women made room for us around the kitchen table where they were cherishing the memories.

"Those sure were great times," Celine mused. "Remember the four of us cuddling up under blankets around the fire pit? Peter still swears he can roast the perfect marshmallow."

"You've all seen it." Peter made an 'oh' with his fingers and kissed it. "You are looking at the perfect marshmallow chef."

Mallory elbowed him. "Maybe so, but I'm the best cook at everything else."

Peter held up his hands. "True, true. Except for my spaghetti sauce, of course. My spaghetti sauce puts all others to shame."

"What? You need to stand up for me here, Ricky. Tell this imposter who makes the best sauce in the world."

I coughed theatrically into my fist. "Actually, my spaghetti sauce is the best."

"Oh come on now," Mallory complained. "Yours comes out of a jar for heaven's sakes."

"But I spice it up. Okay, here's what we'll do. Let's let the kids decide." I called out to the teenagers. "Can you kids come over here a minute?"

Andrew pushed some buttons and put the game on pause. "You want all three of us?"

"Please. Come on over here. We're taking a survey."

The three stood and approached warily.

"What kind of survey?" Andrew asked.

As the children gathered around I explained. "As you know, there is an art to creating a great spaghetti sauce. We're looking to you three as judges, sort of like American Idol. You need to judge whose spaghetti sauce is the best. The contestants are Peter, Mallory, and myself." I turned to Celine. "You want in on this Cici?"

"No. And don't call me that."

I saluted her with my glass of scotch. "Sure. Sorry." Turning back to the teens, I continued, "You may use any criteria you choose, and we want a vote from each of you. Sarah, as the young lady present, you may go first."

Sarah blushed as her hands covered her mouth. "Oh I wouldn't dare choose one of you. That would be rude."

Peter guffawed. "You take yourself too seriously. This is all in fun."

Mallory nodded her agreement. "Really. Make your answer funny."

"As long as you're sure no one's feelings will be hurt. Hmm. Well, I have had some great spaghetti sauces from each of your kitchens." Sarah grabbed a bit of her hair and twisted it, directing it into her mouth for a moment. "Okay. I remember on Travis's seventeenth birthday party we were all starving while waiting for Uncle Peter to tell us his sauce was ready. At around five o'clock he said it was almost ready, but needed another hour or so. At six o'clock he sampled a spoonful, and begged for one more hour. We agreed, but when seven o'clock rolled around and he started to speak we booed him down. And you know what? By the time we finally got to eat we were so hungry that everyone said it was the best sauce we had ever tasted in our lives!"

Peter lifted his arms in triumph. "One vote for me, and truer words never spoken. The key to a great sauce is the simmer, and, of course, starving your judges first. I appreciate your vote and bow to your wisdom, my dear. Later I'll slip you a twenty-dollar bribe."

She curtsied. "No bribe necessary."

I held up a finger. "The score stands Peter ahead with one vote, Mallory and I tied for second with zero. It's time to hear from our next clearly impartial judge. Travis, tell us your decision."

Travis stroked his chin, his brow wrinkled. Only his grin challenged the solemnity of his expression. "This matter requires 'much due consideration,' as my dad would say. Without question all three sauces have merit, what with the spiciness of Uncle Rick's, the chunky vegetables in Aunt Mallory's, and the meaty flavoring of my dad's. And so, in the spirit of the holidays, I must award one third point to each of your sauces. They are all awesome and all deserve to win the prize!"

"Spoken like the true son of a lawyer," I shouted. "Very well. The score stands at Peter ahead with one and a third, with Mallory and me tied still, now at one third vote each. It's time for our last judge to step to the plate."

I put a hand on each of Andrew's shoulders and stared into his face. "You have an important decision thrust upon you today, my boy. On your word alone rests the valued award of Best Spaghetti Sauce Cook. Consider wisely. I'll say no more."

I watched Andrew's face. All the fun he'd been having with his friends showed in his glowing cheeks and sparkling eyes. I again wondered if I was making the right choice keeping him here.

He put on a mischievous smile. "One day last summer I had forgotten my lunch and Mrs. Perkins heated up some spaghetti she had brought from home and shared it with me. Man, it was to die for. I have to give Mrs. Perkins my vote."

The room grew deadly quiet.

Mallory snarled. "How dare you bring up that whore who's trying to steal your father from me?"

Andrew's face blanched. "Whore? You're calling Mrs. Perkins a whore? Dad!" He turned to me, but I just bit my lip, turning my gaze to the floor. "Dad? Why don't you say something? Why don't you defend her?"

Sarah and Travis exited the kitchen for the safety of the living room. Andrew put his hand on my shoulder. I looked up slowly. "She's angry with me, Andy. I don't know where I stand."

."What do you feel, Dad? Do you love her or not?"

I stared into my son's eyes, seeking the answer that could only come from my own heart. "Yes. I do love her." I turned to the adults. "In fact, I invited her to join us at the party tonight."

Mallory dropped her glass on the ceramic floor, sending shattered pieces skittering across the room. "You invited that bitch to our party? Surely she had the graciousness to decline?"

I glared at Mallory. "She declined all right. But maybe I should just give her a call right now and re-invite her."

"Oh crap," Mallory said, turning to Celine and Peter. "He's gone off the deep end again. I think I'll have another drink and go sit in the living room with the kids. Anyone care to join me?"

Celine glared at me. "Let's clean this up first. Everyone out of the kitchen, and be careful not to step on glass. Rick, where's your dustpan and broom?"

When I left the kitchen I saw Andrew standing in the hall with his back to the crowd. I walked over and put my hand on his shoulders. "Thanks for encouraging me, Andy."

Sarah and Travis came up too. "That was quite the scene," Travis said.

Sarah nodded. "It's a good thing Mrs. Perkins isn't coming. Seems like it would be very uncomfortable."

"Well I think she should have a chance to defend herself," Andrew said. He took out his cell phone. "In fact, I think I'll call her right now."

Travis guffawed. "Really? That's grand. I was wondering if you still had a sense of humor hidden somewhere, Andy. Glad to see it surface."

"You think it'd be funny if she shows up?" Sarah asked him.

"Hilarious. Wouldn't miss it for the world. Tell her we ALL want her to come."

I felt certain Sylvia wouldn't be visiting. But I sure didn't think it would be hilarious if she did.

I stood by as Andrew called and could just hear Sylvia's voice, though not make out her words.

"Well, I sure'd like to see you," Andrew said, before disconnecting.

We returned to the living room where we resumed our partying. Outside the wind howled and, for a time, hail bounced off the windows. Mallory had been right about the portions, most of everything was eaten as the evening went on, though it seemed like there'd still be enough leftovers for the next day or two. Andrew found a New Year's trivia game on the Internet and we formed two teams, having a grand time, laughter echoing off the walls.

***

Aunt Frances stood watching Sylvia pour herself another drink. She splashed in the vodka, more than a shot, and the spillage, before adding orange juice and stirring.

"How many of those have you had?" Aunt Frances asked.

Sylvia took a healthy gulp. "Doesn't matter. Itsa …" she paused to separate the consonants back with the appropriate vowels. "It is a *known* fact that orange juice counters the effect of the vodka."

Aunt Frances eyed the glass. "No one really cares if you actually last until midnight."

Sylvia shrugged. "Okay. Maybe I'll take a coffee break." She glanced at her watch. "It's only nine o'clock. I could use a little caffeine."

"Why don't we go into the kitchen and we'll each have a cup?"

Sylvia allowed her to lead through the swinging doors to their bright kitchen, perfused with the aroma of biscuits. Sylvia slumped into a comfortably padded wingback, leaning her head on the palms of her hands. The smell of the coffee Aunt Frances brewed made Sylvia look up, and in doing so, she saw Aunt Frances pouting her lips.

"What bee's stuck in your bonnet?" Sylvia asked.

"You want to tell me about what happened between you and Richard?"

Sylvia shrugged and took a sip of her coffee. "His ex-wife came to visit."

"And ...?"

Sylvia ran her hands through her hair, squeezing her eyelids closed in hopes of holding back her tears. "They're sleeping together."

Aunt Frances tut-tutted, her ostrich feathered hat shimmering in the track lighting. "I'm so sorry, Darlin'. Are you sure?"

"She's staying in the condo. What else can I think?"

Aunt Frances took a sip from her coffee, setting it down daintily on its saucer. "So the ex-wife comes down to fetch her hubby back home. Do you think he'll move back to Chicago?"

Sylvia shrugged, her eyes red, a smudge of mascara forming at each edge. "I don't know. I don't even know what I hope for. On the one hand, if he left, it would be final. I could go on with a clear conscience. But on the other hand, oh Hell, it would just break my little heart."

Sylvia sobbed on her aunt's shoulder until her tears couldn't flow any more. She pulled back and reached for a napkin. "Look. I got mascara on your dress."

"Don't worry about it, Child. Baking soda will get it. Sit back down and tell me everything."

Sylvia settled into her chair, relaxing in its leather embrace. She closed her eyes and grasped her hands in her lap. A deep sigh seemed to dispel the alcohol, opening up her mind to her heart. Her voice drifted across the space, across the years, as visions of Gus and then Michael left their ghostly touches.

"I had finally begun to believe again," she said. "I had this dream that Rick, Andy, and I were living together, like a real family. Andy would be home from college on weekends, and we'd work on his homework together, and take little trips to local historical sites. Did I mention he's likely to receive a full scholarship at Southern? That's hardly an hour away."

She smiled through her tears. "For years this most treasured dream of sharing my life with someone again was like a tiny seed, buried deep in my heart, safe from the freeze. Over the last month or two, letting myself fall for Rick, I felt the sun come out, that the world was warming in anticipation of spring. And now winter has set in again, a blizzard named Mallory who's suffocating my hopes."

She sighed and stared at the window where a cold rain beat against the frosty panels. Her words drifted there and echoed back from the threatening world. "I had so hoped to enjoy a beautiful spring."

The phone rang and Aunt Frances grabbed it. "It's for you," she said, handing it over.

"Hello?" Sylvia said. "Andy?"

Aunt Frances watched, her face questioning.

"No, Honey. I don't think I'd be welcome."

She hung up with a sigh.

"What did he want?" Aunt Frances asked.

"Andy asked me to come to the New Year's Eve party."

Aunt Frances tilted her head, a smile pulling at the corners of her lips. "And?"

"I have half a mind to just show up and tell that ex-wife off! You know what? Rick invited me too."

"He did?"

"This very morning!" She turned to her aunt with a triumphant smile. "I'm going to do it!"

"That's my girl."

Sylvia laughed. "I may need some fortification."

"Coffee or vodka?"

"Vodka. Didn't I just make myself a drink?"

"You left it at the bar, Darlin'. If you're drinking, I better drive."

"What? I wouldn't hear of it. We have a house full of guests!"

"They can take care of themselves. Besides, they're old fuddy-duddies. Half of them will be asleep by eleven. Come on, I wouldn't miss this for the world. Run upstairs and fix your war paint, girl. We're going into battle!"

A short time later, the rain pummeled their car as Aunt Frances negotiated the streets.

"You know," Sylvia mused, staring out the window at the nearly indistinguishable landscape. "I told him I wouldn't come to the party unless hell froze over."

Aunt Frances reached over to pat her hand. "Well it's raining like hell and it's beginning to freeze over."

Sylvia continued to stare solemnly out the window. "I reckon it was meant to be."

***

I glanced at my watch, stood, and stretched. "Two hours to midnight. I'm ready for another drink. Anyone else want one?"

"I'll take a refill," Peter said, holding up his glass, which I took.

Celine stood too. "I'll get another wine. How about you, Mallory?"

"Please." She held up her glass for Celine.

"How about me?" Travis asked. "I'm almost eighteen. Surely that's legal in Mississippi?"

"Nope, twenty-one," I said.

Peter said, "I don't think it would hurt for the kids to have a sip of champagne at midnight, if it's all right with everyone else."

I glanced at Andrew who looked up hopefully. "I suppose that wouldn't hurt anything." Celine followed me into the kitchen.

"That finishes off this bottle," she reported, draining the last drops into her glass. She retrieved a fresh one from the refrigerator and handed it to me, along with the corkscrew. "Please?"

"No problem," I said, working the instrument and extracting the cork. I handed Celine the bottle and returned to fixing the drinks for Peter and me. Though I'd taken a buzz early with the bourbon, the shower had cleared my head, and I'd been limiting myself tonight. No sense in taking chances, just in case Mallory tried that seduction routine again.

The Chivas bottle seemed light. Holding it up to the kitchen bulb, I discovered it two thirds empty. I looked over at Peter, but he didn't seem that drunk. Maybe he just held it well?

"It's good to see Travis so happy," Celine said, interrupting my thoughts.

"Hmm? Yeah, Andy too."

"Ever since the accident Travis has been fighting depression. According to his counselor it's a normal reaction both to the grief process and to being without your closest friends. I imagine Andy went through the same thing when you moved him down here, away from everyone he knew."

I took a sample taste of my drink, frowned, and splashed in more of the Chivas. "Yeah. He was pretty sad at first, but he seems to have made the adjustment. Winning the state championship has sure made a difference in his life."

Celine sipped her wine and eased herself up to sit on the counter. "Now that's over, what's next?"

My attention was drawn to her diamond earrings sparkling in the overhead lights, accented by a playful toss of her head. I wondered how much those pretty pieces had cost? Probably more than I used to make in a month back in Chicago. A sparkling broach hung next to her deep cut neckline. I tried to remember what she'd asked.

"What?"

"Pay attention here. We're talking about our sons and their futures."

"Well, Andy's future seems pretty straight forward. He'll stay here 'til he graduates and then take that scholarship at Southern."

Celine stretched her legs, rocking them a little. Both the Adams girls had those legs that just wouldn't quit. In sheer stockings, they seemed magazine perfect. Her little black dress pulled up high on her thighs and with those gams spread just a tad, I forced myself to look at her face.

"Rick, it's not fair for you to keep Andy down here away from all his friends. It's not just Travis and Sarah, but the dozens of kids he's known all his life. I'm asking you for his sake, as well as Travis's. You've had him down here for a semester and he's proven himself and he's kept you company. Now it's time to let him come home."

I shook my head. "It's not good for him up there, Celine. You know what happened last time. And that was only last month."

"Things have changed since then. It's a whole new year. Personally, I think you're a fool to give up Mallory. She's the best thing that ever happened to you. But, if you're determined to stay here, please give Andy the courtesy to graduate with his friends. It's something he'll remember the rest of his life."

I looked out at Andrew, laughing and playing. I didn't want to believe that Celine was right. "He told me just last month he wanted to stay here."

"Maybe it's time to ask him again," Celine suggested

"How about, instead, you drop the subject, Cici? This is a party."

She snorted, hopped off the counter, and slithered back to the living room with the two glasses of wine. I finished my drink, poured another, and followed her, handing Peter's glass over. "How many have you had?" I asked.

He looked at me puzzled. "Three or four. Why?"

"We were just talking about New Year's resolutions," Sarah said. "Mine is to get a part in the Chicago Playhouse sometime this year."

"How can you make that kind of resolution?" Travis asked. "You don't have any control over who they choose."

"Whom," Celine murmured, but everyone ignored her.

Sarah stood, spun a couple of pirouettes, and motioned for applause. We all obliged enthusiastically, with Travis and Andrew adding hoots and cheers. "You see, Travis, I'll make it on my talent."

Travis shrugged. "Don't want to bust your bubble, but it's not what you can do; it's who you know." He turned to Peter. "Isn't that right Dad?"

Peter picked up a napkin and wiped off the powder from the sugar cookie he'd been eating. "It's both."

Sarah said, "You may be right. There are tons of people with talent who'd like to be on stage, so I'll need to work extra hard to prove I deserve a chance. I've been hanging around the Playhouse after school, trying to make friends. I'm going to make it, you'll see."

"I'm sure you will," Celine agreed. "You have tremendous talent."

"Thanks, Aunt Celine. So who's going to be next with their resolutions?" Sarah asked. "Uncle Peter, how about you?"

Peter gave a thumbs up. "Sure. Mine is easy. My goal is to do fifty-million dollars in business this year."

"Fifty million! Wow!" Andrew said.

"Don't be that impressed," Celine said. "He only receives a portion."

Andrew replied, "Even a small part of fifty million is a heck of a lot."

The doorbell rang, bringing abrupt silence to the room.

"Oh my God," Mallory said. "It can't be her."

"I'll get it," Andrew said, jumping up. He opened the door to Sylvia and Aunt Frances and turned, announcing "Hey everybody! Mrs. Perkins is here with a friend."

I hurried to the door. "Hello?" Her face lay hidden from me as Andrew helped her out of her coat.

When Sylvia turned, she broke into a big smile. "Why, hello Rick. Happy New Year."

Delighted, I leaned forward and kissed her. She tasted of alcohol. I stepped to Aunt Frances and kissed her cheek. "I'm so glad you could come. Let me introduce you around."

I indicated Andrew. "This is my son."

"A pleasure. Sylvia has told me so much about you." Aunt Frances held out her hand palm down. Andrew stared at it in confusion.

"You're supposed to kiss it," I explained, and he did.

I led them into the living room and Travis and Sarah walked up.

"Hi, Mrs. Perkins. Welcome to our party," Travis said, offering his hand. Sylvia took it graciously, and Sarah's that followed.

Sarah said, "Nice to see you again, Mrs. Perkins."

Sylvia wobbled a moment, grabbing the wall. She kicked off her high heels, knocking them against the hallway door near my feet.

Indicated the children, she said, "Aunt Frances, I'm pleased to introduce Sarah Ryan and her cousin Travis Wilburn, two of Andrew's close friends from Chicago. Sarah, Travis, this is my aunt, Frances Hewes."

"A pleasure to meet you, Mrs. Hewes."

"Please call me Aunt Frances. It's such a pleasure to meet young people with manners."

Sylvia swept her arm in the direction of the Wilburns and Mallory. "These others I'm not going to introduce."

Aunt Frances walked up to the three adults and offered her hand. "My Southern manners will-out. Please allow me to introduce myself. I'm Frances Hewes, Sylvia's aunt."

Peter reached forward immediately and shook it. "Nice to meet you. I'm Peter Wilburn. Rick and I have been friends practically our whole lives."

"Ah, lifelong friends. How nice. And related too?"

"Yes, through our wives," Peter said, indicated Celine.

Aunt Frances offered Celine her hand, who gave the fingertips the barest squeeze.

"Celine Wilburn."

Aunt Frances turned to Mallory. "And you are?"

Mallory ignored her, walking around the elderly lady and standing a few inches from Sylvia's face. "What the hell are you doing here?"

Sylvia turned her back on her. "I don't believe we've been formerly introduced."

Mallory stepped up and leaned into her ear. "Don't give me that crap. I'm Ricky's wife and you're the hussy trying to steal him."

Sylvia turned to me. "Did you know you have a visitor here who's hallucinating? She claims to be your wife. My understanding is you don't have a wife."

I looked from one to the other, ending my focus on Sylvia. "That's right, I don't."

Mallory glared at Sylvia. "You need to leave. You're not welcome."

Sylvia's eyes shone as cold as the icicles forming on the porch eaves. "Both Rick and Andrew invited me. As they are the two residents of this home, I certainly feel welcome. Did either invite you?"

Mallory turned to me. "Ricky, this is impossible. She's ruining our party. Please ask her to leave."

I glanced at the Wilburns. Peter's face held a bemused smile, while Celine's was statue flat. Turning back to Mallory I said, "Sylvia is my date."

"And how long have you been dating?"

I counted on my fingers. "We first went out the middle of last month. So, it's been six weeks."

Mallory glared at me. "Six. Weeks. You've been dating her six weeks? How could that possibly compare to almost thirty years of marriage?"

I smiled. "It compares very nicely. Sylvia's here as my guest, and here she'll stay."

Mallory harrumphed and walked away towards the kitchen. "Well, if she's staying I'm going to have another glass of wine." She poured herself a full tumbler and gulped half of it down. She refilled the glass, grabbed the bottle, and brought it with her.

Travis and Andrew brought extra chairs from the kitchen and Aunt Frances settled into one. Sylvia asked, "Aren't you going to offer us something to drink, Rick?"

"Of course. What would you like?"

"I've been having screwdrivers."

"Coming right up. Something for you Aunt Frances?"

"Coffee would be lovely. A teaspoon of sugar and a dollop of cream, please."

I carried myself off to the kitchen to make their drinks. From there I heard Sarah speak and I looked through the pass-through window to watch. "We were just talking about New Year's Resolutions. Would either of you like to tell us your New Year's Resolution?"

She looked at Sylvia who shook her head. "Maybe in a bit." She turned and waved at me in the window. "Rick? Make mine a double."

Aunt Frances held her finger to her face as she considered. "Youngun's nowadays talk about saving the world, global warming and the like. I remember when I was your age; our resolutions were more on how to survive. I grew up in the Great Depression, when we lived on hardtack and collard greens. We worried more about getting through the winter than about New Year's resolutions."

She paused and looked around the room. "Oh my. Listen to me carry on. You shouldn't let an old woman ramble. I look back on my years and have few regrets. My resolution is to enjoy to the fullest the time I have left."

"I'll drink to that," Peter said, finishing off his scotch. "I'm heading to the kitchen for a refill and some food. Would you like something to eat, Aunt Frances? We have a table full of goodies."

She shook her head, and Peter went off, passing me as I returned with the ladies' drinks. I handed Aunt Frances her coffee and Sylvia her glass before settling back into my armchair. I watched Sylvia down hers.

"Who wants to go next?" Sarah asked.

Travis spoke up. "I criticized Sarah for having a resolution that depended on other people's choices, but mine is similar. I'd like to win a debate tournament. I've done the research, I just need to sharpen my speaking style. The next tournament is January 10th at Buffalo Grove. If I can win a tournament or two, that should chinch my acceptance into U. of Chicago."

"Admirable ambition, Travis," Celine said. "I remember watching your father at a debate tournament once." As Peter came back into the room, she called to him. "Remember that, Peter? You were young and thin and so sure of yourself."

"I still am." He settled back on the couch next to her and she lay her head on his shoulder.

"How about you, Aunt Mallory?" Sarah asked. "What are your plans for the New Year?"

Mallory took another gulp of her wine and stared at the tumbler. She'd finished half of it and took a pause to fill it to the top. Standing, she walked to the patio window where the rain had finally stopped. She looked out into the darkness of the night, the unseen future echoing the bleakness of the past.

"Resolution?" she mused. "I want everything to be like it once was, the happiness of a familiar home, the comfort of my husband and son. I just want my family to be together again."

Celine came up and stood next to her, grasping her sister's hand. "As Travis pointed out, sometimes our resolutions can only be accomplished by the willingness of others." She turned to me and asked, "Are you willing to help Mallory with hers?"

I stood and took the last swallow of my drink. "I'm sorry, Celine. I've made other plans. My resolution is to get this smelting plant up and running. My life is in Mississippi now, not Chicago."

Mallory spun from the window and pointed one red-nailed finger at me. "You're not going to be anything but a failure here. Give it up Ricky. Give it up and come home."

The faint tones of the wind chimes being tossed by the storm pervaded the otherwise quiet room. Sylvia stepped up to me and I pulled her into my arms. The alcohol had her Southern drawl stretching her words.

"Ah believe in Rick. Ah know if he puts his mind to this project, he'll get it done. Maybe Ah haven't known him as long as you others, but Ah have confidence in him. Ah think he can accomplish most anything he puts his mind to."

Mallory tilted her head back and chortled. "You'd be surprised what Ricky is capable of. I'm dying to reveal his secrets. Just dying."

Celine squeezed her arm. "Don't say anything you might regret."

I scoffed. "You think you can control me by threats, Mal? Someday I'm going to ask this lady to marry me!"

I bent towards Sylvia who gazed up at me wide-eyed. "Marry?"

Mallory drank the rest of her wine and pushed Celine away. She staggered up to us, looking down into Sylvia's face. "You think he's Mr. Wonderful don't you? Is that what you think? Well he's not. He's eee-vil." She stretched out the 'e' in evil, creating a long moaning sound.

Sylvia leaned against me for support. "If he's so bed," she paused to correct her speech. "So bad. Ah'm saying, if Rick's so bad, why do you want him back? Huh? Answer me THAT if you can, Missy!"

Mallory reached over to the wine bottle, snagged it from the coffee table, and took a large gulp. She held it out in front of her and Sylvia grabbed it, taking a large draught too. "Well?" Sylvia demanded.

"He's done an awful thing, that's what," Mallory said, struggling to keep her balance.

"Awful?" Sylvia leaned away from me, looking me in my face. Her pupils danced wildly. "What did you do, Honey?"

I shook my head. "Shut up, Mallory. You're a despicable drunk. Always have been."

"Yeah?" she screamed, shaking her fist. "At least I'm not a murderer!"

"Mallory!" Celine yelled.

"A what?" Andrew, who had been lying down against the couch, mesmerized at the exchange, jumped to his feet. "What did you say, Mom?"

Mallory turned to look at him, and her mouth dropped open. "I … I didn't say anything." She made her way back to the couch and collapsed into it, burying her face in her hands.

Sylvia pushed away from me, her face gaunt. I couldn't meet her gaze. She stepped back. "A murderer? You're a murderer?"

Andrew came up in front of me. "What the hell is she talking about, Dad? You're no murderer. Tell everybody."

"Ah, she's just drunk," Travis said.

Andrew walked over to his mother, reaching down to touch her shoulder. "Mom, is that right? You're just drunk, right? Dad never killed anybody, right?"

She looked up at him slowly, and then dropped her head back in her hands. "Ask him, not me."

Andrew strode the two steps back. "What's going on?"

I stared into my son's eyes. "Let it go, Andy. Please."

Sylvia pulled on my arm. "No. We need to know. What's she talkin' about?"

I stepped towards the window where I could see their faces mirrored in the glass, all eyes watching my back. Staring out at the deep black, my mind drifted across the waters, imagining other cities, other states, even other countries where people were celebrating the coming of the New Year. They partied. They laughed. Their troubles washed away.

My troubles would never wash away. No matter how many New Years passed, no matter how much alcohol I consumed, no matter how much water washed onto the shore. "Jenny, oh my precious Jenny. You were the one who was murdered. Not Rod-Rod. He was merely punished for his crime. That's all. Just punishment."

I turned from the window, looking at my guests without seeing them. When I spoke it was to one not seen, one now dead two years. "An eye for an eye. A tooth for a tooth. You've been revenged. Now you can rest in peace."

The ensuing silence was shattered by Andrew's wail. "You killed Jenny's murderer? Dad! How ... how could you murder someone?"

I stepped towards him, but faltered on seeing the abhorrence in his face. "Andy, you have to understand."

"Understand? There's nothing to understand! I trusted you, believed in you. You were my role model. Now I find out you're a murderer? I ... I've got to get out of here."

"Wait!" I pleaded, but Andrew ignored me, running back to his room to come out with his coat.

"Travis," Peter ordered. "Go! Stick with him and make sure he's okay."

"I'll go too," Sarah said and jumped to her feet. The two hurried to the coat closet and retrieved their jackets. As Andrew tried to push past them on his way to the door, Travis grabbed his arm. "We're going with you."

Andrew shook his head. "I don't need you."

Sarah placed her hand on his other arm. "Please, Andy."

He stared at her blankly. She stood on tiptoe and kissed him gently. He blinked, shrugged, and held the door open for them. It slammed behind them.

Sylvia had her back to me. "Aunt Frances, could we leave now? I'm not feeling well."

Aunt Frances stood and waved at Peter and Celine. "I apologize for our hasty exit, but under the circumstances, I'm sure you'll understand." Sylvia took her arm and led her to the coat closet. I stood from my crouch on the armchair and called out. "Wait, Sylvia. Please."

She stopped just before the door. "I gave you my love, Rick – but you've been one disaster after another. When you talked about forgiving you for something ... well ... I had no idea! We have nothing more to talk about Rick. I don't expect to hear from you again." She spun away, hesitated, and bounced her last word off the door. "Never." She left the door open, the cold air rolling in.

Aunt Frances buttoned her coat, draped her scarf around her neck, and donned her black leather gloves. Just before leaving she threw me a last wave. "It was a most interesting evening, Richard. Good night." The door's click brought a striking silence.

I sprawled in the armchair; my face drooped into my hands. Peter and Celine stood at the window, holding each other tightly and looking out into the dark.

Mallory rose slowly and headed for the kitchen. I heard her pull another wine bottle out of the refrigerator and pop the cork, refilling her tumbler and taking a long drink.

"I told you she'd ruin the party," she said. "I told you so."

Sarah: Wednesday, December 31st

Sarah followed the two boys into the elevator, and out to the parking garage. "I didn't know you had your own car," she said.

Andrew held up a set of keys. "Dad's. You don't have to come."

Sarah snatched them from him. "You're too upset and the roads are icy. I'll drive." She climbed in behind the wheel, buckling her seatbelt. Andrew sat shotgun, and she insisted he buckle his too. Travis took the back and refused to buckle his, leaning forward to talk with them.

She started up the Camry, drove it down the ramps, and nursed it out onto the icy street. "Where to?" she asked.

"Turn right out of the driveway," Andrew answered. "We're heading to Devonne's New Year's party. At least it's somewhere to go."

Travis held up a thermos. "How about some scotch?"

"Travis!" Sarah exclaimed with disgust.

Andrew took it from him and sniffed. "Never had scotch before. Where'd you get it?"

"I took it from the bottle on the bar. Hey, Dad said I could drink tonight."

Andrew took one more sniff and handed it back. "Nah. I'm going to stay straight."

Sarah was glad the freezing rain had scared most of the other traffic off the road. She eased the car to a stop at the light. "How about we just head over to Waffle House? Or better yet, back to the Beau? We could go up to my room and watch TV."

"Heck no," Travis said. "My parents are going to be coming home soon and I want to celebrate."

Andrew agreed. "I really need to get away."

"You sure you don't want some of this?" Travis asked, holding out the canister again. Andrew took it and tried a small sip. "Yuck! How do people drink this stuff? It's awful."

Travis laughed. "Dad says it's an acquired taste. I plan to acquire some tonight." He took the thermos back and Sarah watched in the mirror as he took a gulp before closing it up.

She followed Andrew's directions to the Devonne homestead, where they found a score of cars parked in the yard. Colored bulbs blinked on all the columns, lights blazed in every window. She pulled on the gloves she'd removed during the car ride over.

"So what are you going to say to all these adults?" Sarah asked. "You know they're going to want to know why you're arriving at almost midnight without your parents."

"We're not going in the main building yet," Andrew explained. "There's an out-building, sort of a playhouse in the backyard where the kids our age hang out. Or at least, they did at the last party. Let's go there first."

Sarah walked gingerly behind the boys as they made their way across the icy lawn and around the path to the back building. Its few windows glowed dimly through their fog covering. Soul music drifted out through the walls. As they approached the door Sarah stopped abruptly, grabbing Andrew's arm.

"Stop. Don't you smell that?"

"What?" He stood still and took a sniff. Travis did as well.

"I smell the funny cigarettes," Travis said, his face breaking into a big grin. "And I thought I was going to have a straight New Year's Eve."

Sarah grabbed both their arms and tried to pull them back. "This isn't a good idea, Andy. Let's just go."

He stomped his feet. "It's freezing out here. Where do you think we should go? For a walk on the beach?"

"Anywhere else."

Andrew shook his head. "I'm not going to get stoned. I can control myself."

Travis shook her arm loose. "Come on," he said. "If we find we don't like it once we get inside we can always leave."

She followed them into the little clubhouse, coughing out her first breath of the smoky air. A space heater's glow wavered through the haze while a boom-box played mournful tunes. Three teenage African-American boys sprawled around a table, which held bottles of alcohol and a bong. She held her nose against the stink of sweat and pot.

"Hey, Andy," Lebron called. "Your friends cool?"

"Sure," Andrew said. "This is my best friend from Chicago, Travis, and his cousin Sarah. They're visiting for the holidays. This is Lebron, and Jamerion from my track team. I don't know the other kid."

Through the haze Sarah saw the other boy raise a hand. "Rand'ee. Waz up, Bro'?"

"Pull up a place on the floor," Lebron said. "We're just about to load the pipe. Oh, I remember. You don't do this, right?"

Sarah pulled his arm. "Please, Andy. Let's get out of here."

"I need to get my mind off of what happened tonight," he insisted, removing her hand. He pulled out his cell phone. "It's eleven thirty. I'll set the alarm for one minute to midnight. We'll celebrate the New Year here and afterwards we'll go into the main house. Okay?"

She closed her eyes and dropped her head. "This sucks. You shouldn't treat your girlfriend this way."

They settled on the floor, Andrew and Travis at the table, with Sarah sitting behind them, her back against the wall. She tucked her legs under her, pulling her jacket around them. Her stockings had gotten wet during the walk across the yard and now her feet ached.

Lebron offered Travis a hit from the bong.

"You know you can't do that," Sarah called. "You're being drug tested."

Travis glanced her way and then back at the pipe. "School doesn't start for another six days. It'll be out of my system by then, right? What's one hit going to hurt?"

She watched him take in a long deep breath of the hallucinating smoke and hold it for what seemed like forever. He let it drift away in little smoke trails dancing from his nose followed by a slight cough.

"Oh, that's good stuff!"

Lebron laughed. "Mississippi grown! Second to Hawaii as the biggest pot producing state in the country."

Travis took a gulp from his thermos, wiped off the top, and offered it to Lebron. "You want some Chivas Crown Royal?"

Sarah saw Lebron's eyes flash. "I always wanted to try that." He lifted it to his mouth and took a gulp. His face turned sour, followed by a forced smile. "That's … that's great."

Andrew and Travis laughed at him. "It's an acquired taste," they both said.

"What time you say?" Jamerion asked.

"Eleven thirty."

"Damn, I gotta get back to the house. My mama said we're leaving the party 'fore midnight."

"You reek of pot," Sarah said. "You think your mother isn't going to know what you've been up to?"

Jamerion laughed. "My mama? She'll be into the weed as soon as we get home. Say Lebron. Come on over later if you're still up. Bring your friends."

He left, letting in a burst of the frozen air, the mist sizzling when it reached the space heater. Rand'ee grabbed the bong and took a long hit. He settled back against the worn pillows with a sigh.

Sarah watched Andrew rest his cell phone on the table and listened briefly as the boys talked about sports. Looking around, she decided it probably had been a horse stall once. With piles of straw in the corner it retained the smell of hay, though the marijuana odor overpowered. Watching Andrew she wondered about their future. *He's got to move back to Chicago.*

She drifted off into dreams.

     ***

Beep. Beep. Beep.

"Fifty seconds to midnight!" someone shouted.

Sarah struggled to open her eyes. *Why do I feel so strange?*

"Twenty seconds." She managed to crack them open, spotting Lebron and Rand'ee huddled over Andrew's cell phone, counting down.

"Nine," the boys said together. "Eight..."

Sarah looked around. Travis was lying propped up on one arm, staring through slitted lids at the space heater's glow. Andrew sat hunched with his back to her. She wondered if he'd turn around and kiss her at midnight. *He better!*

"Two. One. HAPPY NEW YEAR!" Lebron shouted. Rand'ee blew a noisemaker.

Sarah leaned forward, waiting for Andrew to turn around. When he didn't, she reached out and touched him. He jumped, turning to her wide-eyed.

"Andy?" she asked, hesitantly.

He squinted at her. "Who?" Walking to a corner he picked up a handful of straw. Crumbs drifted to the floor from his clenched fists.

Sarah called gently, "Andy? Are you okay?"

He jerked around, hiding his hands behind his back.

"Lebron," Sarah whispered. "Andy's gotten stoned. Did you see him smoke any pot?"

"Nah. Maybe he got stoned just from breathing the air. You feel anything?"

Sarah grabbed her chest, trying to breathe shallowly. She felt like laughing and crying. Leaning forward she shook Travis.

"Travis! Get up! We have to get Andy out of here."

He turned his head slowly in her direction, but didn't get it more than halfway there before his gaze returned to the heater.

She turned to Lebron. "Travis and Andy need help. Is there someone at the main house I can get?"

Lebron laughed. "You sure you want to do that? You were just telling Jamerion that he smelled of pot. Betcha you stink too."

She felt her heart pounding. "I can't believe how crazy this is getting!" She shoved Travis with her foot.

He collapsed flat onto the floor. "Whatta ... whatta want?"

Sarah kicked harder, and he barely muttered, "Don't."

Turning back to the two boys she admonished, "You stay here and watch Andy. Don't let him out of your sight, no matter what. I'll go get help."

Rand'ee laughed. "Sure, Mama!"

Sarah stepped outside and flapped her jacket, trying to air it out. The cold night helped clear her mind. Hurrying across the dark yard she stepped hard into a puddle, splashing freezing water up her legs. She stopped, her clenched fists tight against her side. Turning her head to the skies she yelled. "Shit!"

Gathering her resolve, she made her way to the house and knocked on the back door. No one answered. Slipping in, she felt stunned by the heat, her sinuses complaining at the quick transition. She passed by stacks of food trays and dirty dishes in the kitchen. Following voices down a hallway she found herself in a large room, lit by a blazing fireplace. A dozen African-American adults turned in surprise, laughter interrupted in mid-syllable.

A pretty woman came up to her, eyes radiating concern. "Yes, Miss? Can we help you?"

Sarah reached out and the woman took her hand.

"You're trembling child, what's wrong? Uh-oh. You smell like that old shed."

Sarah nodded. "Yes ... yes ma'am," she managed to stutter.

"Come in and warm up by the fire. What's your name?"

Sarah allowed the woman to lead her towards the hearth before Sarah stopped abruptly. "No! The shed! We need help in the shed. Please! Someone?"

The woman called, "Erskine. Better take some men with you."

He nodded and pointed at a teenage boy and two of the men. The four grabbed their coats and rushed out the back door. Sarah allowed herself to be led to a chair someone pulled in front of the fire.

"My name is Keisha Barnes. This is my home," the woman said, placing a cup of hot cider into Sarah's hands.

Sarah felt tears running down her cheeks. "Thank you so much, Mrs. Barnes. My name is Sarah Ryan. I'm down here visiting with Andrew Lewis."

Keisha gave her a reassuring smile. "Rick and Andy are our family. If you're their friends then you're our friend too."

Sarah shivered. "I'm sorry I have to meet you this way. Andy said it'd be okay. Oh, but it's not!" She twisted around to check behind her.

Keisha patted her hand. "It'll be all right. The men have gone to check."

Sarah took the cup and sipped gently, cuddling up under the warm blanket Keisha draped over her shoulders. She kicked off her shoes, alternately holding each foot to the fire as she kept her attention turned to the kitchen. In a few minutes she heard loud voices and the door slam shut.

"We got him," Erskine announced, carrying Travis draped in his arms. He laid him across the couch and loosened his clothing. Sarah watched Keisha rush over. "How is he?" Sarah called.

Keisha bent and felt his forehead. "He's flushed. Take off his jacket." While the men bent to the task Keisha turned to Sarah. "What was he doing out there?"

"Drinking alcohol and smoking pot. At least, that's all I think he was doing. I wasn't really paying attention."

Keisha raised an eyebrow.

"No, no," Sarah insisted. "I don't touch either of those … I mean, anything. I don't do alcohol or drugs. I was supposed to be supervising I guess. Where are the others? Where's Andy?"

"Andy?" Erskine and a teenager looked at each other and then at her. "This was the only one out there. Do you know who this boy is?"

"Yes, of course. This is Travis Wilburn, my cousin."

Erskine's teenager stepped up and offered his hand. "You must be Sarah. Andy talks a lot about you. I'm Andy's friend Devonne."

"Oh, nice to meet you." She took off the blanket and tried to stand, but collapsed back down as a wave of nausea passed through her. "I need my coat, please. We need to find Andy right away."

Keisha and Erskine exchanged worried looks. "Is he in danger?" Keisha asked.

Sarah covered her mouth with her hand.

Devonne turned to his folks. "Sarah's feared of telling you, but Andy can't do no marijuana. Ends up in the hospital. Where are the flashlights?"

"I'll get them," Erskine said. "Rashad, organize two search parties of three men each." He left the room.

"Was there anyone else there?" Keisha asked.

"Yes, a couple of other boys," Sarah said. "I don't remember their names."

"One of them Lebron?" Devonne asked.

"Yes! That's right. I told them to keep an eye on Andy. Is he reliable?"

Devonne and his mother exchanged a glance and Sarah could read their expressions.

"Fred!" Keisha called.

A fellow broke away from talking with Rashad. "What's up, Keisha? Rashad says we're going out to look for Andy?"

"This is Andy's girlfriend," she paused to see Sarah's tentative nod of agreement. "She says Andy and Lebron might be together. Could you please give Lebron a call on his cell phone?"

Fred shook his head. "No can do. I took his cell phone away from him for failing algebra this semester."

"How about calling Andy's phone?" Devonne asked. He pulled his out and gave it a push. A ring came from Erskine's pocket.

Devonne's father pulled the phone from his jacket. "I picked this up from a table in the shed. I thought it belonged to this boy."

Sarah placed her cup on a table as she stood. "I've got to go find him!"

Keisha grabbed her arm. "The men will find him, don't worry."

Sarah felt coldness rise from her toes and race to her brain. She slumped back into the armchair.

Keisha knelt in front of her, rubbing her arms. "Where are your parents?"

"I'm staying with Travis's parents at the Beau Rivage. Ask for Peter Wilburn."

"Fine. Let's get you upstairs into a warm shower. I'll loan you one of my nightgowns and tuck you into bed."

"I don't want to impose. Besides, I'm not sleepy," Sarah replied followed by a big yawn.

"I can see you're not sleepy." Keisha held out her hand and led Sarah up the stairs. "Hand me your clothes I'll wash them."

Sarah hugged her tightly. "Thank you, Mrs. Barnes. Please find Andy for me."

"We'll find him. Don't worry."

Thursday, January 1st, 2008

I yanked open the door, rubbing my hand through my seaweed hair. Peter stood there, looking about as scruffy and boggled as I felt. I asked, "What? You left your wallet here or something?"

Peter smirked. "You look great. Nothing like waking up after a couple hours of sleep on a big drunk, huh Buddy?"

I snorted. "Come on in. I'll mix us some hair of the dog." I shuffled into the kitchen, pulling my robe closed. "You want a scotch?"

"I wouldn't mind. But this isn't a social visit."

"Yeah I figured." I continued to the bar and began pouring the two drinks. "So, I suppose you want to hear more about me and Rod-Rod."

Peter leaned against the pass-through opening watching me. "Not really. If you don't mind, I have a memory lapse about everything we talked about earlier tonight and I'd like to keep it that way. You making yourself a double?"

"You want a double too?"

"Just a splash, please. We might have to go get the kids."

I looked up at him. "Where are they?"

"You know someone named Keisha Barnes? She called us at the casino, saying the kids were out at her place. How far is that?"

"Fifteen minutes in nice weather, longer with icy roads. I wonder how the kids got way out there? And why did she call you and not me?"

"Apparently you wouldn't answer your phone."

"Guess I was passed out." I returned from the kitchen with the two drinks, handing one to Peter. "To the New Year." We clicked glasses and drank.

"Well at least they're safe," I said.

"She said Travis and Sarah were there."

"What does that mean?"

Peter looked at his drink and then up at me. "I'm not really sure what that means. She said Andy wasn't there. You want to call her?"

I gave them a call and Keisha answered.

"Hey, it's Rick. What's up with Andy?" I felt my heart pound as I waited for her answer.

"Apparently he and his two friends came over here last night. They went straight to the old barn in the back and I never saw them. Sarah Ryan came rushing in just after midnight, sending us out to the shack. We found Travis there, but no sign of Andy."

"That's strange. Any reason to think he might be in trouble?" I stretched, trying to relieve a catch in my neck. Mallory had gone to the Beau Rivage with the Wilburns and I was finally back in my own bed.

"Sarah says he was exposed to marijuana smoke. What do you think?"

I took a deep breath, releasing it slowly. "Yeah, could be a problem." I looked out to the icicles hanging off the eaves, shark teeth biting at my soul. "It's two-thirty. What's been done?"

"Rashad and Erskine organized search parties and I notified our neighbors to be on the lookout. He may be with Lebron." She hesitated. "Rick?"

"Yeah?"

"Should we call the police?"

I turned to Peter and asked his opinion.

Peter leaned against the back of the couch and sipped his drink. "I'm considering that it's a couple hours past midnight on New Year's Day. If you were the police and someone called to say their seventeen-year-old boy was a few hours late getting home, what would you say?"

I nodded. "I get your point. But what if he's lost in the woods or something?" I closed my eyes and imagined Andrew lost, freezing and hallucinating. "I'm getting my coat and joining the search. Jesus Christ."

Peter reached for the phone. "Let me talk to Mrs. Barnes, please."

"Sure."

"Mrs. Barnes, it's Peter Wilburn again. Should we come over tonight and help with the search, or perhaps pick up my kids?"

I brought my coat back from the closet, pulling it on over both arms and zipping it up.

"Okay," he said. "We'll be there in the morning." Turning to me he said, "She thinks that would be pointless. The kids are sleeping and the search has been called off; too dark and dangerous."

"I don't give a crap what she said. My son's out there somewhere, maybe freezing to death. I'm going to go look for him."

Peter stretched out on the couch. "I understand you think that's what you should do, Rick. But stop and think about it. The Barneses know the layout of their land. They've searched the obvious places. If you go out there you're just going to get lost yourself. You're going to make the situation worse, not better."

I stood helpless, fisting my hands. "So what? Just stay here and wait?"

"Nothing else to do. Look, I'll stretch out here and keep you company. That way if there's any word we can go together."

I walked over to the glass door, laying my head against it and sighing. "This New Year sure is starting off crappy."

"Then it can only get better," Peter replied.

Returning to the kitchen pass through I picked up and raised my cup. "In that case, here's to a happy New Year."

"Many happy returns."

Saturday, January 3rd

I stood out on the balcony smelling the salty air brought in by the morning breeze. One brave jogger journeyed along the walk, gray sweat suit and pulled cap covering almost all skin. I had seen Andrew on that walk every morning for six months, and now, for three days, there hadn't been a word. Celine and Peter had kept Mallory calm, but everyone agreed if we hadn't heard from Andrew by this afternoon we'd bring in the police. The impending departure of everyone tomorrow had built a steam-kettle of pressure.

I downed another couple of Tums, little relief from a two-day stomach ache. The one person I thought might be able to help had told me never to call, though I'd picked up the phone several times. I wanted to call, needed to explain, but would she listen? Once more I raised the phone, but this time I pushed in her number. It rang, and rang, and rang.

"You have reached the Hewes residence. Please leave a message."

"Sylvia, please pick up. Andy needs your help."

I heard Sylvia pick up the phone, but she didn't speak.

"Please, Sylvia. Andy's missing. I'm desperate."

When she answered, her voice sounded hoarse and halting, as if she'd been crying. "I … I …" Her voice trailed off.

I struggled to speak, too. "Sylvia. I'm so sorry."

I waited, wondering if I should keep talking. Sylvia finally broke the silence. "What's happened to Andy?"

"He's been missing ever since he ran out of the condo on New Year's Eve. I'm frightened."

Her breathing sounded deep and slow, as if each inhalation hurt, each exhalation an effort. "Is this why you're calling me? Over two days pass and you only call me because you need my help again?"

My mouth went dry. "You ordered me not to call."

"You are so stupid." She hung up.

I took the phone back into the kitchen where I poured myself the second cup of morning coffee. Bringing it to the kitchen table, I looked over the city map I'd laid out, a black star marking the Barnes home, with red circles applied during the first few hours indicating how far he might have wandered. I'd given up drawing those by the first afternoon. I stared at the map, a puzzle that hid my son.

I hit the redial number, listening through the message.

"Sylvia. I love you. Please forgive me. Please talk to me." The silence lengthened until the machine beeped, and I was disconnected.

I redialed again. This time she picked up after the second ring.

I listened to her breathe, before saying, "I love you Sylvia."

"How dare you say that to me? How dare you?"

My grip tightened on the phone. "Because it's true. I've never loved anyone like I love you. I've never understood the meaning of the word until I met you. Please, Sylvia. I need you. You've given me hope. I can't live … I need you in my life."

"How can you love me and not tell me you murdered someone? How can I love you, knowing this?"

"I'm not a murderer, Sylvia. You have to let me explain. You have to forgive me."

"How can I?"

"Because … because you once promised me you would."

I listened to her breathe, picturing how she would look, her deep brown eyes, bloodshot with tears, her bright red lips sagging with her sweet pout. That image carried me to other memories, the walk on the beach, the kiss under the mistletoe, the ecstasy of our love making.

"Sylvia. The first moment I set eyes on you I was captivated by your strength and your gentleness, your inspiration and your determination. I fell in love with you for caring about the most important person in my life. You inspired him. I pray someday you'll give me a chance to tell my side of the story. But right now, Andy needs you."

I remembered how Andy had looked when she first saw him, the dejected longhaired boy angry at the world. She knew she had saved his life. I felt certain she wouldn't abandon him.

"What's the situation?" she asked.

Thank God. "Andy was last seen just after midnight on New Year's Eve. When they left here they drove out to Erskine and Keisha's spread. You remember how Andy had been around smokers the last time we were there? We think he got into some marijuana and went off with one of Lebron's friends. Lebron claims he doesn't remember who was there, but we think he's just covering up for his friends. I was hoping you'd have some suggestions about which of Lebron's friends might be hiding Andy?"

I waited, wondering if she would help. When she finally answered she sounded resigned rather than hopeful. "I'll see what I can do."

"Thank you so much Sylvia. You can't imagine what this means to me."

"You? Don't for a moment think I'm doing this for you. I'm doing this for Andy."

I clutched my stomach as it roared with pain. "Sylvia. I'm not a bad person. Please give me a chance."

"I'm tired of you hurting me, Rick. I'm not going to open my heart again." She clicked off.

Saturday Afternoon, January 3rd

By the time I arrived at Memorial Hospital's emergency department, relief that Andrew had been found battled with my fear of his condition. The nurse who called had been unwilling to tell me anything beyond the fact that he wasn't injured. I had called Mallory at the Beau and left for the hospital.

This was my first ever visit to the facility, and I was surprised that this, the county hospital, appeared clean and well maintained. Five patients waited in the triage line when I arrived, and the nurse took care of each with efficient briskness. When my turn came, she didn't introduce herself, just asked "What brings you to the hospital today?"

"Someone called and told me my son is here. Andrew Lewis."

The nurse examined her monitor. "Hold on a minute and I'll check." She picked up her phone, pushed the buttons, and talked in hushed tones. After hanging up she gave me a weary smile.

"I'm sorry Mr. Lewis. Andrew isn't ready for visitors. Would you mind waiting in that small area to your left? The clerk will want to get registration and insurance information."

"But, how is Andy? The nurse who called advised me to come quickly."

"He's in stable condition."

I shoved my gripped fists into my pockets. "But ... how is he? I've got to see him."

The nurse's smile stiffened. I could see she expected people to do what she said. "Please have a seat, Mr. Lewis. Someone will come out and talk to you shortly."

I obediently left the desk and found a seat in the area indicated. In one corner, an old woman riding herd on a flock of young ones jabbered in Spanish on her cell phone. A middle-age man with a ragged beard sat on an old armchair and read a magazine. I picked up another ragged journal, trying to read, but making frequent checks of my watch. Fifteen minutes crawled towards twenty before the clerk called, "Mr. Lewis?"

In the clerk's banana-colored office I fidgeted while a chubby woman with strong laugh lines keyboarded Andrew's information into her data bank. I read "Pam Riley" off her nameplate.

"Insurance?"

I grimaced. "I'm unemployed and without any insurance right now. Will you still be able to treat him?"

Mrs. Riley waved her hand, wiggling her fingers as if fighting off gnats. "Of course. We treat everybody. We can have the social worker talk to you about applying for Medicaid."

The questions seemed endless, followed by a stack of forms to sign, most of them reading like some lawyer or politician had designed them. While I was signing the last one I asked, "When can I see my son?"

Mrs. Riley let out a cackle I had already grown weary of. "I'll give them a call and ask." When Mrs. Riley turned back her expression wasn't hopeful.

"I'm sorry Mr. Lewis. The nurses are all tied up at the moment. The psych nurse assures me the counselor will want to talk with you shortly."

I walked back past the triage area through sliding glass doors into a large room, its couple dozen seats half-filled. A couple cooed to a crying baby. A mustached man held a bloody bandage on his arm. Mostly the people stared aimlessly. I settled into an empty chair and brought out my magazine, but couldn't concentrate.

If I had just been honest with Andrew months ago, maybe none of this would have happened. Would it have helped if I had insisted he take those medications? On the other hand, if Mallory hadn't made that stupid accusation, none of this would have happened. She was just being petty and jealous. And now she's driven Sylvia away again. Damn it. Mallory is nothing but trouble. It's all her fault.

Mallory burst into the waiting room. I stood, instinctively extending my arms, and she rushed into them. I hugged her, wrapping her in my protection. The familiar smell of her hair, the warmth of her body against mine knocked my breath away.

"Have you seen Andy?" she asked, her voice quaking. "How is he?"

"So far all they've told me is that he's in stable condition."

Mallory snuggled against my chest. "How long has it been since you checked?"

"I got here about half an hour ago I guess. They said they'd come let me know."

"I wasn't dressed, and then I couldn't find the room key … and then the taxis. Oh my God, Ricky, I've been frantic. I'll go let them know I'm here, and ask if there's any more information."

I watched from the waiting room as she joined the short triage line. In a few minutes she made her way back. "Any news?" I asked.

"They promised that a counselor would be out here shortly."

I nodded. "I'm not sure their definition of shortly is the same as ours." I noticed she was staring at me. "What?"

"I'm just thinking how awful this has been … and wondering if something could have prevented it."

"Something?"

"Like … you know. Like maybe if we were living as a family."

I snorted. "Hypothetical question."

"I'm serious, Ricky. Jenny's death and our separation has been awful for all of us, but clearly hardest on Andy. He needs a stable home. Come back with me, Ricky. Let's give it another chance."

I turned from her and paced a few steps. "Mallory, this isn't the time."

"It's the perfect time. If you and I hadn't divorced, if we still lived together as a family, our son would never have gotten into drugs. Can't you see how happy he's been this week with us back together again? If that woman hadn't crashed the party, he'd never have run off. By putting our family back together we can salvage his life. Come home, Rick. For Andy's sake."

I looked off to the glass doors, beyond which my son was probably hallucinating and heavily sedated. What did the nurse mean by "stable condition?" It sounded so ominous, like maybe he was on life support or something.

Could Mallory be right? Was I being selfish depriving Andrew of an intact home? *Could we remake our family?*

I gazed into Mallory's face. The green eyes that had caught my attention the first time we'd met gleamed with unshed tears. At forty-nine her features had matured, but in some ways more beautiful than ever; her body trim and sexy. As husband and wife we'd learned about love, about how to raise a family, and about how to appreciate the little things that made two individuals a couple.

She reached her hand up and stroked my cheek. "Ricky, I leave tomorrow. Why don't you and Andy come home with me?"

I returned my gaze to the area beyond the glass door, remembering Andrew's stricken look when he heard me being accused of murder.

What if he refused to see me ever again? It would be so ironic to trade places with Mallory in his love/hate emotions. Should I give up on this project and let Peter place me as a corporate cog, where once again a head of Human Resources would tell me how to engineer?

And what of Sylvia? Why am I saying "No" to a woman who wants me, when the one I want has told me she prefers to never hear from me again? Never talk to her, never touch her, never feel her gentle breath in my ear. Never again share the love of a book. Never relish another stroll on the beach. Never yield to the ecstasy of her lovemaking. Never again?

I thought back to New Year's Eve, when everyone had urged me to give up my dreams, to abandon my life here and go back to Chicago. *Sylvia had stood up for me, had believed in me. If I went back to Chicago how long would it be before Mallory was ragging on me about how I wasn't as good as Peter, wasn't making enough money, didn't have the social graces for the big parties she cherished? How long before I regretted having given up the chance to prove myself here? Sylvia accepts me for who I am, and loves me this way. I can't give her up.*

Somehow, some way, I WILL win Sylvia back. Or at least give it my best effort.

I gazed into Mallory's lovely face. I still loved her for our history together. But the desire was gone. "It's just not going to work, Mallory. Our time is past, and I've got to move on."

Mallory shook her head sadly. "You're a stupid, stubborn man, Ricky. Always have been. You know this means we'll never see each other again?"

"What do you mean?"

"I don't want to live alone the rest of my life. I'm going to find someone who loves me; someone who will be there for me. And, of course, I want Andy to come home with me."

I forced my jaw to relax enough to talk. "And I want him to stay with me. Why don't we wait and see what Andy wants?"

Her reply was interrupted by a stocky man with a walrus mustache who came up to us. "Andrew Lewis' parents?"

I shook his hand. "I'm Rick Lewis, and this is Andy's mother, Mallory."

"I'm Walter Evans, the counselor assigned to your son."

"You've talked with Andy?" I asked.

I watched him look me over, appraising me. "I've seen him. Would you mind following me?"

He brought us into an unkempt lounge where we settled onto a handful of exhausted chairs. Walter swept crumpled fast food bags off the small table and placed a clipboard stuffed with papers in front of him. I wondered how they could have generated so much information already. Studying the counselor's face, I decided he couldn't be more than forty, though his worry lines added another ten years.

"You look tired," I said.

Walter gave me a grim smile. "I'm fine. I am concerned about Andrew, though."

Mallory said, "We are too! How is he?"

"Sedated. Could you tell me what happened?"

Mallory and I looked at each other but neither spoke. A small beat-up refrigerator in the corner kicked on with a loud wheeze.

Walter looked from one to the other. "Neither of you have any idea?"

I leaned forward in the chair. "All we know is that he's been missing for three days. We're very glad he's been found and we're eager to see him. Could we do that now?"

This didn't seem to impress Walter because he began thumbing through pages he'd put together in a bulging manila folder. He didn't look up to comment, "I understand this isn't the first time your son's had problems?"

Pointing at his file, I asked, "You have information from Chicago there?"

"Yes." Walter shuffled through his clipboard and brought out a faxed page. "Andrew was at the private Humana facility the end of May. Is that right?"

He looked up to check our nods, and returned to the paper. "Dr. Hopkins diagnosed him with latent schizophrenia. She recommended long-term counseling and medication." Walter's eyes flicked back and forth between Mallory and me. "What medications is he on? Who's he been seeing?"

Mallory pointed at me. "He's been with his father."

I scowled. "He hasn't needed medication or counseling. He's been doing fine."

Walter picked another page from his stack and studied it for a moment, glanced at me and back at the paper. Returning it to the stack, he looked squarely at me. "You say he's been doing fine, but my records say he was back at the Humana emergency room on November fifth. Why did you check him out against medical advice, Mr. Lewis?"

I stood and walked over to the sink. Pouring a cup of water, I rinsed and spit, hoping to relieve the desert that had settled in my mouth. Turning, I stared down into Walter's eyes, trying to drill in understanding. "He didn't need to be in the hospital. He needed to be home, with me caring for him. I'm certain it was the right thing for him then, and it's the right thing for him now."

I continued glaring at Walter, though the mustached man didn't so much as blink.

Walter turned to Mallory. "Mrs. Lewis, what do you think?"

"We agreed to Andy coming down to live with his father as an experiment. But I naturally assumed he'd get proper care." She glanced my way. "I called and reminded Ricky of that."

I popped my fist into my open palm. "He just had an unfortunate relapse, that's all. He'll be all right if you just let us see him, let me take him home."

Walter put his hands together and looked placidly at their intertwining. "Andrew is quite ill. Although I can let you observe him through the isolation window, it would be better if he didn't have visitors for the next few days."

"Now wait a minute," I shouted. "We're his parents. If we want to take him home you have to release him."

Walter's mouth formed a thin grim line. "Mr. Lewis, these papers show a clear case of parental neglect."

My voice squeaked, "Neglect? You can't be serious."

"Perfectly serious. Twice you withdrew Andrew against medical advice. You failed to obtain proper follow-up, and you refused to administer prescribed medications. As a result, he's suffered what could have been a fatal relapse. Social Services has taken temporary custody of Andrew."

"Wait a minute," Mallory cried, sitting forward in her chair. "My plane leaves tomorrow morning. I'd like to take Andy with me and have him admitted under Dr. Hopkins' care in Chicago."

"Our doctors have already arranged for admission to our psychiatric hospital, Mrs. Lewis. You can discuss transfer next week with your physician."

Mallory and I looked at each other and Walter stood. "You want to take a glance at your son before you leave? I'm not sure I'm supposed to let you."

I entered the observation room first, observing Andrew's contorted face, his hands grasping at the unseen. Memories of November caused me to hang my head. Mallory pushed me aside and gasped. Holding her hand over her mouth, she ran from the room.

Sylvia: Monday, January 5th

Sylvia thumbed through the files in her cabinet, looking for one of a child who had transferred out of the school at Christmas. Her phone rang for the seventh time this hour.

Cradling the instrument under her chin, she said, "This is Sylvia Perkins." She pulled the found folder out of the file, shoved the drawer closed, and settled into her chair. "May I help you?" She opened the folder to skim through it as she listened.

"My name is Walter Evans, a counselor at Memorial Behavior Health. I'm calling about one of your students, Andrew Lewis. I understand that you're his school counselor?"

Sylvia shut the folder and moved it to the back of her desk. Snatching a pad and pen from the drawer, she wrote Walter's name, underlining it three times and adding exclamation points. "Yes, Andy Lewis is one of my students. I presume he's one of your patients then?"

"Yes ma'am. I make it a policy to call the student's counselor as soon as possible after they've been admitted. He came in Saturday night. Do you have a few minutes to talk?"

Bianca, the chubby nineteen-year-old assistant, stuck her head in the door, pointing at her watch. Sylvia shook her head. Covering the mouthpiece she told her, "I'm going to need ten minutes. Sorry." Sylvia pulled Andrew's file from where she'd stored it on the corner of her desk.

"Of course, Mr. Evans. Thank you for contacting me. How's he doing?"

"I'm not authorized to give out information yet, Mrs. Perkins."

Sylvia remembered how Andrew had looked when Rand'ee had brought him out to the curb, hallucinating and incoherent. Visions of how sick he was when she helped Rick take care of him flashed through her mind.

Walter said, "I'd appreciate anything you can tell me about Andrew."

Stay professional, she told herself. "Besides being his counselor, I'm also his teacher for Mississippi Studies. He did very well in my class, consistently achieving the highest score on the exams."

"A good student then. What else can you tell me?"

Sylvia recognized the open ended questions, the gentle probing. She wanted to keep her relationship with Rick out of the conversation. *After all, it's over anyway.* This thought made her choke up and she had to force her voice to sound casual. "What would you like to know?"

"Have you noticed Andrew displaying evidence of mood swings, or perhaps exhibiting out-of-the-ordinary behavior?"

Sylvia thought of how sad Andrew looked when she first saw him, and how exhilarated he had been when he won the state championship. *Were these mood swings normal, or a sign of his underlying problems?*

"All teenagers have moodiness, Mr. Evans. At the beginning of the year Andy was clearly depressed. But since, he's made some friends and become involved in extracurricular activities. He's qualified for a full athletic scholarship to the University of Southern Mississippi for next year."

"So you never saw anything suggestive of mental problems?"

She let the question simmer. This could be the first step on a slippery slope. "Last month I was aware he missed school for a week. My understanding is that issue involved mental illness."

Walter paused, causing Sylvia to tighten her grip on the phone. *What's he going to ask? Will I have to admit that I was sleeping with his father?*

When he spoke, his voice maintained his soft solicitation. "Are you familiar with his medical records?"

After working so hard with Rick nursing Andrew, Sylvia had ordered the Chicago hospital records, marking them confidential. She had reviewed them more than once. "Yes. They're a part of his file." Sylvia shuffled the papers as if she were reading them. Images of Andrew smashing his hand against the window, and of having to pry his fingers off the rail, came rushing through her mind. "Since he was just admitted two days ago, I presume he's still fairly ill?"

"I'm not sure what I'm at liberty to share." His voice kept its professional tone, and Sylvia felt her heart ache.

She closed her eyes and took a deep breath. "Just as you care for your patients, Mr. Evans, I care for my students. Andy's been a special case. Please tell me what you can. How is he now?"

After a moment of hesitation he said, "As you suspect, Mrs. Perkins, he's having a serious relapse. He'll be out of school for several weeks."

"Oh?" Sylvia tried to make her voice sound casual. "I'll help his teachers gather his assignments. When would be a good time for me to bring them by?"

"I suppose you could drop off whatever you have at the front desk near the end of the week."

She squeezed her eyes tight, knowing she had to get past this man's guard. "You see, as his counselor, I would like to make a personal visit as soon as possible."

A hesitancy preceded his reply. "The psychiatrist makes all decisions about visitors. Especially under these special circumstances I suspect there will be severe limitations."

"Special circumstances?"

"We have court-ordered custody and commitment."

A gasp escaped her lips. She had expected him to be admitted, but to strip his parents of custody? *Poor Rick!*

"Mrs. Perkins? Are you okay?"

She struggled to catch her breath. "Yes," she managed. "Excuse me. Frog in my throat. I understand he had a close relationship with his father."

"Have you ever met Richard Lewis?"

"Yes." Sylvia held her tongue, forcing herself not to volunteer information.

"He seems to be in denial about his son's mental illness. I'd appreciate your impressions of him."

Images of their making love just three weeks before clashed with her current anger and pain. "Yes, I know him well. He seems like a good type – perhaps a little shell shocked."

"Oh?" Walter let the silence drag.

"You probably already know about his daughter's death and his divorce?"

"Yes, ma'am. As a matter of fact, I'm concerned those issues are instrumental in Andrew's problems. I don't suppose you had the opportunity to meet Andrew's mother?"

Sylvia thought of New Year's Eve. *What a bitch. She and her sister. Both bitches.* "Yes, I've met her. She was visiting from Chicago, but I believe she's returned home."

"In a few days I'll need to make recommendations about Andrew's disposition. Since you've met both parents and the child, perhaps you could give me your insight into which home would be better. Do you know if either parent is dating again? That could be a factor in my decision."

Sylvia rested her forehead on her hand. "Yes, Mr. Evans. Andy's father has been seeing someone."

"Hmm. This could be important in explaining Andrew's recent relapse. You wouldn't happen to know anything about the relationship, would you?"

She placed her hand on her chest, feeling her heart pound. "Actually, Mr. Evans, I've been the woman in Mr. Lewis' life."

There followed a long silence from Mr. Evans's end of the phone. Flipping to the opening of Andrew's chart, she stared at his picture. She promised herself this one would find a place of honor on her corkboard.

Mr. Evans voice, when it came, echoed with his disbelief. "You're Andrew's teacher, and his counselor, and you're personally involved with his father?"

She allowed her silence to provide the answer.

"Mrs. Perkins, do you see any conflict of interest here?"

"Teachers are allowed to socialize with parents, Mr. Evans. I once had a close relationship with Andy's father. But that's over."

"Over when, Mrs. Perkins?"

Sylvia swallowed hard. "Quite recently."

"Within the past week?"

"Actually the night of Andy's disappearance. There was some disagreement in the home."

"Oh? Were you there?"

"Yes."

"Who else was present?"

Sylvia relived those terrifying moments, Mallory's stunning accusation, Rick's wide-eyed confession, followed by the teenagers' flight, and finally, ultimately, Sylvia's own rejection of her lover. She squeaked out her answer. "Besides Andrew and his parents and myself, there were a few friends, both adults and teenagers."

"Please, tell me what happened?"

Sylvia felt a tear running down her cheek. "Rick told me that he loved me, that he wanted to marry me."

"And what did Andrew say, how did he react?"

"There was more to it than that."

"I'm all ears."

Sylvia's tears flowed heavily now. She tried to talk but couldn't. She began sobbing.

When Mr. Evans' voice returned it was soft, sympathetic. "I'm sorry about your problems, Mrs. Perkins. They're Andrew's problems now, too. That makes them my problems. Perhaps you could call me when you feel better, or stop by the hospital and talk. I could let you know if the psychiatrist will allow Andrew to see you."

Sylvia composed herself enough to say, "Thank you, Mr. Evans."

"Oh, just one more question. Do you know who made the 911 phone call about where he could be found?"

Sylvia realized her voice would be on the recorded phone message.

"That was me."

"I'm wondering how you happened to find him?"

She took a moment to examine her heart for the answer. "Because, I love him."

His answer took a long time in coming. "He's a lucky boy then, because he needs people to love him. I tell you what. I think Andrew will be ready for visitors by Friday. Perhaps you'd like to come by after school?"

"Yes, that would be perfect."

"Good. If it turns out that you've made up with his father, you could bring him as well."

Sylvia held the phone long after the counselor clicked off, listening to the dial tone dissolve into beeps before she hung up. She looked up to the sound of a knock on her door. Bianca stuck her head in and pointed up at the clock.

Sylvia placed the piece into the cradle. She flashed the young aide a wistful smile. "We never have time for the important things, Bianca."

"What do you need more time for, Mrs. P?" she asked.

"Grieving, Bianca. Grieving the death of a friendship."

"Someone died?"

Sylvia reached up and pushed her wayward lock of hair back behind her ear. "No, just the friendship. I'll be all right."

"You got three students waiting."

"Give me just one minute more."

Bianca stepped out and Sylvia took a deep breath, counting to ten. She fixed a smile on her face and buzzed the assistant to call in the next needy child.

Sylvia: Monday, January 5th

Sylvia savored the spices on the roast chicken. "Aunt Frances, you're such a marvelous cook."

"Thank you, Darlin'. I figured you'd appreciate a hot meal after your first day back at work. How did it go today?"

"Busy as anything!" She thought back on some of the students she'd worked with today, smiling faces, happy to be with their friends and back in school, rattling on about their holidays, and then … there were those who were distressed. Teenage years were so hard. "I had four new transfers, and, of course, the first day of the new semester for Mississippi history. During my office hours, they brought me one boy who was caught smoking in the bathroom. Just what I needed on top of the rest of the madness."

She stopped talking to take another bite of her meal. Looking up she noticed Aunt Frances' keen eyes staring at her.

"Any word from Richard?" the older woman asked.

Sylvia shook her head. She returned to her food, cutting a small piece off her chicken breast and dipped it into the sauce. She chewed slowly and swallowed. "Actually I heard from the fellow taking care of Andy in the hospital; a Walter Evans. He said I might be able to visit in a few days."

"That poor boy. From what you described he must be suffering horribly."

Sylvia smiled reassuringly. "I'm sure the professionals in the hospital will take excellent care of him. In retrospect, I can't believe I ever agreed to help Rick take care of the boy in his home. Not only did it put me in a compromising situation, but it could have been disastrous for Andy."

The phone rang and Sylvia rose to get it. Reading the caller ID she pointed to it and whispered to Aunt Frances, "It's him!"

"You want me to leave?"

"No." Sylvia stared at the phone, counting the rings. Three. Four. Five. Click. The answering machine picked up. "You have reached the Hewes residence. Please leave a message."

"Sylvia, please pick up." Rick's voice pleaded.

She waited, the message machine recording the silence.

"Sylvia. If you refuse to see me again, I'll understand. But please, oh pl…" The machine clicked off.

She turned slowly to her aunt. Aunt Frances' eyes shone with sympathy.

Sylvia's eyebrows arched. "Please what?"

She turned back to the instrument, and they both stared, willing it to ring.

"Will you answer it this time?" Aunt Frances asked.

"He may not call back." She wrapped her arms around herself, her head bowed.

"He will," Aunt Frances insisted, smiling gently. "He loves you, Darlin'."

Sylvia returned her gaze to the phone. It rang. She jumped back a step, watching it, as if it were a snake poised to strike.

Second ring.

She reached out one trembling finger.

Third ring.

She drew it back, staring.

Fourth ring.

Once again she reached out.

Fifth ring.

Her hand froze over the receiver.

The answering machine gave the message and Rick's voice came on.

"Sylvia, for all we've been through, for any love you once had for me; please. Oh, please listen to my explanation. Give me one more chance."

She grabbed the phone. "Hello?"

Rick's gasp came through. "Sylvia? Oh, thank God. Sylvia, I love you!"

Sylvia felt a flush flow from head to toe. "You love me? Do you understand the meaning of the word? Let me tell you. Love means faith, honesty, and trust. It's about telling the truth, the whole truth. We had two months together, several dates. When I told you my deepest secrets, did you tell me yours? No. Not a word! Not a single hint you were hiding something so horrible."

She paused to breathe. When she continued, her voice changed to slow and sad. "I loved you, Rick. I opened my heart to you. How could I have been so mistaken?"

"Stop it, Sylvia. I'm NOT a murderer. You have to listen to my side."

She pulled her head back, her eyes closed, taking a slow deep breath.

Aunt Frances came up beside her and took her hand. She murmured in her ear, "Listen to your heart, my pet. Is it really saying you don't ever want to see this man again?"

Sylvia opened her eyes slowly. She felt her features soften, her muscles release. "Rick, I do want to hear your side of the story. You may pick me up Wednesday at five."

She listened as a moment of silence stretched into a lifetime. His voice cracked when he said, "Thank you, Sylvia."

Sylvia laid the phone back on its cradle and turned to her aunt. Gently she lowered her head upon her matron's shoulder and enjoyed her aunt's patting her back.

Wednesday, January 7th

I held the door open for her at the pizzeria, enjoying the flush of jukebox music and garlic aroma. Walking up to the counter together, we ordered our pizza and beers and took the bottles to a booth in the back to wait for our order. I consumed half of mine, grabbed a breath, and took a few more gulps. I watched Sylvia taste hers. She was a slow drinker, a sipper rather than a chugger.

I hadn't rehearsed what I'd say, and seeing her downcast eyes, I wasn't sure how to begin. Everything in my life had gone so wrong, well, that seemed as good a starting point as any. "Life used to be so sweet," I said. "I had a good home, a happy family, a successful career." I paused to take another gulp of beer. Even on my empty stomach, I didn't feel any of the alcohol's effect.

"We've all suffered disappointments," Sylvia murmured.

I clutched my bottle. "Disappointments? Having your seventeen-year-old daughter murdered goes far beyond disappointment."

She looked into my eyes, her lips in a small pout. "You can't keep using that as an excuse, Rick. It was terrible, yes, but not adequate for throwing away all your morals."

I blushed at the rebuke. I knew she was right, and yet, I hoped she could sympathize. "You said you'd give me a chance to explain."

"That's why I'm here."

I picked up my bottle and finished it, setting it down carefully on the ring it had left on the table. Standing, I said, "I'm getting another one. You want anything?"

She held up her mostly full bottle. "Bring me some water."

"Sure."

I returned with drinks in each hand. Sliding into my seat, I stared at my beer, picking it up, sipping it, putting it down, and repeating.

"Well?" Sylvia asked.

"I'm not sure how to tell you."

She seemed calm on her side of the booth. "I always like a history that starts from the beginning."

"I suppose that's best. It was a chilly Saturday night in Chicago, December second, just over two years ago. Jennifer and her boyfriend, Brent, were out on a date. They'd gone to an experimental play, a rap music show they'd read about in one of the underground papers. Bad neighborhood, part of the 'hood.

"Reportedly they were standing outside the theatre during intermission. There were a lot of kids around, including some gang members. A white van drove up, a kid leaned out a window and started yelling. A couple of the boys next to Jenny pulled out guns. Shots were fired and the van sped off. One of the gang members was wounded, and an innocent bystander was killed. My sweet Jenny." I picked up my beer and drank half of it down. Looking down the barrel of the longneck, I stared into its pool of tears.

"It didn't take long for the police to identify the triggerman in the car, Rodney Carter, Rod-Rod to his friends. I sat in on every moment of the four-day trial, from jury pool selection on. Defense brought up a lot of doubt about who actually had fired first, how unreliable were all the witnesses, and even trying to make some sort of excuse about Rod-Rod being the victim of a shattered home. All sorts of garbage. No one seemed to care about Jenny. It was all about the murderer and not the murdered. Just before it went to jury, someone cut a deal. Two years for manslaughter, with a year of it suspended. Only served seven months. By November he was back on the streets."

I picked up my beer and finished it, setting it next to the other one, forming a small wall. "Maybe I'll have another."

"Why don't you wait until our pizza is ready?"

I shrugged, and sat back in the booth, closing my eyes. "From the time he got out until the first anniversary of Jenny's death I had about a month. I'd already lost my job, so spent my time spying on Rod-Rod, figuring out who were his friends, and which were his enemies. I learned where he hung out and hatched my plans for revenge."

I faded into silence again, my memories as desperate as my needs to suppress them. I picked up Sylvia's beer, mostly untouched. "You mind?"

She shrugged. "Just keep talking."

I drank about half of hers and set it on line with the other two. "When's that damn pizza going to be ready?"

"When it's ready. Go on with your story."

"Okay. I planned it all for December second, an anniversary present. It was a Sunday. On past Sunday evenings Rod-Rod'd been hanging out in a pool hall. I'd moved out of Mallory's house to an apartment by then, but I still used the lab I had set up in her basement. I made up some poison and took it with me to the pool hall."

"Didn't you stand out? I mean, you're a middle-age clean-cut white man in a hangout of young blacks."

I chuckled grimly. "It's not that hard to look disreputable. Three days of beard growth, ratty clothes, disheveled hair … no one looked at me twice. I drank and acted drunk and they ignored me."

"So you poisoned his drink?"

I picked up her beer and finished it off, again setting it back in alignment. I turned them so that the labels all faced me exactly and connected the rings in front of them into a moat.

"I had my chance. He went off to the toilet, leaving his beer half-finished. I slipped up to his table with the poison in my hand. No one was watching. I wanted to drop it in that bottle. I really wanted to."

I fell into silence, staring unseeing at my fortress of beer bottles. Images of that evening danced through my mind; Rod-Rod's smug face as he played pool with the boys and flirted with the girls, the new 'prison' tattoo on his biceps he so proudly showed off. The life he still had, while Jenny's was gone, gone forever. I wiped the sweat off my palms with a damp napkin.

"But you didn't poison him?" Sylvia asked gently.

"No. I walked out of the bar and leaned against the outside wall staring down the street. I hated myself for my cowardice. I just couldn't murder this kid, even though he had destroyed everything I had held dear. Looking off in the distance at the skyscrapers I'd known all my life, I realized I'd have to leave this town. I couldn't stay and face my family and friends. I couldn't look any of them in the eyes knowing that I'd let that monster live."

I fell silent, listening to the jukebox playing a country song of heartache. A lost love. *What did they know of lost love? There wasn't any lost love like the death of a child.*

"You're not a coward, Rick. You did the right thing."

I focused on Sylvia with her concerned eyes and sympathetic smile.

"You may not think so after this next part." I picked up each bottle, one at a time, checking to see if I'd missed any beer. I drained the few remaining drops that had gathered at the bottom of one.

"I crossed the street, collapsing on the curb across from the bar. A trio of members from the rival gang pulled up. One of the creeps got out of the car and asked me if I knew a guy named Rod-Rod. He asked if he was in there and I said yes. He nodded and went back to his car.

"I could have done something then. I could have gone back in and warned him. I could have called the police. Instead, I flopped down next to a garbage can, pretending I was asleep while I watched. About an hour later, Rod-Rod came out of the bar, whistling a carefree song. As he passed their car, the three of them jumped out, grabbed him, and threw him into the back seat. The car sped off."

"And?"

"And a few days later Rod-Rod's body washed up on the shore. Mallory had figured out what I'd been doing, both the stalking and the basement chemistry. She assumed I'd poisoned him."

Sylvia reached out, pushed the bottles aside, and took my hands. "But you didn't do it."

"But I didn't save him either. By not warning Rod-Rod, I passed his death sentence just as sure as if I'd dropped the poison in his drink." I hung my head.

"Why didn't you tell me all this earlier?"

I held both of her hands, feeding off their warmth. "Every day of the past two months I've been certain I wasn't worthy of your love. But I knew in my heart I couldn't survive without it."

I paused, capturing her eyes with my own. "Sylvia. I love you. Please forgive me."

Her mouth lifted into a slow smile. "Rick. I told you I love you. I meant it then, and I mean it still."

I brought her hands to my lips, and kissed each knuckle.

The order desk called my name.

"Pizza's ready," she murmured.

"Yes. And now my appetite, is a-roarin'." I strode to the counter, returning with the pizza and a cup of diet cola. "I decided I didn't need any more beer."

"Good!"

We each took a slice, adding peppers and cheese as to our tastes, and savored the first bites, always the best. After we each had finished a piece, I asked, "Are you available Friday? The counselor said I could see Andy then. I'd love for you to come with me, and I'm sure he would too. I get off from Home Depot at four."

"Yes, of course. I'll be available after four, too."

We ate our second pieces, and I went to the counter, returning with a take-home box for the last two. We sat, relaxed, enjoying each other's company.

"Sylvia, we've been through a lot these last few months."

She stretched her head back, letting loose a chortle. "That has to be the biggest understatement I've ever heard."

I leaned forward and she did the same, and we met in the middle of the table for a kiss. When we eased apart, I softly said, "Sylvia, I love you."

Her reply came soft and slow. "Darling Rick, I love you too."

I reached into my pocket and brought out a small box. "Since we've been through so much, I thought I'd throw one more bit of excitement into the mix." Slipping out of the booth, I lowered myself onto one knee at her feet. I snapped open the box.

"Oh my God. You're asking me to marry you?"

I held my other hand against my chest. "If you'll have me. You know I'm an unemployed dreamer, raising a troubled teenager. I can't seem like much of a bargain. But, Sylvia, I love you more than I've ever imagined I could love anybody. You're the angel God sent down to restore my faith in life. Please, Sylvia Hewes Perkins, do me the honor of becoming my partner in life. Will you marry me?"

She picked up the ring and ran her finger along the narrow silver band, turning the small diamond cluster to catch the rainbows glittering off the various facets. I couldn't resist that arrangement, even though it cost two months of my budgeted spending money.

"Do you like it? We can take it back and get something else?"

"Oh, Rick, it's wonderful!" She tried it on. "Perfect fit. How did you know?'

"Aunt Frances."

She laughed. "No wonder she's been acting so strange today." She handed it to me and held out her finger. "Let's make it official, sweet boy."

I slipped it on her finger and she cried softly, "I'll love you forever."

Friday, January 9ᵗʰ

At the psychiatric hospital the receptionist confirmed our appointment and brought us back to a small interview room, promising that Mr. Evans would be with us shortly. She offered us sweet tea, which Sylvia accepted, and promised to find me some coffee. Sylvia settled into a ragged-edged armchair. I looked at the other places to sit, three plastic chairs surrounding a wobbly kitchen table, and chose to lean against the mustard-colored wall. Tubular fluorescent lighting created a stark glare. The receptionist brought us our drinks, and left. The clock on the wall ticked loudly.

"Stop chewing your nails," Sylvia said.

"This counselor guy, Evans, he's a mean man. Andy's already going to be miserable when he returns to reality in this place. I think he'd do a lot better with someone who offered sympathy."

"We'll see in a minute. When I talked to Mr. Evans I got the impression he was quite empathetic."

"Bullshit!" I stomped my foot. "He stripped me of my parental rights!"

She gave me her "calming" smile. "I'm certain he has Andy's best interest at heart." She picked a small book from her purse and I asked, "What have you got there?"

She read from the cover, "Autobiographical Sketch and Narrative of the War Between the States by Jubal Anderson Early. I had to have our school librarian special order it out of Atlanta. You get such a better feel for history reading autobiographies."

"The War Between the States? You mean the Civil War."

She laughed and covered her face with the book. "Yankee," she stage whispered.

Walter Evans entered, carrying a large file. He set it on the scarred table and Sylvia and he exchanged introductions. He turned, extending his hand to me, but I kept mine clenched behind my back. Walter dropped his, his expression unreadable.

He settled into the plastic chair on the far side of the table. Sylvia lowered back into the armchair, while I kept my stance by the wall.

"I thought we were coming in to see Andy," I said.

"How's he doing?" Sylvia asked. "We've been very worried."

"Better," Walter replied, though he didn't sound reassuring. "On medications now." Turning to me he added, "And will be for some time."

I could feel my fingernails digging into my clamped fists. "Medication? You mean you're tranquilizing him out of his mind, right? That's all you psychiatric people know how to do, and it's NOT what Andrew wanted. You're doing this all wrong! He's lived with me his whole life. You've known him fewer than a handful of days."

Walter leaned back in his chair, crossing his hand behind his head. "I read that you're an engineer, Mr. Lewis."

"That's right."

"What do you engineer?"

I forced myself to calm. "Right now I'm designing a small smelting plant. I'm hoping to have it operational by early this summer."

"I've never been inside a smelting plant, but I bet I could pick up a pencil and paper and put together a reasonable design right now."

I scoffed. "You're being ridiculous."

"Exactly. You attended years of school to become an engineer, and decades afterwards improving your expertise. Yet you seem to think that psychologists and psychiatrists, people who've made a career of studying the human psyche, can't possibly be as smart as you are when it comes to mental health."

I gritted my teeth. "I'm sure you have plenty of degrees and lots of sick kids under your belt, Mr. Evans. But I've been there for Andy. Twice I flew up to Chicago to rescue him. I've hand fed him and cleaned his messes. You have no right to tell me what's best for my son. By God, you're not even a doctor, are you?"

That last remark brought a flush to his cheeks and the muscles around his left eye twitched.

"Rick." I turned to Sylvia's call and saw she held her finger to her lips. Turning to Walter, she said, "Mr. Evans, would you give us just a minute, please?"

He knocked the chair backwards on the floor as he stood, not bothering to pick it up. Turning his back, he walked towards the hall. "There's a bell on the table. Give it a ring when you're ready." He popped the door closed behind him.

"Rick." She had her lips tight.

"What?"

"For a very smart man you can be incredibly stupid."

"What the hell are you talking about now?"

She rose from the chair, her strong calves tensing smoothly. She stepped across the space to stand three feet away from me, her arms crossed. "Who do you think is going to make the decision about what happens to Andy?"

I shuffled one foot. "Well I … I guess … I don't know. Who?"

She pointed at the door. "The man you just insulted, that's who. Is that what you wanted to do?"

I leaned harder against the wall, no longer certain my legs would support me. "Mr. Evans has that right? He could continue to deny me my son?"

"Most likely send him to his mother's care, or, failing that, perhaps foster care."

"But … but that's not right! We love each other, and you … you're going to be part of the family now, too! Don't you love him? Can't you say something?"

She turned away, and I watched her cross the room, leaning her head against the wall. When she turned, her cheeks held tears. "I love that boy. He's smart, he's gentle, he's determined. You know what? In those ways he's like his dad. I love those traits in you, too."

I smiled and started to come to her, but she stopped me with a wave.

"But there's one important way he's not like his dad. He needs medication. He seems okay at times, but even then, you don't know what's going on inside. It's not fair for you to deny him his needs. Suppose he had diabetes? Would you refuse to give him insulin?"

"Now that's a different thing."

"No, it's not."

I examined her stern face. "I've seen what those medications do to people. Dr. Hopkins had Mallory hopped up on so much it was like being married to a sleepy zombie."

"Maybe she needed it. At least she's dealt with the death of her daughter."

I grabbed the chair back for support. "Now? You bring that up now?"

She crossed the room again, grabbing me by both shoulders, indenting my skin with her nails. "Yes, God Damn It. Jenny is dead! Dead, gone forever."

I pushed her off, backing away until hard against the wall. "Why are you hurting me?"

"You? You always think everything is about you, don't you?"

She stepped away, leaning her head on her arm against the wall. "Fate is not kind, Rick. Marriages break up. Fathers drop dead on the golf course. Lovers betray you. You lost a child, so true. But I … I never even had a child to lose."

I came up to her and she nestled into my arms, cuddling close as I closed my arms around her, rubbing her back gently.

"How come you're so sure he needs drugs, Sylvia? Andy was doing fine. He really was."

She pushed herself away and swept her arm, indicating the somber room. "You like it here? Look at the desecrated furnishings. Smell the sweat and terror. Andy's barely seventeen years old, and here he is institutionalized for the third time in less than a year. You really think keeping him off medication is worth this?"

The sounds of some child's scream leaked through the thin walls. "You ... you really believe if he'd been on medicine this wouldn't have happened?"

"To me the answer is obvious. What matters now is how much more Andy's got to go through before you're convinced!"

How much indeed? "I ... I guess you're right."

"You mean that?"

I picked up her right hand and kissed it. "Yes. I may be stubborn, but not totally stupid. I'll tell Mr. Evans I'll keep Andy on the medicines."

"And?"

"What?"

She shook her finger in my face. "You need a major change in your attitude. If you want Andy to come home, I advise you to be as nice as you can to Mr. Evans."

I pulled her towards me to share a lover's kiss. When she broke away I lifted up her left hand, fingering her new ring.

"To have my son back ... for the sake of your love, I'll do my damndest."

She handed me the bell from the table and I took it out to the hallway to give it a shake. In a minute Walter returned to the room.

He leaned against the door, watching me warily. I noted again his over-wrinkled brow, the premature gray around his ears, and the droopy sad mustache. He waited for me to speak.

I forced myself to smile, and held out my hand. "I'm very sorry I've been such an ass Mr. Evans. I promise to work with you one hundred percent of the time. It's clear that Andy needs medications and I appreciate how you're determined to make sure he gets the care he needs."

Walter took my hand and studied my face intently. "Those are the right words, Mr. Lewis. Are they sincere?"

I locked into his gaze. "Yes, sir. Whatever it takes." Moving next to Sylvia, I placed my hand on her shoulder.

Walter picked up the chair from the floor and settled onto it, the flimsy plastic groaning in response. "In that case, we need to discuss Andrew's future. By that I mean his immediate future."

Sylvia asked, "When do you think he'll be stable enough to leave the hospital?"

Walter pursed his lips. "We're not a long-term facility here, Mrs. Perkins. The psychiatrists plan on discharging Andrew on Monday. The question is, to where? He needs a stable environment. His mother would like him to go to Chicago under Dr. Hopkins' care."

I gripped the chair for support. "Back to Chicago? Send Andy away?" I looked over to my fiancé. "Say something."

She turned to Walter. "Until this setback Andrew was doing quite well here, both academically and socially. And as for your concerns about a stable environment ..." She held up her ring hand. "I accepted Rick's proposal of marriage two nights ago. I'll be around to help."

Walter reached up to twirl one corner of his generous lip hairs. "A change in plans, eh Mrs. Perkins? Congratulations are in order, I presume. Will you be moving in together right away?"

Sylvia blushed. "Of course not. We've set our wedding date for summer, after Andy is finished with school."

Walter studied her, his hands resting calmly on his stack of papers. After a bit he pulled a sheet from one of the folders and handed it to me. "This is called a 'Contract for Safety.' It's a legal document you'll sign and we'll have notarized."

I read the paper, its straightforward style specifying my agreement to keep Andrew under close medical care, following the psychiatrist's orders to the best of my ability. I whipped out my pen but hesitated. "I like the idea of a signed contract. So, your part of the deal is that Andy lives with me?"

Walter raised one eyebrow. "There is no deal. Realistically, at seventeen, he will need to make his own decisions, unless the court determines those choices are dangerous."

I scanned the paper again, signed it, and handed it over. Walter placed it back in the folder.

"Are you going to bring Andy out now?" I asked.

"In a minute. First off though, in my discussion with your son he seems to have some issues."

I felt my breath catch. "Issues?"

"Developmental tasks of teenagers include establishing trust in their relationships and defining their role with their parents. Andrew has been through some tumultuous times. He rejected his mother and put all his faith in you. He feels that trust has been broken. This is not going to be a simple problem, Mr. Lewis. As he seems to respect Mrs. Perkins, perhaps she can help."

Sylvia stiffened in my grasp. "I love that boy, Mr. Evans. He will be my first real son ever."

"Very well." The counselor stood. "If Andrew is up for it, I'll send him in." He turned at the door. "Anything else you need?"

"Just my son."

After the counselor had shut the door, I settled onto one of the plastic chairs. Turning to Sylvia, I said, "I'm frightened."

"Of what?"

"You heard him. Andy hates me."

She laid her hand on my shoulder. "No, he loves you. Show him you deserve that love. Be gentle and sincere."

I stood and began pacing again, hardly completing two-dozen tours of the room's perimeter when Walter opened the door and Andrew shuffled in, dressed in blue jeans and a faded t-shirt. His eyes rested on his shoes, untied laces dancing as he walked. He crumpled into one of the plastic chairs.

"I'll leave you three alone," Walter said. "I've told Andrew he can return to his room whenever he wants." He closed the door behind him.

"Andy?" I asked tentatively. "How are you, Son?"

He continued staring at the tabletop.

I walked over to him, gently lifting his chin. Instead of focus, he had shallow blue pools, water left behind by a receding tide. When I stepped back, his head drooped.

"Andy, can you hear me?" I settled in a chair across the table.

The answer, when it finally came, seemed disconnected, a sigh as much as a word. "Yeah."

"I'm sorry I couldn't keep you out of here. That counselor wouldn't listen to me."

Andrew looked to me, his eyes struggling to focus. Sunken cheeks suggested weight loss. I wondered if the nurses had force-fed him during his crisis, like Sylvia and I had. When he spoke his words stretched out dreamily. "New building, same story. Back with the crazies."

Sylvia spoke. "How are you feeling?"

He looked at her to ask, "What happened to me?"

I answered. "You were in a closed shack with kids smoking pot. After that I'm not sure. Mrs. Perkins found you at someone's house where they had been supplying you with more marijuana. But I'm here for you now, Andy. I'm here, hoping to bring you back home."

I watched my son breathe slowly.

"Home? I don't have a home."

I closed my eyes, images of Andrew flashing through my mind. *Andy when he first arrived, canvas bag slung over his shoulder. Andy sitting at the kitchen table, studying. Andy and I standing at the balcony rail, talking about life.* "You'll always have a home with me," I said.

He cocked his head, his brow wrinkled, struggling to remember. "Something. Important." He squinted in my direction. "Murderer?"

I held my head high, my gaze steady. "No, Andy, I'm not a murderer."

The silence stretched, a background of human sobs soaking through the walls like a distant thunderstorm riding over the waves.

Andrew turned to Sylvia. "Murderer?" he asked again, his eyebrows arched in confusion.

Sylvia shook her head. "No, Andy. Your father's no murderer. Your mother was wrong."

Andrew rose and walked to stand a foot away from me. His brow lines sharpened. "You and Jenny's killer?"

I reached up and placed one hand on his shoulder. "I had nothing to do with it. I swear to God."

He shook off my hand and meandered across the room, ending up facing a blackboard speckled with unreadable smudges. "I'm like … adrift."

Sylvia walked over to him, stretched on tiptoe and kissed his cheek. "You have a place with us."

"Us?"

She showed Andrew her ring. "Your dad and I are getting married."

He stared at the ring and then at me. Turning his back to us both, he went to one of the chairs and turned it so it faced the wall, sitting with his face draped into his hands.

"Andy?" I asked. "What are you thinking?"

It took him awhile to answer. "Mom's out?"

I walked over to Sylvia and we kissed. "Life goes on, Andy."

"Where do I fit in?"

Sylvia broke from my embrace and squatted in front of him. "Your counselor says you get to choose where you want to live. Your father and I would understand if you decided to move back with your mother. Your friends are there, including your girlfriend Sarah."

She paused until he glanced up at her. "S'pose."

"But there's another choice," she resumed. "Your father and I both love you very much. If you choose to stay here, nothing would make me happier than to raise you as my stepson."

He stood and held out his hand, helping her to rise. Turning to me his eyes pulled me across the room until the three of us were standing closely packed.

"Dad?"

"Andy. I love you. Please come back."

His face broke into a smile, that golden shine that warmed my heart. The three of us wrapped our arms around each other, Sylvia, Andrew, and me, celebrating the formation of our new family.

"Guess I'll be comin' home then," he said.

Made in the USA
Columbia, SC
28 August 2018